I0729102

ELUDING DESTINY

ELUDING DESTINY SERIES

BOOK ONE

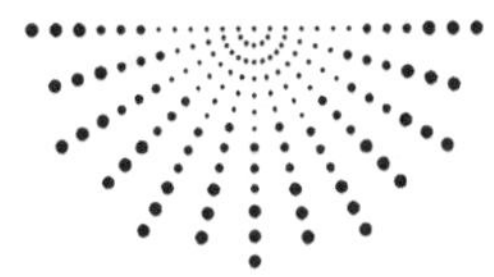

CHARLIE NOTTINGHAM

LIQUID MIND PUBLISHING

Copyright 2021 Charlie Nottingham
All rights reserved.

Liquid Mind Publishing

This work may not be duplicated, redistributed or exchanged without permission granted by author Charlie Nottingham. This work is entirely fiction. Characters, names, places, media, brands and incidents are purely a product of the author's imagination. Author Charlie Nottingham acknowledges the trademark status and trademark owners of products and brands mentioned in this fictional story. The author is in no way associated with nor sponsored by any brand mentioned within this book.

THE ELUDING DESTINEY SERIES

Eluding Destiny

The Horrors That Created Us

Aftershocks

The Precipice

Land of Light

The Quiet Army

Sacred Sins

Flash Back

The Shift

Lost to Time

Gods Among Us

The Cover Up

Blank Slate

Sign up for Charlie's newsletter and receive a free copy of the Eluding Destiny prequel, Blood Bar:

https://liquidmind.media/eluding-destiny-prequel/

Mom

You have always been my greatest inspiration and my biggest supporter.
Though I can only remember a few of them now, those stories you used to
tell me and Steph as kids created a trickle of creativity that would
continue to overflow and flood well into my adulthood. If it weren't for
your stories, I never would have written mine. I never would have found
the love of my life. Writing.
I bet you didn't think those little fairy tales would mean so much but
look, Mom.
I did it. I'm an author.
Thank you for always inspiring me to follow my dreams.
I love you.

PROLOGUE

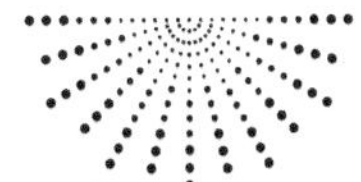

THE PAR ANIMARUM

Humans tell their children stories of glass slippers and red apples before bed each night. A kiss to awaken a dead princess, a carriage set to turn to a pumpkin if the woman doesn't return home by the time the clock strikes, a girl with hair as long as a tower for the prince to climb and rescue her from the evil queen.

The other races though, they tell another fairytale to their young. One whispered from generation to generation in the shadows as the sun sets and the moon rises. The story of the par animarum.

It is said that in the beginning, there were lovers with bonds stronger than any magic in the cosmos. A binding robust enough to break any spell, one that time and space could not disturb, a love that could create and destroy worlds.

Together, the par animarum were unstoppable. Even when not standing side by side, they remained entangled within their other half. They could hear what the other had to say without uttering a word. They could see through one another's eyes. They could feed off of their counterparts' strength in moments of weakness. They could feel one another's agony. They were one within two.

Their mission was simple. To love, to create love, and to spread love.

But a jealous god feared their strength. After all, they were twice as he. Two more legs, two more arms, double the hearts, and double the minds.

He sought to tear them apart. After playing tricks on the pairs, he ripped them in two. Then he laughed from above as they trudged the earth desperate to find the half of themselves, they strived for as much as air in their lungs. Searching and searching, reincarnated life after life, left with an immeasurable sense of agony upon their deaths as mere fragments of who they were meant to be.

The story says that one day, once each broken soul unites with their counterpart through an act of intimacy, they will rise up and take their power back from the god that tore them apart. They will destroy the one who imprisoned them to roam alone for centuries. And when they do, a war unlike any this world has ever seen will wreak havoc on the land.

But it was a story. A myth, nothing more. One that was diluted and misconstrued each generation as it passed down by the word of mouth.

Rumors would surface every few hundred years within the supernatural world of a suspected pair that found one another, but they always fell to the back of minds.

That is, until a young couple in a small American town completed their bond in 2016. Not just any paired souls, but the two most important of all.

Laila Callidy and Jeremy Skoulda.

The supernatural community held onto their doubts, but the young lovers knew they'd been a part of each other for as long as time has existed.

They were no longer two roaming alone. They'd become one within the other.

And still, the pair only strived for what they had in the beginning of time. To love, to create love, and to spread love.

But they never got what they strived for without a battle. Or in this pair's case, *many* battles.

CHAPTER ONE

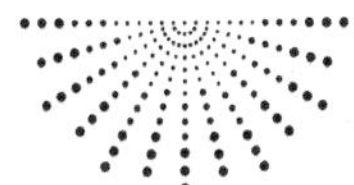

LATE OCTOBER 2018

Normally when you take a DNA test, you're trying to learn *whose* you are. Not *what* you are. But since I received my results in 2016, my job managing Moe's Diner was the only remotely normal part about my life.

The smell of greasy fries and burgers filled my nose. I spun the rag from side to side in the warm cleaning solution bucket, trying to rinse off the crumbs from table four. *Across the Universe* by The Beatles swayed into my ears from the little speakers in the corners. I glanced out the windows above the booths into the parking lot. Snow fluttered to the ground like something in a Christmas movie.

Damn snow. I hoped it'd slow down by the time my shift was over. My car and winter weather did not mix.

"Excuse me, waiter," an old man said. He sat at the corner booth with a newspaper and his meal.

I dropped my rag back to my bucket and wiped my hands on my apron. My teeth tightened to a line behind my smile. It was the third time in ten minutes he'd asked for my assistance.

Walking his way, I said, "What can I do for ya, sir?"

"Yeah, um... There's something off with my burger."

"Oh, I'm sorry about that. What's wrong with it, exactly?"

"I don't know, it doesn't taste right." His nose crinkled, making a gesture to his plate.

"Oh, well that's no good. I can get you a new one if you'd like."

I couldn't help but wonder what the hell was wrong with it. The bun looked crisp, cheese dripped down the edge like something on a fast-food ad, and it smelled like heaven. Aside from the chunk he'd eaten, I was considering lifting it to my lips and having a few bites myself.

"No, no." He stared down at his plate. "I just...I don't know. I expected more."

"What do you mean?"

"Well, I don't know. It just tastes so plain."

I gritted my teeth behind my smile. He'd ordered a plain burger. I specifically asked if he wanted any seasoning or condiments and he said no. "Would you like to order something else? Maybe some sautéed mushrooms or onions?"

"No, no. I don't like mushrooms or onions."

Nothing was gonna please that guy. He wasn't one of my favorite regulars, he never tipped more than three bucks, but service with a smile—that was my motto. No matter how much I did want to punch his wrinkly little face.

"Do you need more condiments?" I asked.

"No, no."

I fought the urge to snip and held my smile. "Well, sir, do you want to order something else?"

"Oh, I don't know. The burger was the only thing in my price range for a diner, you know?"

For a diner. As if our little place was a shit-shack or something. Granted, we were cheap, but our food was bomb.

"Well, how about I get you something else and we'll just charge you for the burger?"

"That'll be great." A smile came to his lips. "How's the baked chicken?"

"It's pretty good. I usually get it with our house-made lemon sauce." I expected him to complain regardless, but it genuinely was delicious.

"I'll go with that then."

"Sure thing." I smiled, turned back to the counter, and rolled my eyes. I walked behind the bar, scribbled on an order note, and hung it on the wheel above the serving hatch.

"Hey, Lai, I need a hand back here." I heard Max yell from the kitchen.

"I'm coming." I hurried past the counter to the swinging, stainless steel door. There, Max struggled with an array of canned goods that had started to fall from the shelf. He used his left hip to stave off the ravages of gravity upon the bottles and jars while balancing a crate of glass cups against his right hip. "Jesus Christ, Max. How do you do this shit to yourself?" I grabbed the glasses and set them on the counter.

"Being both cook and dishwasher isn't an easy job, ya know." He wiped sweat from his cheek with his shoulder.

"Yeah, well neither is manager, server, and busboy. Blame Dan; it's not my fault he didn't show." I leaned against the counter. "Get the chicken out ASAP, please. I'm begging you."

"Guess I better get on it then."

Max was easily the best employee we had at Moe's. He'd been working here for as long as I had, and no one loved it more than the two of us. Maybe I was biased though, since he and I went way back. Maybe not diapers, but definitely kindergarten.

He was a husky guy with big shoulders who stood about my height —near five foot five. A greasy mop of brown hair rested above his muddy brown eyes. He almost always wore the same pair of ten-year-old Levi's and some food stained, white T-shirt that could never stretch far enough to cover the bottom of his hairy belly. He always had a meandering aroma of pot and two-day old beer, even if his clothes were clean.

He was the typical small-town white boy who sold weed out of his '98 Subaru WRX. Basic, relatively normal, I suppose, not nearly as exciting as most of my friends those days. But I loved him all the same. He was about the only human friend I had left since Adrian died. Max

—and Moe's Diner—were the last remnants I carried from my human life.

The bell rang over the door at the front of the house. "I'll be right with you!" I yelled.

"Take your time," a familiar voice called.

My heart raced and a smile pulled at my lips. I ran to the front. Jeremy stood near the counter in a pair of jeans and a gray zip up jacket. He held a small bouquet of lilies in his hand. His lips twitched into a smile that reached his big blue eyes. He pushed long black waves behind his ear.

"Hey, you." I brushed past the counter and hurried to him. My toes lifted me toward him, lips pressing together for a moment. It wasn't one of those long, heart racing kind of kisses. I was on the job; we'd get there later. But it was enough to tie me over.

"Are those for me?" I pulled back and gestured to the flowers.

"Oh, these? Nah, they're mine." He grinned.

I laughed and snatched them from his hand. "They're beautiful, thank you."

"Well, I figured if you'd been gone for three weeks, I'd expect some flowers. So, ya know." He sat at the barstool with a playful grin.

I leaned against the counter beside him. "Well, I'll keep that in mind if I ever get out of here."

He smiled. "You love it here, shut up."

"You aren't wrong. But I thought you weren't getting back until next week."

"Mary called, apparently I'm needed here." He wrapped his arms around me in a gentle hug. The seat brought him down to a height where neither of us needed to crane for a kiss. His lips pressed to my forehead. I rested my head against his shoulder and relaxed into his embrace for a second. "But I'd rather be here than Maine any day."

I smiled, hoping he was back for good this time. He'd been in and out a lot lately. And sure, he'd popped in from time to time, but it wasn't the same as falling asleep beside one another each night. This was it though. Once this case was over, he was back. Mary had said it herself. She wasn't sending him on any more cases out of town until February at the earliest.

"Hey, miss?" the old man said again. An internal sigh echoed within me.

"Except for today." I pulled away. My tennis shoes squeaked against the checkered linoleum, walking towards the old man with a forced, friendly smile. "Yes, sir?"

"My water's getting a little low. Would you mind?"

"Of course not." I grabbed the pitcher from the counter and topped off his glass. "Anything else you need?"

"I think that'll do for now. Thank you."

"Just doing my job." I smiled. Seriously contemplated going to jail for battery on an elderly citizen, but service with a smile. Service with a damn smile, Laila.

I headed back to the counter, grabbed a glass from below, and poured Jeremy a cup of Sprite. "So, are you just stopping by? Or is that case over?"

"Back for good. Finally." He smiled wide. "When does your shift end?"

My stomach filled with warmth. Perfect. I had a few solid months with my man before he left again. That is, if he didn't withdrawal and refuse to work more cases before then.

"About an hour," I said. "I can meet you back home if you want."

"That's alright, I don't have my car so I'll just hitch a ride with you." He sipped his drink. "Need some help closing tonight?"

My smile lifted. "I'd *love* some help closing tonight. We had a call off and a no-call no-show."

"Dan again, huh?" He swiveled from side to side on the barstool.

"Yet again." I nodded. "I think you're right. I hate firing anybody, but at least if I weren't counting on him, I'd know what days I'm gonna be pulling extra shifts."

"Well, I'm back now." He shrugged. "There hasn't been anything major going on lately, I can help out."

"Might take you up on that." I smiled. "But are you hungry? Can I get you something?"

"I'd kill for a burger," he said.

"Coming right up." I scribbled his usual in my notebook, ripped the paper, and placed it on the wheel above the serving hatch. Then I walked around the counter and sat next to Jeremy at the bar. "No rush on the burger, Max!" I called.

"Hey, miss," a woman said behind me, standing from the red leather booth lined with chrome trim.

I turned to meet her gaze. "What can I do for you, ma'am?"

"Do you guys have a restroom?" she asked.

"Oh, yeah, it's right down that way." I pointed past the autographed Abbey road poster on the dingy white wall. "It's the first door on the left. Not the one on the right, that goes to the venue downstairs."

"You guys have a venue downstairs?" she asked.

"We sure do. Local bands play every Friday and Saturday night. Ten bucks for entry, free soft drinks, and ten percent off anything else you order." I gave her a big smile. "Grab a flyer, come check it out some time."

"That sounds so fun, my daughter would love that. Thanks," she said. "You don't rent it out for special occasions, do you?"

"We do actually. My number's on the bottom of the flyer, give me a call if you'd like to set something up." I put my hand on Jeremy's shoulder. "And we have loads of musicians always looking for a gig."

He let out a quiet laugh, shaking his head. "Not this musician."

"I definitely will. You just made planning my girl's sweet sixteen so easy. Thanks so much." She smiled as she started toward the bathroom.

"Any time." I lifted my hand in a gentle wave.

When I saw the woman open the bathroom door, I turned back to Jeremy and lowered my voice. "So did Mary give you any information?"

"Nope." He sipped his Sprite and raised his shoulder in a shrug. "Just that I needed to get back before the day was over, and that I had to bring you. So, I picked up the flowers and headed here. Figured we could eat before we went back to the insanity of our other life."

"Ah, yes. Well, the thought was nice, but I just ate."

"Then I guess you can watch me eat." He smiled.

"I guess I can." I smiled back.

The food finished cooking and I served it. The old man still seemed unhappy with his meal, but I wasn't going to offer him another free plate. After he left, I put the closed sign on the door. Jeremy helped me buss the tables and sweep the floor. Then I told Max he could leave after he cleaned his dishes and to lock up on the way out.

Jeremy and I headed to my car, hands clutched tightly together. Snowflakes danced around us. I turned his way next to my old Beetle. "So, what are the plans for tonight?"

"Well, I figured we could go get started on this case." His hand at mine moved to my waist. His lips lifted to a smile, gingerly backing me into the car. "Then I thought me and you could hang out in the bedroom for the night."

"Oh yeah?" I grinned. I lifted my arms around his neck and reached onto the tips of my toes. "And do what?"

"I don't know, what do you wanna do?" His hand at my waist slid to my lower back and pulled me into him. The warmth of his body radiated against my chest. The smell of his soft, citrus scented cologne wafted up my nostrils.

"Hmm." I reached higher onto my tip toes and touched my lips to his. The familiar texture molded into mine. His hand at my waist slid to my neck, lifting my face closer to him. "I'm pretty tired, you know. I could go for a massage."

"That so?" He grinned against my lips. My smile widened. I nodded, nose brushing his. Then he laughed and rested his forehead to mine. "I think I can work with that."

"And I mean, *full* body massage." I gave a flirty smirk. "Like, every part of me."

"Oh, I'd expect nothing less." He laughed and gently touched his lips to mine once more. Then he pulled me into him and held me tight against his chest. "I missed you, Lai."

Butterflies danced in my stomach. He'd popped in a few times throughout his trip, but he was *home* this time. There in each other's arms, snow flying past us in the dark autumn evening beneath a billion twinkling stars, we were *both* home.

"I missed you too." I twisted my arms around his back.

To put it mildly, Jeremy and I had a complicated love story. It just got more and more intricate as the years went on, but even at that point, things were far from simple.

Before he came along, my life was pretty *un*complicated; I had a normal, happy, and healthy childhood. Then at sixteen, my dad died. I was already young and full of teenage angst, but suddenly I had to grieve for the first time. I went into something of a downfall. I drank more alcohol and did more drugs than any sixteen-year-old should. Somewhere at the tail end of that is when my then best friend, Adrian, started dating Jeremy's older brother, Adam.

I didn't understand why then, but I found myself caring more for Adam than I did for Adrian. At the time, I thought it was just because I felt bad for the guy. The games she played with his head were beyond fucked up. She cheated and broke up with him more times than I could count, and he just kept desperately clinging to her.

Regardless, Adrian, Adam and I went to a concert one night and got stranded a few hours away after hitting a deer. Neither Adrian nor I wanted to call our parents, so Adam called Jeremy. And as they say, the rest is history. Although in my case, that's a bit more literal.

Things between me and Jeremy were almost instantly serious. In every way imaginable, he treated me like a goddess. We took things slow, but I think we were in love long before either of us had the balls to say it.

Despite how serious we were, we had no idea that things between us would be what they were or mean what they meant. We thought we were just two kids in love. We couldn't have imagined how big the picture really was.

As things got heavier, we made love for the first time. It wasn't either of our first times, but somehow it felt like it was. Granted, while it was occurring, I just thought he was great in the sack. Little did I realize I was breaking a binding my father placed on my powers as an infant.

Little did *either* of us realize how much fucking was going to change our lives forever.

CHAPTER TWO

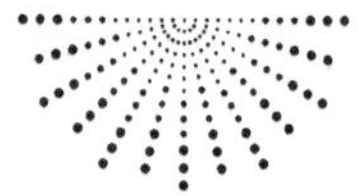

To call Jeremy's family's property a house didn't really do it justice. Estate's more like it. You turn off a bumpy back road to a long gravel goat trail, also known as the driveway. I counted the distance on my Fitbit once. From the edge of the drive to the house itself, it measured a good mile and a half.

Just before the house sat a gorgeous garden with a stone bench and a small fountain. Behind the garden lay the beautiful monstrosity we called home; situated in the center of I'm not even sure how many acres. Suffice it to say, a shit ton.

The house was built from solid brick. On the first floor were two bay windows into the formal dining and living room with two small windows on each side. Ivy climbed the walls, stretching to the eight windows to the bedrooms on the second floor.

From the outside, it always reminded me of The Luthor Mansion from Smallville. Inside though, it was rather quaint. The ceilings weren't as high as you'd expect, and the décor was somewhere between mid-century and modern. Classic, dark mahogany wood lined the baseboards and staircases. Light grays and warm neutrals covered the walls, aside from the bedrooms which each had their own custom colors.

Of course, none of us could afford the place on our own. Even with our combined incomes. But the Skouldas dad bought the property twenty some years ago and their grandparents paid to have the house built. Since there was no mortgage, all we had to pay for was the utilities.

As you may have guessed, Jeremy's fraternal grandparents were loaded. They owned a vineyard in a beautiful little town in France, where a few of the Skoulda children were born. Although, their falsified birth records say they were all born there in small town America. But the trust funds they were given at eighteen provided them to work their duties in the supernatural community rather than hold day-to-day jobs like yours truly.

"Look what the cat dragged in." Leah walked towards us to welcome her brother home. She pulled her lilac locks into a ponytail above her warm brown skin. "Long time no see. How was your trip?"

"Long." I pulled off my jacket as they spoke. "I can't tell you how much I've missed this place."

"I bet," she said. "Want a drink, Lai?"

"Yeah, just some water." I kicked off my shoes.

"Everybody's in the sunroom. I'll meet you in there with it."

"I'll grab 'em." Jeremy lifted his jacket to the coatrack. "Go have a seat."

"Are you sure?" Leah pointed to the kitchen. "I was just about to—"

"Yeah, I have to pee anyway. I'll be in in a second." He kissed my cheek and continued down the hall.

I placed my hands at my hips as my eyes met Leah's emerald stare. "Any idea what this is about?" I asked.

"Mary wouldn't talk about it 'til we were all here." She shrugged. "But now you are, so let's get on with it."

Over the past few years, Leah and I had grown incredibly close. She was my best friend. I suppose all of the Skouldas were in different ways at different times, but if I had to say who I connected with on the deepest level, it was Leah. Maybe because she was constantly inside of our heads—so long as we weren't blocking her out—and knew us better than we knew ourselves. Nonetheless, she and I were sisters long before Jeremy and I were ready to get married.

I hurried to the sunroom off of the kitchen where the whole family was gathered. Brody, Jeremy's younger brother, stood in the corner clutching a crystal glass half filled with scotch. Adam, the eldest of the boys, stood next to him, smoking a joint with their little sister Hannah on the couch beneath them.

Brody was my age, the second youngest Skoulda. To put it lightly, Brody was a dick. His smiles were rare then, but when they did come, they always looked falsified over his flawless teeth and dull gaze. That may be why we became good friends—because we were opposites. I was the glass half full kind of person, while Brody thought it was empty if only a drop was taken from an overflowing cup. I guess we balanced one another in that sense.

Adam was the first of the family I'd met and my oldest friend within the clan. After we'd lost Adrian, our relationship did feel strained. His dewy blue eyes were sadder when they crossed mine, but his broad shoulders were always there when I needed one to cry on.

Hannah was the youngest of us all. Her innocent ocean eyes were always glued to the pages of some ancient, classic novel. That simple, sweet demeanor was easy to overlook. Almost everyone did, including her brothers and sister. Half the time, I think they forgot she existed because she played a little part in the supernatural world the rest of us wrestled within.

The powerless, nearly human sister. They knew she was telepathic like the rest of us, but they thought that was it. I was the only person in the living world who knew otherwise. That in some ways, she was more powerful than any of them.

"Ooh." I hurried over to them. "Can I hit that?"

Adam passed it to me. "Long day?"

I shrugged. "Same as ever. Bitchy customers and shitty tips."

"Had a visitor?" Brody gestured to Jeremy coming in from the kitchen.

"Yeah, Mary called him in for this meeting."

"Long time no see, man." Adam smiled.

Jeremy handed me my drink. "Yeah, tell me about it."

"How was your trip?" Adam asked.

"Yeah, tell us, Jeremy. How *was* your trip?" Brody chimed in, exchanging an odd look with his brother.

I squinted at him before a voice echoed from the hall.

"Alright, alright is everybody here?" Mary stood in the doorway. She looked around taking a quick head count. She pushed short brown hair behind her ear, pursing her lips and shaking her head. "Yeah, looks like it. Jesus. Would you guys stop getting high back there and sit down? We have a dire situation on our hands that everyone needs to be briefed on immediately."

I should have paid more attention to Mary when she spoke, but she always faded to the background. Her monotone voice and emotionless face bored me regardless of how "dire" the situation at hand may have been. Not that I hated the woman, but she was that near parental figure none of us took seriously until shit hit the fan and we needed her.

I plopped on the couch next to Hannah. "Hey, how'd that midterm go?"

She shrugged. "I don't know, I feel like I did pretty well on it, but we'll see what I get."

"I'm sure you did fine. You've been studying all week."

"Fine won't do; I need at least a ninety-five percent to keep my GPA over three point six."

"You did great, I'm sure. You always do." I put my arm around her shoulder. Jeremy squeezed in next to me. He grabbed my water, took a sip, and passed it back to me. Then he wrapped an arm around my waist and kissed my forehead.

"Not alw—"

"Everybody needs to shut up and listen to me. This is important, so pay attention." Mary snapped over our obnoxious chatter.

"Yes, ma'am." Jeremy gave a mock salute.

Mary narrowed her gaze at him. Then she continued, "I've been informed that there was an unauthorized tear in our planetary structure."

"A tear in our what?" I asked.

"A portal," Jeremy said. "Any idea where from?"

"Why didn't she just say portal?" I muttered, sipping my water.

"Well, we know it wasn't from Heaven, and Hell isn't taking credit for it. And we can't speak to the Council without a meeting, which takes months, sometimes years to arrange. But we know where they came out, and it was about a half hour by car from here. The powers that be want the closest clan of Guardians to assess the situation and report back upstairs. That's us, so here we are. Any leads are to be brought directly to me. No one is to engage."

"So, like the multiverse in the Flash? 'Cause that'd be really cool," I said.

"Kind of a similar idea," Jeremy said. "But not really."

"Our people come from another one of the planes." Leah looked my way. "The Fae, I mean."

I'd researched a fair deal about my Angelic heritage since I discovered what I was back in 2016. But I knew next to nothing about the Fae world and its intricacies, despite the fact that I was more in tune with that side of me than either of the others.

The Fae part of my existence did fascinate me, but I strayed away from it because those abilities overtook my body in a way that terrified me.

"Oh, right. Gotcha."

"Whoever it was, it was definitely from one of the Earth planes." Mary leaned against the arm of the couch. "It wasn't a very large opening and it closed very quickly. We do believe it was a Fae. It isn't easy for us to identify much of anything from that place though, so we aren't sure. But we don't have evidence of anything right now, so let's not jump to conclusions."

"Is it possible that this is just someone hopping the planes? Are we certain that they're hostile?" Leah asked.

"No, of course not. We can't be sure of that until we make contact. Temporarily, the Elders have put a ban on moving between planes. Hell obliged but contact with the Fae is never very clear. Still, whoever they are, unless they're incredibly powerful, they're stuck here until we can find them and figure out their intentions."

The Elders and the Council went hand in hand. The Elders took on larger problems, like the unidentified breach we investigated that day and major political issues in the supernatural world. The Council made up of Archangels ranked just below them. They were the ones who sent Angels like Mary to instruct clans like ours to investigate simple situations. Like Demons on murder sprees and Vamps that had a hard time staying off the human radar.

"Has anyone checked it out yet?" Brody asked.

"No, that's why we're here. A few of us will visit the site and then report back. But everyone needs to approach with caution. It's most likely an intelligent race, but it could've been some freak incident where a beast crossed through. We don't know. So, everyone needs to be—"

"Very careful," I finished. "We got it, Mary."

"So, who's going?" Adam asked.

I didn't particularly feel like going on a mission that night. All I wanted to do was cozy up in bed with my boyfriend, drink a glass or two of wine, and rub my tired feet. But that breach was what brought him home. So, I'd do what Mary asked, investigate the point of entry where the portal had opened, then come home and get the alone time with Jeremy I'd been craving.

"Well, Hannah you'll need to be ready to do research on whatever the search team finds. Leah, we'll keep you here so if there are any injuries, you'll be ready to heal. You four" —she pointed to me, Jeremy, Brody, and Adam— "will be on the site. Laila, stay with one of the boys at all times in case something happens, and you need to teleport out quickly. If anything—and I do mean anything—goes wrong or seems suspicious, get out immediately. Do not let your curiosity get the best of you. Are we all on the same page here?"

There were a few mumbled *Yeah's* and some *Mhm's* before she gave us GPS coordinates. We loaded up into Jeremy's old '69 Dodge Charger and started towards the location.

CHAPTER THREE

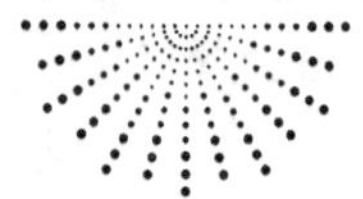

Cool snow, now mixing with water, slammed from the sky to my cheeks. The icicle covered trees ahead twinkled against the bluish cast of the moon above. Wind whistled into my ears. Jeremy's warm hand held mine tight—maybe a little too tight, but he knew my dumb ass was one wrong step from plummeting to the ground.

My feet froze as I trudged through the slushy, muddy snow. It left my tennis shoes and pant legs drenched with pieces of ice clinging to the edges.

"This is why we can't have nice things," I muttered, giving up and stepping in all the puddles.

"I hate this time of year." Brody passed me his thermos.

"We can literally go anywhere in the world that we want at any given time, and this is where we choose to be. Soaking wet in thirty something degree weather," Adam mumbled.

"It's way too cold for October, don't you think?" I said. "I mean, I know it's Pennsylvania, but still. Way too damn cold."

Adam pulled a cigarette from his pocket and searched for a lighter. "Dammit. Laila, mind helping me out here?"

I brought a flame to my fingertip and held it out toward him. He leaned forward, puffed the cigarette against the flame, then muttered a thanks.

My most notable Fae ability. The first that manifested, the easiest to manipulate, and the biggest pain in the ass.

"That never gets old," Brody said in amusement.

"It's really convenient in the middle of the night when I'm looking for my phone," I said. "How much longer, baby?" I asked Jeremy.

"We should be there by now." He glanced down at his phone. "But it's dark and it's been raining all day, so god only knows if we'll find anything."

"At least the temperature would've frozen any tracks." I ignited my hand into a fire ball and shined it toward the ground.

"Maybe we should split up," Brody said.

"Mary said we should stick together as much as possible," Jeremy said.

"We need to cover more ground, Brody's right. Laila has fire, Jeremy has energy, so we'll both have a light source. If anything goes wrong, teleport back to the car and honk the horn. Regardless, let's meet up back at the car in a half hour."

"Fine," Jeremy said.

"Works for me," Brody said.

Jeremy shrunk down a bit to reach my lips and gave me a kiss. "Be careful, alright?"

"Always am." I smiled, kissed him back, then we parted ways.

<hr>

"Doesn't that get, like, too hot after a while?" Adam asked, gesturing to my hand.

"Nah," I said. "It actually feels cozy. The rest of me is freezing."

"Huh. You're lucky, you got all the cool abilities. It's bullshit too, once you get the hang of your Angel powers, you'll be able to teleport too. What good will we be then?" He bumped his shoulder against mine with a grin.

I laughed. "It has its ups and downs. Like waking up from a nightmare to the bed being on fire. Again." I shrugged. "The worst part is that I don't even feel it. I could burn the whole damn house down and I wouldn't even know until the ceiling fell on top of me."

About two years prior, I'd done just that. Well, almost. That fire set off the security system and sent a host of firemen to my mom's at three in the morning. I knew good and damn well what had started it, but I lied and told Mom my phone overheated while it was charging beside my pillow. After that though, I moved in with Jeremy. Because the heat might not wake me, but it definitely woke him.

"You're still pretty new to all this. Give it time, you'll get a better handle on it."

I glanced up at him as snow fell in his dark hair. "Do you ever do weird shit like that?"

"What, like teleport in my sleep?" I nodded and he continued, "Nah. Not that I can remember, anyway. But I've had my powers my whole life. You just got yours last year."

"Two years ago, actually."

It was almost three, in fact. February 2016, that's when I learned what I was. It wasn't one of those typical, "Someone's trying to hurt me, I need to protect myself." sort of awakenings. Nope. Sleeping with Jeremy for the first time. That's what awoke the powers within me.

"Yeah, yeah. Either way. Our powers are wonky, they do weird shit."

"Wonky." I laughed. "That's a new one."

"You know what I mean. All I'm saying is that it takes years and years to gain complete control. How's air coming along?"

"It's alright, I guess. I've started to lift objects but usually I just drop them."

"You know what you should try?"

"No, what?"

"Jump off a building. Or a cliff or something."

I furrowed my brows above my smile. "Geez, what'd I ever do to you?"

He laughed. His sweet, bubbly smile creeped up through his thin scruff. "No, I mean jump off and then your instincts will kick in. You'll manipulate the air and catch yourself."

"I don't know about that."

Adam held a branch open for me. I grasped another for stability, striving to avoid a puddle beside a large log. Once I'd made it to the other side, he said, "Have one of us stand at the bottom. So, if you don't catch yourself, we'll teleport you."

A chuckle. "That sounds like a death wish."

"It's worth a shot."

As I gazed down at the slushy snow at our feet, I noted a mark on the ground that didn't appear to be from an animal. I put my arm out to stop Adam. "Wait, do you see that?"

He stopped and I lowered myself to the ground. I pulled out my phone as a light source, not wanting to melt the track back to water.

Clear as day, there were footprints stamped into the snow. They weren't *shoe* prints; they were impressions of a foot. You could see the curve of each toe fashioned in the slushy ice. It was a bit bigger than mine but not quite as big as Adam's.

"This must have been where the portal opened." I squinted at where the footprints began.

He glanced at it, then scanned ahead. His pointer finger raised to the dimly lit distance. "Look, they only go about thirty feet in that direction and then they stop."

I turned up to him. "Think they covered their tracks?"

"Not in this weather. You can't just dust the snow back over; it clumps because of the rain."

"Teleporter?" I asked.

"Maybe. Could be someone like you that controls air, they can fly. Looks like an adult male to me though."

"A barefoot male." I chewed my cheek. "Mary was probably right, must've been someone from the Fae realm. I'll take some pictures then we'll head back to the car. Shoot Jeremy a text and let him know we found something."

It wasn't uncommon for Fae to cross onto the Earth Realm. It wasn't particularly frightening either. Fae tended to be relatively peaceful. But it was frowned upon by the Angels. I didn't really understand why yet, but it left me feeling at ease with the situation. Demons were a concern to me, Fae were not. With that handled, I figured the rest of my night would be relaxing. I'd go home, cuddle up with Jeremy, maybe watch some Netflix, and just chill for a while.

"Yeah, we'll call Mary when we get better service."

I snapped a few shots and ignited my hand again. Then we turned and started back to the car. After a few quiet moments, Adam cleared his throat.

"So, have you heard anything about Adrian recently?" he asked.

"No," I muttered. At the mention of her name, my hand raised to the phantom pain in my chest. "Unfortunately."

"It's alright," he said. "Just figured I'd ask."

A long silence crept up. Since that night, Adam had been in a state of constant, hidden depression. He still smiled. He still laughed. But it was clear that he was far from happy.

About a week after my eighteenth birthday, I learned what Hannah was. It was also the night that one of my best friends killed my childhood best friend.

Everything had been wonderful. Normal, even. At least, as normal as imaginable after the discovery of my abilities. We were all having a blast, drinking and smoking, listening to music, and enjoying s'mores around the fire pit at Jeremy's.

Then Adrian asked if I wanted to walk with her while she smoked a cigarette. Of course I said yes, she was my best friend. I had no reason to think anything suspicious of it.

I walked a few feet ahead of her, laughing and gazing up at the Pennsylvania winter sky, glistening with a million stars, feeling as alive and free as ever. I remember saying something about how I felt like I was walking on air. Then a knife pierced its way through my sternum.

I can still see the tip of that sparkling crimson colored metal protruding from my chest. The pain didn't sink in at first. Just the shock. Pure disbelief.

She held me by my shoulder. She pulled me close to her. Crying, she whispered that she was sorry, and that she had to. I didn't even process what had happened until I fell to the ground.

Jeremy was yelling my name, teleporting between the trees—having felt my pain when I was stabbed—searching for me when Adam found us.

He saw Adrian with the knife and first asked her what happened. Then she collapsed to the ground and tried to stab me again. I could hear them tussling as he tried to get the knife off of her, but all I could see were their feet.

I'm not sure what Adrian hit in my spine when she stabbed me, but I felt nothing. No pain, no cold of the snow against my bare chest. I was completely numb. I couldn't stand to help him get it off of her. My eyes slowly sealed shut, and I knew. I was about to die. I wasn't scared —it didn't hurt—it was just this profound realization that my life was over.

And somehow in their battle over the blade, that piece of metal ended up in Adrian's chest instead.

Leah tried to heal me, but I was already gone. I don't even hold any memories from that moment or two of death. I vaguely remember hearing my dad's voice, but that's about it. Everything else was just blank. Total, complete darkness.

That's when Hannah yanked my soul back to my body. I didn't see her, I didn't hear her, but when I opened my eyes, my gaze met hers before anyone else's. Her dewy blue eyes glimmered with an almost cunning smile. Then she wiped the tears away.

As Hannah held my essence inside my dying body, Leah was able to heal the wounds. Everyone thought that Leah got to me just in time, despite knowing that Fae can't resurrect the dead.

But I knew it was Hannah.

Regardless, the damage was done. Adam killed Adrian. And we had to cover it up. There was no way to explain my miraculous recovery to the local police and report it as self-defense. Adam would have gotten manslaughter at the least, and he didn't deserve that. Plus, it would have drawn too much attention to us. And to the countless bodies buried around the property.

I don't know the details of how her body was disposed of, and no part of me has any desire to.

My stomach still churns when I think about it.

I couldn't understand what was going through her mind that night. We had our fair share of problems and adolescent arguments over the years, but nothing that would equate to murder.

Adam and I had been trying to get to the bottom of it for almost two years, not that anyone else cared enough to question the events. Everyone figured she flipped like a switch. She wasn't exactly known for being a passive person and she and I had our fair share of disagreements over the years. But Adam and I *knew* her. And we knew it had to be more than that.

We were like the three musketeers. Always together, always partying and having a good time. It didn't make sense.

It took decades before I learned why Adrian tried to kill me that night. But that's another story for another time.

"You did the right thing. You know that, right?" I said, trying to break the quiet.

"Yeah. Yeah, I know." He pulled a flask from his coat pocket. "I know it, I just don't believe it, if that makes any sense. She tried to kill you. And it's not that I'm not happy you're alive. I just…"

"You just miss her?" I wrapped my arm around his back. "Yeah. Me too."

CHAPTER FOUR

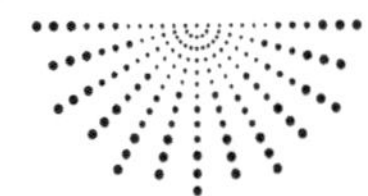

As we arrived at the car, Adam and I explained what we had found. We headed back to the house to brief Mary on the new information at hand and to relax for the night. Of course, everyone else was planning on relaxing, but I hadn't been alone with my boyfriend in some time, so I had other plans for the evening.

It was still before nine and I figured there'd be enough time to have a little bonfire when we got home. I made Jeremy stop at a grocery store where I grabbed some marshmallows, chocolate, and graham crackers.

We got back to the house around eight fifteen. I took Jeremy's hand, gestured upstairs, and muttered something about how I was soaked from the snow and needed to get some fresh clothes on. He happily obliged.

When we rounded the corner to his bedroom, I pressed my lips to his and wrapped my arms around his neck. My mouth opened in a strong, warm kiss. His hand caressed the side of my leg, pulling my body closer to him.

"You really did miss me." A playful grin tugged at his lips.

"It's been a while, what can I say?" I leaned forward, kissing his neck and fiddling with the hair behind his ears.

"Yeah, because two weeks is just so very long." He gave quiet laugh. Two weeks since he'd last visited, although he'd been staying in Maine for three weeks.

"With my libido, it really is. My vibrator just isn't cutting it." I kissed his neck a few more times and fiddled with the zipper of his jacket.

He breathed heavily for a moment, hands tight around my ribs. Then I reached for the button of his jeans. "Baby, can we talk about something?" he whispered.

"Sure." I tugged down the zipper. "We can talk." He let out a deep breath, resting his head against the wall behind him. "Or we could talk after."

My hand crept into the bulge of his pants. His throat bobbed with a swallow. "After works."

His eyes met mine. He snuck his hands behind the back of my thighs, pulled me up until my legs wrapped around his waist, and carried me into his bedroom.

Giggling as he sat on the bed with me around his waist, I found the zipper on his jacket and tugged it down his chest, hurriedly yanking it off his shoulders.

But his touch was slower. Gentle. He cradled my face in his hands, thumbs taking in each pore on my skin, as though he'd forgotten what I felt like and wanted to envelop himself as deeply as he could in the feel of my body.

Warmth filled me at that thought. He was always a passionate yet sensual lover, but usually, if we hadn't seen each other in a while, he was a little bit more intense. It was a seldom occasion that he was aggressive in the bedroom, but he was typically faster in pace than he was right now.

Since he was being so ginger, though, I slowed my pace too. My rushed hands halted, trailing over his chest, feeling the race of his heart beneath my fingers. One of his hands slid around my back and tightened my torso close to his, allowing me to bask in the peace that always settled within us when our bodies were so tightly pressed together.

Lips still touching, he tugged back enough for me to see his eyes, forehead resting on mine. His voice was hardly more than a whisper when he said, "I missed you so much."

A smile stretched across my lips. I kissed him softly, murmuring, "I missed you too."

He squeezed me tighter, touch tender, yet somehow firm. Like it meant the world to him that I was in his arms again, and like he never wanted to let me go. "I don't want to leave again." His voice trembled when he spoke. "Don't let me leave again."

For the last year or so, Jeremy had been talking about ending his alliance with the Angels. He was tired of working cases, and he wanted to stop. I encouraged his decision one way or the other, but I understood why it'd been hard for him to take that step. Working for the Chambers—working with the Angels—was a noble duty. He saved lives; we both did, although he worked more cases than me.

Still, I knew how draining the job could be, and if he was done, I would support that decision.

My head tilted, smile dwindling. "Is this what you wanted to talk about? Do you want to withdraw?"

His breathing slowed, and he grew quiet for a few heartbeats. Eventually, he brought a smile to his lips and cleared his throat. "I don't know. I'm thinking about it. It was... It's been a rough couple of weeks." He squeezed me a little harder, kissing me again. "But I don't want to think about that right now. I just want to be with you for a few minutes."

We'd talk about it later then. Or maybe he'd do what he always did when something bothered him and push it to the back of his mind. He was good at that. But that tremble in his voice had me worried, so I'd bring it up again later.

Right now though? He wanted to be happy, and I wanted to help with that.

So I slid my hands down his chest to his jeans, unclasped the button, and pulled down the zipper, feeling the bulge beneath his boxers grow.

"Then let's forget about it all for a little bit." My lips grazed his with each word, tingling, sending pleasant shivers down my body.

A breathy laugh left him as he helped my jacket off my arms. "I like the sound of that."

Grinning, my kiss traveled from his lips down his jaw to his neck.

Slowly, each article of our clothes fell like rain around us as our touches grew more intense.

Pushing him backward onto the bed, I kissed my way down his chest.

It wasn't like giving head was my favorite thing to do in bed, but it looked like he could use a pick me up.

So I got to work. He gasped when my tongue traced over the head, and he let out a soft sigh when my mouth opened and I took him in.

His eyes held mine, and he pushed hair from my face, caressing my cheek. I loved that expression. His always wide blue eyes grew soft. They weren't closed, but he didn't look so alert. It was like he let himself go, and that was a rare moment for Jeremy. My heart palpitated with pride, knowing I was capable of bringing him to that point.

But it couldn't have been more than a minute before he shook his head and said, "Come here."

I stopped, question lightening my gaze. "You aren't enjoying this?"

A faint laugh. "I am, but that's not what I want right now."

"What do you want?"

He sat forward, tilted my chin up to his, and our lips met. He trailed his along mine so softly, so tenderly, that those barely there caresses were enough to moisten my panties and fill me with anticipation. "To hold you." He kissed me again, voice low. "To kiss you, and feel you come around me."

My cheeks warmed, and I smiled against his lips. "Well, I won't object to that."

He let out a faint laugh, touched my hip, and tugged me closer. As I straddled him, he pulled my panties aside, sliding from my opening to my clit.

When he applied just the right amount of pressure, swiping a seductive circle over it, a faint gasp dropped into my lips. Typically, we'd spend a while on foreplay, but now that he'd said that, I wanted him too much to wait.

I settled over him, quiet moan falling from my mouth into his as I stretched to take him all the way in. He did the same, finding my cheek and holding it softly as I ground into him. I loved the feel of his fingers on that tender button, but I wanted what he wanted.

The intimacy of being held and holding him.

I touched his hand, guiding it toward my hip. He squeezed me close, gasping as I rolled my body in a wave toward him. My clit rubbed that firm spot on his pelvis, bringing me the same pleasure as his hand, and I locked my arms around his back.

He nuzzled his head into my neck, kissing gently.

I closed my eyes, holding him for stability, but it was for more than that. His arms around me were the safest, most comforting place in the world, and I wanted to give him the same thing. He needed sensuality, and I enjoyed giving it to him just as much.

That feeling of comfort combined with the intimacy and magnified the pleasure by a thousand.

His cock massaged something glorious inside of me, and I lost myself in the haze it brought me. Moments like this, in my eyes, were the epitome of romance. Sure, we had rough, dirty sex from time to time, but it wasn't any better than occasions like these. Both strengthened our connection, both brought us ecstasy, and neither was better than the other.

Each little rock of my hips brought me closer to that finish I yearned for. The pressure building within me increased with every heavy breath he released at my ear, and part of me wanted to stop just to make it last longer. Although, I wasn't sure that I could.

The pleasure fastened a rope around me, and it wouldn't allow me to escape.

I had no choice in the matter. I was a few gentle strokes from finish, and his fingers embracing my bare back, filling me with comfort and safety, only brought me closer to that climax I craved.

"Lai," Jeremy whispered in my ear, kissing my neck again.

"Yeah?" I made out between deep breaths.

He tugged back slightly, hand sliding to my face. It glided to the back of my head. He gingerly grasped a fistful of my hair, wide, entranced eyes on mine. In a raspy whisper, he breathed out, "I love you more than anything."

Somehow, that simple phrase was the most erotic thing I'd ever heard. My body gave way, muscles contracting around him. The orgasm crashed over me like an incapacitating wave, locking up my legs, trapping him inside. My vision grew hazy, and suddenly, he was all I could see. There was nothing in this room aside from his comforting, sensual embrace and the passion that shined behind those electric blue eyes.

He let out a groan of his own, hauling me tighter against him, finger kneading tighter into my scalp. "Damn it," he murmured as my contractions slowed. "I wanted this to last longer."

A quiet laugh escaped me. I closed my arms around his neck and laid my head on his shoulder, whispering, "I love you too."

CHAPTER FIVE

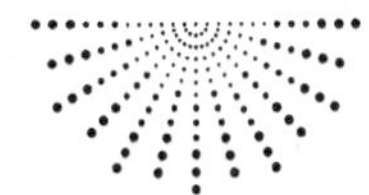

Rummaging through the dresser drawers, I found a pair of Jeremy's sweatpants and an old Lynyrd Skynyrd T-shirt. "Hey, baby, can I wear this?" I asked.

"Go for it." Jeremy stood and buttoned his jeans.

"Okay, good. I'm literally out of everything. I need to wash clothes so bad but I'm so incredibly lazy."

"You're busy, not lazy." He walked behind me and wrapped his arms around my naked waist. He kissed my shoulder and his eyes closed.

I looked over him in the mirror and smiled. He looked so relieved. Like the weight of the world had been on his shoulders and had finally fallen off. Being away from home was always hard on him, so I didn't think much of it.

Eyes still closed, taking in a deep inhale against my hair, he whispered, "God, I missed you."

"I missed you too." I turned and locked my hands behind his neck. "Wasn't there something you wanted to talk about?"

He paused. "Yeah, yeah there was."

"And?" I smiled. "What is it?"

Silence lingered for a moment. His eyes shifted between mine.

Then he smiled and shook his head. "Nothing really. We can talk about it later."

"Are you sure?" I asked.

With a nod, he smiled. "Yeah. Yeah, it can wait. But they're going to run out of wood for the fire out there."

It was a cool, quiet night. The crackle of the burning wood resonated in my ears. Smoke coasted up my nose. I leaned my hands closer to the fire for warmth, rubbing them together. The sweet taste of white wine lingered on my tongue. As I stumbled forward a bit, Jeremy caught my hips.

I laughed, turning to meet his gaze. "Oops."

He smiled and kissed my shoulder. I smiled back, leaned onto him, and crossed my legs over his. It felt so good to sit on his lap surrounded by friends and family again. Things felt normal again. Familiar, like home. Bullshitting, sipping drinks, and munching on s'mores.

"So, what'd you even do in Maine?" Hannah asked Jeremy from the other side of the fire pit.

"Yeah, did ya' keep busy up there, Jeremy?" Brody asked a few seats to my left.

"We were tracking a pack of rogue wolves." Jeremy licked his lips. "I was on my toes the whole trip, there wasn't much down time."

"Ya don't say." Brody gave an expression I couldn't quite place. Gaze narrowed, lips nearly pursed. Then he guzzled the rest of his beer and stood. "Anybody need another drink?"

"I could go for another glass of wine." I held my glass up.

"Moscato, right?"

I laid my head back on Jeremy's shoulder. "You're the best."

Brody took my glass with a "Mhm."

"That's pretty vague," Leah said. "Give us some stories. You were gone for weeks; you've got to have something juicy in there."

Brody scoffed at the other end of the patio. Shaking his head, he turned back into the house, trotted up the steps, and walked through the French doors to the kitchen.

"I dunno, there wasn't anything very memorable," Jeremy muttered. "The wolves cooperated so there weren't any crazy fights. It just took a while to get concrete evidence that they were feeding off of humans. They had a Fae working with them and she'd wipe the memories of their victims. It was a really smart plan, but there were over fifty people having hour or more blackouts on several different occasions. Once we saw the bites, it was just a matter of figuring out which wolves were responsible."

"What kind of punishment do they get for that?" I asked. "I mean, I know it's wrong to feed off a human excessively but as long as they're careful, there wouldn't be any real damage done."

"The issue wasn't what they fed on; it was more so the quantity they were feeding."

"Exposure risk," Adam said. "Makes sense."

Jeremy said, "Yeah, a lot of people were starting to question what was going on with their bodies. They had these strange bites and black outs of time. They were getting suspicious; it was just a matter of time before someone put two and two together. They just got a slap on the wrist though."

Brody appeared to my left. He handed me my drink and said, "And it took a month to figure it out?"

"About," Jeremy muttered. "There was a lot of undercover work."

"I bet." Brody rolled his eyes.

Something was off with them. "Am I the only one who can taste the salt in the air when these two are near each other?" I teased.

"It tastes like the warm breeze on the ocean coast." Hannah grinned. Leah and I laughed, Leah raising her hand for a high five.

"We're fine," Jeremy said quickly.

"Oh, yeah," Brody replied. "We're fan-fucking-tastic."

"Ouch," I murmured.

Jeremy and Brody loved one another and all, but it wasn't uncommon for them to fight. Maybe if I wasn't so tipsy, I would have been a little more suspicious. But I was happy. The group was back together again, banter and all, and that's the only thing that mattered.

"You boys need to quit acting like little bitches and work out whatever you're all bent up about," Leah said.

Brody gritted his teeth. "I'll get right on that, Leah."

"Ladies and gentlemen, let me give to you the one, the only," Adam slurred, "the king of all things sarcastic."

"Ya know, you guys always point the finger at me and make it out like I'm being petty and you don't even know what we're fighting about," Brody said.

"Well, share with the class." Leah placed her chin on her hand. "We can hear either side and pick which one we like more."

"Won't be Jeremy's," he muttered, taking a swig of his scotch.

"What's that supposed to mean?" Adam asked.

"Let's just drop it, Brody," Jeremy said.

Brody took a deep breath. "Just forget it. I shouldn't have said anything."

"Well, we can't forget it now," Leah said. "That was, like, the ultimate teaser. You can't do that to us."

"Jeremy will talk about it when he's ready." Brody guzzled back the rest of his drink.

My head tilted to the side a bit. Jeremy wasn't usually one to keep things quiet. If he were arguing with his siblings, he'd probably bitched to me about it at some point. Yet, he hadn't.

"Does this have anything to do with what you wanted to talk about earlier?" I whispered to Jeremy, arms still around his neck.

"We can talk about this later."

The only thing we didn't openly discuss in front of the family was our sex life. And even that did come up from time to time. But a disagreement between the brothers? Working through it as a group was typically how we handled it.

I felt his heart begin to race beneath my hand that rested on his chest. "Why can't we talk about it now?"

"It's personal, that's all. I'd really prefer to be in priv—"

"But Brody knows, doesn't he?"

"Yes, but—"

"You really aren't going to tell me?"

"This just isn't the right time. Let's just talk later."

"Should I just get it from Brody's thoughts?"

"No," he said quickly. "No, Lai. Everything's fine. Really. We can talk about it later."

I moved my arms from his neck and turned to face him better. "Why are you so nervous?"

"Now is just a bad time. Let's enjoy tonight—"

"You're hiding something." I tilted my head to the side.

Not once since he told me what he was had he kept something from me. Not once had he tried to cover something up.

He did something and he didn't want me to know about it. Maybe the timing was wrong, but damn it, he was lying, and I knew it. I had to know what about.

"Baby, please. Let's just talk about it later..."

I didn't hear anything after that. I was already in Brody's head looking for what was bothering him. And without much digging, I found it, floating around in his conscious mind. Memories were a complicated thing to divulge but reading present thoughts was as easy as watching television.

Brody was walking into the house Jeremy was staying at with his team while he was in Maine. He walked up to Mary, who made quick conversation. Then she pointed him to Jeremy's room. It was choppy, of course, as all memories are.

He opened the door, and there lay Jeremy. His feet hung off the foot of the bed, jeans around his ankles. But I couldn't see his face at first. No, because all I could see was a naked, porn-star perfect woman, sitting on his lap, turning to meet Brody's gaze.

Brody nearly gasped. "What the fuck are you doing?"

The girl moved and Jeremy jumped to his feet. He pulled his pants up. Brody turned away, shaking his head. Jeremy chased after him with open jeans and wide, shocked eyes.

I flung myself from Brody's mind and staggered to my feet. Suddenly that homey feeling I got sitting on his lap turned to sickness.

My stomach churned. I raised my hand to cover my mouth. I heard Jeremy quickly begging me to listen, but I couldn't even look at him. He reached for my hand and I ripped mine back.

Without thought, I ran to the edge of the patio and vomited on the grass. My heart thudded in my chest louder than a drum at a concert. It echoed in my head, slamming against my skull. My chest ached. I gripped the snow covered, wooden handrail to the steps, trying to cool my fiery hands.

"Laila, please let me exp—" Jeremy's hand touched my back.

"Don't touch me," I said.

"If you just let me—"

"Don't fucking touch me!" I yelled, shooing him away with my palm.

Then I heard a loud, echoing bang. The back of my head throbbed, and my shoulders ached. I turned around. Jeremy was on the ground beside the house. I'd thrown him through the atmosphere with the wind. He stumbled up and rubbed the back of his head.

I hadn't gained full control over my ability to manipulate air yet, so when my emotions ran rampant, so did my powers. Guilt flooded over me, but I was still tied up with rage. I'd normally ask if he was okay. But my head was spinning, my fingers were flicking with fire, and I was worried I'd do it again.

"I-I have to get out of here." I ran up the steps and into the house, searching the counter for my keys. I didn't want to hurt anyone. Part of me did, part of me wanted to light his ass on fire. But regardless of how hurt I was, I knew I wouldn't forgive myself if I did.

"Laila," Jeremy called, running close behind me. "You've had way too much to drink. You can't drive—"

"You can't tell me what I can and can't do," I snapped.

Jeremy drew closer. I knew he was right; I'd had too much to drink. But he needed to leave me alone before I unintentionally hurt him again.

He took another step toward me and I shoved him. He stumbled backward, barely, then took another step forward, holding his shaking hands upward to his sides in a surrender motion.

His wide, sad blue eyes shifted between mine. "You're mad at me, and you have every right, more than every right, but you can't get yourself killed—"

"Mad?" I felt my eyes warm to a glow in their sockets. "You think I'm *mad*, Jeremy?"

He took a step back. "I can't begin to imagine how you're feeling..."

"You're damn right you can't."

He licked his lips. His electric blue, guilt filled eyes stayed locked on me. "But please stay. I'll sleep somewhere else. I don't want you driving like this."

"I'll have someone come get me." I felt my breaths getting deeper and closer together. "Please just leave me alone."

My hands began to tremble. I bit back tears of anger, holding my fiery hands in tight, closed fists. Who would I even call? I didn't want Mom to see me like this. My sister had to be up for work in a few hours. So did Max. All of my other friends were here, and no one was in any shape to drive.

"Laila." He leaned forward and placed his hand on my bicep, the way he often did when I was trying to prevent my powers from getting the best of me. Usually, that touch was about the only thing I needed to calm down. But all I could think about was his hands on that woman's body and fury washed over me once more. "Just take a deep breath."

Sparks ignited at the tips of my fingers. I turned and pushed him. "We're done, Jeremy. Don't fucking touch me. Leave me alone, damn it."

He didn't budge. "Baby, just—"

"What part of leave me alone do you not understand?" I yelled that time, angry spit splattering from my drunken lips. "You fucked someone else, dude. You don't get to touch me. We're done. We're fucking done." I turned back to the counter and panted, trying to level my racing heart.

"Okay," he said quietly. "I'll sleep in the cabin. You can take my bed. Just please don't drive."

"You mean the one I just sucked your dick in?" My stomach

swirled and I gripped the counter for balance, unable to even look at him. "Fuck that."

"You can take my bed," Adam said as he entered the kitchen. "Get out of here, Jeremy."

"I just need to—"

"You need to get the fuck out." Adam gestured to the door.

Behind me, I heard Jeremy mutter, "I'm so sorry. I love you."

He loved me? Really? Because you cheat on someone you love and then fucking lie about it?

I picked the glass off the counter and threw it where he'd been standing, but he'd already disappeared. Maybe not the most responsible decision but it was better than setting him ablaze.

I didn't want to hear that shit. I didn't want to talk about it. Regardless of the reasoning, none was good enough to fuck another woman. And he knew good and damn well that I couldn't control my abilities when I was angry. Granted, that anger had never been aimed at him before. Still, it shouldn't have taken his brother stepping in for him to leave me alone when I asked him to.

"Brody filled me in." Adam wrapped his arms around me. Tears I struggled to contain streamed down my face and snot ran from my nose. "It's gonna be okay," he whispered.

"How? How could he do that?" I swallowed the lump in my throat. "I don't understand. I don't—I don't get it. We were—we were happy, we were good. Why would he do that?"

"I don't know. Jeremy's a lot of things, but I never thought he was a cheater."

"Me neither." I pulled away. "But clearly we were wrong."

He was quiet for a moment. "I don't get it. He loves you more than anything."

"Obviously he doesn't." I wiped my wet face, trying to compose myself. "Not if he's going to go out and fuck whoever he wants."

"You're right," he said. "I'm just... I don't know, I didn't see that coming."

"How ya' doin,' babe?" Leah gingerly wrapped her arms around my shoulders. Hannah was close behind, hugging my stomach and laying her head against mine.

"I'm so sorry," Hannah said. "That was one wicked throw though."

"Is he okay?" I asked, suddenly remembering that ache in my head wasn't just from my pounding heart.

"He'll live," Leah said. "Are *you* okay?"

"Yeah." Wiping my eyes, I nodded, trying to convince myself that I was. Tears welled in my eyes once more, but I managed to blink them away.

———

The myths about soulmates were so beautiful. They talked about how the bond makes you so incredibly in love that you wouldn't even think of being with someone else. That you're the most perfect person to your mate. That no one else even compares. That you couldn't even dream of hurting them. That you would give your life for theirs.

It had built up these inhuman expectations. I never thought Jeremy would cheat, it never even crossed my mind. I thought that I was perfect for him the way that he was perfect for me.

Those myths were full of a lot of bullshit. There was truth to them, but I was only just beginning to see that the stories of the par animarum had been grossly diluted since they'd first been spoken.

My mind kept racing though. I'd always thought Jeremy and I were a flawless match, even prior to learning we were soulmates. Our personalities complimented one another effortlessly. Our souls were literally bound as one.

We were best friends. And that's what hurt the most. I'd been betrayed by my best friend yet again. He hadn't literally stabbed me in the back the way that she had, but it hurt just as much. Maybe even more.

I had to deal with my own, personal Brutus, so I knew betrayal. But somehow, this hurt worse than a knife between my ribs. It was different. Jeremy was my partner. I trusted him with every part of me. I trusted him with my life. Then I saw him fuck another girl.

Maybe if I hadn't drunk so much, I would have been able to process it better. Maybe I would have at least let him try to explain. Not that I would have forgiven him. Not that it would have made a difference. I was hurt, and angry, and that wouldn't go away just because he said he was sorry.

But maybe I should've listened.

CHAPTER SIX

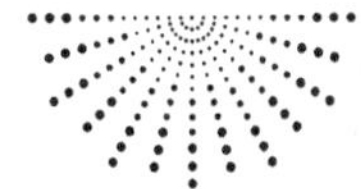

In the morning, I awoke in Adam's bed, and for a minute, I forgot about the night before. I forgot about Jeremy cheating until I saw it flash behind my eyelids again. My stomach flipped and I fought the urge to vomit.

All of the wonderful memories we shared moved through my mind. Our day trip to Hawaii the month before. Our midnight giggles in his bed. The first time we made love. They all made my stomach dance with butterflies. Then the image of him with her turned the butterflies to a gurgle and I swallowed down bile that rose up my esophagus.

Tears burned across my eyes. Then my tears turned to a quiet sob I muffled into Adam's pillow. But I only cried for a moment. I had to get to work.

I stumbled to the bathroom and took my shower. I stood there, letting the water cascade over my clammy, hungover body. My mind wandered as I watched the water slide down the drain, thinking that I should have listened to Adam all those years ago.

When Jeremy and I started talking, Adam was entirely against it. Not that I blamed him. Jeremy wasn't without faults. He said once that I had no idea what I was getting myself into by talking to his brother.

He was right, I didn't have a clue. Not only his connection to the supernatural world, although I do think that's what he referred to then.

Jeremy was a broken, beautiful disaster. There were a million good reasons that Adam didn't want us to be together. Although, cheating had never been one of them.

At eight years old, Jeremy found his dead father dangling from a ceiling fan. If this world hadn't fucked him up already, then that definitely did the trick. His mother had died a few years prior, leaving him and his siblings as orphans. Had it not been for their mother's sister, Annie, they would have been split apart. Nonetheless, their aunt stepped in. But I think he would have been okay if it weren't for the traumas that followed.

I don't know the details, but at fifteen, he got caught up in a fight with a Werewolf. Leah wasn't able to heal yet, so he had to go to the hospital. His injuries were pretty severe, and opioids were administered to deal with the pain as he healed. But within a few months, it became more habitual than just pain relief. He was healthy and still taking the pills.

I guess he got better for a while. A few months, that is. Until his oldest brother, Chris, was murdered at his high school prom. Jeremy was closer to Chris than either of his other brothers, and his gruesome murder hit him like a sack of bricks.

When Chris died, Jeremy went into something of a downward spiral. He fell back into the world of addiction. He stayed in it for quite some time, until he was about eighteen.

Before her death as well, Annie managed to trap him in his room which she lined with morion and hematite—grounding stones other races used against the Guardians to block out their abilities—to prevent him from teleporting. He was trapped inside that bedroom when she died. Tragic as it was, as all stories of addiction tend to be, it acted as a catalyst. He was overwhelmed with guilt over his helplessness due to his dependency on drugs. He still says that if he hadn't been detoxing, maybe he could have saved her. Her death was his wake-up call.

When the two of us met, Jeremy had barely more than two years of clean time. Besides the supernatural world itself, Adam's biggest fear at the start of our relationship was Jeremy falling out of love with me and back in love with drugs.

A relapse I could have handled. At least, that's what I thought then. But cheating on me was different. I couldn't tolerate it. It wasn't a problem within himself, it was a personal attack. It was an intentional deception of my loyalty.

Somehow, I found the strength to crawl out from under the black cloud and made my way to the sink when I'd used up all of the hot water. I threw on some foundation and a little red lipstick, deciding that I wasn't going to throw myself a pity party. My wings came out perfect over my green eyes and my tears were not going to screw them up.

I headed to Jeremy's room where Adam was sleeping and grabbed my knee length, red swing dress. Figured it'd be easier than looking for separate articles of clothing. I hurried back to the bathroom, got dressed, and quickly lifted my black hair into a ponytail.

When I reached the bottom step, I heard Jeremy in the kitchen and started towards the door. I didn't want to see him. I didn't want to talk.

Then I remembered my keys were in there. Leaning my head back, I started that way.

"Morning." Leah slid a plate of pancakes, sausage and eggs down the island. "Coffee's already made if you want to grab a cup."

"Thank you, but I'll probably just eat at work—"

"You don't have work for another two hours," Hannah said from the breakfast nook behind me. "Just stay for breakfast."

"Hannah." Leah caught her gaze and shook her head.

I looked down at the plate, stomach bubbling from the alcohol I'd drunk the night before. Gritting my teeth, I took a calming breath. "Alright. Thanks."

"Course, babe. I added some cinnamon to the pancakes." Leah smiled. "Coffee mugs are in the dishwasher."

"Gotcha," I muttered. After I got my coffee, I sat at the counter across from Leah, unwilling to turn and look at Jeremy. "The cinnamon was a good idea. It's subtle, but enough to spice it up."

"I thought I'd try something different." She shrugged. "They were out of Mrs. Butterworth and I won't use the knockoffs, so I figured I had to add something, ya know?"

I nodded, eating quickly. I made small talk about the weather and Hannah's grades. When my plate was clear, I rinsed it off and threw it in the dishwasher Leah had just unloaded. "Thanks for breakfast, guys."

"Any time." Leah smiled. "Are you staying here tonight?"

"I'll probably stay at my Mom's. Thanks, though."

"Course." She smiled back, although I could tell it bothered her.

I was always there, even when Jeremy wasn't. Technically, I lived with my mom. But this was home. They were my best friends, and I was theirs. But I needed time. I was too angry to be here.

I grabbed my purse and keys and started towards the front door. "Laila?" I heard behind me.

"What, Jeremy?" I pulled my shoes over my tights and put my coat on.

"I know you hate me right now, and you—"

"Here we go," I muttered. He stopped, not saying anything for a moment. I turned and met his dreary gaze. "What do you want me to say?"

"I just want to talk to you." His big blue eyes looked sadder than I'd ever seen them. He looked like a lonely, abandoned puppy on the side of the road.

"About what?" I snapped.

He raised his hand to rub his tense forehead. "I don't know, anything. I just want to be with you."

"A little late for that." I zipped my jacket.

"I know what I did was unforgivable, and I can't ask for your forgiveness because I don't deserve it. I don't deserve you, not after what I did, and I know that. But I love you so much. And I can deal with not being your boyfriend, but I-I need to be in your life. I need to see you and talk to you and—"

"Stop with the guilt trip. Just stop. You..." A dry laugh escaped my lips. "You did this, Jeremy. You hurt me. I didn't hurt you."

"You're right." He looked down at his feet. "You're right. I'm sorry."

I rubbed my forehead with my palm. "When I look at you, all that I see is what you did. I *see* it, Jeremy. Every time I close my eyes, it's right there." I clenched my hands to prevent myself from catching fire. "And it hurts so bad. It's like this giant weight sitting on my chest and it keeps pushing and pushing and I can barely breathe. I feel pathetic and weak. I'm not the kind of girl to cry over some piece of shit who thinks it's okay to cheat on his girlfriend. And I'm pissed. I just want to fucking..." I gritted my teeth to a hard line, tightening my sparking fingers to my palms. A gust of wind spun around us, pushing stray hair into my face. "I don't want to hurt you. I need to calm down. I need to process this before we talk so I don't kill your ass."

"I understand," he said. "Just please, talk to me when you're ready. I'd really like to explain—"

"I don't want an explanation, Jeremy." My tone sharpened, gaze narrowing. "I wanted you to live up to the soulmate hype you roped me into. I want you to be the person you convinced me you were. But apparently, you're just a great actor."

As he opened his mouth to speak, I pulled the door open and made my way down the steps.

At work, I let everything else leave my mind. I just waited my tables, cleaned the bathrooms, and prepared for the performances Friday night. After the morning rush, I went in the back by the dumpsters and lit a joint.

I laid my head against the aluminum bin filled with garbage and took in a long, deep drag. I wasn't going to cry. I refused to cry. I felt pathetic enough already. I wasn't going to sit there and wallow like a little bitch.

Instead, I started manipulating the air. Not surprisingly, that power seemed to be controlled by large bursts of energy, the same way my ability to produce fire was. The difficult part was distinguishing between fire and air, because they felt pretty similar when I was moving them. But the impulse that came with air wasn't as angry as fire.

Fire came from a place of fury, and passion. Air came from a place of focus. It was kind of hard getting it to work in my current state of mind. Unless I was flinging someone away from me, I guess.

When it did work, it was in small bursts, or long currents. The hard part was holding it in place, as if to levitate something. I could send something flying but to keep something still required concentration I was too frustrated to hold onto.

The back door clicked open. I looked up, ready to stow away the joint. But Max's brown eyes met mine.

"You alright back here?" Max sat beside me on an old milk crate.

I let out a half laugh. "I've been better."

"What's the matter?" He held his hand out for the joint.

"Jeremy fucked someone else while he was in Maine," I said. Blatant, yes, but that was me and Max's friendship. We weren't ones for beating around the bush. I took another long drag and passed it to him.

"Damn, really?" I nodded. He took in a long drag. "I really liked that guy."

"Yeah. Yeah, me too," I murmured. "And ya know what the worst part is?" He kept my gaze and I continued, "I never even thought about it. It never even crossed my mind that he might sleep with someone else. I thought we were better than that. I thought we were one of those couples that would never betray each other. I thought he really loved me, ya know?"

"The guy definitely loved you," he said. "Even yesterday when he came in for dinner. He looks at you like you're a goddess."

"Probably because I am. Duh." I gave a sarcastic grin.

"Shut up." He laughed, jokingly pushing his shoulder to mine.

He wasn't wrong. We'd been perfect. Truly, the happiest, sweetest, most perfect couple. We talked about everything. I was there for him and he was there for me any time we needed one another. We were best friends. And that's what made this so hard. Because I really needed my best friend in that moment. But he was the one who hurt me.

"He wasn't going to tell me, either."

"How'd you find out then?" Max asked.

"Brody told me. Apparently, he walked in on them when he went up to visit."

"Woah. Major bro-code violation right there," Max said. "You don't do that to your friend, let alone your brother."

"What do you mean?" I asked.

"Well, think about it. If Jenna cheated on her boyfriend, would you tell him? Or would you let your sister decide if one mistake should destroy their relationship?"

"Are you saying I didn't have the right to know?"

"No, that's not what I'm saying at all. I'm just speaking hypothetically here. If your sister made a one-time mistake while she was away for work and you found out about it, you'd let her deal with that, right? You wouldn't bring yourself into it?"

Jen had never really been the dating type, so I didn't have much experience in that situation. But I couldn't see myself butting into a relationship of hers regardless. Then again, I was closer with the entire Skoulda family than I was with my sister.

"I don't know. Probably not, I guess. Brody and I are friends though," I said.

"I'm just saying."

I let out a sigh. "Regardless of how I found out, I did. And my pride tells me there's no way I could ever forgive him, but every other part of me wants to forget it happened."

"Well, if you stay with him, you've got to teach him a lesson."

"What do you mean?" I asked.

"Make him feel as bad as you do. Go fuck someone else." He grinned. "Or don't and say you did. Make it hurt or he'll think he can get away with doing it again."

"I don't think that's how it works." I laughed. "That just starts an endless cycle of distrust."

"That's how it should work." He shrugged again.

"I pushed him into a brick wall, think that's enough punishment?"

"With your minuscule amount of strength?" He laughed. "I'm not talking physical pain, that shit heals. Emotional pain never goes away, not really. It might dull after a while but it's always there."

"I dunno. I'm over it. We're done."

Obviously, I was not over it.

After the lunch rush, there was one guy who stayed in his booth through dinner. He had an accent that I assumed was Irish, although it may have been Scottish. I watched a fair amount of BBC, but it didn't match any particular accent I'd heard before.

There was something familiar about him that I couldn't place. He had messy dark brown hair, a scruffy short beard, and bright emerald eyes. If we'd met, I was sure I'd remember him. But no memories came to mind. Just a sense of familiarity.

I asked him if he wanted anything, but all he had was tea. All day. Usually, that annoyed me. I hated when someone took a table for hours upon hours and ultimately gave me a twenty percent tip on their three-dollar drink. But he was kind and didn't bug me. The day was slow, and he stuck to himself.

Nonetheless, it was Monday, and we closed at six on Mondays. So around five thirty, I approached the guy and asked if he needed anything before I had to shut the store down. He said no, but thanks for the tea. Before he left, I asked him if we'd ever met. He assured me he was new to town, but that it was possible.

At six, I sent Max home and finished cleaning up on my own. I started with the tables and wiped everything top to bottom. When I say everything, I do mean everything. The salt and pepper shakers, the trim along the windowsills that lined the Formica tables. The light fixtures, the baseboards, it all got a good scrub. Cleaning was my way of staying out of my head.

As I took the garbage to the dumpster, I heard a thump behind me, as if something fell or maybe as if someone were walking. I prepared myself for an attack, knowing I'd need to keep my hands free in case I needed to throw fire.

The steps grew louder. The rustling of pants. My heart picked up speed.

I tossed the garbage in the dumpster, knowing with certainty that there was someone behind me now. It may be a minute before I got another. Abruptly, I turned myself around, grabbed the person by their throat, and slammed them into the wall of the diner.

"Who are you?" I growled, squinting to get a better look in the dim moonlight.

"A friend. A friend, I swear." His hands clutched my fingers at his throat. "I din't mean to scare ye."

His voice made me jump. I dropped his neck. I moved my hand to his shoulder. "Shit, you're the tea guy. Oh my god, I'm so sorry."

"No, no it's all right. Wow, ye're strong." He bent over, taking in long breaths, trying to regain a normal rhythm.

"I'm so sorry about that, I wasn't trying to hurt you. Alleys just aren't the best place to approach a lady. Did you forget something inside? Need me to unlock the doors for you?"

"No, nothing like that." He rubbed his throat. "I got somethin' to tell ye, and ye need to keep an open mind, because I wouldn't be here unless I was absolutely certain."

"Alright, how about we go talk about this up front?" I said, looking around the empty parking lot.

"This isn't the kind of conversation you want to be overheard." He straightened up and met my gaze. "Your name is Laila Callidy, daughter to Luka Callidy, born August 18th, 1971, correct?"

I'd read a million testimonies about stalkers online and immediately became uneasy. "Alright, listen, buddy. I don't know who you are, or how you found me, but I'm having one hell of a day, and I'm in no mood to—"

"No, Laila, you don't understand. You were born February 12th, 1998, no?" he asked.

"Okay, this is the last time I'll tell you. You need to walk away right now, or you'll find yourself in a world of—"

"The reason I know this is because I was born February 12th,

1998." He spoke fast. "My father was Luka Callidy. And I ken none of this makes any sense to you—"

"Okay, I'm sorry, dude. You're crazy, and that's a shame, but I know for a fact that my mother only gave birth to two children, and that was me and my sister. So, you need to go on about your day—"

"Ye ken our mum?" He moved in closer. "Please, ye've got to take me to her. I've been searching and—" He reached out to grab my wrist and I brought a ball of fire to my palm. Simultaneously, he brought a ball of water to his.

My mouth fell agape, and I shook my head. "This doesn't make any sense."

He took a step back. He absorbed the water back to his skin. "I'm sure this is confusing, but I have proof, Laila. Just let me reach into my trousers here. I've got a photo." I didn't rest my fire but watched as he rummaged through his jeans. "Just please don't burn it. I don't have many."

I let the fire go out, but kept on hand held upright in case I needed it. He passed me an old polaroid of two babies. Infants, to be specific, no more than a month old. They lay side by side in matching green and purple rompers on my family couch we'd thrown out a decade before.

There were pictures of me in that same romper on that same day on the mantel at Mom's. Of course, there were no other babies in those, but that baby was certainly me.

"This can't be real," I muttered, shaking my head.

"My name is Kai. Kai Callidy. I wrote the hotel I'm staying in on the back of that photo. If ye need some time and to talk to yer mum, that's fine. But please get back to me soon. My adoptive mother, she just passed away and I'm looking for family because, well..." He cleared his throat. "Well, I don't have any."

I nodded, still staring down at the photo in disbelief. "I uh, I've got to go."

CHAPTER SEVEN

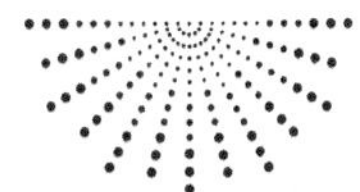

When my abilities presented, tests at an underground hospital for supernaturals like us confirmed that my DNA was vastly different than most. I wasn't just a Guardian like Jeremy with a couple of abilities. I wasn't just Fae like his adoptive sister, Leah. I was a hybrid with more power than anyone ever imagined.

One half Angel, one quarter Fae and one quarter Guardian. My powers, once mastered, were practically infinite. Those abilities, plus my relationship to the notable Skoulda clan, was quick to send a shiver down the spine of anyone in the supernatural world. It didn't seem to do that to Kai though.

Either way, sometimes abilities skip a generation or simply lay dormant, so I assumed Mom and Dad didn't know what we were. Admittedly, a stupid assumption. But I didn't want to fathom the idea that my family knew something like that and kept it from me. A habit of mine, ignoring obvious signs to protect my emotions.

My dad died three years prior. Just a few months before Jeremy and I met, in fact. I found out about my powers after the car accident that took his life. I had no way of asking if he knew what he was or if his powers were ever active. I just assumed they weren't, because then he would've shown me how to use them as a child. He would have, he wouldn't have hidden all of that from me.

Regardless, after meeting Kai, I needed answers. There was only one living person left that could tell me what my true origins were and if Kai was telling the truth.

Mom.

I pulled into her driveway at a speed that'd never be acceptable on a gravel path. Slamming the car into park, I ripped the keys from the ignition, clutching the picture tight in my hand. Sludge and icy water slushed beneath my feet, soaking the edges of my shoes in cold, dirty icicles.

I opened the door without knocking. Mom stood at the other end of the open floorplan making something in the Dutch oven on the stovetop. She jumped, turning to face me. "Oh, hey honey. I wasn't expecting you tonight, but that's alright. Want some chili?"

"No, that's okay. Thanks though." I sat at the bar that overlooked the kitchen.

My eyes shifted over her. She and Jenna were blonds with green eyes. Dad had green eyes too. I always assumed that I got his dark hair, both of their pale skin, and a combination of their eyes. But her jaw was a bit stronger than mine. My face was round with a pointed chin, hers was cleft. Jenna had a cleft chin too. I remembered learning about genes in biology and discussing how that trait was dominant, yet never questioned why my sister got it and I didn't.

"Mom, I need to talk to you about something."

She dropped her ladle in the pot, turning to face me. "Oh, no. You're pregnant, aren't you?"

"What? No, I'm not pregnant."

"Oh, thank god." She put her hand to her chest. "Alright, what is it?"

Shaking that thought away, I said, "This might sound insane, and if it's just some crazy kid talking out of his ass, that's great. Well, I guess it's not great, and it'd still be a little creepy, but it'd be better than the alternative."

She laughed. "You know how you do that thing where you start at XYZ and just skip A through W?" I sighed and she continued, "You're doing that."

"Alright, I'll just get straight to the point then. Are you... God, how do I say this..." I looked at her high cheekbones. Why were mine so soft? I didn't know how to say it without being insensitive. So, I just jumped straight in. "Are you my mom?"

Her eyes creased and she turned back to her chili. "Of course I'm your mom, Laila. Don't be silly."

"Then, did you give up my twin brother for adoption?"

I expected her to immediately tell me of course not. But she stopped stirring and looked at me with wide, quizzical eyes. It was like she'd just met Medusa's gaze, suddenly freezing to a statue. Her hands gripped the counter on either side of the stove, and she let out a deep breath.

"You *are* my mom, aren't you?"

"I'm going to need a drink. Do you want a drink?"

"Mom." My heart began to race. A knot formed in the back of my throat, and I swallowed it down. "Did you? Did you give up my brother?"

"No. No, I didn't." She pulled a bottle of Jack Daniels from the freezer with a glass. "I wish I'd been given that opportunity, but unfortunately, that wasn't in the cards after Jenna."

I knitted my brows in confusion. "But Jenna and me, how did you..."

She grew quiet for a moment. Then she walked around the counter, sat beside me, and poured a glass. "It's a long story, sweetie."

"I've got time."

She was quiet for another long moment. Then she took a gulp and cleared her throat. "Before I met your dad, I was with another guy. He was a really great man. But while I was pregnant, he died. It was devastating, but I had Jenna and she was born happy and healthy. But she was breach, so they did a C-section and I guess something went wrong. I had a lot of scarring on my uterus. I wasn't able to conceive again after that." She gazed down at the liquid in her glass. "That's how Jenna fits into this picture, anyway."

I blinked hard in a trying attempt to grip that concept. Jenna and I weren't related. That's what she was telling me. My big sister was only family by adoption. Not that I ever thought we looked alike anyway but taking that in was not an easy conclusion to grasp. It felt...Not like anger or betrayal, but just confusion. I didn't understand. None of it made sense.

"What...What about me?" My voice shook in a whisper. My hands started to tremble too, and my heart raced. "What about Kai?"

"When I met your dad, you weren't born yet. Jenna wasn't even two." She was quiet for a moment. "Your biological mother was still pregnant with you and your brother. She...She wasn't a very good woman, Laila. She made me swear that if I took you in, that I tell you that you were my baby, and that Jenna was your sister. It was your dad's idea to tell Jenna he was her dad too. For all intents and purposes, he was. He changed her diapers, he financially supported us, he treated Jenna exactly as he treated you. And I didn't have anyone else, Laila. My parents died years before then and I didn't have any siblings. I wanted a family so badly. And then this beautiful baby girl just fell into my lap and I..." Her lips turned up in a smile. She took my hand. "I just had to have you. I wanted to keep your brother too, but your dad... He said it wasn't an option."

That's when the anger set in. I mattered but my brother didn't? Dad cared about me but not him?

"So, what...he just gave away his child? Just threw him to a stranger without caring what might happen to him?" I stood. "That's appalling. How could you let him separate us?"

"Laila, it wasn't that simple. Your dad said it wasn't safe to keep you two that close together. God, I'm going to sound crazy." She rubbed her tense forehead. "I wanted to keep you both, but I barely even got to meet the baby. They took him…" She trailed off, wanting to say more, but unable to find the words.

I crossed my arms against my chest. The answer was right in front of me, but I was too confused to tie it together. "They took him where, Mom?"

"You're not going to believe me," she muttered.

"You'd be pretty surprised at where my imagination is going right about now considering the kid has a god damn Irish accent."

"It's not Irish," Mom said with a shake of her head. "They took him to another dimension."

For a second, I couldn't believe those words came out of *her* mouth. As far as I knew, she had no knowledge of my world, and I'd liked it that way. She was safe and sheltered and that had always been the best way to keep it.

"Another what?" I asked, making sure I'd heard her correctly.

"Another world. It's still Earth but it's like another layer of Earth, I guess. I'm not really sure, to be honest, Lai. They call it the Fae Realm," she said. "I know it sounds crazy, and you don't have to believe me. But that's the truth."

That's when the breach started to make sense. It was Kai, he'd come to Earth to find me. And to find our mom.

I blinked hard a few times. "I know what the Fae Realm is. I'm just trying to understand how you do."

Her hand raised to her mouth. "You…You know about what you are, don't you?"

"I have. For almost as long as Dad's been dead."

She gazed at me with wide eyes, blinking a few times. Then she chugged the rest of her glass. "Dear god, I'm a horrible mother."

"No, you're not," I murmured under my breath. Mom was always quick to turn the blame on herself. It didn't bother me; I loved her compassionate heart. But I was just trying to let it all settle in.

"Your dad told me that if you started displaying your powers, I'd know about it. He said you'd have mood swings, and you'd break things and… Jesus Christ, how could I have not realized." She paused, eyes growing dreary. "God, Laila, I'm so sorry. Your dad, he should have been here. He should have showed you how to live with this."

"I've got a handle on things," I muttered.

"What can you do?" Her reaction shifted from nervousness to excitement. "Show me something. I always loved watching your dad use his."

I awkwardly lifted my hand and conjured a fire ball. Her eyes widened in amusement. "So it wasn't that damn phone charger that caught your bed on fire." I laughed. Mom's sweet joy always had a way of bringing a smile to my lips, even if I didn't want it. "Is that it?"

"No, but we can't just jump straight into a tutorial of my powers." I absorbed the ball and crossed my arms back to my chest. "Why did Dad separate us?"

"I don't completely understand it all, Laila, but I'll explain what I do. Your father, he was part Fae and part something Latin that translates roughly to—"

"Guardians of humanity," I said. "Yeah, I know what they are. And my mother?"

"She's an Angel." Mom chewed her lip. "Apparently that combination of gifts produces a very powerful child. In this case, two very powerful children. A type of strength that, even when suppressed could attract creatures that may want to do horrible things to the two of you. Use your powers or raise you as their own. Nowhere on Earth would be safe enough for the both of you. So, your dad and," she gritted her teeth, "that *woman* decided the safest option was to put you on this plane, protected by your father, and your brother on the Fae Realm, protected by his people and the realm itself."

I blinked hard for a moment, trying to come to grips with everything she was saying. It sounded like nonsense, but it was coming from the woman who raised me.

But it made sense, in a way. The only people who had access to the Fae Realm were Fae. It was safe for him there. And it's not like Dad planned on dying. God only knows what he warded off to keep me sheltered before I learned what I was.

"My mom, my biological mother, I mean. Is she still alive?"

"Last I heard."

"Who is she?" I asked.

Mom guzzled down the rest of her drink. "I wish I could tell you."

"What do you mean?"

"When I adopted you, when you became my daughter, the condition was that you become *my* daughter. I'm bound by blood to keep who she is a secret."

A confused wave of anger and fear washed over me. If she'd made a deal with an Angel to keep it a secret, I couldn't be angry. I knew what Angels were capable of. I knew what going back on your word to one meant. But it wasn't fair to me either.

I stared down at the sandy colored countertop. "Don't you think I deserve to know?"

"Of course you do, Laila. And I wish I could tell you. I really do. But I don't know what would happen if I did. This agreement I made was with a hierarchy of very powerful Angels. Believe it or not, they aren't all harps and naked babies, they're actually very nasty creatures."

I wasn't particularly keen on the Angels either. They were abrasive, they were violent, and they had their heads so far up their own asses that everything they said wreaked of shit. But I was one of them. Whether I liked it or not.

"Warriors," I muttered. "We're warriors. I know."

She was about to say something but stopped, realizing what she'd just implied. "Oh, baby, I didn't mean that."

"I know what you meant. And you're right. Angels are dicks."

She laughed. "How 'bout another drink and you can ask all the questions you want?"

Admittedly, I was in shock. But Mom was innocent in all of it. She took in an unwanted child and raised her as her own. All she ever did was love me for every fault and flaw I had, even when I was the hardest child in the world to handle. Part of me was angry, but not at her. She'd been the perfect parent to me for as long as I could remember.

"No...No, that's okay. I, um...I need to go talk to my brother." I stood, grabbed my purse, went to my mom, and wrapped my arms around her. "Thank you for telling me the truth."

"Of course, sweetie."

"And Mom?" I asked.

"Yeah, baby?"

"Mind if I take this?" I gestured to the Jack Daniels.

She laughed. "Go ahead. I've got more in the cupboard."

CHAPTER EIGHT

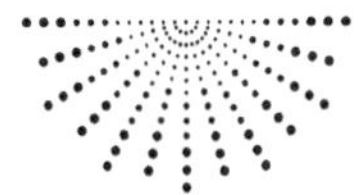

My hand shook and my heart raced, knuckles tapping on room 24 of the shitty motel. I was so rude earlier; I wouldn't answer the door if I were him. I'd literally held him against a wall by his throat. What a warm welcome to America. Although, he was an illegal immigrant, so I guess it wasn't that unusual.

The door swung open, and there he stood, messy brown hair falling in front of his bright green eyes. He turned his head to the side a bit, then smiled.

"Hey, are you busy?" I asked, holding out a pizza and the bottle of whiskey. "I don't know if you guys have this where you're from, but it's kind of an American treasure and I really think you should give it a try."

Kai nodded with a big smile. "Sure. Sure, of course. Come in."

He pulled the door open, exposing a messy room lit by an array of candles. Every visible surface was covered with newspapers and thick, uneven, nearly yellow papers, with beautiful letters scribbled across the pages. He must have brought them with him from the Fae Realm. "Sorry for the mess. I've just been working on this for a very long time and, well" —he laughed— "As ye can see, I ain't the neatest bloke."

"No, that's alright." I set the pizza on the table next to the TV. "Hey, I want to apologize for earlier. I had no idea who you were, and I shouldn't have called you crazy. Or, ya know. Almost killed you."

"Prolly wouldn't've killed me if ye tried." He laughed and pushed the door shut. "I shouldn't've approached ye in the dark like that. Things are far different here than they are back home. It's much safer there."

"Yeah, that's probably true. What's it like there?" I put my hands to my hips. "I've heard different things. Is it true that it always smells like honey and sugar?"

"Perhaps. But I don't ken what those are." He smiled and sat on the bed. "It smells a lot better there than it does here though, that's for certain."

I laughed. "Right. You guys speak English, but not entirely. And I'm sure there's a lot of cultural differences. You guys don't have electricity, right?"

"Elec...?"

"Um, lights that glow without fire? Like that thing?" I pointed at the TV, then the lights on the walls. "Or those?"

"That's a light?" He nodded toward the TV.

"No, not exactly. It makes light, but it's actually used for entertainment. Do you have plays back home?"

"Theater, you mean?" he asked.

"Yes, exactly. Theater. TV is like theater that never stops. There are different shows on all day, every day. You can use these too." I reached for the light switch and flipped it on.

His eyes widened in amazement, looking around frantically. "How'd ye do that, lass?" I laughed, flipping the switch on and off a few times. "This place is very strange." He laughed. "But I'm sure ye didn't come here to discuss culture."

"No, I didn't. Actually, I came here to talk about us."

"Yer mum confirmed my stories, did she?"

"She did. But unfortunately, I don't know who our real mother is. My mom..." I trailed off as I sat on the bed beside him. "She told me a lot of stuff I wish I'd known my entire life. But maybe it'd be better if you told me what you know, 'cause it seems like you might have more information than I do." I gestured to his papers scattered throughout the room.

"Sure. Of course." He glanced at the pizza. "But before we get into all that, ye should ken that I haven't eaten since I got here and that smells delicious."

I laughed, passing him the box. "It's basically a massive heart attack and diabetes in cardboard, but honestly, it tastes so good that it's entirely worth it."

"I don't ken what most of that is, but I'll take yer word for it. Smells heavenly."

"It's the closest you can get to it on earth. That, and turtle ice cream."

"You eat turtles here, too?" He asked casually.

"No," I paused. "Well maybe in some places, but it's called turtle ice cream because it looks like there's a turtle in it."

"Huh. Strange place."

As we ate, we discussed our families and what it was like growing up where and how we did. He made the Fae Realm sound like the garden of Eden in certain places. He said he always dreamed of moving to either Earth, where he could find me, or a place he referred to as the Open Lands.

He held my hands and telepathically showed me a few snapshots of his life back home. It wasn't exactly as I'd expected from his descriptions. He lived in a colder climate on a farm—not the Open Lands that he made out to be a gorgeous eutopia. His life there was mostly tending to animals, some that looked just like our cows and goats and others that I couldn't begin to think of names for. Life there, at least in Kai's upbringing, was like living in colonial America.

He told me what he knew about our birth mother. Which was about as much as I knew.

She was an Angel. Apparently, his mother had taken the same oath as mine.

It was disappointing, because now that all the things I thought I knew about my genetics were not true, I was wondering a lot about myself. Did I look like her? I didn't look much like Dad had. Did I sound like her? What about our mannerisms, were they similar?

But it wasn't devastating. I still had a mom and sister who loved me and that was enough. Sure, I was curious, but I'd be okay without knowing.

Kai wasn't. He'd only met Dad the few times he'd gone to the Fae Realm to visit him and his mother was a lurking question his entire life.

He said that his mom had made the same deal mine had, that nothing she knew about our birth mother could ever be released. But my dad wanted him to know that he existed, and that I existed. He brought him pictures while I was growing up, showing him what his baby sister—by twelve minutes—looked like. However, when he was ten, he would see our father one last time before he was never heard from again.

It was odd, finding out that someone knew me so well and I didn't even know he existed. Although, it was exhilarating in a way, learning first-hand about another world from my own flesh and blood. There we were, twenty years later, finally reconnected. I was mesmerized.

After an hour or two of serious conversation, I pulled out the whiskey. Kai nearly spat his first shot out but manned up for the following three. I don't know how many shots I'd downed when I got a text from Jeremy asking how I was doing.

"What's that?" Kai gestured toward my phone. "I see 'em everywhere."

"Oh, wow this is so cool. It's like talking to an alien."

"Alien?"

"God, I love you." I laughed. "It's called a smart phone. Anybody who has one is assigned a number, and with other people's numbers, you can call them, send them pictures, even send videos. Actually, you can have a live video with someone on the opposite side of the planet."

"Sounds like some pretty powerful magic," he murmured.

"No, it's not magic at all. It's science."

"This world is utterly mad; I'll never catch onto it all."

I laughed. "I'm sure you'll figure it out. Do you know how to read?"

"Of course I ken how to read, you think me a bloody idiot?"

I laughed. "I only asked because if you can read, then this little thing can teach you just about anything you could ever want to know."

"How's that?"

"They call them smart phones because they're actually way smarter than us. Basically, everyone all over the world can make something, anything, and upload it to the internet. Then you type in whatever you're looking for and it takes you to an article or a website about the subject you asked about."

"I'm lost," he muttered.

"Alright, let me show you. Give me a question, any question pertaining to Earth."

"Oh, I dunno. Uh, how many people live on this plane?"

I typed it in and said, "See? 7.442 billion as of last year."

"Wow." He looked at the screen in amazement.

I went into explaining the basics of our society and culture, trying to not make the stupid jokes I often did so I wouldn't completely lose him. He seemed uninterested, other than the texts that Jeremy kept sending.

"Who might that be?" He gestured to Jeremy's contact photo of him kissing my cheek while I stuck out my tongue. "A lover, perhaps?"

I laughed. "Yeah, I guess. Not really. Kind of. I don't know. It's a really long story."

"Well, I've got nothing but time."

"To make a long story short, I found out that he slept with another girl."

"You don't share beds here?" he asked.

"No, we do. Not usually with girls that aren't your girlfriend, but... How do I say this? He... Um... Well, I'll just say it. He had sex with another girl."

"Ah. I see now. And he still sends you love letters?"

"I mean, I wouldn't call a text a love letter." I shrugged. "But I guess. I just found out yesterday."

"Well, do you still love him?" he asked.

"I wish I didn't," I muttered. "But yeah, I do."

"What's unfortunate about love?" he asked. "It's a wonderful thing."

"Sure," I said. "Until they betray your trust."

He shrugged. "It's all relative, idn't it? Is the pain of being with him worse than the pain of being without him? Because being happy is more important than having pride."

"But if I lose my pride, I lose my confidence, and if I lose my confidence, I lose who I am."

"Confidence is found within yourself, not by what those near you perceive you to be."

While I agreed about confidence being something within yourself, that didn't mean I agreed enough to take Jeremy back. A slap to the face was a slap to the face, and that's what hurt the most with our breakup. The fact that I loved and trusted him without question only for him to betray me.

But I wasn't about to start an argument with my new brother. I was enjoying the distraction from Jeremy and wanted to shift the conversation away from him.

"You, sir, are wise beyond your years." I raised my glass to his. "Now I know you don't know this yet, but when someone raises their glass, you're supposed to clang yours against it and say cheers."

"A rather odd tradition, I'll say," he replied, touching his glass to mine.

For clarification, Kai didn't know what a toast was because he was poor. Not because it wasn't done on the Fae Realm.

CHAPTER NINE

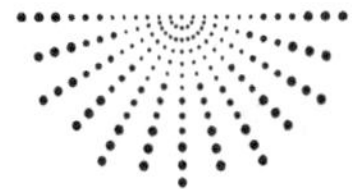

I didn't know how much I'd had to drink, but I knew it was too much. And from the looks of it, Kai was in the same boat. He was out cold, hanging halfway off the bed.

It was times like that when I wished that I had more friends, because it was four in the morning and I was not capable of getting behind the wheel. Sure, I could've called Adam, Leah, or Brody even. But there was only one person I wanted to tell about my shit storm of a day. And I had to share what I'd learned with the clan anyway.

So, I dialed.

"Hey, you," Jeremy answered after two rings. "Are you alright?"

"I am great," I slurred. "A wee bit tipsy, and a wee bit stranded, but way better than I was last night."

"Stranded?" he asked. "Do you need a ride?"

"Well, um. Well, yeah. But also, I've had an insanely, very crazy day and I really want to tell you about it. Did I wake you up?"

"No, I couldn't sleep. I was working on a song," he muttered. "But where are you? I'll flash there and drive your car home."

"That would be great. How soon can you get here?"

"I just need to get dressed. Where are you?"

"I'm at Motel Six off of 70. You know where that is, right?"

"Uh," he sputtered for a second. "Yeah. Yeah, I think so. What're you doing at a motel at four in the morning?"

"Oh, you know, making my rounds. Selling my body, making that bread." I grinned.

He chuckled. "Oh yeah?"

"Nah." I shrugged and lifted my purse over my shoulder. "But ya know, that'd probably be more believable than the rest of my day has been."

"I guess you can tell me about it when I get there. I'll meet you at your car?"

"That'll work." I chomped down on a piece of cold pizza.

He laughed. "Alright, I'll be there soon."

"Okey dokey." I clicked the shutter button and stood. I wrote Kai a quick note on the motel stationary, explaining that I'd gone home and that he could call me from the hotel phone if he needed to get ahold of me.

Then I wobbled my way to my old yellow Beetle and climbed in the passenger side. With a yawn, I rested my head against the cold window and started the engine for warmth.

After a moment or two, Jeremy appeared in the driver seat, startling me and causing me to hit my head off the window.

He laughed, and I exhaled. "Why am I not used to that by now?"

"Probably because you're shit faced."

"I am not." He gave me a once over. "Okay, a little. But you're not going to believe my day, baby, it was crazy." His eyes widened and his lips pulled into a smile. "That just slipped out, I'm still mad at you. Like, really mad—"

"It's alright." As he shifted the car into drive, he cleared his throat. "So, what happened? What's so crazy that I won't believe?"

"I have a brother," I said. "And I also found the breacher. Ya know how?"

He glanced from the road to me. "I do not, but I bet you're going to tell me."

"Because the breacher—Get this—He's my brother. My twin brother. From another dimension."

He raised a brow. "I would love to try some of whatever it is you're tripping on."

"No, Jeremy, I'm serious. This is real. I have a twin brother. His name is Kai, and my dad took him to the Fae Realm when he was a baby to keep him safe."

He let out a quiet laugh. "Okay, so you ate a bunch of shrooms and watched Star Wars. That's okay, we've all been there. They'll wear off in a few hours."

I huffed. "I told you that you wouldn't believe me."

He held my gaze as we stopped at a red light, examining my eyes. "You're serious."

"As a heart attack."

"Really?"

"Really, really," I said.

He paused for a minute, taking it all in. "Well, we need to talk to Mary."

I nodded in agreement. "We do. But I really need a cheeseburger first."

He laughed. "We'll stop at McDonald's on the way."

"Thank the lord."

CHAPTER TEN

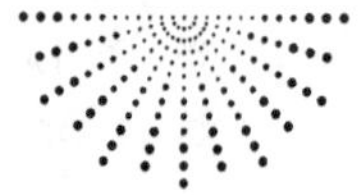

"Okay, listen." Leah yelled as she trudged down the steps. "Someone had better have died or I'm going to kill one of you. I need my eight fucking hours."

"Seriously." Adam lied down on the couch and put his head on the armrest. "This better be important."

"It is," Jeremy said. "You guys aren't going to believe this."

"Get on with it then." Mary stifled her yawn and gestured to Jeremy.

"Laila, do you want to tell them?" Jeremy asked.

I stood. "Well, guys, I found the breacher, and he's not a threat."

From there, I went into the story from start to finish. That Kai showed up at the diner, that Mom confirmed his identity, and that she and I weren't biologically related. The whole nine.

"Okay, so your parents kept you and got rid of your brother. Why, why would they do that?" Brody asked.

"Something about sending off too much power. Apparently, we'd act as a beacon for anything that could sense large amounts of power."

"Which makes sense," Jeremy said. "When Laila got her powers, we all felt it. From miles away. And when I picked Laila up from his hotel room, I felt something similar. I thought that it was just her until she told me about all of this. A huge source of energy. As strong as twenty of us combined."

"So, he's like Luke and you're Leia." Adam paused. "Woah. Leia. Laila. And your dad's name was Luka." He turned his head to the side a bit. "Were your parents Star Wars fans?"

"Focus, Adam," Brody said.

"I said the same thing." Jeremy grinned and they exchanged childish snickers.

"Did he tell you why he's here?" Mary asked.

"He said he was looking for me. And our mother."

"So, did you take him to meet your mom?" Brody asked.

"Well, see, that's where it gets crazy." I sat on the edge of the coffee table. "Apparently, my mom can't have kids. Well, I guess she could, which is how Jenna came to be, but there were complications with her birth, and she couldn't get pregnant again. I don't know the science behind it. Anyway, my mom met my dad when my biological mother was pregnant with me. Or us, I guess."

"Plot twist," Adam muttered.

"Does your mom know who she is?" Brody asked.

"She does. But she can't tell me."

"Why not? I'd kill to know who my real mom was," Leah said. "Mom tried to figure it out for years. Kids deserve to know who their parents are."

I started to relate to Leah on a whole other level in that moment. Annie adopted her as an infant too. She didn't talk about her biological parents often, but she'd shed a few unusual tears for them on some drunken nights.

She'd said that she didn't care to have a relationship with them, but she wanted to know where she came from. She wanted to know what they looked like. If they shared any mannerisms or things of the sort. And I felt the same way. I had a mom; I didn't want anyone to replace her. But I did want to *know* my real parent.

"She made some deal with the Angel, 'bound in blood,' she said? Whatever that means," I muttered. "I don't know. She can't tell me."

"That's bullshit," Brody said.

"That was smart on her part," Mary muttered.

"Why's that?" I asked.

"When you make a deal with an Angel, breaking it is suicide."

"What do you mean?" Leah asked from her perch on the stairs.

"Think of the life as collateral. If she doesn't hold up her end, the Angel takes the soul as payment, so to speak," Mary said. "Metaphorically, anyway."

As in, kills them. Just as I'd thought. I wanted to know, but was digging worth my mom's life? Although, if Mom didn't tell me, then it wouldn't put her at risk. So, if I figured it out on my own, Mom couldn't be killed for it.

"How are we going to find her then?" Adam asked.

"We're not," Mary said.

"What?" Leah said. "What do you mean we're not?"

"Exactly what I said. We aren't going to find their mother. Whoever she is, she doesn't want to be found. Don't you think that should be respected?" Mary asked.

I did understand that perspective. A woman's right to choose is her right. She could have gotten rid of me and Kai, but she didn't. She made sure I went to a beautiful family. I wasn't sure if that was enough for me, I still felt like I had the right to at least know who she was. But I did understand.

"No, actually. I don't," Leah said. "You're an Angel, and if Laila's mom is one of you, then you're our best chance at finding her."

"I don't think you've understood me. I'm not going to find her, you're not going to find her, neither are you, or you, or Laila's brother." Mary pointed a finger between us. "If an Angel is instructed to procreate, their job ends at the birth of the child. They have no obligation to meet them, talk to them, or even be near them. In fact, their meeting is frowned upon."

My perspective shifted a bit then. She created us with the intention of getting rid of us. We weren't a mistake with a hookup she wanted to forget. She intentionally became pregnant just to abandon us. We were an order from someone who ranked above her.

Then again, her right to choose was out of the equation as well. She was *told* to conceive us. Essentially, she was used as an incubator. Maybe meeting us would be a painful reminder of something she was forced into that she never wanted in the first place. Or maybe it'd be a moment she'd wished for every day over the last twenty years.

"So that must be where the myths of demigods come from," Brody muttered.

"We shouldn't give them such an admirable title," Adam said. "We should call them what they are. Dead beats."

"Well, that's not fair," Mary said. "They made sure the children went to good families and lived good lives. Look at Laila. She has a sister, a mother. She went to school; she grew up with a dog. It's not like they throw them to the wolves."

A fair argument. Yet the fact remained. Regardless of how we came to be, we did. We existed. And I didn't care to meet her. But Kai did.

"Well, maybe that's true, but Kai doesn't have anyone. He didn't have an adoptive father and his mom just died. He has the right to at least know who she is."

"I agree," Leah said. "Children should know who their parents are."

"Let's take a vote then," Jeremy said. "All those in favor of searching out Laila's birth mom, raise your hand." Everyone raised their hand except for Mary.

"Looks like you're out numbered," Jeremy said.

"And where do you suppose you start?" Mary asked. "Because you know Laila won't let her mom die just to find out what her genome looks like. And her father's dead, so it's not like you can ask him. Kai doesn't seem to have any leads, and no Angel will help you."

"We'll figure it out," I said.

"Yeah, because you kids are so good at solving mysteries." Mary laughed.

"What's that supposed to mean?" Leah said.

"You let a murderer come into your home and nearly kill your best friend, and you still have no idea why."

A phantom pain vibrated through my sternum. My gaze turned to the ground. That's exactly what happened. Adrian walked right in the front door and attacked when we all least suspected it.

"Wow, really? You're going to go there?" Adam asked. "Because you were there too. You saw her countless times and you never suspected a damn thing."

"I wasn't saying it to hurt you," Mary said. "Just as a fact, Adam. I didn't mean to—"

"Shove that apology up your ass." He stood and hit his shoulder against hers. She pressed her lips together. He walked up the steps. "We'll work on this in the morning. I'm going to bed."

"That was low. Even for you," Brody headed upstairs.

"I'm going to bed. We'll talk about this tomorrow." Leah followed the boys to bed.

Mary rubbed her forehead with her thumb and pointer finger.

"That was pretty shitty," I muttered.

"I need to learn to bite my tongue, I know. You kids are just so sensitive." She paused. "That wasn't the right thing to say either."

"Ya know, I see your point to some extent," Jeremy said. "Whoever she is, she has a right to her privacy. And if you don't want to help us find her, that's fine. But why tell them they can't try? This kid has no one, all he wants is to find his family."

"That's the thing though, Jeremy. He has a sister now." Mary gestured to me. "Isn't that enough?"

"I don't think that's for you or me to decide." Jeremy shrugged. "That's up to them."

"How about you then?" She nodded to me. "Do you want to find her?"

"I'm curious. But I have my mom. And she loves me more than this woman ever did or could. Obviously. She never would have given me up if that weren't the case. Plus, I know Angels, and I know what to expect from them."

"What do you mean?" Mary asked.

"Don't get me wrong, I appreciate all the ways you've helped me. Between saving my life and helping me get a handle on my powers, you've been a huge help. But it's not like an Angel could love us like our mothers did." A half laugh left my lips. "You guys don't feel, or at least, you suppress whatever you do feel." I shrugged. "You're all kind of assholes."

She let out a quiet laugh. "Yeah, I guess we are."

I smiled. "Woah, I don't think I've ever heard you laugh before. Now that I think about it, I don't think I've ever seen you smile."

"Once in a while," Jeremy said.

Mary frowned. "That's not true. I smile."

"You're, like, five-hundred years old and you don't have a single laugh line. I think the evidence speaks for itself." I grinned.

"Closer to a thousand." She shrugged. "But fair enough."

CHAPTER ELEVEN

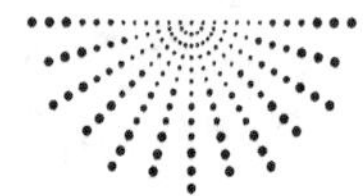

I leisurely rested my head against the arm rest of the sofa and closed my eyes. "I'll take the couch." I heard Jeremy say from the steps. "I'm not getting much sleep any way."

"It's alright. Thanks, though." I grabbed the throw blanket from the cushions behind me and bunched it beneath my chin.

"Your back's going to be killing you tomorrow," Jeremy said. "C'mon, just take my—"

"I'm not going to sleep in your bed. I'm just not." I covered my head with the blanket.

I wanted to. There was nothing I wanted more than to sleep in our bed together. But how could I? How in the hell could I?

"Alright," he muttered. "Alright, I'm sorry."

"It's fine," I said, closing my eyes and hoping to get a few hours of sleep before I had to get up for work again.

A few seconds passed, then I heard him exhale deeply and say, "Laila?"

"Yes, Jeremy."

"Can we talk for a minute?" He asked.

"I'd really like to get to sleep."

"I know, I know. I'm sorry." His voice was soft, sadness touching the edge. "It's just...I've been trying to talk to you, and you haven't answered my calls, and I don't blame you, I wouldn't answer my phone either if I was you, but it's just that there's been a lot of thoughts running around in my head and if I don't tell you, I think I might explode," he said in one breath.

Did I want to hear him apologize again? Did I want to hear him beg me to take him back? Did I want to see his big, sad eyes make me feel guilty for ending things? No, no, and no. But fine. We'd talk.

I pulled the blanket from my head and let out a deep sigh. Then I sat up until my back was flush with the arm of the couch. "Fine. But I've had a lot to drink, and if I say something wrong, don't say I didn't warn you."

"Thank you." He sat on the coffee table and rubbed his forehead.

I pushed messy hair from my face. "What do you need to say?"

"Well..." He licked his lips, eyes shifting between mine. "Well, I want you to know how sorry I am. I never wanted to hurt you and..." I rolled my eyes and he stopped. Then he looked down. "You have every right to be pissed. I just..." He glanced up. "Look, I've been running through that night in my head and I ... I can't remember most of it."

I crossed my arms. "So, what, you were drinking too?"

"No. No, of course not. You know I don't drink." He shook his head, rubbing his clean shaved jaw. His hand moved to massage the back of his neck. "But it felt like I was. Or maybe like I was high. I don't know, it's hard to explain. But it doesn't make any sense. It's there in my mind, but it's fuzzy and distorted. This chunk of time is just, like..." He trailed off, letting out a huff. "It's like erased. And I don't understand it. I wouldn't do that to you, but I did." He raked his hand through his long hair. "I don't get it. I was just sitting there, playing some Rolling Stones song and then the next thing I know, I'm running after Brody, begging him not to tell you."

"You were drugged? And raped?"

As awful as it may sound, I wished he would have said yes. Because then I wouldn't be angry. Then I wouldn't be hurt. If he had no choice in the matter, then I'd never blame him for it.

"No, it's not that." He let out a slow breath. "I'm not trying to get out of it, I know I fucked up. But I just don't get it."

My eyes burned with tears. He fucked up. That's what he told me. That he knew he fucked up and wasn't trying to get out of it. I hardly heard that last line. "Okay, let me ask you something then. Are you attracted to her?"

"Who?"

"Scarlett Johansson," I snapped. "The bitch you fucked. Do you want to sleep with her?"

"Laila, I—"

"Just answer the question. You wanted to sleep with her, right? You thought she was pretty?" I asked.

His brows creased. "Well, I didn't find her repulsive, but that doesn't change that I wouldn't have—"

"What you think you would and wouldn't do obviously doesn't hold true to who you are and what you actually do." I bit my lip to keep it from trembling. "You took your pants off, right?"

Attraction isn't consent—I knew that. But it just sounded so fictional. Guys lie when they get caught cheating. And that's how it seemed. Plus, he'd explicitly said 'I know I fucked up.'

"I don't think you—"

"I know that you did, Jeremy. You slept with her. And clearly, you wanted to. Did you say no? Did you tell her you were in a relationship and that you weren't interested in a one-night stand?" He rubbed his forehead. "No, you didn't."

"But it's not... I..." He paused, licking his lips with dopey big eyes. "I just really think there's a bigger picture here that we aren't seeing. There's a lot of gray area and maybe if we can—"

"Gray area or not, I'm seeing a lot of black and white," I said. "You slept with someone else. And I don't want to be with someone who thinks it's okay to cheat and lie—"

"I never lied to you, and I never said it was okay to cheat," he said quickly, not as sheepish as he'd been a moment before. "I was happy with you, Laila. I'd never want to be with someone else." His gaze softened, eyes growing sad. "I know this sounds ridiculous, okay? I know.

But there's more to this than we can see, I know there is. And you don't have to believe me right now, but I'm going to figure it out."

I grew quiet, gazing him over. "It looks to me like you can't own up to what you did."

"Laila, I'd never cheat—"

"But you did!" I raised my voice. He turned to the ground. "You did, Jeremy. And I can't forgive you right now. Maybe someday, maybe somehow. But..." I paused, frowning. "But right now, I've had a really long day. And to be honest, I kind of hate you at the moment." He winced a bit, shaking his head slightly.

That expression hurt my heart. This was exactly why I didn't want to talk about it. He'd hurt me but I didn't want to hurt him and that's what I was doing.

"I'm just not feeling up to this conversation, Jeremy. I don't trust you and I..." I paused again, watching him lick his lips and struggle to look up. "I can't be with someone I don't trust. And right now, I don't trust you."

He cleared his throat. "I understand. I'm sorry, I know you're tired. Probably a bad time to tackle this conversation. I'll let you get to sleep." He stood and started towards the steps.

A stiffness settled in my chest. I didn't like where we were, or how this had been, and I... I felt bad. "Jeremy?"

"Yeah?" He turned to face me.

"I'm not trying to be a bitch. I just can't do this right now."

"I get it." He managed a wan smile. "I got myself into this mess, right? I'll get myself out."

I gave a quiet laugh. I shifted back down to the couch and pulled the blanket to my chest. "We'll see."

He shrugged. "And Laila?"

"Yeah?"

His soft but serious eyes shifted over me. "I love you. You know that, don't you?"

"I do." He smiled. Then he started back up the steps.

"Jeremy?" He turned to meet my gaze. "I love you too. I just... I can't do this right now."

His lips lifted in a sad smile. "I know. It's alright. Sleep tight."

Jeremy's ability of understanding was one of my favorite qualities in him. Throughout this, no matter how frustrated I was, he stayed calm. I didn't appreciate it as much as I could've in each moment, but it did make all of it easier than it could've been.

CHAPTER TWELVE

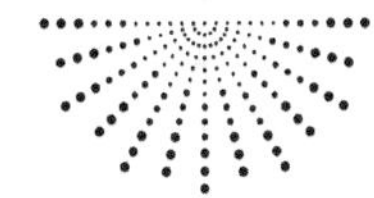

The sun peeked into my eyes as I flipped over on the couch. The scent of warm coffee eased into my nose. My stomach rumbled with desire. But to drink that glorious bean water, I'd have to take off that cozy blanket.

I knew I needed to get up, but I was drained. Emotionally and physically *drained*. I hadn't fallen to sleep until close to five and when I did, my dreams were like a rerun of my hectic day. Kai's voice trailed through my mind. Mom's somber face as she apologized for being unable to tell me what I needed to know. Then Jeremy, and his sad eyes as he pleaded for me to hear him out.

I just wanted to sleep.

"Rise and shine." Leah plopped onto the cushion by my hip.

"Five more minutes." I pulled the blanket over my head.

"Your phone has been going off all morning. It's some random number."

My eyes shot open. "Kai," I muttered, looking around but blinded by the daylight. Leah handed it to me.

Suddenly, I was wide awake. I'd left my phone in the kitchen when I came in the night before. I usually charged it beside the bed as I slept, but with everything that had happened with Jeremy, my routine was completely destroyed. I barely knew what day it was, let alone where I'd left my phone.

"Should I have answered it?" she asked.

"No, it's okay."

I called the number back and asked to be connected to Kai's room. The man told me that he had just checked out. My heart thudded. What if someone had found him? What if something had felt his energy and gone in for the kill? Oh god, what if he was dead?

The diner. He'd met me at Moe's. He probably would have gone there if he needed me.

I called Moe's and Max answered. "Moe's diner, this is Max speaking. How can I help you today?"

"Hey, it's Laila. Kind of have a weird question." I leaned forward and rubbed my temples.

"Of course you do," he muttered. "What's up?"

"Has there been a weird guy in today?" I stifled a yawn. "Maybe six feet tall, skinny, dark hair, drinks a lot of tea?"

"Um, yeah. Actually, I think there was."

The erratic beats in my chest slowed. "Okay, great. Can you tell him to stay put? Or better yet, can you put him on the phone?"

"I would, but he already left." My heart skipped a beat. If he'd left Moe's I had no clue how to find him. "Sophie was his server though. I can put her on."

"That'd be awesome, thank you."

"Sophie!" he yelled. "Hey, Laila's on the phone. She's got a question for you."

"Don't say it like that, you're going to make her think she's in trouble," I said.

"Oh, and you aren't in trouble," Max said. I rolled my eyes.

"Hey, what's going on?" Sophie said in a nervous tone.

"Nothing really, I just had a friend that was supposed to be stopping by. Max said you served him. I was wondering if he told you anything."

"Oh, okay. Who was he?"

I pondered how to describe him for a moment. He stood out in our small, suburban town, that was for certain. "Weird, kind of tall, dark hair. Thick Scottish accent. Drinks a lot of tea?"

"Oh, yeah. Tea guy. What do you want to know?"

"He doesn't have a phone right now so I can't get a hold of him. Any idea where he went? Did he mention anything at all about where he was going?"

"He didn't say where he was going, but he said he'd be back for dinner if that helps."

The tense feeling in my chest subsided and my eyes closed in relief. "Dinner. Yeah, that helps a lot. If he shows up, give me a call and tell him to stay put."

"Can do. Anything else I can help you with?"

"Nope, that about covers it. Thanks, Sophie."

"No problem, but while I have you, could I ask you a quick question?"

I rubbed my tense forehead. Sophie never asked for much, but I was tired and grumpy. "Yeah, what's up, hon?"

"I've had this cough for a couple weeks and I think I might have an infection or something. I've been trying to schedule an appointment, but my doctor's office is booked all afternoon tomorrow and I know you hate opening, but I was hoping that maybe you could work my morning and I could do your evening? It's just because I don't have another—"

The easiest request anyone had asked of me all week. "Oh, sure. That's fine. Just get to the doctor. I'll see you at one then?"

"Thank you so much, Laila. I owe you one."

"It's no big deal. I hope you're feeling better."

I got off the phone. "Is there coffee left?"

"Always," Leah said. "What's going on with this brother of yours?"

"I don't know. He checked out of his hotel. He went to Moe's and left. Told my server he'd be back for dinner though, so I guess that's where I'm eating tonight."

"Well at least you know he's alive."

I started to the kitchen. "At least there's that."

As I poured my cup of coffee, I heard footsteps trot down the maid stairs off the kitchen. "Morning," Brody muttered as he made his way to the coffee pot.

"Morning," I said. "How'd ya sleep?"

"I've had better nights."

"Oh, yeah, sorry for waking you up. I figured you'd want to know." I stirred my coffee with a spoon.

"No, it's not that," he muttered. "I'm glad you told me."

"What was it then?" I asked. That was the first time he'd turned to face me since he'd come downstairs. I gasped. There was a deep, black ring around his eye. "Holy shit, how'd you do that?" I stepped forward to examine it and took his face in my hands.

"Your boyfriend. Or rather your..." He raised his voice so Jeremy could hear him upstairs. "*Ex*-boyfriend."

"Jesus Christ, what did you do?" I leaned in closer for a better look.

"You really need to ask?" He laughed.

Jeremy and Brody weren't known for being the best of pals, but I'd never seen him resort to violence. Especially not on my behalf. "He did this because of me?"

"Not exactly. We were talking about how I shouldn't have put my nose where it didn't belong, and I made a snide comment. I deserved it."

"Well, at least you're not a pussy about it." I patted his shoulder and started to the front of the house.

"Hey, guys," Leah called from the living room. "Can everybody come down here, please?"

I followed Leah's voice, set my mug on the side table and plopped next to her on the couch. A minute or so later, we all were seated around the coffee table, except for Hannah who had already left for school.

"Alright, guys, we need to devise a plan," Leah said.

"A plan for ...?" Adam asked.

"To find Laila's birth mom," Brody said.

"Oh shit. That wasn't a dream. Right. Go on." I laughed and Leah continued.

"Any ideas, guys?"

"We could check out local records, right?" Brody said.

"No Angel would give birth in a hospital." Jeremy shook his head.

"That's true. And my birth certificate says my mother is Rachel Callidy, so that's also a dead end."

"There'll be a lot of those if we're working against the Angels," Brody said.

"This won't be easy," Jeremy said.

Working against Angels and the powers that be never was. That always irked me. When they said jump, we had to ask how high. But when we needed something? They couldn't give two shits less.

"Maybe we should talk about this later whenever Kai's here. He's been researching this for months, or maybe even years. I'm sure he has some leads," I said.

Leah said, "That's a good idea. But maybe in the meantime, we could do some research underground. See what we know about Angels mating with Fae."

"But Laila's also part Guardian," Jeremy said. "That won't make finding information any easier."

"Yeah, races don't usually mix," Brody said. "I doubt we'll find much in the books."

"No, but it might give us another direction to look in," Adam said. "I mean, I've never heard of a hybrid like you, Laila. But I'm sure there's a reason for that. Mary said that Angels are ordered to reproduce with certain people, right? Maybe if we can figure out why they wanted Laila to exist, we can figure out what all of this means."

"That's a good point."

Kind of a gross thought though. I was created for a purpose. And probably not the good kind. When people do artificial insemination or surrogacy, it's 'cause they want a baby they can love and care for. Because they want another piece to fill out the puzzle of their family.

But nope. My mom didn't want me. Just wanted to pop me out and give me to a stranger because someone told her to.

"I think why they wanted a hybrid is pretty obvious," Brody said. "Power."

"Right, but if that's what it was about, then why would they give me to my dad? And Kai to his parents? Wouldn't they want us to fight for them?" I asked. "Doesn't make much sense to order someone be born for their power, only to have their power hidden."

"The lady makes a good point." Jeremy chewed his lip.

"Alright, well let's all simmer on what we've got so far and regroup tonight," Leah said. "And don't eat when you go to get Kai, Laila. I'll make something and we can talk over dinner."

Come to think of it, eating at the diner probably wasn't the best move after all. We were going to talk about supernatural issues. It wouldn't be good if anyone overheard.

"Sounds good," I said. "But try and cook something simple. Something he might be able to identify with a bit? Vegetarian's probably the safest bet."

"Oh yeah, he's from another world," Adam muttered. "I wonder what he'd think of a taco."

"You should've seen his face when he tried whiskey," I said.

CHAPTER THIRTEEN

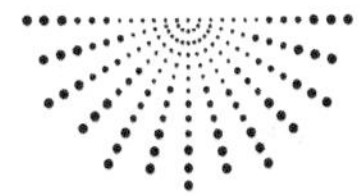

Afew hours later, I got a call from Sophie saying Kai was there. I rushed to Moe's, surprised to see a familiar green jeep in the parking lot. I thought maybe it was a customer, but the closer I got, the more details I made out. I knew the scrape on the back bumper, because I was the one who put it there.

Moe was in town.

When I was thirteen, Moe gave me my first job washing dishes. At sixteen, he bumped me up to server. When I was seventeen, I was unofficially managing the diner. At eighteen, he gave me the title.

Generally, Moe wasn't around. His wife died about ten years prior, and he promised her that he'd go out and see the world for the both of them. For the past five years or so, he did just that. Travelled the world.

When he was around though, I was always thrilled to see him. Unfortunately, I didn't know how to explain anything about Kai to him. He was a good friend of my dad's before he died, so maybe he knew something about it. Or maybe he didn't. Regardless, I couldn't say, "Hey, Moe, this is my long-lost brother Kai. He lived on another dimension his entire life and just came here to meet me and look for our mom."

I decided I'd lie. I'd say Kai was a distant relative visiting from Scotland. Anything else I could make up along the way.

I opened the door to see Moe behind the counter. He shifted some papers around, fiddling with his mustache. "Moe!" I walked around the bar. "It isn't Christmas yet, is it?"

He smiled; a touch of an English accent pierced the edge of his words. "Oh my, look how you've grown. You're a woman now, huh? Last I saw you; you were still in high school."

"Has it really been that long?" I put my arms around him in a tight embrace. His chunky arms tightened at my waist, big belly pushing into mine.

"I think it has. Wow." He pulled away and gave me a once over. "How's that bug doing for you?"

I shrugged. "She runs. Some days better than others. But she's my baby."

"Well good. I'm glad you still have her. Agnes loved that car."

I smiled. "I remember. So, what're you doing here? Wasn't enough snow in Bora Bora?"

He laughed. "Oh, no. I had some business to take care of in New York, so I figured while I was state side, I'd stop and see how things were going here. Not too bad, I gotta say. I picked a good manager."

I smiled. "So, how's your stay been so far?"

"Great." His smile stretched up his cheeks. "I went up and saw Agnes's grave. I visited your dad while I was up there. Then I went to Beverly's Bakery and picked up some doughnuts. You know, I've had pastries all over the world and somehow, nothing tastes as good as Beverly's."

I laughed. "They are delicious, I'll give you that."

I made a mental note to stop by there one day soon. It'd been a while since I had one of Beverly's bearclaws and I was craving one. Ooh, and a chocolate covered Oreo. I'd have killed for a chocolate covered Oreo. I wondered if Kai would be into something like that. Then I wondered if he even had chocolate or anything of the sort where he was from in the North.

He smiled. "Yes. Yes, they are. But I just checked the schedule, and you're off today. What are you doing here?"

"I'm actually meeting up with a friend." I looked around, seeing Kai tucked away in the corner booth. "That's him over there."

"Ya know, I thought he looked familiar. Honestly, I had to do a double take. He looks exactly like your father did at that age."

I laughed. "Yeah, well. He's family so."

"Well stay for dinner," he said quickly. "On the house, anything you want. I'd love to get to know him. Any family of yours is family of mine."

"Aww, well thanks for the offer, Moe, but we actually have plans. But ya know what, I'm opening tomorrow. How 'bout I come in an hour early and we can have breakfast?"

"Don't come in early, we'll just open an hour late." He smiled. "Go ahead, enjoy your night, Laila. I'll see you in the morning."

"That sounds great, I'll see ya then."

He held his friendly smile and waved as I started across the diner.

I went over to Kai. He sat with his head in his hand, a cup of tea in the other, and a duffle bag over his shoulder. In a hushed tone, I said, "How ya doing, big brother?"

He shrugged, rubbing his stomach. "Not feeling too good today."

"It's just the whiskey." I slid into the adjacent side of the booth. "You'll feel better after dinner."

He reached in his pocket, pulled out some crumpled ones, and laid them on the table. "I don't ken if I can eat the food here. It don't taste like food."

"Pizza isn't exactly real food. We'll have an actual meal this evening."

On the way home, I explained to Kai that we'd be having dinner with my ex-boyfriend's family. He didn't seem to grasp it, so I just labeled them as my friends. We arrived back to the house with many warm greetings and odd introductions. I explained who everyone was and what all of us could do. He was amazed by Jeremy's power to create and control electricity considering he'd never seen it before.

It was bizarre, constantly explaining what everything was and what it was used for. Fascinating, but bizarre.

Throughout dinner, I had a hard time keeping my mind from traveling. As much as I wanted to focus on Kai and what he must have been experiencing, I kept thinking about my dad. How he'd torn us apart. How he'd told Kai about me but didn't tell me about Kai.

I thought about how he lied to me about my mom. And then how they both lied to me about my birth, and about my sister.

Then I started thinking about Jenna in greater depth. Should I tell her about dad? He raised her; he was her dad as much as Mom was my mom. I couldn't take that away from her. But didn't she deserve to know who her real father was? Or that we weren't related at all? Or about the fact that dad kept his son from us our entire lives?

I tried to chime in on the conversation as Kai spoke and laughed with my surrogate family. But I wasn't sure what to say. The reality was just dawning on me.

Everyone around me had been lying. My dad before his death. My mom for as long as I could remember. My boyfriend. The mysterious biological mother I'd never met.

My entire life had been a lie. I didn't know who I was, but my parents did, and they kept it from me. My boyfriend, my *soulmate*, had cheated and hid it from me. The people who were supposed to love me the most put so much effort into deceiving me.

There I was, in a room full of friends and family, and I felt alone. Nothing felt right. The world seemed different. It felt dark, cold, and sad. I was trying to be happy, but I just couldn't slow my racing mind.

After dessert, I headed to the back porch. I chugged my bottle of water and let the crisp air cool my sweaty skin. I leaned my body against the brick wall behind me, slowly collapsing against it, enjoying the frozen brick on the backs of my arms.

"Hey," Jeremy said in the doorway.

"Hey," I said. "Nice party in there."

Nodding, he gave a smile. He lowered himself beside me. "Yeah, he's a nice kid. It's a little surreal though, isn't it?"

I let out a huff of a laugh. "Ya know what the weirdest part is?"

"Hmm?"

"He's a spitting image of my dad. Couldn't figure out where I knew him from at first, but Moe said it earlier and that's it. He looks like a younger version of my dad. Even the expressions he makes. It's bizarre."

"You look a lot like him. A prettier, female version." He smiled. "But he's definitely your twin."

"Really?" I asked. "People always tell me how much I look like my mom. That's clearly bullshit."

"Yeah, I guess so." He chuckled a bit. "So, how are you? Are you alright?"

"I'm great." I forced a smile. "Everything's great. I have a brother. It's...it's really exciting."

He took a long look over me. "Uh-huh." He got quiet for a moment, big, electric blue eyes resting gently on mine. "You sure you're alright?"

I gave a fake smile. Tears welled in my eyes. "No. Not really."

He leaned in closer. His arm wrapped around my shoulders. For a moment, I wasn't mad at him. I didn't think about what he'd done or what we were. I just let him hold me tight as I fought back tears. Being with him just felt right, no matter what he'd done.

After a moment, I pulled back and rested my head against him. "I wish things were different, ya know? My dad... He never got to see us together. He never even told me he existed. And I'm so mad at him for separating us. I get it, I do, but he could've at least told me about him. He told Kai, why couldn't he tell me?" I said, still lying my head against Jeremy's chest. "I'm having dinner with a stranger. He knows me but I hardly know a thing about him. And it sucks because I want to relate, but we're literally from two different worlds. I've only known that supernatural things exist for a couple years, he's been raised with his powers. And I just..." I trailed off. "I don't know how to do this."

"You're doing great." I scoffed and he smiled. "No, I mean it.

There's no Wikihow that tells you how to build a relationship with your long-lost brother. At least it's not as bad as Luke and Leia."

I rolled my eyes. "Again with the Star Wars references."

"No, I'm serious. You could've made out with him, that'd definitely be the wrong thing to do." He smiled wider, jokingly nudging his shoulder against mine.

I pulled away, hitting his chest with a laugh. "I hate you."

He laughed and smiled wider.

CHAPTER FOURTEEN

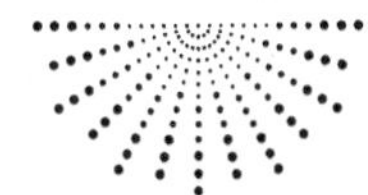

At five, my alarm sounded. I'd passed out on the couch around ten, so I'd gotten enough sleep to function. I threw on some makeup and made my way to my car. Groggily, I climbed in and went on my way to work.

I put on some Nirvana, blasting the radio so high that I could scream the lyrics without hearing my disgusting singing voice.

It had been a rough week. But I had no idea how much worse it was about to get. When it first started, driving down the back roads of our boring town, I had no idea how important that day would be in my story.

It was just a day. Another page in another chapter in the story of my life.

But that's how every pivotal moment starts out. Just another day. You never know when your entire world is about to change.

The only car in the lot was Moe's dingy Jeep, dusted with a layer of peaceful snow from the night before. I didn't see any fresh tracks stamped on the sidewalk; I didn't feel the presence of another person.

Everything looked as peaceful and quiet as it always did at five o'clock in the morning.

I made my way to the door, expecting it to be unlocked since Moe was there.

But it wasn't.

Maybe he'd locked it while preparing for the morning rush. But the lights were out. Still, I went on, pushing any suspicion from my mind.

I dug in my purse for the keys I'd just dropped in, pulled them out and unlocked the door. I stepped inside, hearing the bell ring above my head as it always did.

I set my things on the counter and started around the bar to clock in at the register. Just as I rounded the edge, I saw it.

Everything froze. The seemingly meaningless morning quickly went down in mental history as one of the most significant days of my life.

I'd seen dead bodies. Most more gruesome than the one I stood before. But that type of horror couldn't be forgotten or brushed off. It wasn't a Demon or a Witch we'd killed to save lives.

It was someone I knew.

Someone I loved.

My limbs went numb, and my brain stopped processing. I stumbled backward, cupping my hand over my mouth.

That anxious, fight or flight reflex kicked in and I couldn't help the scream that made its way from my lips. It tore through the silence like stepping onto a frozen lake, only for it to snap and crack, falling apart and sending me down into the icy water on a quiet day.

There on the old, checkered tiles in a pool of his own blood, Moe lay. A look of outright terror frozen on his wrinkled, age spotted, blood splattered face. His eyes were wide open, casting a dark, cold gray gaze over the room.

What looked like a thousand stab wounds stared up at me from his torso. So wide, so deep. The drops of crimson from the impact splattered against every wall, the counter, even the ceiling.

For a second, it felt like a blade through my own torso.

I dug in my purse for my phone.

It's all a blur after that. I called 911. The woman who answered told me to check for a pulse. I told her he didn't have one and she told me not to touch anything. So, I didn't.

I was horrified. Who would kill Moe? The man didn't have a mean bone in his body.

My stomach churned and I ran outside, puking all over the sidewalk.

I dropped to the ground. My hands shook. The terrified trembling turned to sobs. I didn't know what to do. I didn't know who to call. I didn't know... anything.

Suddenly, it was like the world had stopped spinning. I couldn't hear my breaths moving in and out of my chest. I couldn't hear the woman on the phone anymore.

Before my powers, I'd had panic attacks on a regular basis. At least once a week. But when I got my abilities, I had no choice but to control my emotions, because my emotions ruled that part of me. If I weren't able to control my powers, someone would get hurt.

But after what I had just seen, I wasn't able to rationalize. I couldn't take the step back that I normally took. I couldn't help it.

My vision went blurry, and my body quaked. I cried and I cried. I didn't even know if I was still breathing.

I held the handrail for balance, trying to steady myself and keep from falling over. As things started to go black, I lowered myself to the ground. I braced my body against the chipped handrail, knowing from experience that it was better to faint in a seated position than from standing.

I must have passed out because when I came to, there were sirens and flashing lights rushing into the parking lot.

An officer leaped from his patrol car and rushed toward me yelling, "Are you Laila Callidy?"

I wiped black mascara tears from my cheeks. "Yeah, I called 911."

"What's going on here, miss?" He looked at the pile of vomit next to me.

"I-I." I paused, taking in a deep breath before I continued, "Moe, my boss, the man who owns this place. I ran into him here yesterday and he-he asked me to stay for dinner but I told him I couldn't so he told me that we'd have breakfast this morning and I came in and he was just lying on the floor all covered in blood and I don't know who would've—"

"Okay, miss. I need you to slow down. Your boss, Moe?" I gave an expression of confirmation, and he continued, "Okay, Moe asked you to come in this morning for breakfast. Is he just your boss?"

"Well, no, he was a friend of my dad's. He gave me my job here."

"Okay," he said. "So, Moe asked you to meet him here for breakfast. You came in, was the door locked?"

"Yeah. I don't know why, 'cause he doesn't lock the door. Just at night, and he knew I was coming in. I-I used my key, I'm the manager."

"Okay, so you walked in, and what did you see?"

"I set my purse on the counter and I went to the register to clock in and that's when—" I paused, choking back tears. "That's when I saw him on the floor."

"Okay. Stay put, alright?" He turned to walk away, then looked back at me, then back to the puke. "Was this here when you got here?"

"No, that's–that's mine."

He started into the diner.

A few moments later, another cop approached me. "Miss, we're going to need you to come down to the station and give a full report of what you saw."

"Yeah. Yeah, of course."

"Can someone pick you up? You don't seem to be in a good condition to drive."

"I'll figure something out. Thank you."

CHAPTER FIFTEEN

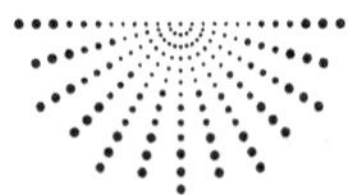

When the officer said I'd be going to the police station to give a report, I thought it'd be that simple. Give a report, then go home and cry like a baby.

I didn't realize I'd end up here. Sitting at a cold metal table, on an even colder metal chair, drinking watered down, lukewarm coffee cluttered with grains. In front of me was a two-way mirror, and I couldn't help but wonder why.

The door swung open, startling me. Steaming coffee spilled over my hand. "Shit," I muttered, using my hoody to wipe up the mess.

"Hello, Miss," a man in a fancy black suit said as he entered the room. He was older than me, but still young. I'd say somewhere in his mid-thirties based on his salt and pepper colored hair and supple brown skin. His eyes were a warm, medium brown and his hair cleanly cut just above his ears. He glanced at his paperwork, approached the table and sat across from me. "Callidy?" I nodded and he continued, "I'm Detective Ray Ramirez. I need to get your recollection of this morning's events that led to the discovery of Moses Bakers' body."

"Yeah. Yeah, of course," I said.

"Alright, now let's start from the beginning. You manage Moe's

Diner, is that right?" I nodded and he continued, "You're pretty young to run a business."

I shrugged. "My dad was friends with Moe, he hired me when I was a kid. I went from dishwasher, to server, to manager. It's a small place, there really isn't much to it."

"Yeah, I've been there a few times. It's very quaint." He paused, shuffling over some notes. "So, we checked the schedule. And it said that your shift didn't start until one p.m. Why were you there so early?"

"I went to the diner last night and I ran into Moe. He said we should have breakfast. Well, no. Actually, he said we should have dinner and I already had plans, so I suggested breakfast. We haven't seen each other since I was in high school. And I switched with one of my waitresses so she could get to the doctor, I wasn't supposed to come in 'til lunch," I said. "I'm glad I did though. I can't imagine what she would've done. Probably would've lost another server."

"We'll have to get her information and cross check that," he muttered. "What about contact with Mr. Baker? Did you talk on a regular basis?"

"Not really. We'd talk on the phone every few weeks or every other month about issues at the diner. But mostly, I just faxed him quarterlies."

"Right." He glanced over his papers again. "So, you came in early for breakfast with Mr. Baker. When you arrived, was there anything out of the ordinary? Cars that shouldn't be there, maybe a person somewhere there usually isn't?"

"No," I said. "No, it seemed like a normal day. But the door was locked, and Moe only locks it if there's no one there."

"Yeah, I see that in my notes. And you're the manager, so you have a key, I'm sure." I nodded and he continued, "Tell me, does the diner have security cameras?"

"Not many, but there is one on the entrance and one on the back door. They're really old. Like VHS tapes old."

"We're going to need copies of at least the past twenty-four hours."

"Of course."

His warm brown eyes lifted to mine. "So, you unlock the door, step inside, and what happened after that?"

"I walked to the counter and set down my things. Then I walked around the bar to clock in and... and that's when I saw him."

His expression showed no emotion. No sympathy, no uncertainty. He was utterly blank. "What'd you do?"

"I went in my purse and found my phone and called 911. She told me to check for a pulse. He...he didn't have one, so she told me to wait outside and that dispatch was on its way."

"And the vomit outside. Care to. . .?" He made a rolling motion with his hand, as if asking for an explanation.

"After seeing him like that, I just felt sick and I ... Well, ya know."

"And what happened after that?" he said.

"I thought I was going to have a panic attack, so I sat on the ground and waited for the officials."

"Did you?"

"Did I what?"

"Have a panic attack."

"I guess, yeah," I said. I didn't see how that was relevant. But okay, pal. "I haven't had one in a while but... Well, that was a lot."

"I can only imagine. It's been a rough couple of years for you, huh?" he added in a casual tone.

"To put it lightly," I muttered.

He gave a half chuckle. "It must be tough."

"Yeah, Moe was like a second dad." I raised my hand to my face and rubbed my eye.

"Right. Sure, and your best friend, and your father." He read from a sheet in front of him. "I can't imagine what it's like to lose so many people that close to you. Especially at your age."

Why bring up Adrian and my dad? "Yeah, it's been hard. But this is about Moe, isn't it?"

"Sure." He looked back down at his papers. "Sure. I was just wondering—Your friend, Adrian Montgomery. She went missing in February of 2016, correct?"

I put my best poker face on. "Yes. She did."

"So, tell me about that night."

"About what night?" I asked, heart starting to pound in my chest.

"The night Adrian went missing. She was last seen on her way to your birthday party, isn't that right?"

"Yeah. Yeah, she was, but she never showed," I lied.

"Huh," he said. "Are you sure about that?"

I'd seen enough cop shows to know it was time to lawyer up. No, I didn't kill Adrian, but I knew who did. And clearly, he had some suspicions of his own. There hadn't been much investigation into her disappearance, and I'd thought she'd been forgotten. Clearly though, Ray Ramirez hadn't.

I narrowed my gaze. "Okay. I'm sorry, but wasn't I here to give a report?"

"Yes, you were. But while you're here, I figured I'd ask you a few questions."

"It feels a bit more like an interrogation to me."

"Well, should it be?"

My head jolted back a bit. "Of course not."

"So then answering my questions shouldn't be a problem. Homicide and missing persons aren't common around here. This isn't a city; this is a very small town. It's my job to make connections, and you're connected to three homicides in three years. I mean, you can't deny that people you're close to seem to be dropping like flies. Your father in 2015, your friend in 2016, and now your boss, in 2018."

"You can't be serious," I said. He huffed, crossed his arms with a smile, and leaned back in his chair. "It's been a hell of a day, and I really don't feel like being harassed about my dead friends and family. So, if you'll excuse me ..." I stood and started to the door.

"Dead?"

"Pardon?" I said.

"You said, 'dead friends and family.' Adrian's body was never recovered."

I glanced at him over my shoulder. "She was declared dead in May."

"Right, but generally when someone goes missing, families and friends don't call them dead."

"If you're suggesting I had something to do with Adrian's disappearance, you're sadly mistaken. Adrian was my best friend and I think about her every day of my life. Implying that I'd do something like that isn't only ignorant, but also extremely offensive." I reached for the door handle. "I have nothing more to say here."

He gave a little half chuckle. "Well, you have a great day, Miss Callidy. I hope you enjoy your new business."

I squinted and looked over my shoulder again. "What are you talking about?"

"You didn't know?"

"Know what?"

He smiled. "You're the executor of Moses's will. At the very least, I know you'll get his business. Probably a sizeable inheritance too."

CHAPTER SIXTEEN

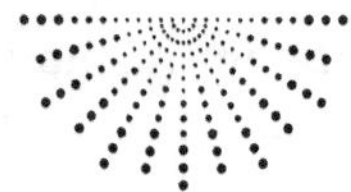

By the time I'd left the police station, I had no idea what time it was. It could've been midnight for all I knew. I checked my phone, realizing I had ten missed calls from staff members at the diner. I wasn't sure what I should do. Hold a staff meeting? Send out a group text?

I dropped to the sidewalk and sat with my feet off the curb. People stared, giving me questionable and some judgmental gazes. But I didn't have a single fuck to give.

I started with Max, because he was my closest friend at the diner. When I told him that Moe was dead, he thought that I was joking. Then I broke down into tears and he apologized profusely.

I didn't get into the details of what I'd seen, or that he left the diner to me. I didn't know how.

As we wrapped up the conversation, I asked if he could spread the message. I wasn't in any place to tell my employees what had happened, and I certainly wasn't ready to tell them that I was taking over the diner. He said he'd get the word out, apologized, and to let him know when the diner would be reopened.

There I was, sitting on the sidewalk of a busy street. Just watching the cars go by. I was there, but I wasn't. I wanted to cry, but I couldn't. I felt numb. Everything just felt numb.

When I checked for his pulse, he was still warm. Not hot, but warm. Maybe if I'd come in an hour earlier, maybe he'd still be there. Maybe I would've been able to save him.

I kept seeing the blood. All over the floor, strewn against the counter, splattered on the white ceiling. Everywhere.

My stomach churned and I knew I couldn't sit there anymore. So, I stood up and started walking. The diner was about two miles from the police station. I could've had someone pick me up. But that would mean I had to talk. And I wasn't ready for that. Not yet.

I started walking, and I didn't stop. I barely even looked up from the ground. Probably would have walked right past the diner if not for the flashing red and blue lights.

When I finally made it there, I had to duck under the caution tape to get to my car. There were still three cops parked out front, but the ambulance was gone.

Then I remembered I'd left my purse inside.

With a heavy heart, I approached the diner. Reliving this morning. Seeing it all in my head for the thousandth time.

I made it to the doorway and knocked to get the officers attention. The one I'd talked to this morning turned around. "Oh, hi, ma'am. Do you need something?"

"Yeah, my keys are in my purse on the counter. Do you mind if I …?"

He turned to the other cop. "Hey, Johnson, is she allowed to take her purse?"

"No, that'll be logged as evidence."

"Sorry, I can't give it to you. But I can get you your keys."

"Sure. Can I have my wallet too?"

"Yeah, I don't see a problem with that." He walked across the room, slid on some gloves, carefully opened my purse, and grabbed out my keys and wallet.

My eyes fixed on the blood splatter. Suddenly, I couldn't picture

Moe without seeing that blood. I couldn't remember what he looked like alive. Those frozen eyes and blood speckled cheeks were all I could visualize. It was like that feeling once you get a haircut and don't remember what you looked like before it.

As he handed them to me, I cleared my throat. "So how do we go about cleaning this up?" I gestured towards the counter. "Is there someone to call or do you guys…?"

"Yeah, I can get you some numbers. There are services for this sort of thing. But you won't be able to get them in here for a few more days, maybe even a week. Everything has to be cataloged and inventoried. All evidence will be bagged and photographed."

"Right. Well, I'm going to need to hold a staff meeting to let everyone know what happened. When do you think I should schedule it for?"

"Honestly? I couldn't tell ya. But if I were you, I'd find somewhere else."

"Alright. Thanks."

"Sure thing," he muttered. "And I'm very sorry for your loss, by the way. We come by here all the time, always loved that old man. He built a great place, and you've kept it running just the same. Always liked that about this diner. If it ain't broke, don't fix it, right?" He sent me a sad smile.

"Right," I muttered. "Thanks."

CHAPTER SEVENTEEN

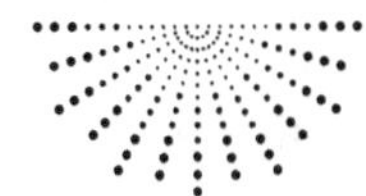

Walking through the door, I tossed my wallet on the entry table and kicked my shoes carelessly onto the welcome mat. I heard the TV in the living room. I took a glance in, noting Brody sprawled out on the couch watching *Game of Thrones*. I thought about saying hi, but I decided I wasn't in the mood to talk. At least not with Brody.

I made my way to the kitchen and read a note on the counter for me.

Hey Laila, me and Hannah took your brother out to see a movie and get dinner. Just so you don't think he disappeared. -Leah

It was a bit of a relief to not have to see him in my current state of mind. Not that I didn't want to see my brother, just because I didn't want to talk about our long-lost mother or our dead father. I was a little more encompassed by my friend's murder.

I made my way to the wet bar, pulled out a bottle of wine, and poured a glass. It started with a sip and before I knew it, the glass was gone.

"Fuck it," I muttered to myself. I pulled the bottle of whiskey off the shelf. I poured about a shot in my glass and decided that wouldn't be enough. Raising the bottom of the bottle higher in the air, I filled the glass until it was nearly at its brim.

I lifted it to my lips, leaned my head back, and guzzled for a few moments. It was bitter and my throat burned like fire, but it was worth it, because by the time I set the glass down, my body felt warm. My hands tingled and my stomach felt as toasty as the sun.

"Jesus, Lai." I heard Jeremy say from the landing of the steps. "Bad day?"

I scoffed, pouring another shot of whiskey. "You could say that."

"What happened?" He took a few steps forward. He looked closer at my eyes, examining me for a moment. "Hey, have you been crying?" I wiped my eyes, turning my gaze back to the drink on the counter. "Oh, god, Laila. I'm so sorry for all of this. I wish—"

"No," I said. "No, it's not you." A knot formed in my throat the size of a golf ball. "I went into work early this morning to have breakfast with Moe and... Fuck, I can't even say it." Tears welled in my eyes and my breathing became uneven.

He reached forward and thumbed a tear from my cheek. "It's okay." He pushed messy hair from my face behind my ear.

"No." I shook my head, trying to contain my blubbering sobs. "Moe's dead. He's dead, he's gone."

As the words left my mouth, I couldn't hold it in anymore. My face became drenched in tears in less than a second and my body quaked violently.

"Oh god," he said quietly, opening his arms and wrapping them around me. "What happened?"

I hugged his waist. "I don't know. I don't know, he was on the floor and he-he was covered in blood." I made out between weeps. "There was so much blood."

"Someone killed him?" he asked.

"And I can't shake this feeling that somehow it's my fault."

"How could that be your fault?" His fingers ran through my hair as his other hand thumbed tears from my cheeks.

"I don't know. But it doesn't make sense. It doesn't make sense;

Moe couldn't hurt a fly. The only high-risk thing he's ever done in his life is associate with my family."

"Try to breathe," he whispered, holding me tight. "It'll be okay."

"No, it won't," I said between gasps. "He-he didn't deserve that. No one deserves that but Moe—he-he was the best person in the world."

"Geez, who died," Brody said as he came into the kitchen. Jeremy gave him a look and he quietly muttered, "Oh, shit. I'm sorry, I didn't realize."

I raised the back of my hand to my eyes, wiping away tears and goopy snot. I swallowed the liquid running down my throat in a trying attempt to collect my composure. "My boss was murdered this morning."

"Damn, I'm so sorry." Brody's gaze softened. "Are you alright?"

"I will be," I murmured, trying to dry my face.

"Do you want to smoke a bowl?" he asked.

A typical Brody response. But no. I definitely did not. "I'm good. Thanks."

He walked to me and gave me a tight hug. "Do the police have any leads?"

"Yeah. Me." I huffed.

"What? Why?" Jeremy asked.

Brody pulled back with wide eyes.

"I'm the beneficiary to his life insurance policy. I... I get the diner."

"Why?" Brody asked. "All you do is manage his restaurant. It's not like you were screwing him." He paused. "You weren't screwing him, were you?"

"Really, Brody?" Jeremy said.

"It's a legitimate question."

"Who do you think I am?" I narrowed my gaze.

"Just checking," he muttered.

"No, I wasn't screwing him. I've known him my whole life. He was my dad's best friend. He never had kids and he was an only child. He treated me and Jenna like we were his, and—Oh god, I have to tell Jenna. And my mom. They're going to be devastated." I put my palms to my face, rubbing my temples. "This is officially the worst week of my life."

"So far," Brody said. "Worst week of your life so far."

"Why the fuck would you say that." Jeremy shook his head. "Do you want to go lie down, Lai?"

"No. Not yet. I just want to shower and change into some comfy sweatpants and a big sweater and drink this whole bottle of whiskey."

"Are you sure about that?" Brody asked.

"Listen, Brody, right now is not the time to lecture me on my alcohol problem," I said in a stern, yet sarcastic voice.

"No, I just meant there's Jack Daniels in the back. You don't have to drink the cheap shit."

"Fuck yeah." I reached to the top shelf and pulled the bottle from the back.

CHAPTER EIGHTEEN

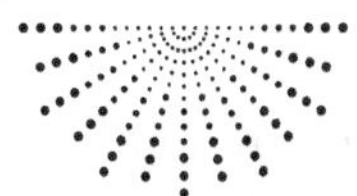

After I showered and got ready for bed, I stumbled my way to Jeremy's room guzzling the bottle of whiskey. I knocked on his door. He pulled it open.

"You don't have to knock." He gave a gentle smile.

"Kinda do."

"Why's that?" He leaned against the doorframe.

"Because, if I don't knock, then it's our room. And this is not our room anymore. This is your room."

"Uh-huh." His shoulder raised. "Well, my closet, full of your clothes, would probably disagree with you."

I stepped through the threshold and plopped onto the bed. "I'll start moving those tomorrow. I'm going to have at least a week off before I have to go back to work."

"Well, you really don't have to do that." He sat beside me. "But if that's what you want." He struggled a smile. "If that'll make you happy."

"Happy." I leaned back onto his pillows. "Can't really be happy right now."

"I know the feeling," he murmured.

"I'll settle for numb." I raised the bottle to my lips and chugged. "I just want to forget the rest of the world exists. Oh, I know." I jumped to the edge of the bed.

"You know what?" He cocked his head to the side.

"Serenade me," I said. He laughed and I smiled. "No, really. Play me something."

He let out a quiet laugh. "What do you want me to play?"

"Anything?" I asked.

"No Backstreet Boys." He grinned. "But yeah. If I know it, I'll play it."

"Hmm. I don't know. Oh, how about Bon Jovi?" He grimaced a bit. That just made me want it more. I smiled wide. "No, you said anything. And I want to hear some Dead or Alive."

His brows raised, unwilling smile pulling down at the ends. "Please don't do this to me."

"Can I record it?"

"Absolutely not," he said.

"Worth a shot. But c'mon now. I wanna hear some Bon Jovi. You said no Backstreet Boys, you didn't say no Bon Jovi."

"Close enough," he muttered.

I smiled, crossing my legs beneath me as he stood. Didn't really see the correlation between the artists, aside from the fact that they were both amazing. But he was gonna do it, so I wasn't bitching.

"You're lucky I love you." I giggled. He walked to the corner to grab his most expensive, exquisite guitar from the wall mount.

"You're getting out the Gibson?" I nearly bounced with excitement.

Jeremy's hair fell in his face in front of his boyish grin. "Only because I really want to see you smile."

I grinned wide, showing all of my teeth. "Goal accomplished; I'm smiling."

He laughed and sat on the bed next to me. "It's been a while, I'm not sure if I remember all the chords."

"Shut up and serenade me."

Laughing, he shook his head. "Well, since you asked so nicely."

He began, starting with a sick guitar solo and then working into the opening. When he sang Bon Jovi, he didn't use his real voice. He sang this weird, almost Johnny Cash sounding pitch that practically killed me. I laughed and he smiled, making his way to the chorus.

His expressions were priceless. They reminded me of the faces you make when you're really pissed off, scrunching down your eyebrows and holding your mouth the whole way open. I laughed and so did he.

I tried not to think about the breakup as he sang. Because I really needed him that day. I didn't want to be mad. I just wanted my best friend.

As the song ended, I smiled. "That was perfection."

He shrugged, sarcastic smirk against his lips. "Yeah, I don't like to brag, but I think I've mastered the raspy tone."

I laughed. "Oh yeah. Nailed it."

He smiled. "I got you to smile though, so it was worth it."

"So, there's something I didn't tell you about today."

A slow exhale left his nostrils. His smile fell. "That's never good."

I was quiet for a moment. "I went to the police station, and they were asking me questions about what I saw and the chain of events that led us there. But then once I'd answered everything, he made a hard left onto the topic of Adrian."

His gaze hardened and he turned to face me head on. "What did he ask?"

"It wasn't so much what he asked but how he asked it. I don't know what he knows, but he thinks I have something to do with her death."

His shoulders stiffened. Deep breaths moved in and out of his chest. "You stuck to the story, right? She never made it here?"

"Yeah, of course. But it was shady. He asked if I was sure she didn't come."

"What'd you say?"

"That she never showed. But why after all this time?" I nibbled on my lip. "I don't know. It was weird. I have all these puzzle pieces and I'm trying to figure out how they fit together." I ran my fingers through my hair. "They won't be able to find the body, right?"

"Not unless they go to Egypt, Austria, New Zealand, South America and Africa. And even then, they'll only find pieces."

"Ew." My lips turned down in disgust. "How did you—Ya know, what? I don't want to know. Ever."

"Good call," he said. "But back to what you were saying, about the puzzle pieces?" I nodded and he continued, "I agree. This week's been a train wreck and the whole thing feels orchestrated."

"What do you mean?"

He pulled his leg onto the bed and shrugged slightly. "I don't know. It started with Mary, with this whole breacher thing. And as it turns out, the breacher isn't only your brother, but he lands in an area that is purely our jurisdiction. And he's from the Deep North, that's, like, Canada on the other realm. Which is really lucky on Kai's part, because if it were anywhere else, the Angels might have taken him hostage for interrogation, possibly even execution." He set his guitar down, pausing for a moment.

"Especially when they realized he was looking for one of them. And then there's the whole matter of what I did and how I have no memory of it, even though I've seen it in Brody's head, and I know that it happened. And then Moe. He just so happens to be in town for the first time in two years and gets murdered hours before he's supposed to have breakfast with you?" He paused. "There's just a lot of things here that can't be chalked up to coincidence."

Biting the inside of my cheek, I said, "It does feel a little suspicious, doesn't it?"

"And the only common denominator I see here is you. More specifically, that all of these things *hurt* you."

"Who would want to hurt me?"

"I don't know." His gaze met mine, softening a bit. "But I know that a few years ago, your best friend tried to kill you, and the only thing she had to say was, 'I had to, and I'm sorry.'"

"Are you thinking mind control?"

"Maybe, I don't know. But whatever or whoever put her up to it, they had her convinced that killing you was the only solution. And even so, who would've done it? She was human, she didn't even know what we are." He licked his lips. "There's just too many coincidences for it to be a coincidence."

"Well, I'm going to sleep like a baby tonight."

"I'm not trying to scare you. I just don't understand this and…" He pressed his lips together. "I don't know if you believe me when I say this, but whoever did this wanted us broken up. So badly that they literally made me sleep with someone else and timed it out perfectly so that Brody would walk in. And it had to be Brody, because any of my other siblings would have let me talk to you about it before blabbing until you read their mind."

"That's not true. All of your siblings would tell me."

He laughed, eyes creasing a bit. "Sure, if I didn't. Eventually. But Brody knew I was going to tell you. We talked about it when we split up at the portal. I just wanted to spend some time with you before I did. I wanted to talk about it. The way it came out made things way worse. I hadn't even been back for a day and he opened his big mouth."

Those words did bring me a shred of comfort. His voice sounded genuine when he said he had every intention of telling me. And his eyes were so soft and sincere.

"So what, he can't keep a secret."

He laughed. "Right over your head, huh?"

"What are you talking about?"

"Brody," Jeremy said. I raised a brow and lifted my shoulder. He laughed. "Wow, okay. I thought you'd figured it out by now."

"Figured what out?"

"Brody. He's in love with you," he said in a matter of fact, obvious tone.

"Shut up." I laughed. He held my gaze. "You're kidding."

"Why do you think he has a black eye?"

"'Cause he made a snide comment about what you did."

"Yeah." He chuckled. "Something like that."

A laugh left my lips. "Brody is not in love with me. That's crazy talk."

"Ask him then. I bet you fifty bucks."

I narrowed my eyes. "If you're right, and he does have a thing for me, then why are you talking about it like it's not a big deal?"

"First of all, I am right. I know I'm right. We've all talked about it, we all know it." He shrugged. "And secondly, because I know it's all one sided. You don't have a thing for him, there's nothing for me to be jealous about."

My head tilted. In his shoes, I'd probably be jealous. If he were right, which I wasn't convinced he was. Brody was my friend. I was closer to Adam by far, that'd be easier to believe.

"What do you mean?" I asked.

"How could I be mad at you for what Brody feels?" He shrugged again. "Aside from that, you're easy to love. It's not like I can really blame him."

I smiled. He smiled back for a second. Then his smile slowly fell. "But anyone else would've given me a little bit of time to prepare myself. If I'd been able to think about what I was going to say, things wouldn't have been as bad as they were." He finally met my gaze, voice slowing with soft eyes. "I had every intention of telling you, Lai. I really did, but you were so happy, and I'd missed you so much and..." He trailed off, turning his gaze to the floor. "And I didn't know how to tell you something I knew was going to break your heart. I was just trying to figure it out before I did. The way you found out...That wasn't fair. None of this was, but you didn't deserve to see that. And I'm really sorry that you did."

I turned away, feeling like I'd just been kicked in the chest. All the while, butterflies still danced in my stomach. "Where'd that bottle go?" I muttered to myself, rustling blankets around.

"Laila," Jeremy said quietly. His hand reached out to take mine. His warm, strong hand held mine, fingers twining together. "Laila, please just stop for a second."

I paused, turning to meet his gaze. He reached forward and wiped a stray tear from my cheek. I leaned into it, relaxing my head against his warm hand. My eyes closed for a moment. I wished all of this would have happened at a different time, because I needed my best friend then. I needed to not be mad at him. I needed my relationship with at least one of the people I loved most in the world to be normal.

When I opened my eyes, his gaze was still on me.

"What?" I smiled.

He shook his head, flashing a quick, gentle grin. "I just miss this."

My fingers tightened around his. And I felt safe. I felt at home. I felt like I was where I should be.

I'm not sure if it was the alcohol or the emotional turmoil, but something clicked. And it occurred to me that no matter how badly he screwed up, no one in the world could make me happier. Maybe it was the soulmate bond thing. Maybe it was just who he was. But regardless of it all, the only thing I wanted was him.

I leaned in and pressed my lips to his. His hand found its way to my neck and into the back of my hair. His lips opened on mine, slow and gentle. He inched closer; mouth still pressed smoothly to mine. The painful pound in my chest shifted to an excited race. And that hurt in my stomach turned to the flutters of butterflies flapping their wings.

His bottom lips caressed mine until our tongues touched. It wasn't one of those intense, sexual kisses where you eat each other's faces. It was slow and sensual, like kissing for the first time. So safe, and familiar, and comfortable.

After the week it'd been, that's exactly what I needed. The safety and comfort that his hands on my body gave me.

I moved closer and tugged at the buttons on his shirt until it opened. He lay down and pulled me with him, holding our kiss. His hand went around my waist while the other rested at my neck. Mine traveled down his chest to his jeans, playing with the button and pulling down the zipper.

He caught my hand and pulled away, meeting my gaze. "You've had a lot to drink."

"If you wait until I'm sober to sleep with me, you'll probably never get laid." I smiled, watching my damp hair drip to the pillow beside his head.

He let out a quiet laugh. "I want to. You have no idea how much I want to." His hand made its way to my ear, massaging it gently. "But I don't think it's a good idea."

"Why not?" I whispered at his ear, touching my lips to his neck.

"Because you'll regret it," he whispered.

"I'd never regret you." I kissed his collarbone. His breathing shortened, getting closer together with each second. My hand at the bulge of his jeans reached for the zipper.

Then he let out a quiet chuckle and pulled away to meet my gaze. "You will, baby." He moved his hands to my hips and carefully shifted me to the other side of the bed. Then he stood, reached up, and scratched his head. He lifted his hand to push long black locks from his ivory cheeks. "I'm going to sleep on the couch. I'll see you in the morning."

"Don't." I sat forward in the bed. "We don't have to kiss but I just..." I trailed off, hand moving to my face and rubbing my eyes. "I don't want to be alone tonight. Please stay."

A gentle smile came to his lips. "Alright. Alright, I'll stay."

CHAPTER NINETEEN

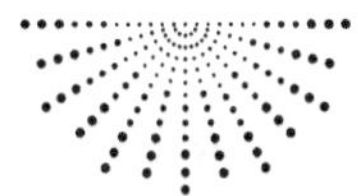

hen I woke the next morning, Jeremy's arms were tight around my waist. For a moment, I wanted them to stay there. I didn't want to let go. But the more I thought about it, the more I knew I had to.

I squirmed out of his grip, threw on my slippers and started downstairs.

When I got to the kitchen, I wasn't surprised that everyone was asleep still. The sun was barely up. I headed to the coffee maker, brewed a pot and looked in the fridge. I pulled out the bagels and cream cheese then popped one in the toaster.

I heard a strange tapping in the yard and headed to the window. Kai was on the patio, holding a ball of water in his hand, throwing it into the air and catching it with the opposite. I watched as it grew, then shrunk and grew again. Then he tossed it in the air and caught it in his opposite palm.

I stepped outside. "And just how in the hell do you do that?"

He jumped, dropped the ball to the ground, and laughed. "With much focus."

I smiled. "Sorry, I didn't mean to interrupt."

"Oh, no. I'm glad ye did, I miss having someone to practice with. Would ye care to join me, lass?"

I shrugged. "I dunno, it's pretty cold out here."

"Refreshing though. Nothing like watching the sun rise and exercising." He placed his hands at his hips. "That sister of yer boy's, the dark one. She told me about yer friend. I'm very sorry."

"Leah. Her name's Leah," I said. "But yeah, thank you."

"Right, course. Sorry, I din't mean that in a bad way. Just how we talk back home," he muttered. "But ye really ought to come give it a try. I bet it'd feel great, all that stress built up in ye and all."

I could use a good paranormal unload. "Sure. You're probably right. Just let me get dressed, I'll be right back."

<hr>

I formed a ball of fire in my hand. "Still orange, I see," Kai muttered.

I turned my head to the side. "What do you mean?"

"Yer fire." He gestured to my palm. "It's still orange."

I laughed. "What's that supposed to mean?"

He smiled. "Little weak, is all."

"Weak?"

"Aye." He absorbed his water. Violet flames shot from his palm. My eyes widened. "Once ye've learnt it enough, it ought to look like this."

"No shit," I murmured, watching the flames of purple ascend from his hand.

He closed his palm. "But go on, then. Let's see what we're working with."

I expanded the flames over each finger. Then I tossed it to the ground, rolling it like a bowling ball.

"Why'd ye throw it down?" Kai asked. He gestured toward my flame that burnt out in the snow with a chuckle. "Won't do ye much good all the way down there."

"I could burn the house down. Or start a forest fire."

"I doubt that. But I can be sure it don't happen." He smiled, a ball of water forming in his hand.

"I dunno, I don't want anyone to get hurt."

"Flame don't hurt me neither, ye ken." He took a step back. "Just let it out."

"It's not that simple. I wouldn't be able to live with myself if I hurt anyone, even if it was just a squirrel."

"Ye can't think like that. Ye can't be afraid of yer strength. When a babe learns to walk, they idn't afraid of stumbling, are they?"

I laughed. "Right, but a baby falling won't burn down a forest."

"If it gets too big, I'll take care of it. Ye've got to let it all out, Laila."

He was right. I had to apply myself to grow my abilities. I knew that. But applying myself could get ugly fast. I'd nearly killed Jeremy a good fifty times by then, a few times while we were fucking. When I let go, when I contained the abilities, I went up in flames.

But I was in a field. Thirty feet from the house, and about five hundred from the woods. I had to just do it.

"Fine. But be ready, okay? Because this can get ugly fast."

He laughed and gave a nod.

I formed a ball of fire in my hand and looked out into the distance. There was a stretch of woods that started further back than the rest of the other trees, about a thousand feet from where I stood. I gestured toward it. "I'm aiming over there."

"Ready when ye are."

I leaned back, swung my arm back, and tossed it underhand. Then I watched as it soared through the air and flew forward into the trees. My heart raced, terrified of watching the trees go up in flames. It landed, smacking against one, and burned the stump. Then Kai shot water at it like his hand were a fireman's hose to put the embers out.

"You've got some distance there." Kai grinned. "Care to try again?"

At first, I was stand offish on the subject. But after a few more tries, I didn't want to stop. We started with the tree, but then we moved onto each other. I'd throw fire and Kai would put it out before it hit him.

Then he'd do the same, throwing water in my direction before I evaporated it.

It made me think back to my dad and how he'd separated us. I could've been doing this my whole life. Instead of playing tag with Jenna, I could've played fire and water catch with Kai. I was having so much fun, it was like being a kid again.

Standing here with him, laughing and enjoying time with someone like me, comfort bubbled deep in my chest. I hadn't realized how deeply I craved familiarity until now. Truthfully, I wanted to forget everything else, pack a bag, and run off into the middle of nowhere with Kai for a few days.

I didn't want to think about what happened to Moe. I didn't want to think about what happened with Jeremy. I wanted to get to know my brother and catch up on all the years we'd missed out on.

But that wasn't the reality I was living in. I had to get to the bottom of all of this.

I guess building a relationship with Kai would have to simmer in the background for a while.

Before I knew it, my body was so warm, all of the snow in a ten-foot radius had melted. Leah stepped onto the porch, saying, "That was probably the coolest thing I've ever seen."

I laughed. "It was pretty cool, wasn't it?"

"I made breakfast. Why don't you guys come in and eat? There's some stuff I think we should talk about as a group."

"I'm starving."

CHAPTER TWENTY

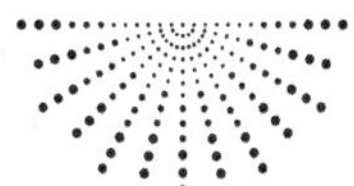

Brody sat next to me at the kitchen table and put his arm around my shoulder. "How are you doing today, Lai? You alright?"

"I'm hanging in there."

"Did you go home? I didn't see you on the couch."

"No, I stayed with Jeremy last night."

"Oh," he muttered.

Jeremy sat down across from me, glanced at his brother, and let out a quiet chuckle. I still hadn't given much thought to what he'd said about Brody. Maybe he did have feelings for me, maybe he didn't, but things were too much of a mess for me to think about all of that. It's not like it mattered anyway. There was only one Skoulda boy I'd ever have an interest in.

"What're you laughing at?" Brody asked.

Jeremy shook his head. "Me? Nothing." He glanced at me. "Nothing at all."

"Alright, guys, we've got to have a serious conversation to try and figure out what the hell is going on in this god forsaken town," Leah began. "By the way, I'm really sorry about Moe."

"Me too." Adam sat down at the table. "He was such a nice dude."

"Thanks, guys," I muttered.

"I'm sure this isn't really what you want to talk about, but..." Leah said.

"No, it's exactly what I want to talk about. I need to figure out what happened."

"Alright, well, let's recap then. You went into work at six to have breakfast with Moe and when you walked in, he was dead behind the counter."

"Yeah. He'd been stabbed multiple times."

"Was there a knife nearby?" Adam asked.

"No knife, no footprints. Nothing."

"Was all of the money still in the drawer?" Leah asked.

"No, the drawer gets emptied every night and then locked in the safe in the office. But I didn't get to check the money. I really don't think it was a robbery though. I guess it could've been, but if someone tried to rob him, Moe would've given them whatever they wanted. When he trained me as manager, he specifically said that if the place was ever held up, no amount of money was ever worth your life. Whoever was that desperate for money probably needed it more than us."

Leah sat at the breakfast nook beside Jeremy. "We'll give it a couple of days. Let the cops do some digging. If we don't hear anything by then, I'll make a trip down there and do some telepathic investigating."

"You said he was stabbed, right?" Brody asked. I nodded and he continued, "Correct me if I'm wrong, but Moe was a big guy, wasn't he? Stabbing him repetitively wouldn't be easy, even for a body builder."

"Yeah, and if someone was robbing a diner, they wouldn't do it with a knife. Plus, Moe kept a gun under the register. If he's standing there and someone walks in with a knife, his first thought would've been to grab it."

"Unless it was someone he knew," Adam chimed in.

"Or if he didn't see them coming." Jeremy raised his shoulder.

"Like a teleporter?" Leah asked.

"Or an Angel," he said.

"That's ridiculous," Brody said. "Angels don't just kill people."

"Not usually but think about it," Jeremy said. "Moe comes into town one day after Kai arrives from the Fae Realm. Keep in mind, Moe is the only person alive besides Rachel who knew Laila's dad before she was born."

"You think he knew who our real mom is?" I asked.

Jeremy shrugged. "I don't know, maybe. It'd make sense, right? Mary told us that if a human went against their agreement with an Angel, they'd kill them. And I wouldn't put it past Mary to spread the word to other Angels she knows. Maybe your real mom came to tell him to keep his mouth shut and things got heated."

The theory lined up. Whoever this woman was, she was willing to kill my mom. Why not kill Moe if he knew something, she didn't want me to?

"Ye think she'd do that?" Kai asked sheepishly. "I've heard lots of bad things about Angels but I... I thought that was just scary stories. I'm not like that, Laila idn't like that."

"The Angels we've met are pretty ruthless," Jeremy said.

"Yeah, makes perfect sense to me," Adam said.

"But that would mean Moe knew about us, wouldn't it?" I asked.

"Maybe," Leah said. "Maybe he just knew of a fling your dad had."

"Well, we can ask your mom," Adam said.

If Jeremy was right, that meant asking Mom about Moe was the equivalent of asking who my mother was. The stakes were getting higher. My friend was murdered. I couldn't add her to the list of dead people Ray Ramirez so graciously pointed out had a connection to me.

"I dunno, maybe that's not such a good idea."

"Why?" Brody asked. "We're not asking who the Angel was, just who else knew about it."

"I don't want to bring her into this," I said.

"But she's already at the center of it," Brody said.

"We can ask her, and if it goes against her agreement, she doesn't have to answer," Adam said. "She's the only lead we have."

Maybe he was right. She already divulged pieces. Confirming Moe knew may be another piece she could relay.

"Fine. I'll ask if Moe knew who my real mom was but nothing

more. I have to tell Jenna and my mom what happened anyway, so I guess I'll talk to her then. Then I have to host a staff meeting to break the news to everyone today. And at some point, I have to get in touch with Moe's lawyer." I rubbed my eyes and stood. "I'll see if Max will let us do the staff meeting at his place."

"You could host it here," Leah said.

"No, that's alright. It's probably not a good idea to have traffic going through here right now, especially with my innocence in question."

I started towards the door. Jeremy stood behind me and Leah said, "Where are you going?"

"I've got some loose ends to tie up in Maine. I was going to flash but with all this legal stuff going on, it's probably a good idea if I drive," Jeremy said. "I'll be back later tonight."

"It's a long drive, isn't it?" Brody asked.

"I'll be alright," Jeremy said.

CHAPTER TWENTY-ONE

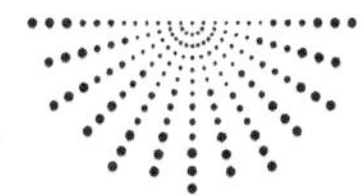

I called Jenna on the way to Mom's and told her I needed her to get there as soon as possible. When I arrived, I could see Mom's worried gaze peeking through the living room window. She probably thought I was going to tell Jenna what I'd discovered days before.

When I made it inside, I sat down on the plushy couch and searched for the words. My stomach ached with anticipation. I didn't know how to explain it. I certainly didn't want to relay it. But it'd be better coming from me than reading it in the newspaper.

I nervously pulled a thread on the edge of couch cushion. Mom handed me a warm, steaming cup of chamomile. I managed a smile and sat it to the coffee table. Then my gaze caught on the mantel. The picture of me in that green and purple romper. And Moe's big belly in the background.

"So, what's this about, hon?" Mom asked.

"I really don't think there's an easy way to do this." I cleared my throat, rubbing my forehead. "I guess I'll just get to it." I rubbed my temples. "Moe was in town the night before last and we ran into each other at the diner, so we decided to have breakfast yesterday morning. I went in early and um." I paused. "Moe was...I walked in, and I went to clock in, and he was…he-he was on the ground behind the register. I found his body."

Jenna's eyes scrunched down in confusion, but Mom didn't seem so surprised. Sad, surely, but not surprised.

"What… what do you mean you found his body?" Jenna asked, "He's dead?"

I gave a slow, sad nod.

"But… but who would do that? *Why* would anyone do that?" Jenna asked.

"I don't know who. I don't know why. But the cops seemed pretty interested in me."

"In you?" Mom asked. "Why would they think that?"

"Because he left the diner to me. Some cars and stuff too, I don't know exactly. I haven't talked to the attorney. The cops told me I was executor of his will."

"Wow, he left it all to you?" Jenna asked. "Rude."

"Seriously, Jenna?" Mom said.

"What? It's not like I expected anything, or I wanted him to die. It's just kind of offensive," she muttered. "I mean, I knew the guy too. I wasn't as close to him as you are, but we were friends. Kind of, anyway. He made a damn good milkshake."

My loving, bitchy big sister. "He might have left you stuff too, Jen, I don't know. Like I said, I haven't talked to the lawyer."

"What makes you think the cops are looking at you?" Mom asked.

"They brought me in to give a report of what'd happened and then the detective brought up Adrian and Dad," I said. "I dunno, he said something about how people close to me 'drop like flies.'"

"Well, you didn't, did you?" Jenna asked.

"Didn't what?"

"Have anything to do with Adrian or Moe."

I made a face. "I can't believe you'd even ask that."

"It's not like I'd turn you in. I just want to know. I mean, you love that diner, and you and Adrian always had a love-hate relationship."

"No, Jenna, I didn't have anything to do with any of it." I brought myself to my feet. "I just wanted to tell you guys before you heard it from someone else. With the diner under investigation, we won't be able to open for a few days, so I've got to host a staff meeting." I grabbed my wallet from the end table and started towards the door. "I love you guys. I'll call you after I talk to the lawyer."

"Wait, before you leave, what happened with you and Jeremy?" Jenna asked.

"Huh?" I swiveled to meet her gaze.

"I saw Hannah Tuesday at school." She pushed up her glasses. "She asked if you were coming back home because of what happened with you two, but she didn't mention what that was."

Jenna was three years older than me. She got her degree as a registered nurse last year and landed a job at the local high school because it was her alma mater. The beloved old nurse had retired the summer that Jenna got her degree, so it was great timing. Being a perfect, upstanding student while in high school, I guess she was a shoe in.

Jen was always the good girl. Dad used to say it all the time with a sarcastic laugh, that I was the problem child, and she was the one who'd have a 401K before she hit twenty-five. And he was right. She never partied, got great grades, and always looked beautiful, even on her worst days. She looked a lot like my mom would with dustier blond hair. Her eyes were a pale, crystal blue, trimmed with long, blond eyelashes. She had this simple, breath taking beauty that required almost no effort. Her lips were small, but they fit her tiny, heart shaped face perfectly. She was the typical American beauty.

"Something happened with you and Jeremy?" Mom asked as she stood and cleared the distance between us.

"This has been a really tough week, guys. I don't want to get into it—"

"Laila Rose," Mom said with narrowed eyes.

"We broke up," I muttered, reaching for the doorknob.

Mom held the door shut with the palm of her hand. "You two were so happy. What went wrong?"

I didn't want to get into it. But if I didn't tell her, she'd keep pushing. She wouldn't let me leave until I did.

"He slept with someone else when he was in Maine. Alright? Can I leave now?"

"Oh, honey." Mom's brows pulled together, tears nearly welling in her eyes. I wasn't sure what she was sadder about. What he'd done, or the fact that she couldn't like him. She regularly talked about how he was the son she'd always wished she had. "I'm so sorry—"

"God, I'm so sick of hearing that. If one more person tells me they're sorry for me, I'm punching them in the face," I snapped.

Mom made a face at my attitude.

"I'm sorry. I'm just really stressed right now."

"It's alright, hon. Can I walk you to your car?"

Her expression said more than her voice, as if she didn't want to mention something in front of Jenna. We walked to the car and my suspicions were confirmed.

She reached her arms around me in a hug, whispering in my ear, "Moe knew about you and your brother. He wasn't as simple as you think he was."

Well, that answered that question.

"I didn't want to ask," I said quietly. "But what do you mean by that?"

Her voice was almost impossible to hear. "He was like you. Like your father. Not that other thing, the Guardian thing. But the other one. The Fae. He came from there, your dad helped him get started here."

"No shit," I muttered, thinking hard for a moment.

Moe wasn't human. I hadn't had the slightest clue that he was anything other than ordinary. But then again, the last time I'd seen him before his death was the first time since I'd gotten my abilities.

I looked back to Mom. "You telling me that...it won't get you into any trouble, will it?"

"I was never told I had to keep that a secret. Moe had nothing to do with our deal. So no, I don't think so."

"You don't think my birth mom did it, do you?"

She raised a shoulder in a half shrug. "I don't know, baby. But I wouldn't put it past her."

"Did Moe know what I am?" I asked.

"Yeah, he did. But I can't give you much more than that."

I pulled open my door and sat down. Then another thought dawned on me. When Moe saw Kai, he said he looked like my dad. Then he invited us to stay for dinner. He said, 'any family of yours is family of mine.' He meant that in the literal sense. We were from the same people and he knew. Either he felt my energy, or he knew the moment he laid eyes on Kai what I'd figured out on my own.

Jeremy was right. He was going to tell me. But my birth mother got to him first.

"Alright, well, don't tell me anything else, Mom. Or Kai. Or anyone. Don't tell anyone, anything."

She held the door as I reached to pull it shut. "I can do that. But, sweetie, I need you to talk to me."

"What do you mean?"

"I know you're probably mad at me for not telling you everything about your life, but baby—"

"No," I said. "I'm not mad at you. Dad, I'm mad at. But not you, Mom. It's just been a horrible week and I haven't felt like talking to anyone."

"I get that, but you've got to be devastated. Let me be here for you."

"I will. I just... I need to keep my distance right now. Moe's dead, probably because of me. And if it were you." I felt a lump form in my throat. "I... I wouldn't be able to live with myself."

Tears welled in her eyes. "Okay. Okay, but please keep in touch."

"I can do that."

"And if you need help planning the funeral—"

"Oh shit. I have to do that, don't I?" I ran my fingers through my hair. "Yeah. Yeah, I'm definitely going to need your help."

She squeezed my shoulder. "And if you want to stay here, so you don't have to see Jeremy, your bed is always open. And the guest room, Kai can stay there too."

"I know, Mom. Thank you."

She smiled. "Plus, I'd really like to meet him. I've always wondered who he'd grow up to be."

I gave a quiet chuckle. "Well, seems to be a great guy. He looks just like dad. It's actually scary how much he looks like dad."

She smiled. "Well, like I said. I'd love to meet him."

"Yeah, maybe we could go out to dinner some time. But Jenna's going to have a lot of questions, Mom. We need to figure out what we're going to tell her."

"Yeah. Yeah, I know."

"I love you, and please be careful. If anything out of the ordinary happens, anything at all, call Jeremy right away. Don't waste time calling me. Call Jeremy."

"What can he do?"

"I can't get into it right now, but he'd be able to get to you faster than I could, so call Jeremy."

She still looked confused but said, "Okay. I love you too, baby. Be safe."

CHAPTER TWENTY-TWO

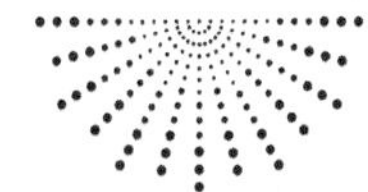

I held the meeting at Max's house, because he lived closest to the diner and he was practically assistant manager. At the staff meeting, everyone asked the predictable questions, most of them I didn't know the answers to.

Someone asked when the diner would reopen. Someone asked who'd killed him. Someone else asked if the diner was unsafe.

Then, someone asked who'd be taking over as owner of the diner. I dodged that one, not ready for everyone to know it'd be me.

Someone asked how they'd be able to pay their bills if they couldn't count on work. Rather than lose my whole staff, I told them I could guarantee them seventy percent of their regular income with money that was put aside in case the diner shut down for whatever reason, which was a lie. I planned on using my personal savings and paying it back with the insurance policy when the money came in.

Then they asked questions about what I'd seen and what had happened. Max interrupted them, saying that I'd just experienced something extremely traumatic and was holding this meeting as a courtesy to the staff. But that wasn't fair to make me relive what I'd seen.

I thanked him and wrapped up the meeting. As everyone cleared out, Sophie approached me with a big hug, saying how sorry she was that we'd switched shifts, and that what I'd gone through was absolutely tragic. I told her it was alright and thanked her for her apologies.

Given my abilities and the life I led, I think it was better that I found Moe than her. I wasn't handling the situation in the best way possible; however, I was probably having an easier time dealing with it than she would have. What was one more trauma to add to my list of reasons for PTSD?

Sophie was the last to clear out, leaving Max and I sitting on his couch.

He sat next to me and handed me a bottle of water. "How ya holding up?"

I laughed, shaking my head as I unscrewed the lid and gulped. Drinking water was one of those simple, basic tasks I always forgot to do. Then someone would hand me a bottle, I'd slurp it down, and realize that dehydration was the source of the throb in the back of my head. I'd tell myself I was gonna remember to drink more later, then completely forget.

"I don't even know how I'm here right now." I huffed. "The past few days have just been a messy blur and I'm surprised I have pants on to be honest."

"Yeah, I can't even imagine what you're going through. It really sucks, all this shit's going down while you're dealing with all that shit with Jeremy."

"Yeah. Yeah, it does. But I don't feel like getting into all of this." I sat forward and chugged the bottle. "I have a lot to get started on today. Mind if I head out?"

"No, of course. If you get any new information, let me know. We can have the meetings here until the diner's back up and running."

"Great," I said. "Thanks, man. That's a huge help."

"Anything I can do." He shrugged. "Want me to walk you to your car? There's a murderer out there. I'd feel pretty bad if you died in my driveway. Then cops would show and shit, and they'd probably have dogs, and then I'd get busted for the half pound in my bedroom. I'd go to jail and miss your funeral."

I laughed, shook my head, and started towards the door. "I've got my taser. Thanks though."

"Be safe out there."

I made it to my car, plopped into the driver's seat, and closed the door. Part of me wanted to cry and part of me wanted to scream. I was so angry, and I was so sad, and I was so stressed. There was too much hitting at once, and I didn't know how to handle it all.

And then it just came out. This long, obnoxious, ear-piercing scream echoed from my lips.

Just as I thought I was relieved, it hit me, and I started bawling again. I laid down, put my head to the steering wheel, and pouted for a while.

It was much easier to hold it all in when I was around other people. Not that breaking down is a weakness, but something about crying in front of my friends always made me feel like a child. Social interaction also kept me distracted; it's easy to forget the pain when you have things that need to be done and conversations that need to be held. But it's difficult to fight the lump in your throat when you're alone.

After a few moments, I decided the pity party had to end. I needed to focus on figuring out the mess I called my life. I started the car and headed home.

Not long after I pulled into the drive, I felt a stabbing pain in my leg. It hurt so much that I cried out. Then again, on the left side of my lower ribs. My stomach flipped, as if I was going to be sick. I slowed the car, feeling dazed. Instinctively, my mind began to reach out to something in the far distance.

My eyes were open, but I wasn't seeing through them anymore. At first, I couldn't distinguish what I saw.

I was looking out a large dashboard. My whole body spun through the air, head smacking against the roof. Body slamming to the left, and then again to the right, and then my head on the ceiling again until I was upside down. My breathing was uneven, and my heart raced.

The dashboard was black, with a gold necklace dangling from the rear-view mirror.

"Jeremy," I whispered.

CHAPTER TWENTY-THREE

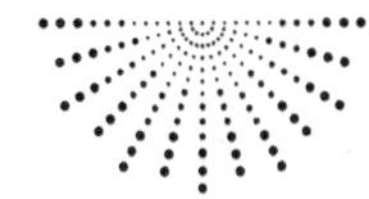

I slammed the car into park, pulled out my phone, and called Adam.

"Hey, what's up?" he answered on the second ring.

"I don't know, but I need you to teleport to the end of the driveway right now and pick me up." I hurriedly pulled the keys from the ignition and opened the car door.

"What? Why?"

"When Adrian stabbed me, Jeremy said he saw it while it happened through my eyes, right?" I stood with my phone pressed between my ear and my shoulder.

"Yeah...?"

"I think Jeremy was just in a bad accident. Please just—"

He didn't even hang up before appearing beside me. "Where is he?"

I dropped my phone to the passenger seat. "I don't know. It only lasted a second."

"If you saw him, then you can find him. You two are tied together. Just go into his mind."

"I've never done that from miles away. I don't know how—"

"Just focus," he said, voice shaky and nervous.

I mentally reached out to his mind. I tried focusing on the energy where I'd felt him.

When I turned the telepathic switch from off to on, there was this nails on a chalkboard sensation in my mind, at least at a distance so far. Kind of like when you hold a microphone up to a speaker.

That retched sound was followed by loud voices. Thoughts whirled in my brain, mostly indistinguishable from one another. I focused harder, trying to find Jeremy's. I thought so hard that I began to feel lightheaded.

After a few seconds, my head started to pound, but I was starting to feel him. It was almost like I could hear him in my mind, although he wasn't saying anything.

I channeled it, focusing on what was in his head. The pain. All he could think about was the pain. Then I was there again, looking through his eyes.

He groaned, looking down at his blood drenched hands. In the corner of my eyes, or rather the corner of Jeremy's eye, I saw his phone, glowing with the GPS open.

"I got it." I took Adam's hand and disappeared with him. Then we landed next to the flipped Charger on a tree covered, winding, ice coated road.

"Jeremy!" I kneeled down to the window and looked inside. He lied face first on the ceiling, struggling to turn over. He was barely conscious and covered in blood. Coughing, he tried to pull himself from the car. "Don't move," I called, looking from the deserted road to Jeremy.

I turned to Adam, expression of desperation flooding my gaze. "Teleport in there and get him to Leah."

"I'm trying, Laila, it isn't working."

"What do you mean it isn't working?" My heart thudded in my chest like a drum.

"I don't know!" He lifted his foot and slammed it through the passenger window. "Me and Laila are here, alright? We're going to get you out."

"My powers..." Jeremy tried to make out between wheezes.

"I know, mine aren't working either. But we'll get you out, just hang in there." Adam lowered himself down to eye level.

"I'm small enough to get inside." I looked from Adam to the window. "I can pull him out."

"Try your powers, are they working?"

I brought a flame to my hand. "But fire won't help."

"Something's grounding us," Adam muttered. "If we find it and get it out, then I'll be able to flash in there and then flash home. Get in there and find it."

"But what could do that?"

"Hematite, or morion maybe? That's the only thing I can think. It's a rock, black and shiny," he said. "It would have to be a decent size to be affecting me from here."

I dropped to the ground and army crawled into the car. Jeremy cried out as I brushed into him.

"I'm so sorry," I muttered, kneeling and looking under the seats.

"Laila, that's not gonna work!" Adam called from outside. "We need to get him out!"

"What's wrong," I heard Jeremy mutter.

"What's going on?" I called.

"The car's on fire," he said. "We need to get him out now."

I moved until I was next to Jeremy's head. That's when I got a good look at his injuries. On his left side, a large shard of glass stuck out of his chest. Another chunk of bloody glass protruded from his upper thigh. I worried it may have severed his femoral artery but pushed that thought from my mind. We had a healer back home, we just had to get him there.

"We're going to have to be really careful," I called to Adam. "Okay, baby, I'm gonna flip you over, okay?"

"Watch the glass," he murmured. "I don't want it to—"

"Hey." I ran my hand through his hair. "Just trust me, okay?"

His disoriented gaze moved between mine. I knew there wasn't a way to flip him manually without pushing the glass further into his chest. So, I did the only thing I could think to.

The air swirled in from the windows, moving slowly as I

summoned it, gently flowing beneath him, until he was levitating a few inches in the air. I lifted him further, high enough that I could spin him around so he was face up.

"Adam, I'm going to put him through the window, help me get him on the ground," I yelled.

"Gotcha," he said, shuffling to the other side of the car.

Balancing him in the air with one hand, I sent a gust of air through the other window to shatter the glass. Adam kicked the stray edges and yelled, "I'm ready."

I held the air around him with my left hand and nudged his body through the small opening with my right. He moaned and groaned a bit, but we got him out of the car.

"You can set him down," Adam yelled.

Slowly, I brought his body to the cement, hearing him cry out in pain as he made contact with the snow.

I hurried out, scooted onto the pavement, and then into the snow.

Jeremy coughed. Blood spat out of his lips, covering his unusually white skin. His eyes moved until he looked at me, revealing a large cut just below his eyebrow. His hand found mine, grasping it tightly.

"It's bad. It's really bad," Adam said quietly, kneeling next to his brother. "I don't know what to do. My powers won't work."

"You think it's in the car, right?"

"That's my best guess."

I moved Jeremy's hand, stood, and walked closer to the vehicle. "Sorry, baby," I whispered to the beloved old car. Then I raised my hands, focusing on the feel of wind surging beneath my arms. Taking in a deep breath, I slammed them forward.

Air rushed from behind me, then around me, sending the car flying in the opposite direction with one big gust. It flipped, roof slamming off the ground, then somersaulting over the hillside of the dingy road.

"Try now," I said, falling to the ground next to Adam.

We were then back home, Jeremy lying on the couch and Adam and I on opposite sides of him.

"Leah!" Adam screamed. "Leah, get down here now!"

"What's the problem?" she called from upstairs.

"Now, Leah!" Adam exclaimed. He looked at me to see if he was okay to flash and grab her.

I took Jeremy's hand in mine. "Baby." He pulled our trembling hands to his lips and kissed my knuckles. "Baby, I'm so sorry," he muttered softly.

"It's okay." I pushed blood coated hair from his face. "It's okay, just relax. Leah's gonna heal you, you'll be fine in a couple minutes. Just breathe. It's-it's gonna be okay."

"No." He shook his head slowly. "I hurt you."

"Stop it. We're gonna get you healed up and then you can apologize all you want."

He coughed. Blood splattered all over my hand. He touched my neck. "Thank..." He coughed again, more blood hitting me.

"It's okay, baby. Don't talk. Take slow breaths, okay?"

"Oh my god." Leah dropped next to me on the floor. "Someone get me a chair."

I started to stand but Jeremy squeezed my hand tighter. He held my gaze and whispered, "Please stay," before coughing again.

"Okay." I tightened my hand around his. "Okay."

"Hang in there, man." Adam dropped the chair next to Leah. She pulled it over and sat next to me.

"Okay. Okay, I'm going to start with the glass in your chest. It's going to hurt like a son of a bitch, but I need you to be as still as possible, okay?" He gave a nod and Leah turned to me. "I don't know if you should see this."

"He wants me here." I warmed my hand around his for comfort. "Just do it."

"Brody!" Leah called, then turned to Adam. "I'm going to get started but I need you to hold his legs down. I don't want that glass out until I'm ready, but I don't want it any further in either."

"I got it," Adam said.

CHAPTER TWENTY-FOUR

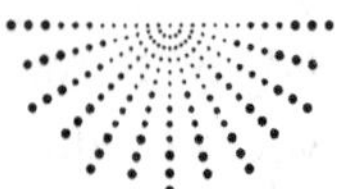

eing healed isn't as simple as it sounds. Sure, all you have to do is lie there. But the pain is excruciating. Your body is healing, but it feels like you're being lit on fire.

It's not just in the spot where you were injured; it feels like the blood coursing through your veins shifts to a rolling boil. Coming from someone who has actually died, death is less painful than being healed by a Fae.

"Jeremy, are you still with me?" Leah grabbed his face and turned it to her.

He gave an odd moan that sounded something like yes. His eyes were crossed and his face whiter than a cloud. His lips, beneath the crimson red blood, turned a ghastly shade of blue.

"Okay, I'm going to pull the glass out of your chest, and when I do, you're going to start losing a lot of blood and your lung is going to start filling with fluid. You're going to feel like you're drowning, but it's only going to last for a second. I need you to fight the urge to cough as long as you can. It's going to take me at least a half hour to get the internal wounds closed. After that, I'll need to take a break before we do your leg. If you feel like you're going to pass out, it's okay. You don't have to fight it. You made it here in time, you're going to be okay. But it's going to hurt worse than any time before because of where the wounds are. Do you think you can handle it?"

He gave a half nod, squeezing my hand, trying to hold Leah's gaze but eyes spinning in opposite directions.

"Are you ready?" Leah asked, looking at Brody and Adam. They nodded, and Leah looked at me. "Are you sure you can handle being here? Because he's going to be in a lot of pain."

"Just heal him, damn it."

She leaned in closer, hand gripping the glass with a sweater that laid on the back of the couch. In one fluid motion, she ripped it out and put her hands in front of the oozing wound. I looked to Jeremy's face, which somehow grew even more fair.

Leah started healing him, blood still oozing from his chest. His eyes grew large, bulging as he let out the most pained scream I'd ever heard. His body quivered like he was seizing. "Hold him tighter," Leah commanded.

"It's okay," I whispered, running my fingers through his hair as he screamed out in pain. His eyes closed and he scrunched down his eyebrows, crying out and biting down on his lip, tears gushing from the corners of his eyes.

Blood formed where his teeth met his lips. I grabbed the sweater Leah had used to pull out the glass, rolled it up, and put it in his mouth to bite down on. He clamped his teeth together, moaning in agony, body quaking in misery. His hands trembled but his fingers tightened around mine.

"You're okay," I whispered, running one hand through his hair and using the other to hold his hand upwards, away from Leah so that she had the angle that she needed.

All I could think was how sorry I was for the way I'd talked to him in the last few days. There was so much blood. Leah was healing him, but that instinct in me kept saying, 'he's gonna die. And you've been a raging cunt to him all week.' I started to hate myself, thinking about how his last memories of me could be when I threw him into the house, or when I told him I didn't care about his side of the story.

And mine would be of all that blood.

Despite his mistake, he was my best friend. He was the darkness to my light. He was the air to my fire, and the electricity that shocked me to life. He was everything to me.

Without him, boyfriend or not, this life terrified me. I didn't know how to face it without knowing he was out there somewhere. A world without Jeremy Skoulda was a world I didn't want to live in.

In those moments, I started to understand how my not-so-permanent death two years ago must have affected him. I started to understand the overwhelming sadness and fear of losing the love of your life. This ten-ton weight in your chest that burns like a star, filling you with nothing but ashes and dust.

If I felt that way about losing him, even though I knew he'd survive, I couldn't imagine how he could give us up by choice, not even three years after watching me take what he thought would be my last breath in his arms.

Maybe Jeremy was right. Maybe there was more to this than we realized.

Almost three years ago, someone tried to kill me. A week ago, I found out that my soulmate "cheated" on me. A few days ago, my family friend was murdered because he knew what I was. And that day, after I had spent the night in his bedroom, someone tried to kill Jeremy.

There was no way those events weren't connected. I didn't know how, and I couldn't begin to imagine why, but I knew there was more to all of it than we could see. These events, these tragedies, they had a purpose. Every single one of them. I didn't understand the reasoning, not yet anyway, but one thing was clear.

Jeremy was right. Someone wanted us apart at any and all costs. Even if it meant killing us.

After about twenty minutes of healing, Jeremy had color back in his cheeks. His lips were pinkish rather than blue. His chest was still open on the side where the glass had cut him, but he was breathing without a wheeze.

Was it because of what we were? The legends said the *par animarum* were cursed. But this wasn't like any curse I'd seen. It wasn't a curse disguised as bad luck; someone was pulling strings behind the curtain. There was a face behind these atrocities.

Leah leaned back in her chair, looking pale with dark circles beneath her bloodshot green eyes. "How are you feeling?" she asked quietly, hand resting on Jeremy's arm.

"Better," he murmured. "I'll be okay for a few hours. Get some rest."

"I've got to get that glass out."

"Not yet," he said. "You need to rest."

"Really, Leah," I said. The dullness in her skin made it clear how badly she needed a break. "I'll make sure he doesn't move. You need to take a break."

She looked at his leg, then his chest, and then back to me. "I'm just going to nap for a few minutes. Give me a half hour. If he starts bleeding or starts showing signs of shock, call for me right away."

As she stood, she fell to the left a bit. Adam teleported behind her and caught her before she hit the ground. "Thanks," she muttered.

They disappeared, and I turned my gaze to Jeremy.

"I don't think I've ever been that scared." My hand rested at the side of his neck, tears welling in my eyes.

"What happened?" Brody looked between the two of us.

"Yeah, how'd you wreck?" I asked.

Brody gasped. "You wrecked the Charger?"

"Don't worry, I'm okay," Jeremy muttered, although I could still feel the excruciating throb in his thigh.

"I'm serious, what happened?" I asked.

"I... I don't know. I was driving and then out of nowhere, the car started flipping."

"Well, that sounds unlikely," Brody said.

"Stranger things have happened." I held Jeremy's blue-eyed gaze. "You didn't see anyone?"

He thought for a moment, creasing his brows and then shaking his head. "I saw something, but I don't know if it was a person. It might have just been snow. But when I was flipping... I think I might have seen someone."

"What were they wearing?" Brody asked.

Jeremy bit his lip. "I don't know, all I saw was white. It might not have even been a person."

"But wait, the car just lifted off the ground and you landed upside down?"

"No, it lifted and then flipped a few times. It definitely made contact with the ground more than the final impact."

"There was morion in the car." Adam appeared a few feet away. "Or hematite, I'm not sure. But someone didn't want you to be able to use your powers."

"This makes no sense," I said. "Why were you going to Maine?"

He paused. "Guys, can you give us a minute?"

Brody looked from me to Jeremy. "Sure. I should probably tell Mary what happened."

Adam disappeared.

Brody teleported and I turned back to Jeremy. "What were you doing? What was so important there?"

"You're not going to like it." I didn't say anything, just waited for him to continue. "Last night, when we were talking and I told you I felt like everything that happened this week was a setup..." I nodded and he went on, "Well. I didn't know what else to do. I wanted more facts. I needed to know if Ally remembered."

"Ally?" He looked down in shame, unable to hold my gaze. "Oh."

The girl he fucked. I guess it made sense that her name wasn't Girl Jeremy Slept With.

"I figured that maybe she'd know something about that night that I didn't." He pressed his lips together. "I'm sorry. I should've told you. I just...I knew you wouldn't like it and—"

"Did you learn anything?"

No, I didn't like it. But the inkling that all of this was a setup was growing. If he knew something, I was dying to know it too.

"I didn't even make it there. I was still a few hours out."

I pressed my hand to my forehead, biting my lip. "What the hell is going on?" I shook my head, stood, and paced along the couch. "Someone kills Moe and then the next day, someone tries to kill you? Half a state away? This... This makes no sense."

"We'll figure it out," Jeremy said.

"Will we? Really? Because someone just tried to kill you, Jeremy, and we still don't know who wanted me dead a few years ago. Don't you get it? They aren't going to stop."

"Laila, calm down," he whispered, hand going to the oozing wound at his chest. "Please."

Trying to slow my racing heart, I sat on the ground next to him. "I'm sorry. I'm just scared." Water welled in my eyes. "I didn't know if you were going to make it."

"I'm okay." His hand found my cheek and wiped away a stray tear.

I held his gaze for a moment, exhaling a heavy breath. "Yeah, for now." Shaking my head, another deep exhale left my lips. "I have so much power, and somehow... Somehow, I feel more pathetic and help-less than I did in high school."

"You saved my life today." Jeremy took my hand in his. A soft smile lifted at the edge of his lips. "Couldn't have done that in high school."

I let out a slow, calming breath. Then I smiled. "So that's what, one to a hundred?"

"No." He frowned. "Your heart stopped beating on my property, a hundred yards away from me. I was five hundred miles away, and somehow, you still managed to save my life. You aren't pathetic, and you certainly aren't helpless."

Uncomfortable butterflies flapped in my stomach again. "I don't want to watch everyone I love die."

"Then don't," he said, hand grasping mine. "Fight, Lai. Use your powers. Make them afraid of you. Show them that you won't take it. Fight back."

"What am I supposed to do, fight the air?" I asked. "We have no leads, Jeremy."

"Then find one. Don't sit here and wallow. Get out there and fight for what you want."

I knew he was right. If I wanted to end this, I needed to figure it out. Feeling sorry for myself wouldn't make anything better.

CHAPTER TWENTY-FIVE

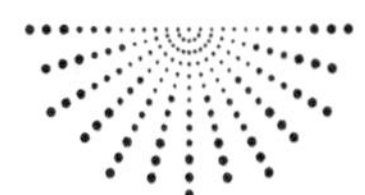

Leah came downstairs about thirty minutes later ready to finish healing Jeremy. She healed his leg, but she didn't have the energy to completely heal his chest wound. She assured him she'd finish tomorrow, but Jeremy was grateful regardless.

When I checked my phone, I wasn't surprised to find five missed calls. The first two were Mom, just checking up on me. There was one from an unknown number, one from Max, and another from the police station. I listened to the one from Mom first, and then from Max, who was informing me I'd left my sunglasses at his house. The unknown number was Moe's lawyer, asking if we could meet up and discuss the situation with his will. The police didn't give me much information, just asked that I give them a call back when I got the message.

First, I called the lawyer and set up an appointment for the next morning. Then I called the police station. After waiting on hold for fifteen minutes, I was finally put through to the detective I'd met a couple days before.

"Hello, Detective Ramirez," he answered.

"Hi, this is Laila Callidy. I got a message from you guys saying to give you a call back when I got a chance."

"Right, sure. How are you, Miss Callidy?"

"I've seen better days," I said. "Do you have any leads on what happened to Moe?"

"We do, actually, thanks to your security camera. That's why I'm calling. I was hoping you'd be able to take a look at the video, see if anything looks familiar."

My heart skipped with excitement. It was late though. Going on seven PM to be precise. "Yeah, of course. Could I come in the morning?"

"I was hoping you'd be able to get here tonight, but the morning will do. What time can you make it in?"

I paused, thinking about what Jeremy had said. If I wanted to get to the bottom of everything, I needed to chase every lead that came my way. "Ya know what? I'll make it work. Will you be there in, let's say, half an hour?"

"Sure thing. Thanks."

Ramirez's office was tiny, but sufficient for a small-town detective. On his desk sat pictures of him and his wife with their daughter who couldn't have been more than a year. The walls were painted an ugly forest green that probably hadn't been redone since the 90's. Other than the picture, there weren't any more decorations, which wasn't shocking, considering the unpleasant man Ramirez seemed to be.

The door opened. He came in and sat down at his desk across from me. "Sorry to keep you waiting, Laila. I got held up at the copy machine."

"Not a problem," I muttered. "Just glad you found something."

"Yeah, so am I." He pulled his laptop from the desk drawer and placed it on the table.

"You don't have a VCR?" I asked, knowing the tapes weren't new enough to be stored on DVD or a flash drive.

"No, we do. It looks better in HD."

"Right."

"Just one second." He clicked a few buttons and turned the laptop to face me. He played a side by side of the front and back camera. "Now if you look here, at four forty-three, we see Moses exit the building from the rear entrance, drop a bag in the dumpster, and enter the building from the rear entrance again. Then at five twelve" —he fast-forwarded— "we see a figure, indistinguishable, enter from the front. Then at five thirty-seven, as you're getting out of your car, we see someone, more visible this time, but still indistinguishable hurry out the back of the building."

I squinted, trying to see the person more clearly. They wore a black hoodie and dark pants. The only thing slightly distinguishing element on the clothes was some type of reflector on the heel of their tennis shoes.

"Does that look familiar to you at all?"

"No. Not really. It could be anybody."

"Except for you," he said.

I blinked, squinting a bit. "Right, because I'm walking in."

"Exactly."

I leaned back in my chair. "I'm sorry, I don't understand."

"I'm just wondering why the murderer sat with his victim until you pulled in. Almost as if they wanted you both on film at the same time, so that you'd have an alibi."

"What?"

"It's a good plan, isn't it?" Ramirez's brown eyes shifted between mine. A cunning grin pulled at his lips. "Promise someone a cut of the insurance. It wouldn't go to you if you were the one to kill him, so you'd have to have concrete proof you weren't the one to do the deed. Really genius, actually. Bravo."

"Are you psychotic?" I snapped, standing quickly. "What country do you live in? I'm grieving the loss of my friend, and here you are, accusing me of—what exactly? Someone wanting me to not go to jail for their crime?" I shook my head, heading to the door and opening it. "You are sick, Detective Ramirez. And if you continue to harass me, I will be filing charges."

He laughed. "Sure, I get that. But then I might have to show them this video, and you'll have some serious 'splaining to do."

"I'm sorry?" I turned to see his computer, now showing another video all together.

Early evening. Me. Holding Kai against the wall. By his throat.

Shit.

"Just wait, this is my favorite part," Detective Ramirez said, pointing at the screen.

A fireball appeared in my hand, and then a ball of water in Kai's.

I pushed the door shut and looked up to meet his gaze. "What do you want?"

CHAPTER TWENTY-SIX

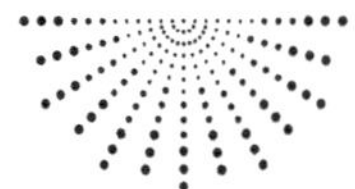

"First of all, I want to find out who killed Moses Baker." Ramirez's eyes flipped back and forth between mine. "Secondly, I want to know what you are and how you did that. Oh, and I'd like to know who Poseidon over here is."

"Yeah, good luck with that."

"Ya know, Laila, I could have taken this directly to the FBI. CNN even. Fox News would eat this shit up. But I didn't do that." His dark eyed gaze held mine without faltering. "What you can do...It's amazing. But if I wanted to, you'd be publicized. The CIA would abduct you and you'd never be heard from again. I don't want that."

That wasn't accurate. The world governments knew about us, and they liked us. Not me in particular, but there were treaties in place high up. We stayed out of their way, they stayed out of ours.

The scary part about being publicized? The masses. Not the government.

"So what do you want then?" I asked.

"It's simple, really. You have fire power and I need fire power."

"Aren't you clever." I narrowed my gaze. "I'm sorry, you believe that I'm a murderer, and you want me to work for you? Jesus Christ, this is what's wrong with this country."

"I don't think you're a murderer," he said. "I did. At first. But after I watched that video, it all clicked."

"Oh, yeah?" I asked. "Hit me with your best shot."

"Well, body language tells everything. In our last interview, most of what you told me was true. You had no idea what happened to Moe. But you lied about Adrian."

"I did not."

He smiled and leaned back in his chair. "You have to cover your ass, I get it. I'm not asking for details."

"Wait, did I hear that correctly?"

"I read her file. Adrian was a drug user with multiple arrests for possession, assault, battery, the list goes on and on. I don't know the whole story, but if I had to guess? She got herself mixed up in some of this supernatural shit and something happened. But you, your record's perfect. You made decent grades in high school. Not great, but enough to graduate so." He shrugged. "You came from a good family, you sometimes work sixty hours a week, just to give most of it to your mom, despite the fact that you're living with your boyfriend of, what is it, two years?" I sucked my teeth, waiting to hear what else he knew about me.

"Oh, and speaking of your boyfriend and his little family. Most of them are pretty smart, but that Jeremy. Wow, he's got a track record. When I first read the police report, I was sure it was a typo. How could one person possibly shut down the entire security system to a massive facility like that *and* manage to steal over a thousand animals from a cosmetic company? Then I watched this video again and it hit me— teleportation." Ramirez smiled as if he'd come to the most amazing revelation of a lifetime.

"First of all, he didn't steal them. He rescued them. And he did that as a minor, so it's really not relevant. And secondly, have you been following me?"

"Researching."

"No, I'm serious. Have *you* been following me? Or has someone else?"

"Just me." He squinted a bit. "And these videos haven't been seen by anyone else either, if that's what you're worried about."

"Look dude, you need to delete every copy you have and forget you ever watched it. This shit is going to get you killed."

He let out a laugh. "I worked in Brooklyn for almost ten years. I don't scare easy."

"Maybe not, but your little girl?" I gestured to the picture on his desk. "She does, right? And the things that exist in my world, even the good ones, they'll do horrible things to her. And your wife. Just for knowing what we are. And what we do..." I paused. "You need to run from this as far and fast as you can. If not for yourself, then for them."

He looked down. "Yeah, I probably would if they weren't already gone."

I stopped, stomach sinking. "Oh. Sorry. I didn't know."

"Yeah, well," he said, "I've got nothing left to lose." He slammed his laptop shut. "Look, Laila, I get that you're hesitant. I don't know what your world is like, that's true. But the things I've seen? Do you know how many people I've seen die? Or how many kids I've found hiding in closets from their abusive parents?" he asked. "Humans are the least humane creatures I've ever met."

I scoffed. "Yeah, because you've never met anything else."

"Sure I have." He grinned. "I met you earlier this week."

I rolled my eyes. "I'll think about it. But there is a lot I need to consider here. I don't even know if I'm allowed."

"Allowed?" he asked. "What, does your boyfriend tell you how to use your powers?"

I laughed. "You're cute. But no. It's a lot more complicated than that. And by the way, I'd appreciate if you'd quit calling him my boyfriend like we're all old friends. You don't know me or my friends or my family."

"Well, he is, isn't he?"

"That's complicated too, and also none of your business."

"It's clear you won't give me any information, so I have to dig in the gaps."

I rolled my eyes. "And by the way, what if I say no?"

He shrugged. "I guess it depends on what you give me. If I believe you to be a threat, I'll send you to homeland security."

"And if I'm not?"

"I'm not sure. But either way, if you want the video deleted, you need to give me answers."

CHAPTER TWENTY-SEVEN

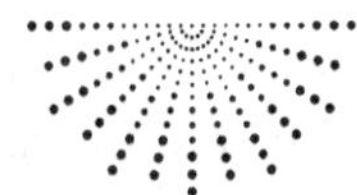

I sat on the couch, buried my head in a pillow, and screamed for a moment.

"I take it the news you got at the police station wasn't very good." Brody plopped down beside me.

"Yeah, well. I'm no longer a murder suspect, so I guess that's a good thing."

"That's great." Brody placed his hand on my lap. I didn't think much of it. We were a pretty touchy-feely bunch. That was kind of my thing then, I didn't pay much attention to most things going on around me. "How are you holding up with everything else?"

"I'm fine. Just really sick of everyone asking me how I am."

"Sorry," he muttered. "I didn't mean to—"

"No, I'm sorry. It's just all that I keep hearing and I don't even know how I am."

"It's alright."

"No, it really isn't." I laughed. "Everyone's being so nice to me, and I can't decide whether I'm pissed or happy or sad." I let out a sigh. "My anxiety level is through the roof."

He laughed. "I don't think anyone blames you. We're all pretty shocked you haven't had a breakdown yet."

I chuckled, shaking my head. "Want to take bets on how long it'll be until someone has to have me committed?"

He laughed. "You'll be alright. You always are. I mean, you've been through worse. Survived a literal knife to the heart. Sounds traumatic, but you handled it pretty well."

I chuckled. "Dying's simple. You just watch everything slowly fade away. Living is what's such a bitch."

"Can't disagree with you there." He grabbed a joint off the table and searched for a lighter. "Laila, would you mind?"

I brought a flame to my finger and held it out in front of him. He struggled at first but got it lit. Ash flew through the air. I extinguished my fingertip. After a few puffs, he passed it to me. I shook my head. "I'm good. Thanks though."

"Yeah, sure." He puffed on the joint and looked me over. "Hey, you've got some ash…" Brody gestured to my chin. I wiped it and he laughed. "It's still… Here." He leaned forward and wiped just below my lip with his thumb.

I laughed, watching the thick gray ash fall to my lap.

Completely blindsided, Brody leaned forward and pushed his lips to mine.

I hauled back and covered my mouth with my open palm. His eyes widened.

"What was that?" I said.

He stopped, face turning red. "I-I'm sorry. It was just. I thought that…" He stood quickly. "I'm sorry, I thought there was a thing happening here."

Well, damn it. Jeremy was right.

My brows fell further. "Brody, I'm sorry if I did anything to make you think that I felt that way about you, but you know that I'm going through—"

"No, you didn't. It was stupid. *I'm* stupid. Just forget it."

"You aren't s—"

"Please. Just forget it. Please?" He walked around the couch and started up the stairs.

"Hey, will you wait a minute and talk to me?" I brought myself to my feet.

"I'm sorry." And he was gone.

"That's not fair!" I walked to the steps and yelled upstairs. "I wouldn't kiss you and then disappear. Even if I could teleport!"

I walked to Jeremy's room and knocked on the door.

"C'mon in," he called.

I spun the doorknob, pushed it open, and met his gaze. "Are you busy?" I leaned against the doorway. "Want some company?"

"No, not at all. Just waiting on Leah to recoup enough energy to heal this. I'd love some company." Jeremy smiled and rested his guitar against the bed on the floor.

He sat shirtless against a pile of pillows at the head of the bed, not wearing anything incase Leah needed to get to his wound immediately. I took him in for a moment, admiring the firm muscles of his chest and shoulders. Then down his arms, studying the beautiful, strong lines.

"Excuse me, Miss, my eyes are up here, and I find your staring extremely offensive." He grinned.

I laughed, walked inside, and sat at the foot of the bed beside his legs. "If you weren't already in pain, I'd hit you."

He grinned. "Good thing I have a gaping hole in my side then."

I smiled, scooting backwards until I was in my usual spot on the right side. I went in there to tell him about my conversation with the detective. Telling Leah first would have been the most responsible option but telling him was the easiest. Still, when I relaxed into the pillows beside him, the whole reason I was there kind of faded away. I didn't want to think about it. I didn't want to think about anything. I just wanted to go back in time a few weeks before my life hit the fan. "Why is this bed so comfortable?"

Jeremy laughed. "You aren't here to talk about my bed, are you?"

"No. Wish I was, but nope."

"I'm sure I can handle it," he said.

"Not so sure about that," I muttered.

"Unless you're going to say that you hate me and never want to see me again, because that, I could not handle." He gave me a playful smile. "But that's not it, is it?"

I laughed. "No. No, but after I tell you this, you may never want to see *me* again."

"Doubtful," he said. "But wait, let me guess. Brody finally came onto you, didn't he?"

"No, that's not—Well, yes, he did. How'd you know that?"

"It was just a matter of time," he muttered. "That, and the fact that he's been blasting Three Days Grace for the past half hour like a little bitch. Probably trying to drown out the sound of his sobs."

I frowned. "Don't be mean to him, I feel really bad about the whole situation."

"I wasn't going to be mean. Maybe just tell him 'I told ya so.'"

"Don't," I said. "He looked so sad. Like a poor little puppy when you walk in the house and don't say hi to them."

Jeremy laughed. "He'll be alright. But what were you here to tell me?"

"Ah, that."

"Yes, that."

"You're not going to be happy."

"I love when stories start this way."

I went into it, telling him what Detective Ramirez had said, first about the video that was my alibi. But then I started explaining just how badly I'd fucked up. We're never supposed to use our powers near a security camera. It's practically common sense, for obvious reasons. Rookie mistake.

To say the least, he wasn't amused. But he wasn't as mad as I'd predicted.

"You know that if Mary finds out about this, she's going to wipe his memory and then kill you," Jeremy said.

"I figured that."

I rubbed my tense forehead and thought back to the moment outside the diner. I used my powers outside of Moe's all the time when no one was around. The parking lot was on the center of an empty back road. No one could see anything from the street. I was the manager, no one else would look at the security cameras. Hell, I'd forgotten they existed until Ramirez mentioned them a few days before.

"And there's no way for you to know with certainty he wouldn't turn on you."

"Yeah, thought about that too."

"I take it you don't need a lecture then."

"I do not," I muttered.

"So what are you thinking? What do you want to do?"

What *was* I thinking?

There weren't many options. I could erase Ramirez's memories, but he was a smart guy. He'd surely have some type of reminder to bring him back to that video. And even if I did track down every copy he made, that'd only solve the exposure problem. But then he'd be back on my ass as a murder suspect in not one, but two cases.

Plus, if he wanted my help, was that really such a bad thing? Wasn't that what we were supposed to do? Protect people? Help them? We were Guardians, it was literally our job.

But he was an asshole from what I'd seen. I wasn't sure I wanted to work hand in hand with someone who blackmailed me. Behind his attitude though, I did see a shred of something that made me want to collaborate.

He worked outside of the law. But so did we. After all, I'd taken part in covering up my best friend's murder.

"I don't know. What do you think I should do?"

"Well, it wouldn't be the first time we worked with a cop. The Chambers work with major governing entities. A little above our pay grade though. But he knows a lot. That's not safe for him. Or us. Especially since he has leverage over you with the whole Adrian situation."

"I know. You're right. I just..." I let out a sigh, "I don't know, wouldn't it be nice? He has resources we don't. Imagine if we had access to local city records and police reports whenever we wanted. He could be our eyes and ears."

"It'd be helpful but is it worth the risk? I mean, how could you trust him? Two days ago, he was accusing you of murder."

"Well, rightfully."

"You didn't kill anyone. Any human, anyway."

"No, but I did help cover it up."

"And you said he knew that?" he asked.

"Guessed. I didn't confirm anything though."

"What did he say, exactly?"

"About Adrian?" He nodded and I continued, "Well, he figured she got mixed up in the supernatural world and somehow ended up getting killed and we had to cover it up."

Jeremy leaned back onto the mound of pillows. "Well, at least he's a *good* cop."

CHAPTER TWENTY-EIGHT

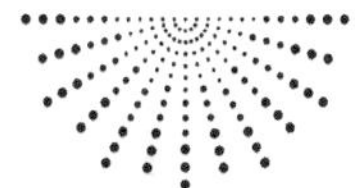

When I awoke, I was in Jeremy's bed with his arms tight around my waist. I glanced at the clock, seeing it was almost ten. Knowing Jeremy wasn't completely healed, I didn't want to squirm out of his reach.

"Jeremy." I tapped on his arm. "Hey, I've got to get up."

He yawned, giving a quiet groan as he released me from his grip. I wiggled my way to the edge of the bed and stepped into my slippers. Then I walked to the mirror and ran a brush through my hair. It was then that I felt something wet and sticky on my back.

A big patch of crimson.

Jeremy's bleeding had picked back up. I walked to him and pulled the covers off to check his wound. There was a decent amount, but I wouldn't describe it as uncontrollable.

"Hey, you're bleeding." I tapped his shoulder.

He opened his eyes, leaned forward, and looked down at his chest. "Well, shit," he muttered. "I really liked these sheets."

"Now you know what it's like to be a woman and wake up in a pool of your own blood."

He crinkled his nose a bit. "Not the same."

I laughed. "I'll go get Leah."

"Probably not a bad idea."

I started down the steps, hearing voices echoing from the kitchen. I made it to the dining area, calling, "Hey, Leah, we could use a little help up..." I trailed off. Detective Ramirez sat on a bar stool at the island, cup of coffee in hand.

"Laila." Leah's darting eyes shot to mine. "So glad you could join us."

"Jesus Christ." Ramirez's eyes locked onto the crimson spot on my shirt. "What the hell is that from?"

"What the fuck are you doing here?"

"Can you handle this?" Leah gestured to Ramirez. I nodded. She started up the maid stairs.

"Out of line." I angrily wagged my finger as I approached him. "Completely unacceptable. You can't just come to my home and—"

"Seriously. Why are you covered in blood? Is someone dead up there?" He glanced up the steps. "Don't have that Adrian girl up there, do you?"

I narrowed my gaze. "Keep interrupting me and it'll be you up there."

He leaned back in his chair. "Just tell me no one's dead or dying in this house."

"No one's dead or dying, but I'm really considering killing you."

"That's just... that's a lot of blood."

I rolled my eyes. Then I inched closer and leaned over the counter. "I told you to walk away."

He looked up from my bloody shirt and met my gaze. "And I told you to think about my offer. It's been twelve hours, you've had time."

"Oh, and you think twelve hours is enough time to decide whether or not I want to work with a crooked cop?"

He crossed his arms against his chest. "I'm not crooked."

"Really? Because, I'm not admitting anything here, but you told me that covering up Adrian's death was 'understandable.'"

"Okay, so maybe I practice outside the law, but clearly so do you." He gestured to my pajamas.

I narrowed my gaze. "What, do you think I'm torturing someone up there?"

"I don't know what I think. But I came here with a purpose." He pulled a letter from his jacket pocket. "When we searched the safe to check for a robbery, we found this note. It's for you."

"Did you read it?"

"Sure did. Doesn't make any sense. Maybe it will to you." He handed it to me.

My name was written on the outside in Moe's beautiful calligraphy. I'd recognize it anywhere. As a young girl, I'd watch in amazement as Moe hand wrote the menus with a calligraphy pen.

I opened it, reading, *"When shall we three meet again in thunder, lightning or in rain? When the hurly-burly's done, When the battle's lost and won."*

Obviously, I knew what the quote was from. Any Shakespeare fan would. But I had no intentions of mentioning that to Ramirez.

"Any ideas?" he asked.

"Nope. Sorry."

He squinted. "This is never going to work if you aren't honest with me."

"This is never going to work if you show up at my home unannounced."

"Fine. Fine, I'll call next time." He stood. "But you should also know that we've collected all of the evidence needed from the diner. Once you get the place cleaned up, you're welcome to resume business."

"Great. Now I have a meeting to get to. So." I made a shooing motion with my hands.

"I hope you don't go wearing that." His gaze traveled over my blood drenched shirt.

"Funny. You're so funny."

He laughed. At his own joke. That dude's sense of humor was pathetic. Dad jokes to the max, even without a kid. "Really, though. You aren't going to tell me why you're covered in blood."

"Real heavy flow this month."

CHAPTER TWENTY-NINE

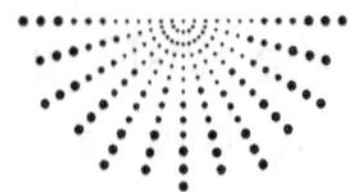

I sat in the sticky leather chair and looked around the small office. Nothing fancy. It smelled like printer paper, moth balls, and shitty coffee. Dust and cobwebs hung at the corners of all four white walls. The Berber carpet beneath my tennis shoes looked like it may have been close to cream once judging by the low traffic area in the corner. But without having looked at that spot, I'd have thought it was gray.

"Laila Callidy?" An old man stepped into the office and reached forward for my hand.

"That'd be me." I extended mine and shook it with his.

"I'm Brian Collins. It's nice to meet you. Although, I wish it were under better circumstances."

"Yeah. Yeah, likewise."

"Let's get to it then, shall we?" He stated a bunch of legal jargon I didn't understand before transitioning into the will. "So it looks like Moe listed you as executor of his will. Do you know what that means?"

"I control the money?"

He laughed. "Basically, yes. You control the money. He had very specific instructions laid out for his funeral, but after that, it's all yours. Although there is a list of people he'd like to give some belongings to.

Your mother, Rachel Callidy?" I nodded and he continued, "She is supposed to receive a portion of the life insurance policy in a sum of fifty thousand dollars. Your sister, I presume, Jennifer Callidy, is entitled to seventy thousand dollars as well as his Dodge caravan. It says here that thirty thousand of that money is to be used for either a home or paying back college tuition. The rest of the money can either be put into savings or towards the purchase of a home."

I turned my head to the side, blinking a few times. "Wait, did you say seventy and fifty thousand dollars?"

"Yes I did."

"Moe owned a diner."

"Yes, but he had a great life insurance policy. Helped him set it up myself twenty-some years ago. He also owned many properties that he would flip and then sell. Not to mention the grocery store he owned in the nineties, as well as his keen sense for following the stock market."

"Jesus Christ," I muttered. "Well, they're going to be some happy ladies."

He laughed. "I bet you'll be ecstatic then."

My eyes widened. "Dear lord, it's more than seventy grand?"

He gave a small laugh. "Once the paperwork goes through, you'll have at least five-hundred-thousand dollars. Before funeral costs, of course. Oh, and he has some stocks. Even bought a few in Google." He laughed again, shaking his head. "I told him that one was a bad investment but boy, was I wrong."

I raised my hand to my chest. "Fifty thousand. You meant fifty thousand."

"No, ma'am."

With wide eyes, I said, "So what you're telling me is that I'm about to have half a million dollars."

"Before taxes, of course. And more, if you sell off his assets and cash in his stocks."

"That's insane. I'm a waitress. I'm—I just manage a diner. I'm not even twenty-one yet."

"Not anymore, you aren't."

CHAPTER THIRTY

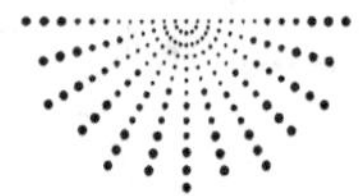

As I pulled out of the attorney's parking lot, a thousand thoughts raced through my mind.

Five hundred grand.

I thought that my thousand-dollar tax return each February was a lot. But five hundred grand. I had no idea what I'd do with that much money. I never expected to see that much money in my entire life. Just the thought made me a little antsy. Also made me a little pissy that Moe had only given me an extra quarter at each yearly employee review. Although, I didn't have much right to be mad now that I realized how much he'd left me with.

But there were more important things to attend to. I had a business to run and a murder to solve.

I'd called the cleaning company earlier that morning after I got the okay from Ramirez, and they said they'd meet me at the diner around one fifteen. So I headed there and parked in my usual spot.

Then I sat down on the stoop outside, unable to actually walk in the door. I'd had a set of keys to the place for years, but now it felt dirty to use them. I couldn't walk in there, not when Moe's blood was still strewn over the walls and floors.

But then I remembered.

Macbeth.

Moe used to sit in a booth with me and Jenna, reading us old novels from his collection. *Moby Dick, Gulliver's Travels, Wuthering Heights.* But my favorite was always Shakespeare. It was our thing. We'd each choose a different character to read aloud. *Macbeth* was a favorite of mine. Being the little sadist that I was, I always chose the part of Lady Macbeth.

Regardless, he wouldn't have left that note in the safe unless he wanted me and no one else to find it.

I didn't want to go in, but I had to.

I'd been upstairs regularly to check on miscellaneous things and flip the breaker when the power went out, but this time was different. Now it was *mine.*

My hand found the hole. I inserted the key, fiddled with the old handle, and pushed it open.

The familiar old bell rang above my head, somehow sounding quieter than I remembered it. Almost as if it sounded sad.

I made it through the threshold, unable to look behind the counter. But to get to the steps, I had to get behind the counter.

Just don't think about it, Laila. Get the book and get out.

I willed my feet to lift beneath me. I didn't look down. I didn't want to see... I just jumped.

When I made it to the kitchen, my shoes squeaked across the floor. Bile rose up my esophagus. Moe's blood. On my feet.

Shaking my head, I hurried down the hall by the office where the stairs to the apartment were. I climbed them slowly, listening to each crack beneath my feet and knocking down cobwebs along the way.

At the top of the steps was a small landing at the door to the apartment. I reached for the key in my pocket, put it into the door, and struggled, bumping it with my hip to get it open.

It was the same as it had always been. The door opened into the small, quaint living room and open kitchen. To the left was a closet and hallway leading to the bedrooms and bathroom. The walls were a weird, retro shade of orange.

The living room featured a large floral print couch and an ugly pinkish recliner made from a corduroy like material. Above all, the carpet was the worst—a pinkish color with weird, textured, swirling patterns.

Just beyond the couch and recliner sat the bookshelves, separating the kitchen from the living room.

I headed towards them, looked through encyclopedias and dictionaries as well as some classics before I found it.

Macbeth written along its binding in large, cursive letters.

I pulled it out, opened the cover... Only to find Moe's beautiful calligraphy. I flipped through the pages.

Only then did I realize that it wasn't Macbeth at all. Just the cover wrapped around an old leather-bound journal.

Downstairs I heard a loud knock on the door. I jumped. Then I clutched the book to my chest, left the cover, and started downstairs, locking the apartment behind me.

CHAPTER THIRTY-ONE

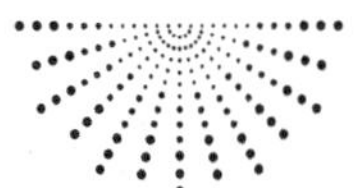

I wrote the cleaning people a check and headed out. I clutched the book tight in my hand, unwilling to part with it until I knew all of its contents.

I made it to my car and headed down the street to grab a coffee from a local shop. Still holding the book tight, I got a cup and a banana nut muffin, then sat at a quiet booth in the back.

I sat down and opened the book, preparing to find any and everything.

Dear Laila,

If you're reading this, it means that I'm gone. I want you to know now, before I give you all of the details, that no matter how it seems at this moment, none of this is or ever could have been your fault.

Unfortunately, most of us in this life are thrown into situations we don't understand for reasons we don't understand. But that's the most beautiful part of being alive, isn't it? Not knowing why you're here but wanting so badly to figure it all out?

I can't tell you why you're here, not really. I don't know every detail of your fate, but I can tell you how you got here.

I've wanted to tell you all of this for an awfully long time. It was always my plan to give you the truth, and I hope you realize that I never wanted to keep any of it from you. Neither did your dad, or your mum, for that matter. But there were circumstances out of my control. Even out of your father's. Even your real mother's.

There is so much to all of this, I'm not sure where would be the best place to begin. So I guess I'll start with your very existence.

Your father, Luka Callidy, was a great man. But he wasn't the wisest. Especially when it came to women. Not until Rachel came along at least, he made a good choice with that one.

When he met your mother, your true mother, he fell more in love with her than I had ever thought possible. It was sweet, but pathetic. He was always like me in that sense, a fool in love.

And your mother knew that. She relied on it. See, it didn't matter that he'd buy her flowers, or take her out on extravagant dates and treat her like a queen. She needed him to love her, not because she wanted to return it, but because those were her orders. At least, that's my entirely subjective view on the matter.

I don't know how to explain this, and I doubt that you'll believe it, let alone understand it all. But your mother wasn't human, not even close. She was an Angel. And Angels aren't the gentle creatures American culture makes you believe they are. They're several hundred-year-old robots. They don't think for themselves, not really, not like you or me. They do as they're told, and that's what she did when she had you.

Around '92, I'd heard rumors that the Council ordered a wider gene pool to be born. They wanted more strength in the next generation of warriors. There was talk of a war in the coming years, a war we still have yet to see, and one I hope you never will.

My phone rang in my pocket. I jumped, closing the book and reaching for it. It was Jeremy.

"Hey, what's up?" I answered, breathing uneven from the entries I'd just read.

"Hey, I was just checking in to see what happened with the lawyer," he said. "You alright though? Sound kind of winded."

"Well, you aren't going to believe it." I gathered my things and stood from the booth. "I'm heading home now. We can talk about it when I get there. How are you though? All healed up?"

"Yeah. Leah took care of me after you left," he said, "I'm good as new."

"Good, good," I said. "Well, I'll be home soon. We'll talk when I get there."

* * *

As I drove, I thought about what I'd read. *They're several hundred-year-old robots... The Council ordered a wider gene pool to be born... A war we have yet to see and one I hope you never will. . .*

He knew. He knew about all of it.

I didn't know much of what Moe was talking about, but after reading that, one thing was clear to me. Moe knew about this world in a way that even our notable clan didn't. And that was enough for me to know that he died trying to tell me all the secrets so many had spent their lives trying to protect.

At that point, I had no doubt about who had taken his life. My mother, or my biologic contributor, more like.

She'd killed one of the only men left in my world. Before, I didn't care to know who she was. But now, knowing this, I needed to know more. Not to build a relationship with her. Not to know my genetic makeup. No, none of that mattered.

All I cared about was taking her life the way she had taken Moe's. Nothing else mattered.

CHAPTER THIRTY-TWO

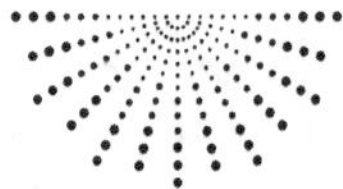

When I got home, I sat down with Jeremy and told him about everything I'd discovered. I started with the book, but then told him I'd get back to that. Then I told him about the money. He was shocked, but also happy for me. The diner was exciting on its own, but an entire estate? I didn't know what I'd do with it all.

Leah said, "Put that shit in the bank."

"No, you need to invest. I hear the real estate market is the way to go right now," Adam said. "That's what I did with my trust fund, you know."

"Yeah, and you lost thirty grand," Jeremy said.

Adam narrowed his gaze and flipped him off. "Like you're one to talk. Where's *your* inheritance, bro?"

"Mostly in my veins."

Changing the topic, I said, "First of all, I'm paying off my credit cards. And I'm probably going to pay off my mom's house if she doesn't have enough from her cut. But other than that, I don't know really."

"What about college?" Hannah chimed in.

"I dunno, college really isn't for me."

"Well you need something to fall back on," Hannah said.

"It doesn't get much lower than waiting tables," I said. "And I love waiting tables. Now that I have to manage the whole business, I'm going to need to put all of my time into it. I can't take time off for school."

"Well, I think you put it in the bank," Jeremy said. "Save it for when Moe's is having a shitty revenue."

"You could always renovate the diner." Brody was unable to meet my gaze as he made his way into the living room.

"That's actually a great idea." I smiled in a trying to make him feel less uncomfortable. "The tile could really use a redo. The bathrooms need…Well, to be completely gutted."

"But all fun and money aside." Kai dropped onto the couch next to Hannah, maybe a little too close. "What's this book ye're rambling about?"

"Right," I said. "Well, Moe left a note in the safe for me and it was a quote from 'Macbeth.' So I went to the apartment upstairs, found his copy, opened it, only to realize that this was what was inside." I pulled out the small, black, leather- bound journal.

Adam reached for it, and I pulled it back. I regretted it immediately. He looked back to my gaze, kind of confused, and said, "Oh, sorry."

"No, it's not you. It's just that I don't want to let it out of my sight. I haven't even read it yet. I'd kill myself if this thing ended up missing after everything Moe went through to make sure I'd get it. It must be important for him to have hidden it."

"Laila, you check the safe daily, right?"

"Yeah, why?"

"Was the letter always there?"

"No. No, I guess it wasn't."

"So he put it in there the day before he was murdered."

"Almost as if he thought someone was going to kill him," Jeremy said.

"Or at least suspected it," Adam said.

"Do you know if he had any meetings the last time you talked?" Leah asked.

"No, no I don't. But he kept all of his schedule on his phone. I can talk to Ramirez and see if he'll let me see it from evidence."

"Speaking of that asshole." Leah met my eyes with a piercing gaze. "What the fuck, Laila?"

"Yeah, what the fuck, Laila?" Adam said with a big grin. Leah gave him a dirty look and he turned back to me with a serious one. "Da fuck, Laila."

"We have one rule." Leah wagged her finger. "You don't bring cops here. Period."

"You're right, I'm sorry. But in my defense, I didn't tell him to come and you're the one who let him in."

"Actually, I opened the door and he just walked in. What if he would've seen something unexplainable? Like, oh, I don't know *your blood-soaked nightgown?*"

"About that. I should probably tell you all something."

<hr>

Then, I explained everything I'd told Jeremy the night before. How he'd caught me on tape, the offer he made me, and all the details, ending it with, "I'm so sorry guys. I didn't even remember we had a camera on the back of the diner until Moe died and I was stupid enough to let them take the cameras before I checked them."

"This could end us, Laila. Do you realize that?" Leah said, green eyes coming to a vibrant, angry glow.

"Relax, Leah—" Jeremy began.

"No, I won't relax. You know how much I love you, Laila, but fucking Christ. You can't possibly be considering this." She angrily shook her head. "Do you know what the government would do to us? What scientists would do to us? If you think Demons are scary, you'll cringe at the human race."

"Woah there, slow down," I said. "Until a couple years ago, I was a part of that race."

"Look, this isn't an argument about how shitty humans are or whether or not they'll accept us. This is a matter of protecting all of us.

You want to be an idiot? Get yourself kidnapped and experimented on? That's fine, that's your choice. A dumb one, but yours. But don't bring that shit to my house."

Truth is, Leah was entirely right. I'd fucked up pretty bad. Humans knowing what we were could end very, *very* badly.

"She just told you she didn't tell him to come here," Brody said. "Yeah, she fucked up, but she can't do anything about it now—"

"I can wipe his memories," Leah said.

"But he has copies. And if he's smart, he probably has them in more than one place. We couldn't be sure we got every one," Adam chimed in.

"Then we kill him," Leah said.

"We can't just kill him." Jeremy gave a nonchalant shake of his head.

"Sure we can."

"He's human," Brody said. "Not only does that go against everything we believe, but it's just wrong."

"So what do you suggest? We work with him? Because that also goes against everything *I* believe. This fucker threatened us, that can't be overlooked."

"Maybe," Brody said. "I don't know. But give me time to think about it and I'll come up with something."

"Well, I hope you come up with something soon because I'll be damned if our family is exposed."

CHAPTER THIRTY-THREE

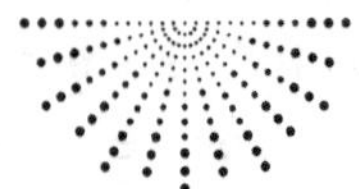

The conversation with Leah ran circles around my mind. She was right in many ways, but in others, she wasn't. Killing the guy was not the solution.

But the stunt he pulled showing up at our house had to be rectified. I still wasn't sure what I wanted to do about his offer. But I had to make one thing clear. If we were going to work together, we were going to do it on my terms. I was going to be the one that told *him* how things would go. He wasn't going to show up at my home unannounced again demanding answers.

After googling Ramirez's name, I discovered an address and found myself pounding at his doorstep at eleven p.m.

A light turned on and the door opened. He was in his boxers wearing a pair of wired glasses, and messy, uncombed hair.

"What the hell are you doing here?" he asked.

"See? Doesn't feel so good when someone shows up at your doorstep without calling first." I pushed past him, walking into his messy living room.

"This is entirely inappropriate—"

"Yeah, yeah. I don't care," I muttered. I ignored the smell of two-day old pizza and stale beer, searching for a place to sit. But nearly everything was covered in clothes, trash, papers, or a combination of all three. "Look, I have a lead on Moe's murderer, and I need some help."

"So that quote meant something to you?"

"*Macbeth*, dumbass." I sat on the corner of his couch because it was the only visible surface.

He put his hand at the edge of his muscular hips. "Ya know, you've got to start talking to me with some respect."

I couldn't help my eyeroll. Did he think that intimidated me? *I've killed Demons, bro.*

A stern, bad cop look wasn't gonna scare me into being a little sweetheart.

"This is how I talk. Either accept it or don't talk to me."

He narrowed his gaze. "What do you want, Laila?"

"I need Moe's phone."

He laughed. "You think I'll break into evidence for you?"

I crossed my arms against my chest. "What if I said please?"

He laughed again. "That's a federal offense."

"So is withholding evidence. And assisting in the cover up of a missing person—"

"For the last time, I did not assist—"

"Are you going to help me or not?" I said.

He grew silent, jaw tightening and eyes shifting between mine. My lips tried to turn up in a smile, seeing that my attitude was a success, but I urged them down. It was dawning on him though. That if this was going to happen, then it'd be on my terms. I was going to be the one who called the shots.

"What are you going to do for me?" he said.

My shoulders raised in a shrug. "Sounds kinky."

He rolled his eyes. "If I do this for you, what will you do for me?"

"What do you want me to do?"

Silence crept in once more. He wanted more from me than just solving Moe's murder, that much was clear. But I wasn't going to play his mind games. If he wanted my help, he'd be met with the same level of intimidation he'd attempted to use on me.

He ran his hand over the scruff of his chin, gaze turning down. Then he let out a slow breath and met my eyes. "Look, can I be blunt with you for a second?"

I narrowed my gaze slightly. "Yeah, that's why I'm here. Quit pussyfooting and tell me what you actually want."

He lowered himself to the recliner across from where I sat. "I wasn't completely honest with you before."

"Got to love hearing that," I muttered.

"When I told you my wife was gone, that wasn't the whole story." I held his gaze, waiting for him to continue. "She's gone. She's been gone, for almost seven years. But we never found a body."

"So that's what you want? You want me to find her body?"

"Not exactly." He shuffled some papers around and sat on the edge of the coffee table.

"What do you want then?"

"Amy, that was my wife." He leaned forward and rubbed his temple. "I've never talked about this with anyone but her, so this probably won't come out right." He took in a deep breath and said, "Amy was... gifted."

"Gifted?"

"She felt other people's pain. She couldn't go in a hospital or even drive near a car accident. And she saw things before they happened. My daughter too, she made things grow."

He knew what I was off the bat and started things out with fear tactics rather than respect? "So you know about my world?"

"No, not really. I didn't know what she was. Her parents died when she was young, and she was adopted before she turned three. *She* didn't even know what she was." I held his gaze, waiting for him to continue. "Well, about a week before Amy went missing, she called me while I was on a night shift and said she had this horrible premonition. She was frantic and she couldn't breathe, and she had me come home right away. And when I got there, she was calm. She said that something was going to happen to her. Something horrible, and there was nothing I could do to stop it. She was delirious, like she always was after one, so I didn't think anything of it. A week later, I came home, and she was gone, Lydia too. Things were strewn all over the floor, there was blood everywhere. And I knew something was going to happen, but I didn't know it'd be that. And I didn't know my daughter would have anything to do with it."

If his daughter could make things grow and his wife could feel other people, that meant that they were Fae. Clearly untrained Fae, but some of my people. I'd never heard of our kind having premonitions. Fae had a specific set of abilities, and telling the future wasn't one of them.

I tilted my head to the side a bit. "So what do you need me to do?"

"She told me I'd meet a girl who could hold fire in her hands. And that after years of searching, she'd eventually bring us back together."

Not only did the woman have premonitions, but she had premonitions about *me*? The girl with only the slightest grip on her abilities? Someone whose only importance in the supernatural world was her tie to the Skoulda clan? Well, I suppose the whole soulmate thing was pretty important. But seven years ago, I was thirteen. I certainly hadn't completed my bond with Jeremy yet.

If he were right and she'd had premonitions, then why would they be about me? Why not about someone in the clan who actually knew what they were doing?

"And you think that's me?"

He raised his shoulders. "Well, I haven't met many girls who can hold fire in their hand."

"Valid point," I muttered, shaking my head. "You didn't care to mention this earlier?"

"We've had, what—Four conversations? The first two, you were a murder suspect."

"Well, yeah, but trust me, that whole security camera stunt you pulled would have gone over a lot better had I known all of this."

"Look, I didn't know how to address it. There's no instruction manual."

"Well, no shit, Sherlock. But maybe honesty would've been a good place to start?"

He huffed. "Working in law enforcement, I've learned that honesty isn't always the best policy."

I didn't want him to see that I was now incredibly curious, so I rolled my eyes. But I wanted to know more. I needed to figure out who this woman who had seen me in her mind was. And where she'd gone.

"I'll look into your wife. But I need Moe's phone."

"Deal." He extended his hand with a cheerful smile.

"But look, I can't make you any promises. Don't put all of your faith in me." I shook his callused palm before moving my hands to my hips. "Solving missing persons cases isn't my area of expertise."

"Don't be ridiculous. I'm not putting my faith in you," he muttered. "I'm putting it in Amy."

"Fair enough. But the future isn't concrete, alright? You can't completely depend on this being true."

"Amy was never wrong."

CHAPTER THIRTY-FOUR

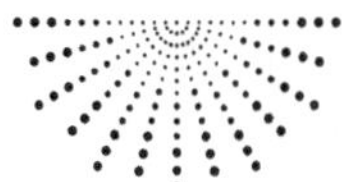

I told Jeremy about the deal I'd made with Ramirez. He was on the fence about the subject. If what he said about his wife was truc, why didn't hc try to prcvent her from going missing? Why let it happen? But more importantly, why not start the conversation out that way after he'd seen the video? Why threaten me?

Was it because he was just a human cop and figured being a dick was the only thing that'd work? Was he that simple? He did seem to be. But I was still hesitant.

Jeremy was right. If Ramirez really did want my help with this, if he believed I'd reunite him with his wife and daughter, it wouldn't make sense to treat me the way he had. But he was a cop who'd worked in Brooklyn. I imagined interrogating drug dealers and gang bangers was much different than trying to get answers from someone like me.

He didn't know our world. Maybe he knew that things larger than him existed. But he didn't know how we operated. He didn't realize that the best way to get things from us was playing the 'I need help' card from the get-go.

But it did explain why he was more amused than shocked after discovering the video of me and Kai.

I lie awake, staring at the ceiling and smoking a blunt. Jeremy's body heat radiated toward me from the other side of the bed.

My eyes shifted over his peaceful, dreaming face. I couldn't figure out how I felt about our relationship. The bigger part of me wanted to let bygones be bygones and move on. Clearly, he was sorry. Part of me wondered if he was even responsible for what he did. But as soon as the thought ran across my mind, I remembered the look of guilt and fear he flashed Brody as he followed him out of the bedroom. I saw what happened, so why was I questioning it?

By that point, I wasn't mad or upset over anything anymore. I was just numb. I'd become an empty pit, a black hole. Something as bright and beautiful as a star had blown up inside me and now, it was collapsing inside itself. I was full of thoughts and questions, but they all twisted around each other. Nothing made sense as they spiraled together.

I sat up and reached for the book I'd slipped under my pillow. I found my place and started where I'd left off.

I don't know if any of that was true, but that's what I was told. And again, I'm sure none of this makes any sense to you, Laila, and I wish I was there to explain it all. I wish Luka could sit you down and piece it together for you.

Most of all though, I want you to know that you are much more powerful than you realize. When you were born, you were not alone. You had a brother. But with the power the two of you held together, you had to be separated.

I'm still not sure how to tell you all of this, but I'd rather you have the full, real story than whatever you can assume on your own.

I didn't want you to know who she is either. I wanted you to believe Rachel was your mother, because she is a damn good one.

When Luka met the woman who birthed you, he thought he'd found a pot of gold. And for a short while, I did too. Until she became pregnant.

You aren't the only child your mother had and gave away. Before you, there were hundreds, maybe even thousands. In the back of this book, you'll find a list of the children, still alive, that I know of. Most of them are like you; they don't know her and probably don't realize they were even adopted. If you want to reach out to them, that's your prerogative, but before you do, consider you may be tearing their world apart. The very reason your father decided to keep all of this from you in the first place.

When she was pregnant with you, she disappeared. She told your father she'd return when you were born. She came back to him about 4 months into the pregnancy and informed him that she was pregnant with twins, and that he could only keep one of you, because together, your powers could not stay bound. You would inevitably amplify one another, making it impossible to mask you from threats.

That's when they decided one of you would stay with him and the other, Kai, would return to our homeland.

This is a complicated situation, because we are more than just family friends. On the Fae Realm (which I have defined for you in the back of this book), life is different. It is run by class systems. Royalty, nobles, and peasants. Different parts of the realm are run in different ways, but this is the common denominator within them, aside from the Open Lands.

Growing up, I lived in the Deep North as a peasant. When I was about fifteen, I heard about a place where these systems aren't used, at least not worldwide. Earth. After years of bargaining, I made it to this plane with the help of my cousin, Bodhi, who was your father's father.

He ran a trafficking system from the Fae Realm to Earth. The Fae didn't care that we left, but the Angels did not want us crossing to this plane. Ultimately, Bodhi as well as his wife, Aadhya, died when your father was young at the hands of Angels, preventing a group of Fae from crossing to the Earth Realm.

When they died, I stepped farther into your father's life. The only relatives he did have were dead, aside from me. Formed quite a friendship, the two of us.

Aadhya was a member of the Elite from the Homeland.

Which reminds me. In the Fae Realm, there are six major sectors of royalty. The Flame, who control fire, The Wave, who control water, The Zephyr, who control wind, The Terra Firma, who control the dirt, and the

Sprite, who control spirit. The last is the Elite, who are descendants of the five sectors. The Elite are considered to be the most enlightened of all.

That was the last thing I remember reading before I fell into a quiet, peaceful sleep.

CHAPTER THIRTY-FIVE

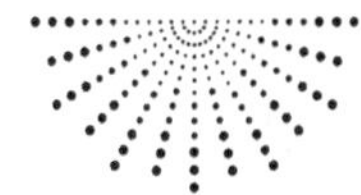

"What the hell are you doing?" Jeremy said beside me, waking me from the first deep sleep I'd had in days. In front of mc was Mary, standing oddly over the bed.

"I wanted to see if you were awake yet," Mary said.

"And you couldn't have knocked on the door like a normal person?" I asked.

I didn't question it. I should have, but I didn't. Mary was an odd one, always appearing simultaneously without a known reason until she divulged it.

"We could've been naked in here," Jeremy said.

She laughed. "I think we all know that's not true."

I stifled a laugh. She was a bitch, but she could be witty when she wanted to be.

"What do you want? Jesus." Jeremy pulled the blanket down and stood from the bed.

"Just come downstairs when you can," she said.

I opened my mouth to say that I was still tired. But she disappeared.

"God, I hate that woman," Jeremy muttered.

"Don't we all," I said. My arms stretched above my head. A yawn left my lips, still disoriented from exhaustion.

Jeremy's phone vibrated on the side table. I reached for it like I always did. But he teleported in front of me.

I pulled back. "What's all that about?"

He scratched his head and rubbed his eyes. "Okay, listen, I wasn't trying to hide this. I just wasn't sure if you'd even want to know."

Not trying to hide it yet jumping so I wouldn't get to it before he did.

I crossed my arms. "Well, now I definitely want to know."

"I've been trying to meet up with Ally so we can talk about what happened that night." I tried to stay levelheaded, but I guess my face showed that I wasn't. "It's not...it's not romantic or anything like that, okay? I just wanted to see if she knew anything. I'm just having a really hard time recalling what happened and it's freaking me out. I thought she might remember something I don't."

He was texting the girl that ended our relationship. An internal huff echoed within me. I found myself questioning my thoughts from the night before. Maybe I couldn't let bygones be bygones after all.

I bit my cheek, stood, and started towards the door. "Well, you should probably do what you have to do, Jeremy."

"Stop for a second." He put his hands on my shoulders, swiveling to face me. His big, honest blue eyes cascaded between mine. "I don't want anything from her other than to find out what happened." His eyes stayed firm on mine, large and unwavering. "Do you understand how hard this is for me? That I can't even remember what I did that ended our relationship?"

I studied his expression. He was in pain, and he was scared. I could see that he was telling the truth. But it didn't make me feel better to know that the two of them were still in contact. He was begging me to take him back. I was sleeping beside him each night. And he was still talking to the girl that ruined us.

He continued, "Laila, I love you more than anything in this world. And it kills me that we aren't where we were. I know it's my fault, but I'm trying to fix it, and I wouldn't do anything to jeopardize that. You have to believe me when I say that all I want from her is answers." I stared him down for a moment, waiting for a stutter or a shift in his gaze. But it didn't come. "You can read the messages. All I'm talking with her about is meeting up to discuss what happened. You can be there if you want."

"I'd rather not." I pulled away to head downstairs. "But I understand if that's something you need. Thank you for being honest with me. But I have a million things to do today. So I'm gonna go get ready."

"But can I ask you something?"

"Yeah, what's up?" I said, pushing messy hair from my face.

"Do you have any plans for tonight?"

"Not that I know of at the moment. Why?"

"I know this is a long shot, and if you say no, I completely get it. But you've had a really tough week, and I know right now is probably the worst time to ask, but I was wondering if maybe you'd like to go somewhere with me tonight."

I stopped. My pride told me to say no. But then I realized how pathetic that'd be. There I was, sleeping in his bed, wearing his pajamas, and I wouldn't get out of the house with him?

I was a little depressed, and I really needed a night out. I needed to do something that would make me feel happy. I didn't like the mindset I'd had recently.

Jeremy licked his lips. "It's okay if you don't want to. I know that we aren't doing so good and everything. I just felt like you deserved a getaway."

"No. No, let's do it. But this isn't a date, right? Just two friends having a good time."

His face lit up, as though he'd expected me to say no. "Right. Of course. Just friends."

CHAPTER THIRTY-SIX

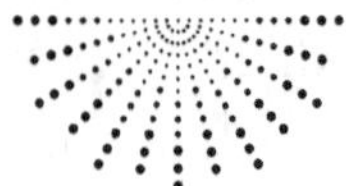

When we made it downstairs, a man with short blond hair stood beside Mary, wearing a pair of jeans and a gray V-neck.

"No fucking way," Jeremy said with a big grin. "Long time no see, man."

"That's what I said," Adam said.

Jeremy approached him and put his arms around him in a strong embrace. The man smiled, returned the hug and let out a laugh. "You look great, Jeremy."

"Well, I'd hope so considering the last time you saw me, I was in a ball on the floor with explosive diarrhea and the shakes, dope sick as shit."

"So charming." Leah plopped to the couch next to Adam.

He turned to me. "Laila, this is Sariel. Sariel, this is Laila, my—" He stopped himself, wanting to say girlfriend but knowing that wasn't right.

"Par animo," Leah answered for him. "They aren't a couple right now, but they do share a bed."

"Leah."

"What? It's the truth."

"Laila, that's an Angelic name, you know." He reached forward and took my hand.

"Angel of conception." I smiled. "And Sariel. Angel of destiny?"

He smiled. "Guidance, but you were close."

I laughed. "Well, it's nice to meet you."

"And you as well. Can we all sit for a moment and talk?" he asked, lowering himself to the recliner.

"We sure can, but it won't change anything," Leah said.

"Change what?" I asked.

"She brought reinforcements to convince us to stop looking for your mom. I've already told them it won't happen."

"You're damn right it won't."

"I'm here to talk, not to tell you what to do," Sariel said. "Please. Just sit."

I glanced at Jeremy who gave a nod. Clearly, they seemed close, and I trusted Jeremy's opinion. "Fine."

"So, Laila, tell me about yourself," he said.

A quiet laugh left my lips and I lowered myself to the arm of the couch. I knew that tactic. Play nice. Pretend you care about their feelings when you could really give two shits less.

"Don't do that."

"Do... What?" he asked with a confused expression.

"Try to get me to open up so I'll be more susceptible to your opinion."

He smiled. "Is that what I was doing?"

"That's how it seemed."

"Well, truth be told, I want to hear your side of this."

"My side?" I chuckled. "Well, Monday night, my brother from the Fae Realm, who I didn't know existed by the way, shows up and tells me he's looking for our mom. Who is not my mom, because my parents lied to me about who I am for the entirety of my existence. Later, I discover that my mom never told me because she's under some bullshit Angel code which will literally kill her if she tells me the truth. My dad, well, he didn't tell me because he was too afraid to stand up to his Angel whore." His brows arched at my choice of words. "But just wait, there's more. My boss, who I just discovered last night is actually my distant cousin, he also knew who my birth mom was, and he was mysteriously murdered two days ago."

"Oh, my. That sounds awful."

I huffed again. His voice said he cared, but his eyes said he knew it all and just wanted me to calm down. "Look, Moe knew who she was and now he's dead. Whenever I find out who it was, I will kill them. My mother or not, they're going to die."

"Those are some strong words."

I smiled. "Well, I feel strongly about them."

"You feel strongly about murder?"

"Justice is not murder."

"Sure, it'd be justice, but it'd also be murder."

"Don't dish out what you can't eat. An eye for an eye and all that."

"Fair enough. But you don't believe in the death penalty, do you?"

Angels killed whenever and however often as they pleased. Killing one of them was no different than killing a Demon. In fact, it felt even more justified. At least Demons openly admitted that they were shitty. Angels acted as though their sins were acceptable because they did it in the name of their lord.

"We're not talking about humans here."

"No, but death is death. And to kill your own blood, whether you know them or not, that would take a toll. Tell me, have you ever taken a life?"

"Couple times."

"But always Demons, right?" I shrugged and he continued, "Aside from that, do you think you alone will be able to stand against all of us?"

I laughed. "I know you won't hurt me."

"Is that right?" He smiled.

I smiled back. "Yes. Yes, it is."

"What makes you say that?"

"I'm one of you. And to be frank, I'm stronger than most of you."

While that may have been true, yet again, my pride was getting the best of me. One day, I'd be able to kill an Angel with ease. But to date then, I'd only ever killed Demons, Vamps, and a handful of Wolves. At that time, there was no way in hell I could take on an Angel. But I was gonna try.

"Is that so?" His head cocked to the side.

"Don't act like I'm not. We both know how powerful I am."

"Not to mention modest," Mary muttered.

"You don't have to like it. But I'm going to find her. And then I'm going to kill her."

"No one blames you for your perspective, Laila. But you have to see this from the big picture."

"Which is what—'any who dare cross an Angel shall perish?'" I altered my voice to sound mighty and god-like. "Your race, or rather our race, is just as evil as the things we are so hell-bent on destroying."

"We're many things, but evil is not one of them."

"Then what do you call killing someone for telling their loved one who their mother is?"

He said nothing, just held my gaze for a moment. "The circumstances you've been dealt are unfair, I'll admit that. But—"

"But nothing. I'm not going to stop looking for her. And I'm going to kill her. There's nothing you can do to sway my opinion."

"Do you even know how to kill an Angel?" he asked.

"I'm sure I can figure it out," I said. "But thanks for your opinion."

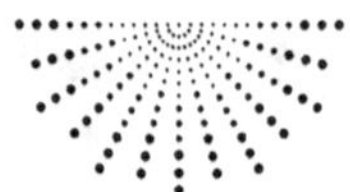

CHAPTER THIRTY-SEVEN

Throughout the day, I called the funeral homes as well as the local paper and set up Moe's obituary. Then I made arrangements for a casket and music to be played at the funeral. I'd never realized how much work went into a funeral until I was planning one.

As the day went on, I found myself looking forward to my night with Jeremy. A part of me wanted to act nonchalant, but god damn, it'd been a rough week, and I just wanted to enjoy something. And if Jeremy was good at one thing, it was making me happy.

I dusted on some foundation, carefully trimmed the edges of my winged eye liner and painted my lips with a bright red lipstick. At first, I wanted to go simple. A pair of jeans and a nice blouse, but then I thought about it for a while, and I decided to go for something a bit fancier. Why not? I wasn't feeling so great about myself since Jeremy cheated and nothing makes a girl feel more beautiful than a little black dress.

Then I headed downstairs and went to the kitchen for a glass of water. Brody stood at the fridge. I figured then would be as good a time as ever to talk about our awkward, one-sided kiss.

"Hey," I said, leaning against the counter.

"Hey." He gave me a once over. "Hot date?"

"Something like that. Can we talk?"

"I'd prefer if we didn't." He poured a glass of scotch. "But we can drink."

"How 'bout both?" I asked.

He pulled another glass from the shelf and poured some whiskey into it. He slid it down the counter. I grabbed it and he raised his glass. "To dumb decisions that fuck up friendships."

I frowned. "I'm still your friend, Brody, you know that. Nothing changed."

"But it has." He sipped from his glass. "It's weird and uncomfortable now."

"No, it's not."

"Sure it is. Maybe not for you, but it is for me. Now you'll question my motives in everything we do, every time we talk. Like with Jeremy cheating on you. I brought it to your attention, and you're probably thinking I did that to break you guys up." His words slurred as he spoke.

"No, I don't think that," I murmured.

"Well, you should."

"You wanted us to break up?"

"Well, I wouldn't have kissed you if you were together." He tilted his head back, chugging what was left in his glass. "Got punched for it either way though, maybe I should have."

"Brody..." I frowned, glancing over him. He was always pissy. But I'd never seen him so... depressed.

He turned his gaze up, finally meeting mine. "What do you want me to say, Laila? Want to tell me there's no chance? I know it's never going to happen. I know that, I do. But it doesn't change how I feel."

"How do you feel?"

"I think it's pretty clear that I'm in love with you. But you're in love with Jeremy. Obviously, I mean, he's your soulmate and all that stupid, cheesy shit." He huffed. "No matter what horrible things he does to you, you're always going to go crawling back to him."

Now, that was uncalled for. Hurt or not, it wasn't my fault that he had feelings for me. And I couldn't help that I was in love with Jeremy. It'd only been a couple days since I found out what he'd done. Were my three years of love with him supposed to just disappear? Still though, Brody was hurting, so I maintained my composure.

I crossed my arms against my chest. "That's not fair."

"Really? Then what're you wearing that for?" He gestured to my dress.

"For me."

He laughed. "Yeah, I'm sure."

I always hated when guys said shit like that. As if, what, exactly? Women have to wear makeup for men? We can't put on a nice dress and a little lipstick because it makes us feel good?

Normally I'd make some quip saying just that. But I felt bad about the whole situation. He really was a sweet guy when he wanted to be, and I was sure he'd make some girl incredibly happy. Just not me.

"Brody, I'm sorry if I did something to lead you on—"

"That's just it, Laila. You didn't. You didn't have to." He looked between my eyes quickly. "I love who you are. The way you stop the car to let animals cross the road and how you take care of every asshole employee at Moe's, even when it fucks you over. And that you bend over backwards to make other people happy. I love how most days you don't wear makeup or do your hair because it's just not worth your time. I love the way you bite your lip when you're anxious. I love the way you fucking breathe, and it's fucking pathetic because I don't want to." He slammed his glass to the counter, words sliding together as he spoke. "You think I want to love my brother's soulmate? I want to love someone who isn't my brother's other fucking half. I want what you have with him. And I hate myself for being so god damned jealous of him. I've never wanted something so wrong for me in my entire life and I just wish it would go away. But it doesn't. I've tried and I just keep loving you. I just want it to fucking stop."

I reached out to put a comforting hand on his arm. "Don't," he said, taking a step back. "Please just..." He shook his head. "Just don't."

"I wish things were different, Brody," I said quietly, biting my lip.

"But they aren't." His eyes locked with mine. Sadness flooded them.

I'd never seen him so upset. He'd always been so fierce and tough but now, he looked vulnerable.

It broke my heart, because I did love Brody. He was smart and strong, and independent. A sheep in wolves clothing. It killed me to see him so hurt over something that was ultimately my fault.

But he was right, I loved Jeremy way too much. Unless he blatantly told me he didn't want to be with me, I'd always go back to him. It hurt my ego to admit, but it was true.

CHAPTER THIRTY-EIGHT

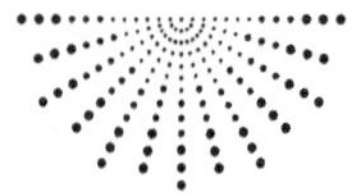

"Wow," Jeremy said. He walked into the kitchen from the steps, carrying a bunch of lilies My gaze traveled from his luscious black waves to his blue button up and dark washed jeans. His eyes shined bright blue on his perfectly even, porcelain skin. "You look beautiful."

I laughed and stood from my perch on the bar stool. "Yeah, well, I'm gonna wear this dress to the funeral so I figured I should get one more good memory in it before I ruin it forever."

He gave a sad smile. Then he cleared his throat. "Are you ready to go?" he asked.

"Yep."

He extended his hand. "You may want a jacket."

"Oh?"

"Yes, ma'am."

I headed to the hall closet and grabbed my black coat. I prayed he wasn't planning on taking me somewhere that was also dusted in a layer of white. The snow had only been around for a few weeks, but I was already over it. "This better be worth all the time I spent on my face."

"I think it will." He extended his hand until I grasped it. "Close your eyes and don't open them until I give you the okay."

"You know how much I hate surprises."

"I know how much you *claim* to hate surprises."

Sighing, I shut them. "They're closed."

"No peeking."

"Yeah, yeah." I murmured with a wave of my hand.

I felt the familiar swirl followed by queasiness in my stomach. Then we landed somewhere unfamiliar. I opened my eyes. I looked around a cold, dark tunnel. Water fell from the cool bricks above, splashing into puddles on the cobblestone at my feet.

A long breath drew into my lungs, inhaling the scent of bread and the moisture of water. I heard crowds, but too far in the distance to make out any words. My arms got chills, adjusting to the cool temperature.

"I said no peeking," Jeremy insisted, putting his hand over my eyes.

"Yeah, yeah," I muttered. "Where the hell are we?"

"You'll know in a second."

"France?"

"No."

"Greece?"

"Since when does Greece get this cold?"

"I don't know, I've never been to Greece."

He laughed. "Just wait a minute." He stepped behind me, keeping his hands over my eyes.

"Fine, fine."

Standing that close, I took in the familiar scent of his cologne. Kind of citrus like, but also musky.

"Alright keep your eyes closed for one more second." He took his hands off my face and moved in front of me. "Okay, open them."

I did, looking up from the grassy hillside in front of me to the beautiful canals. Venice.

My jaw dropped, taking in the gorgeous sparkling water as the moonlight shined upon it like a glistening mirror. I listened, hearing elegant violins in the distance. I drew in air, trying to capture the smell of the salt water and delicious cuisine. It was so gorgeous, I had to fight the lump in my throat that wanted to erupt in tears of joy.

On my first date with Jeremy in a little Italian restaurant in our town, I gestured to the murals on the walls of the Venice Canals. I spent a good twenty minutes talking about how much I wanted to see them in the flesh. I told him how I'd dreamed of floating above the water on a gondola, sipping a sweet, expensive red wine, listening to the sound of a peaceful violin and watching the stars above.

"Oh my god," I whispered, hand covering my mouth in awe.

"What do you think?" He gave a big, boyish grin.

"I can't believe it," I murmured. "It's beautiful."

He smiled. "Wait for it." Just then, a small red gondola turned from a bend in the canal, heading towards us. A violinist stood on the back playing some glorious piece of art.

"Jeremy," I whispered, actually wiping tears from my eyes this time. "How could you afford this?"

"I think what you're trying to say is 'thank you.'" He smiled. "And I've got a little bit left in my trust fund. Not much, but this seemed pretty important."

"I would have settled for a movie." I laughed. "But thank you."

He smiled, taking a step closer. "Laila?"

"Yeah?" My gaze shifted around between the buildings, admiring the old architecture, taking in all of its vibrant hues.

"I have a really crazy question to ask you." His palms gently moved to my forearms.

"Oh god." My stomach flipped. "Please don't propose because I don't think I'd have the heart to tell you no right now."

"No." He laughed. "No, not that."

"Alright, go ahead."

"Tonight, just for one night. Can we pretend that this last week hasn't happened yet?" He asked, holding my gaze. "I know that we aren't a couple right now. And if not, that's okay. I'd just really like to—"

I leaned onto the tips of my toes, grabbed his shirt and forcefully pushed my lips to his. It wasn't a peck. It was one of those long, open mouth, heart racing, wet panties kind of kisses. His hand wrapped around my waist, pulling my body tight against his. The other slid to my neck, thumb resting on my cheek and moving further back into my hair. It lasted for a long moment.

There was such romance in the air, I couldn't help myself if I wanted to. But I didn't want to. I wanted him so bad. Every part of him, pushed against me, moving gently like the waves beside us.

"I'll take that as a yes," he whispered. Our bodies still pressed together, hearts thudding against each other's chests like drums. He rested his hand against the side of my neck.

I let out a quiet laugh. I tried to catch my breath.

The boat drew closer, and time seemed to stand still for a moment. I looked at him, and he gazed at me, admiring one another, just living in that instant. I felt dizzy, and not in a bad way. It was a pleasant kind of disorientation, like a buzz after a few drinks. Not the spinning, sick to your stomach kind of drunk. The peaceful feeling that leaves your body weightless and your stomach full of butterflies. I captured it, taking all of it in, not wanting to forget a moment of how wonderful this night was.

As the boat touched the hillside, Jeremy helped me into it, holding my hand as I climbed over the edge. He followed and sat beside me on the wooden bench. I rested my head on his shoulder. We started to peacefully float along the water.

He reached below us and pulled out a dark green bottle of something I couldn't pronounce. I gasped. "You even got the wine."

"I did, but I should probably inform you that it isn't very expensive." He glanced over it. "The lady at the liquor store said it was good though."

"It's perfect," I said. "This is really sweet. Thank you."

"I just want you to be happy," he said with a kind, joyous smile.

We floated along the canal, peacefully listening to the violin, watching the stars. We argued over what was a plane and what was a U.F.O. I didn't drink the wine though. It was the nastiest thing I'd ever tasted. I made a mental note to never, *ever* drink Pinot Grigio again.

It was perfect, my dream date even, and an excellent distraction. I genuinely forgot about the past week as the night drew on. Maybe it wasn't the healthiest coping mechanism, but for the night, I was completely relieved.

Just when I thought it couldn't get any better, we climbed off the gondola to a lovely, terraced restaurant with a gorgeous view of the vineyards in the distance. Moments like that made me fall head over heels for Jeremy all over again.

Despite it all, I still knew how much he loved me. That was never a question. He knew me to my annoying, obnoxious core, and he was still crazy about me.

That's what made all of it so hard. He cheated on me, but he still loved me. If he didn't care, moving on would be so much easier. A part of me wished he never cared at all, because then I'd be able to convince myself I didn't love him either.

But there he stood, holding my hand tightly in his. His dark brown locks flying in front of his face, brushing past his messy five o'clock shadow. His bright blue eyes stared over the distance, watching the dark green hills.

His ample, dewy lips curved into a half moon. His eyes stopped on mine. They locked, and I was lost in a messy wave of blue. Like the tides in the ocean, beautiful and peaceful—but also strong enough to trap me inside, pull me down and toss me around until I washed along the sand, battered and bruised.

CHAPTER THIRTY-NINE

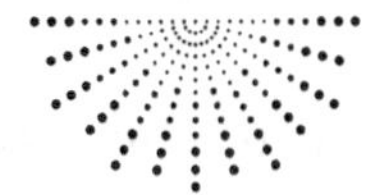

"There's no argument. The Beatles were twice as influential as the Stones." I waved my fork with chicken marsala on its spikes.

"Bullshit!" Jeremy said. "I love the Beatles; you know I do. But c'mon, the Stones are rock and roll."

"So are The Beatles. Just look at 'Helter Skelter,' it is just as rock as 'Gimme Shelter' or 'Wild Horses.'"

"But it doesn't touch 'Paint it Black' and you know it."

"Fine, maybe Rolling Stones are a little heavier than the Beatles, but that just furthers my point that the Beatles were more relatable, expressing a style that is still used now, almost fifty years later. I mean, just look at modern pop music. Although it's not my cup of tea, it still uses a lot of the same dynamics that the Beatles tapped into when making songs like 'Love Me Do.'"

He rolled his eyes. "Oh, please. Don't get me started on that album."

"What's your prejudice against 'Love Me Do?'"

"The whole thing was created in a few hours. Even John admitted that album was made for the purpose of making money. They had what—A day to finish it?"

"Yes, and they locked themselves in the studio and wrote and recorded until it was done. That speaks wonders to the type of artists they were."

"And what does it say exactly? That they waited until the very last minute to record and produce an album that they had more than enough time to create? Face it, if they weren't already famous, that album would have flopped."

"Still a great album." I gulped my water. "It sold over a hundred thousand copies, and for the time, that was hugely successful."

"Sure, if you like the boring, repetitive sing along kind of songs. But real, makes your heart hurt kind of music? Sorry, 'Love Me Do' doesn't cut it."

"Speaking of albums, any new songs recently?"

He laughed. His hand raised to his mouth, shaking his head. He gave a slight shrug. "Nothing worth mentioning. You know I'm not much of a writer. I've got some good beats going though."

"Well, whenever Moe's is up and running again, we can head down to the basement and you can record for a while. If you get a demo out there, you never know where you'll go with it."

"I don't need a demo." He took a bite of his fettuccine.

"Sure you do," I said. "I see musicians at the diner every week and you're easily the best. And that isn't even a biased opinion, it's just the truth."

"I'm not going to go anywhere with my music, Laila—" he said.

"Not with that attitude," I said. "You're a great musician, you should do something with it."

"And you're a great writer, but I'm not pressuring you to go back to school to become a journalist," he said quickly. I licked my teeth, and he frowned. "I'm sorry, I just—"

"No, you're right. Our passions aren't our careers." I smiled. "Your music is your business. I'm sorry."

He reached across the table, hand wrapping around mine. "I'm sorry, it's been a great night. I'm really enjoying this. I don't want to ruin it."

I smiled, clutching his tighter. "So have I." Then I leaned forward and took a bit of his chicken alfredo. He laughed as I chomped away at it. I smiled back.

A little tradition of ours. On our first date, I ordered the chicken marsala, and he ordered the chicken alfredo. I kept picking off of his plate, then he started nibbling off of mine. Ever since, each and every time we ate Italian, we got the same thing and did just as we did then.

It brought me back to those moments. When we'd first fallen in love. When life was so much simpler. And for a moment, I nearly forgot about everything else.

His lips pulled up in a smile. He held my hand beneath his. "Do you ever want to just stop time? Just exist in one moment for the rest of your life? Like the world could be burning around you and you wouldn't know the difference because you're just living in that one instant?"

I smiled. "I have a lot of those when I'm with you." He smiled back for a second. Then he looked down, trying to hide a frown. "What's wrong?"

"I'm fine."

"Jeremy." I squeezed his hand.

He ran his hand through his hair. "I just... I kind of hate myself right now." I creased my brows with concern, knowing why but also realizing for the first time how much it all was getting to him.

"Jeremy," I started.

"Just listen, Laila, please." I paused, holding his gaze. "I know that I hurt you, and I don't blame you for hating m—"

"I don't hate you—"

"But you should. I hate me. I'd hate you if the roles were reversed." He licked his lips. "I don't deserve this night with you. I don't deserve a moment of your time after what I did. I've been cheated on, I know how that feels and I wouldn't wish it on anyone, especially not you. But the thing that hurts the most is that I don't remember it. I try, and I try but it's like a drunken memory that disappears and reappears in waves." He paused for a second, gaze shifting to his hands. Then back up at me. "I get that you're mad. I know that I hurt you. And I'm so sorry for that, and I'm sorry that I'm bringing it up now. But do you believe me?"

"That you don't remember it?" I nibbled on my bottom lip. "In a way. It's not that I think you're lying, if that's what you mean."

"What do you think then?" His big, innocent eyes shifted between mine.

"I think the mind can do incredible things. I think you're mad at yourself and forgetting what you've done is easier than accepting it."

He swallowed, giving a nod. "So you don't believe me then."

"I didn't say that."

"I don't blame you. I wouldn't believe me either."

"That's not what I meant."

"I just…" He paused. "Will you meet with me and her?"

"Ally?" I asked, heart beginning to nervously thud in my chest. He nodded, and I shook my head. "I don't think I can."

"Please, just one meeting. She has something to say but she won't talk about it on the phone. Just one meeting—"

"I can't, Jeremy." I pulled my hand from his. "Look, I would love to say that this is fixable and that we can go back to where we were, but I saw it, Jeremy. I still see it. I don't want to. I don't want any of it to be real, but it is and I can't come that close to it. I can't meet her. I can't look at her. I don't even want to have that memory. You can't expect me to come face to face with the girl you fucked that ruined us."

"Laila." He reached for my hand.

I pulled it away. "I get that you're hurting, but don't you think I am too? Can't you see that this is killing me? I look at you and I want to cry because your loyalty is gone. My trust for you is gone. I have nothing left but love and pain and it's the worst combination because I want you. I *need* you. And it's pathetic. It makes me sick because if you were anyone else, we would have already said our goodbyes. The day I found out would have been the last day we ever had contact. But you're like the drug I never wanted to try but now I can't get off of. I want all of this to go away, but it won't. It can't."

I felt a lump forming in my throat and my eyes stinging with tears.

Bringing myself to my feet, I fought the urge to wipe them away, not willing to let the water escape my eyes.

"Don't leave," he said. "I'm sorry, I shouldn't have brought it up. We were having a good night and I shouldn't have—"

"Just give me a minute, okay?" I asked.

I turned from him and walked to the edge of the balcony. It's not like I could leave anyway, we were half a world away from home. But I didn't want to. I just wanted the last week to disappear. I held my breath for a moment to keep the tears inside, staring out into the distance.

My gaze shifted to the dark empty fields that met the evening sky. I bit back the tears and took it in, ignoring the empty hole in my chest. I stayed there for a moment. My gaze shifted over the planes flickering through the night sky. I wouldn't think about it. I wouldn't ruin this night with the sadness of reality.

A few moments later, I felt Jeremy's hand at my hip from behind. I leaned into him, taking his other hand and wrapping it around my waist. "The rest of the world can fade away for a while." I closed my eyes and molded into the warmth of his chest against my back. "Let's just be here. In this moment."

He rested his head against my shoulder and kissed my forehead from above. "I love you, Laila."

"I love you too." I stared off into the distance. Just basking in the peace his arms gave me.

After a moment or so, I turned and put my arms around his neck. His found their way to my waist. I reached up on the tips of my toes and pressed my lips to his.

Mine opened, parting until our tongues gently grazed each other's. His hands held me tight, gripping the sides of my waist. My hands twisted in the back of his hair, massaging the back of his neck slowly.

He tugged my body closer to his, hand tracing down my side. It slowly slid to my back, then down my ass and rested there, gently grabbing as we kissed. My panties began to moisten, and I didn't want to stop. But we were still at a restaurant, so I pulled away.

"I'm sorry—" Jeremy began before I cut him off.

"Is there somewhere we can go?" My eyes turned up to meet his.

He seemed surprised but nodded. "Yeah. There's a little hotel down the street. I'm pretty sure they'll take cash."

"Let's go then," I said.

He paused, studying me. "Really?"

I shrugged a shoulder. "Just this moment, remember? Let's forget about the rest."

He gave a gentle smile.

Kicking the hotel room door shut, Jeremy's hand found my cheek, hauling me close to him with the other. His body against mine filled me with that same sensation of comfort, and passion, and sensuality that it always did, and I didn't want to think about anything else. I didn't *allow* myself to think of anything else.

Only him, me, and the desire that boiled between us.

There were ten million things on the other side of that door that could destroy this tranquil romance I was encapsulated in, and every one of them could wait. Nothing mattered aside from this moment.

All that mattered was how fucking good his lips felt on mine. How safe I was in his embrace. How deeply I wanted more.

I had to have more.

Yanking his shirt off of his shoulders, he pushed me against the wall, lips back on mine the second his shirt floated to the carpet. Butterflies crowded in my belly as he took my face in his hands, pulling back slightly to meet my gaze. His eyes danced between mine, deep breaths warming my cheeks, studying me carefully. "Are you sure?"

"Yes. All that matters is now," I whispered, grabbing his face and bringing his face back to mine. He kissed me back with passion, pinning me to the stucco wall, knee parting my thighs. "Are *you* sure?"

He smiled against my lips, exhaling a chuckle. Then he grabbed my hips and hoisted me into the air. A squeal of a laugh left me as he spun around and sat me on the entry table, sending the old phone clunking to the floor.

I still felt his smile against my mouth as he arched his hips closer, bulge brushing that sensitive spot between my thighs. "Is that answer enough?"

"I'd prefer to hear a yes," I whispered.

He kissed me again, hands trailing up my thighs beneath my skirt. "*Fuck* yes."

A quiet laugh left me, grazing his smooth shaved jaw with one hand and teasing down his chest with the other. Just when I made it to the buttons and tugged them down his legs, he hooked his fingers around my panties, and then cool air tickled my most sensitive skin.

"You teleported them off?"

Smirking, he tugged my legs further apart, calloused fingers scraping their way up to my pussy. A wave of shivers coursed through me, compiling in my core.

He teased my opening and coasted up to my clit. As he pressed his fingers in and made that glorious, gentle circle, those shivers of temp tation stretched into my pussy, and I gasped with pleasure.

He slid back down to my cunt and pushed inside, thumb finding my clit. As my head rolled back in bliss, he said, "Just like the good old days."

I wanted to laugh, but all I could manage out was a soft sigh.

I hooked a leg around his waist and yanked him toward me. He loved to tease, and I wasn't in the mood. I didn't want time to sit and think. I wanted to get lost in this.

As he entered me, a deep moan fell from my parted lips, and I locked my legs around him. My arms closed around his back, and I dug my nails in. He groaned too. I wasn't sure if in pain or pleasure, but he thrusted in harder, enough to make me hurt too, and I squealed.

It was that beautiful combination of ache and yearn, and I loved every second of it. This was exactly what I wanted. It was why I agreed to forget everything for the night.

Because I needed this.

I needed the release that came with his touch. I needed bliss that would leave me screaming so loud I'd grow lightheaded. I needed ecstasy, and pleasure, and anything that'd fade the rest of the world to nothingness.

And sure enough, it did.

All that I could focus on was this moment. Jeremy's hot breath at my ear as he held me tight. The bliss that gentle massage on my clit filled me with. How passionate his kiss on my neck was as he teleported us to the bed.

His lips stayed on mine as he found a pillow beside my head and brought it below my ass.

When he pulled back, and I reached up to pull him back down to me, he shook his head. "Just lie back."

"But I want to kiss you," I whispered. "I—"

"And I want to make you come as many times as I can," he said. My dress vanished, and his eyes swept down my body, breaths shortening.

He spread my legs wider apart and situated my hips better on the pillow. He dropped his fingertips to my clit and massaged it in slow, even circles. He rested his free hand at the bottom of my belly just above my pelvis, applying just a little bit of pressure. Then he thrusted in, and I gasped with shock, involuntarily squirming with euphoria.

When his eyes came back to mine, a half-smile spread across his lips. "If that's alright with you, anyway."

The next thrust was a little softer, but hit that same spot deep inside my cunt that felt like heaven. What the hand on my stomach was for was beyond me, but it felt like he was hitting my G-spot while simultaneously massaging all of those other places, and I...

My head rolled back with bliss, everything else fading away. Clenching the sheets on either side of me, I closed my eyes and wrapped myself in the sensations of this moment. He was touching all of those spots with such precision, allowing me to detach from reality with ease.

There was nothing else to think about now. Thoughts left me entirely. All I felt were these touches and the pleasure they brought me.

Fuck, I didn't want to leave this moment. I wanted this embrace, this ecstasy, this bliss, for eternity. Nothing else mattered.

"Is it?" Jeremy asked.

My eyes opened, meeting his. He still wore that half smile. Between deep breaths, I hardly made out, "What?"

"This," he said. "Making you come again" —he thrusted in, and that pressure inside me stretched higher— "and again" —another thrust, this time forcing a squeal of euphoria from my lips— "and again—"

I screamed his name as the contractions yanked him into me. My eyes were on his, body writhing closer into him, legs shaking, over-taken with gratification. His smile only widened, pushing his hand deeper on my belly, rubbing my clit at the same pace, rolling his hips, massaging that erotic spot deep inside with the head of his dick.

That pride filled smile was all I could see, vision blurring around the edges. I loved that about this man. It never failed. His favorite part of having sex always seemed to be getting me off.

It seemed a bit different this time. I wasn't sure if it was because he feared he'd never see me spread out for him like this after this week. Maybe it was because, considering the state I'd been in, he was happier than ever to bring me this type of encapsulating bliss.

I didn't know, but I knew I wanted him to feel the same way.

"Come here," I whispered.

He shook his head, smiling. "You're not done."

"I didn't say I was." The most I could manage of a laugh through my uneven breaths left me. "But I want you to hold me."

The pride in his eyes transformed into something else.

Perhaps it was he whose belly was full of butterflies now.

He lowered himself over me, holding my cheek, propping himself up with his free hand. His eyes stayed on mine as he lifted his hips and sunk into me slowly. I craned up for a kiss, taking his face in my hands.

For a few long moments, we stayed just like that. The pleasure hadn't left me, but it was a gentle, coasting stream now instead of a tide of crashing waves. What brought me even more pleasure was that gorgeous gleam in his eyes.

They say that the eyes are the window to the soul, and I swore that in that moment, I saw his.

It was aching, but watching me softened that agony. Each time a moan left me, or my leg shook, that grief would dissipate.

That was the last thing I wanted.

All I wanted was for both of us to be happy. I wanted a way to erase the past few days from history. I wanted to go back to where we'd been, when all I saw in that gaze was love.

Maybe I should.

Maybe we can move past all of this.

The moment that thought came to me, so did the realization of why we were where we were, and I jolted away from it.

Tomorrow, I'd consider the what ifs and maybes, but for now, I had to forget. I had to focus on this intense state of intimacy where he and I were all that existed.

"Laila," Jeremy whispered.

"Yeah?"

He stroked his thumb along my bottom lip, kind eyes holding mine. "I love you."

My heart skipped a beat.

I tightened my arms around his back and held him, bringing him further down so we were chest to chest.

"I love you too," I whispered.

CHAPTER FORTY

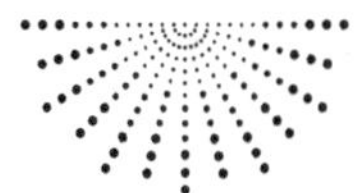

Jeremy's fingertip swept gingerly up and down my arm, peacefully pulling me from my dreams. "Hey." A yawn escaped my lips as I rolled to meet his gaze.

"Good morning, beautiful," he whispered with a smile.

"Were you watching me sleep?"

"Maybe." He smiled and kissed my hair.

I chuckled, rubbed my eyes, and stretched. My glance shifted to the window where bright sun lit the room. "Shit, what time is it?" I sat up.

"It's noon," he began. I flung the blankets from my body and started off the bed. "But it's only six back home. We haven't been gone that long. Don't worry." He gently grasped my hand.

I lowered myself to the bed, leaned back against the pillows, and rubbed my eyes. "How long have you been up?"

"Not long. Maybe half an hour." His hand pushed hair from my face behind my ear.

"What time did we fall asleep?" I reached for my bra that laid messily on the side table.

"I can't answer that with certainty." He laughed. "But I'd say around three. Maybe four."

"Sounds about right." I tightened the hook on it and spun it to its proper location.

"Last night was amazing." He sat up in the bed.

"It was." I grabbed my dress off the floor and slipped into it. Rummaging through my purse, I grabbed my phone. I clicked the home button. And nothing. It was dead. "We should probably get home so I can check this. Ramirez might've called."

"Right. Let me throw some pants on and—"

"Can you just send me back? I shouldn't have been gone for this long."

His eyes grew dreary as he gave a nod. He knew that I was in such a rush because I wanted to check my phone, but also because I didn't want to go through the whole 'What did last night *really* mean?' conversation.

"Yeah. I'll get dressed, check out, and come home. See ya there?"

"Sure."

Before I could blink, I was standing in the kitchen. Leah stood at the coffee pot. She turned around and jumped. "Jesus Christ." She held her hand to her chest.

"Sorry, didn't mean to scare you," I said.

"You're good." She gave me a once over. "Rocking the walk of shame, I see."

I laughed and sat at the bar stool. "Thanks, I guess?"

"Can I be blunt with you?"

"You always are."

"What the fuck are you doing?"

I made a face. "What do you mean?"

"It's quite apparent that you were up half the night with Jeremy, God only knows where. And I'm pretty sure you guys are broken up. So. What the fuck are you doing? Do you want to be with him? Do you want to work it out?"

"I don't know."

Leah lowered herself to the stool beside me. "I get that you're upset. You should be. You should be infuriated. But it's not really fair to act like Jeremy has a chance if that's not what you want."

"No, cheating on your girlfriend isn't fair."

"You're absolutely right. It isn't." She sucked her teeth and shrugged slightly.

"But?"

She rubbed her temples. "I've kept my nose out of this for the most part because I'm biased on both ends. You're my best friend and he's my little brother. But I don't think he actually did it, Laila."

I rolled my eyes. "I saw it. Brody didn't just dream it into existence."

"No, I don't mean literally. I know it did happen, but we live in a very peculiar world."

"Meaning?" I asked.

"Meaning that I've been in Jeremy's head. The memory's foggy and distorted. And not like when you're drunk, and you see flashes of what you did but can't clearly distinguish why or how you did it. It's like he wasn't controlling his body."

"So what are you proposing? Possession?"

She shrugged. "It isn't unheard of."

"Why would someone want to hop in Jeremy's body just to sleep with someone else?"

"I don't know, Laila, but I've been thinking. Back in 2016, when Adrian killed you, she said it was because she had to, right?" I nodded and she continued. "We haven't been able to figure out what that meant but think about how long you were friends with her before she tried to kill you. She had more than enough chances. Sleepovers, acid trips, drunken concerts. She had plenty of opportunity and she didn't make a move until things between you and Jeremy started to get serious, not long after you'd gotten your powers. What if it wasn't about you? What if it was about who you'll be if you and Jeremy stay a couple?"

Jeremy had said it too. I'd flirted with the idea. But it was just so far out there.

My forehead creased. "So you really think that someone out there wants for Jeremy and me to not be a couple so badly that they'd be willing to kill us? And to convince my best friend to actually do it?"

"We both know the stories of the par animarum." Leah paused, biting her lip. "It's said that you guys are cursed. Maybe this is a part of that."

"That's the thing. This isn't a curse. Moe didn't choke on his own blood or have his skin melt from his body. Jeremy specifically said that he fucked up. If there is something that connects all of this, it's a person. Not a curse."

"I dunno. Just a theory. Maybe he did just fuck someone else but that doesn't sound like Jeremy. He's all soft and poetic and sappy, and he's crazy about you. I just can't see him as someone to just say 'Fuck it, I'm going to sleep with this girl I don't even know despite the fact that I have someone back home that I'm madly in love with.' And he didn't even think she was *that* pretty. He definitely thinks you're hotter. Plus, if he wanted to get laid that bad, he would have just teleported home like he did every other time he was horny."

I did see her point there. Just a few weeks prior, he was begging me not to let him go. He said how badly he wanted to stay; how sick he was of being gone all the time. How much he loved me, and how he wanted to leave all of this behind. Nothing about this sounded like something Jeremy would do.

"He did come by a few times to see me. Not like he wasn't getting any."

"I'm just saying. You should look into it. I think there's a bigger picture at play here."

CHAPTER FORTY-ONE

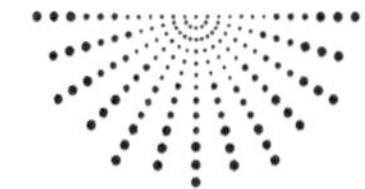

"No, all of the flowers have to be white," I said into the phone.

"I'm sorry, ma'am, but we don't have enough for the displays you're requesting," the guy replied.

"How do you not have enough white flowers? It's not like I'm asking for gold, I just need white fucking flowers. Doesn't even matter what kind, just some white fucking flowers."

"There's no need to cuss, miss—"

"There definitely is a need to cuss right now because he said he wanted all white flowers from you guys, and if you don't have them, I have no idea what to do."

"I'm sorry, miss, but who wanted our flowers?"

"Moe." I rubbed my forehead. "Moses Baker. Apparently you did his wedding flowers in the eighties and it's in his will that all of the flowers are to come from you, and they all have to be white."

"Can you hold for one moment?"

"Sure. I have nothing better to do than to sit here and—" The hold music began playing and my hands flicked with fire. Then the line went dead, and I gritted my teeth to a line.

"Woah, honey." I remembered that I'd left the door unlocked as

Mom's blond waves bobbed through the doorway. She took my phone from my hand and set it on the table. She rubbed my lower shoulders. "Not that that wasn't the coolest thing I've seen in a long time, but maybe you should lock the door if you're going to be doing that?"

"It wasn't intentional."

"Oh?" She sat in the chair next to me. "What's the matter?"

"This is just a mess. My life is a fucking train wreck."

"Aww." She put her arm around me in an embrace. "What's getting to you?"

"This funeral. I'm sure Moe *thought* that planning every finite detail would be helpful, but it's actually really annoying, because nowhere seems to have what he wants. They didn't have any platinum white caskets, or white flowers at the flower shop, and the band he wanted has been dead for fifteen years. Why does he want white anyway? It's a funeral."

"White is like black in the Fae Realm," Mom said. She looked down at the documents laid out on the table. "But I'll tell you what. You fry me up a burger and we'll start making some phone calls."

"That sounds perfect. Thank you, Mom." I stood, stowed my phone back to my pocket, and headed to the kitchen.

"What's this?" she asked. I glanced into the front of the house and saw her holding the leather-bound book Moe had left for me.

"Oh, right. That's Moe's journal. Don't lose it."

"It's not very polite to read someone's journal, Laila."

"No, he left it to me. He had a note in the safe that sent me to it, and I started reading and it's shined a lot of light so far. I've only read a few pages though."

"What's it say?"

"Mostly stuff about Dad. And my powers. I guess he didn't realize that I knew. Did you know he and dad were cousins?"

"No, I didn't."

"Distant cousins, but yeah. I guess Dad's dad ran some trafficking between the worlds. He helped Moe get here."

"Oh, wow. That's something."

"Yeah, go ahead and read it," I said.

I grabbed a burger patty from the fridge and set it on the counter in its wax package. After a moment of rummaging, I found the pre-cut tomatoes, but they'd gone bad since the diner had been closed. I picked up a whole one, a head of lettuce and an onion. I looked for a knife, but there weren't any in sight.

"Figures," I muttered.

"What's that?" she asked from her seat.

"All the knives are gone. The cops must have taken them all. Hope you don't mind a burger with just cheese and lettuce."

"That'll be fine," she said.

"Alright then." I grabbed a piece of cheddar cheese and tore the lettuce. I threw the bun on the griddle to get it crispy. Then I put the burger on and grabbed two glasses and filled them both with Sprite. I carried it out and set the cups on the table.

"Could you get me a Coke, hon?" she asked, still looking down at the book.

"I thought you hated Coke."

"Oh, well you know how taste buds change." She shrugged. "I dunno, I've been having this craving for it recently."

"You're not pregnant, are ya?" I laughed, only saying it because she'd made a similar comment the other day.

"God, no. That'd be horrid."

I furrowed a brow. Horrid? Brushing it off, I headed back to the kitchen.

As I flipped the burger, I felt my phone vibrate in my pocket. I reached in, pulled it out. and read the incoming call.

Mom.

I glanced out into the dining area. "That's weird," I murmured. I slid the green button. "Hello?"

"Hey, baby, how'd everything go with that lawyer yesterday?"

"It went good." My heart began to thud in my chest, gazing into the dining area. That woman sitting at my table was anyone but my mother. "Ya know, boring. But hey, my Mom's here right now, can I give you a call back?"

"What?" she said, clearly confused. "What do you mean, hon, did you find your biological mother?"

"Sure thing, baby. I'll call you back when she leaves, alright?"

"Laila, who's there? Should I call someone?"

"Absolutely. This burger's about to burn, I really need to get a new grill in this place. Anyway, I'll call you back later, Jeremy."

She hung up, and I devised a plan. Act natural, then burn her alive. Wasn't sure if that'd kill her, whoever she was, but it was worth the shot. Shoot first and ask questions later is almost always the worst course of action, but what else was I supposed to do? I didn't have time to compile something better. I would have lit her on fire right then, but she was holding my book.

I took the burger off the grill, despite the fact that it wasn't done, threw it on the bun, and hurried out to the table. "Here ya go, Mom."

"Thanks." She flipped a page in the book.

I saw my opportunity and I took it. The air soared around me. It threw her from the seat and into the wall on the far left of the room. I held her there in a gust of wind. She'd dropped the book as she flew. "Laila, what are you doing? You're scaring me!"

"Cut the shit. We both know you aren't my mom." I approached her and manipulating the air to thin around her. She began to heave in slow gasps.

She studied me for a moment. Then she managed a laugh. "Actually, you're wrong about that."

"Who are you?" I growled, drawing closer and siphoning the air tighter from her lungs.

She smiled. "If you," she wheezed, "Kill me," another wheeze, "You'll never know."

I narrowed my gaze, pulling the air even tighter. Her skin faded to a purple color. I was literally draining her life, and I was disgusted with myself. Not because I was hurting the bitch, because I knew that she wasn't my mom. But she looked just like her.

"What do you want?"

She shook her head, unable to breathe to make words. I released slightly, watching her gasp. The air rushed back into her lungs. I guess

I lost my hold on her, because she was moving freely again. She smiled. "Thanks, kid."

Then she disappeared and reappeared on the floor next to the book. She snatched it up, smiled, and disappeared.

"Son of a mother fucking bitch!" I kicked the counter and knocked a stool to the ground with a bang.

CHAPTER FORTY-TWO

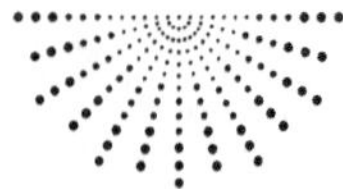

My head clunked against the edge of the booth behind me. I raised a joint to my lips, drew in a deep drag, and held it in until I grew lightheaded. My teeth gritted together, head shaking.

She was right there. She was right in front of me. And I let her go.

The woman that killed Moe, the woman that gave birth to me, the woman that was making my life a living hell. She was right *fucking* there. Then she ran off with the only hope I had at figuring all of this out. The thing Moe busted his ass to make sure I'd get.

Chairs laid on their sides against the linoleum tiles, mounds of shattered glass littered with salt and pepper. I really needed to control my temper. What happened sucked. But why the hell did I decide to take it out on the diner? It wasn't its fault that I fucked up and let the bitch go. Now I had a great big mess to clean up, on top of my shit storm of a life.

Jeremy appeared beside the bar. His head shot from one side to the other, then fell on me. His wide eyes softened. He teleported beside me, dropped to the ground, and looked quickly between my eyes.

He reached out and pushed hair behind my ear. "Are you okay? What happened?"

"Someone took my book." I raised the joint to my lips and drew in a long drag.

"Moe's journal?" he asked.

"Yup."

"Who the hell was it?"

"My mom. Or at least, she was wearing my Mom's face," I said. "I knew I shouldn't have let anyone touch it. I just knew it."

"A shape shifter?" His head tilted. "What would a shape shifter want with Moe's journal?"

"She said she was my mom. At least, I think that's what she meant." I eased in a deep breath, let it out, and took in another. "I didn't know they could shape shift."

"Most can't. But some of the really old ones can," he said. "So this means she's a super powerful Angel. Probably an old one."

I shrugged. "Not that powerful. She didn't even fight back. Just teleported over to the book and disappeared."

"Well, you're her kid. She probably didn't want to hurt you." He accepted the joint I passed to him. His gaze traveled down to my hand. "Hey, you're bleeding."

I glanced down. A cut about two inches long dripped blood down my arm onto the linoleum. "Look at that."

He stood, walked to the bar, and grabbed a clean rag. He brought it over, wrapped it around my hand, and tied it around my knuckles.

"What are we going to do?" I clunked my head against the wall behind me.

"About what?"

"Everything. My biological mother, and Moe, and Kai and just... everything."

"I don't know," he whispered. "But we'll keep moving. It'll be okay."

"Just roll with the punches?" I shook my head, letting out an ironic laugh. "I'm sick of dodging, Jeremy. I need to quit playing defense and start playing offense."

"Well, where do we start?" he asked.

With the book gone, there was only one stone that hadn't been turned. One that made my stomach hurt and my eyes sting. But one that had to be flipped.

"The only lead we have," I murmured.

Jeremy cocked his head to the side.

"Ally."

CHAPTER FORTY-THREE

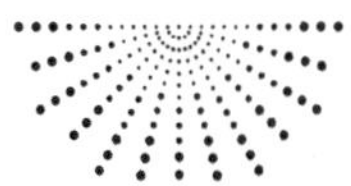

Jeremy spent the day helping me clean up the diner and trying to get ahold of Ally. We started downstairs, picking up the chairs I'd knocked over and the broken, spilt salt and pepper. Then we cleaned up behind the counter. We wiped stray blood speckles with bleach until there was nothing left to wipe. Scrubbing didn't seem to get it off completely though. Little stains of crimson remained in some places. Once the money came from Moe's insurance, I'd have the place repainted, at the very least.

Once that was done, we headed to the apartment upstairs. We knocked down cobwebs and talked about all the updates it needed. The Formica counters had to go, and so did that atrocious carpet. Jeremy pulled up the corner, exposing some gorgeous hardwoods. He said they were a little beat up, but he could sand and stain them any shade I wanted.

I wasn't so sure how I felt about that. A week prior, I'd have been begging him to do it. But now? I couldn't ask him to do anything like that. Helping me tidy up was one thing. Renovating was another.

Regardless, the day dragged on, cleaning with no response from Ally.

I called my mom and explained what had happened this morning.

She was frantic and worried, but I explained that I was fine and there wasn't anything she could do.

Around two p.m., Jeremy said he still hadn't been able to get through to Ally. He suggested that we should just flash up to Maine and see if she was at her apartment.

For obvious reasons, I was reluctant to join him. I didn't particularly want to meet with the gorgeous girl my boyfriend cheated on me with. Part of me wanted to hit her, and part of me wanted to cry. I knew that neither of those were options, but it didn't change how I felt.

Then I thought about what happened to Jeremy when he went alone. I decided with certainty that I had to go. So we did.

We landed in some snowy bushes in a suburb not far from Castine, Maine. The cool air rushed around me, the crisp smell of snow touching my nose. Jeremy held back the shrub so I could make my way out. In front of me stood a large apartment complex with three glass doors leading to a series of different apartments.

Jeremy led the way to the one on the far left. I thought about making a snide comment, like 'Of course you know where her apartment is' but bit my tongue.

We headed up two small, winding staircases until we stopped at apartment B205. Jeremy knocked at the door a few times with no response.

"Ally?" he called. "Hey, it's Jeremy. Can we talk?"

"Call her," I said. "Maybe she's not here."

He pulled out his phone and dialed. Rings sounded behind the door. "That's weird," he muttered, knocking again. "Ally? It's Jeremy. I really need to talk to you. Please come to the door."

Silence followed. I'd worked enough cases to know that something weird was going on. If she didn't want us to know that she was here, she'd have silenced the phone. But it kept ringing.

I reached for the handle. It turned. "It's unlocked."

"We can't just go in. Can we?"

I shrugged and pushed the door open. Didn't have much care for her privacy considering how she'd, ya know, fucked my man.

"Hey, the door was open," Jeremy called. "We're coming in."

Jeremy brushed past me, but I stood in the doorway for a moment.

My gaze shifted around the living room. It was tidy, but little. The décor was boring, decorated in browns and neutral cream colors. There was a small TV, a beige colored love seat, and a bland coffee table. But there wasn't much else. There weren't even pictures on the walls.

"Laila!" Jeremy yelled from the bathroom.

Uh-oh.

I ran towards him, following the sound of his voice. I made it down the short hallway off the living room. My eyes fell on a woman lying on the ground. She was sprawled out on her back. At first, I didn't see her chest moving. I squinted. Her chest lifted upward. Barely, but she was breathing.

There was no blood or vomit, nothing to suggest injury or foul play.

"Jesus," I muttered. Jeremy checked her pulse. A jealous swirl turned in my stomach as his hand touched hers. But I cleared my throat and said, "Is she okay?"

"I don't know," he muttered. "Her pulse is weak. We should take her to the Hospital and see what's going on."

"Does she have any health problems? Or a drug problem?"

"Not that I know of. But it's not like we're close, we just worked together."

"You must've been *kind of* close," I muttered.

Jeremy gave me a look, which I returned, reached out for my hand, and grasped her wrist with the other.

Then we landed at the hospital. Ally gasped for air. She shot forward on the gurney. Her head raced from one side to the other.

Even then, pale and clammy, trying to summon air into her lungs, I took in just how beautiful she was.

Her hair was platinum blond, smooth and silky. Unlike most blonds you see who have achieved their color through hours and hours of sitting in a salon chair, processing the hair until it was as coarse as a horse's mane. It reminded me of a child, that white blond that never lasts into adulthood. Her eyes were large and blue, almost gray. She had a small, ski-slope nose and big pouty pink lips. Her figure was small, and her chest was huge.

It was strange thing, envying someone and being attracted to them in the same instant.

"It's okay. You're alright," Jeremy said. "You were passed out, so I brought you here to see if you were okay."

She shook her head, eyes bulging. "Get me out of here." She frantically tossed her legs off the gurney, pushing Jeremy away. He grasped her shoulders.

"Okay. Alright. We'll take you home."

His voice was gentle and soothing. The same way it was when I was having a hard time. Had it been anyone else, it wouldn't have bothered me. But that soft voice, the one I loved so much, targeted toward the bitch who ruined our relationship lit a fire within me.

"Not home." Her anxious gaze shifted around.

"Okay." He ran his hand along her arm, attempting to soothe her. It made my stomach sink and my blood boil. Rationally, I knew it shouldn't. Clearly something had happened to her. She was scared. And he was just doing what he did to anyone in that condition. But human instinct kicked in and I had to grit my teeth together to keep from saying or doing something I'd regret.

We teleported again, this time into the small hunting cabin on Jeremy's property. "Is that better?"

She nodded, sitting forward on the old couch, still having a difficult time breathing. Her heaves sounded relatively similar to an asthma attack.

"Do you need an inhaler?" I asked.

She struggled between dry heaves. "Water," she said. "Lots... of... wat... er."

I walked to the small counter and grabbed a gallon and a cup. I headed back to the couch and poured a glass. She grabbed it, chugged, and then reached for the gallon. She held it to her lips and guzzled about half of it.

"Jesus," I muttered.

I didn't even know it was possible to drink that much at once. Come to think of it, I knew it wasn't. Not without getting sick. I half expected her to vomit.

Jeremy gave her the same confused, head tilting expression that I did. Ally started to catch her breath. After a few moments, she recovered. She didn't puke. She looked... refreshed. The ghastly color of her skin had softened to a milky white.

Then she said, "Sorry about that."

"Nothing to apologize for," I muttered.

Except for fucking my boyfriend.

She managed a smile. Damn, was she pretty. Like, model pretty. "I'm Ally." She extended her hand.

"Laila." I grasped her dainty palm. Her expression changed from grateful to... To something I couldn't quite place. Guilt? Fear? Overall discomfort would be the best way to describe it.

"Oh. You're as beautiful as Jeremy said you were," she said quickly.

I rolled my eyes. "Thanks. And you're way prettier than I hoped." I chewed my inner jaw. "So there's that."

She started to stand. "Well, thanks but I really should be—"

Nope. Not losing my only other lead in the same day.

"Answering some questions?" I used the wind to keep her pushed down in her chair. "I couldn't agree more."

"What's going on?!" she yelled, trying to push through the gust I used to hold her down.

"Laila." Jeremy let out a slow sigh, eyes shifting between mine. "She's not the bad guy here."

Defending her. He was defending *her*.

My teeth gritted together. "You sure about that?"

"Just let her go. She doesn't have a way to get back to Maine without me anyway."

Fine.

I released my hold on her. She stood and darted towards the door. I grasped the air around her and slammed her back to the chair. I walked in front of her. "Listen, we can do this the easy way, or we can do this the hard way. One way or another, I'm getting my questions answered."

"Please don't hurt me." Tears poured from the corners of her eyes. "Please just don't hurt me."

"Jesus Christ." Jeremy teleported her to the other side of the room.

I turned his way. "What?"

"You don't have to do that. She's not a Demon." He sat on the table across from her. "Nobody's going to hurt you, Ally. We just need to talk to you."

His kind tone with her infuriated me. He insisted the bitch knew something that we didn't and that's why he wanted to talk with her. But if that were true, she wasn't the victim. And he was talking with her like an old friend.

My hands tightened to fists. My jaw clenched.

She looked from him to me. "I'm sorry. I'm so sorry."

"Oh dear god." I rolled my eyes and sat on the table. "Please don't. We're not friends."

She looked down at her hands. Her manicured palms reached up to wipe tears from the corners of her eyes. "What do you want to know?"

"The night you two fucked." I pointed between them. "Do you remember it?"

"Remember what exactly?" Her gaze narrowed slightly.

"Having sex with him. Do you remember it?"

Her tense shoulder softened, as did her fearful gaze. "Of course I remember it."

"And you didn't roofie him or anything?"

"Roofie?" she asked.

"Yeah, roofie." My forehead wrinkled. "Ya know, pills? Powders? Drugs?"

"No, I don't think either of us took any drugs."

"Nothing suspicious about that night? No Demons or Witches nearby?"

"No, not that I remember," she replied. "What's all this about?"

Who the hell doesn't know what roofie means?

"I have no recollection of that night." Jeremy met her gaze. "And I know that in my right mind, I would have never slept with you."

"Gee, thanks," she muttered.

"I didn't mean it like that. You're beautiful." Fire touched the tips of my fingers. Jeremy met my gaze, realizing he'd already put both feet in his mouth. His voice picked up speed. "But I love her. And I don't look at other women the way I did before we met. I'm not a cheater. I've never cheated, and I never would. Except I did and I don't understand how or why." His gaze locked with hers. "You don't have any idea why I can't recall that night?"

"None that I can think of."

Those shiny, manicured fingers started to tremble. But her shoulders were soft and relaxed.

"You sure about that?" I asked.

She seemed terrified at first, and now, she seemed confident. As if she'd expected us to know something that we didn't and now had nothing to fear.

"Yeah," she said quickly.

Something was off. Jeremy was right, she knew something and wasn't willing to say it.

"Walk me through that night," I said.

"I don't think that's the best idea," Jeremy said, meeting my gaze.

"Are you sure?" she said quietly.

"I already saw it. Hearing it can't be much worse. So walk me through it."

"Okay, fine. Well, we were celebrating. We had just closed the case, and everyone was in a really good mood. Jeremy and I were having a drink at the table in the living room. And then he pulled out his guitar, and I pulled out mine. We sang for a while, some old songs and some new. But then some song came on the radio and I asked Jeremy if he wanted to dance with me. He said yeah, so we danced. Then this song came on, oh god, what was it. An older one, but a popular band sings it. Something five." She thought for a moment.

Doubted she was the type to listen to Five Finger Death Punch. I only knew one other band with the word five in it.

"Maroon 5?" I asked.

"That's it. Yeah, Maroon 5. The song came on, and we were danc-ing, and Jeremy started singing, and one thing led to another, and we started kissing. Then Jeremy asked if we could go somewhere more private and we headed upstairs."

At the thought of him asking her to go 'somewhere private,' a lump thickened in my throat. But something clicked.

First, she said they had a drink. She didn't specify what kind, but context clues suggested alcohol. And he hadn't relapsed. If he had, he'd have been eyeing the bottle I was drinking a few nights before like a starving dog to a fresh cut steak.

Not just that. But Adam Levine was a tenor. Jeremy's voice fell somewhere between a baritone and bass.

"You guys were singing Maroon 5?" I asked.

"Yeah, right before we went upstairs."

I narrowed my gaze. "Why are you lying?"

"Excuse me?"

"Why. Are. You. Lying?"

"What're you talking about?" Her tone sharpened.

I huffed, half smile coming to my lips. "You and I both know you're lying. I just want to know why."

She started to her feet. "Ya know what? I answered your questions. I didn't come here to be harassed."

"You didn't come here at all. You were brought here. And good thing too, seeing as how you were unconscious on the bathroom floor. Now sit your ass down and tell me the truth."

She reached for the door handle. "I already did, and it wasn't good enough for you." Her gaze narrowed. "Truth is, you can't accept that your boyfriend doesn't love you as much as he claims to."

Low blow, bitch.

I lifted the wind around her and slammed her into the wall. "Jeremy refuses to sing Maroon 5. He can't hit those notes. Any time they come on; he hums. He won't sing." I felt my eyes brighten in their sockets, pushing the air in front of her. "So why are you lying?"

"You want to believe he's someone he isn't," she said, still up against the wall. "He told you he can't remember it because he's a coward. He'll never admit it, but he loved it. Every minute of it." A slutty, mischievous grin inched up her lips. In less than two minutes, she shifted from terrified to smug. Her attitude completely shifted, and I couldn't figure out why. "God, you should have seen the face he made when I—"

All reason left my body and mind. I reached forward and grabbed her by her throat with fiery hands. Her expression changed, pain racing through her. She screamed out in agony. She reached up to grab my hands but struggled and I squeezed tighter. I held on firm, pushing against her fast pulse under my thumb.

"Laila, you're going to kill her." I heard Jeremy yell.

He yanked my shoulder. I elbowed him away and clenched harder at her throat. My eyes grew bright hot in their sockets.

"Who are you lying for?" I screamed.

"Let... Go." She gasped, smacking my wrist.

I held even tighter, burning her neck. I wasn't sure how I expected her to answer when I was depriving her of oxygen, but she'd pissed me right the fuck off.

"What are you hiding?"

Jeremy grabbed my shoulders, pulled me backwards, and kept his arms around my flailing extremities. She fell to the ground, still gasping for air.

"You stay here," he barked to Ally. Then he teleported the two of us back to the house.

CHAPTER FORTY-FOUR

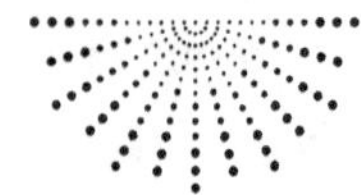

T kicked, slamming my fists down, sending Jeremy to the floor behind me. "Stop," he barked as if trying to calm a rabid animal. "God damn you, Laila."

"Damn me?!" I yelled. "I was defending you! She's lying!"

He stood, gesturing from me to the mirror on top of the dresser. "Look at your fucking self. Look at what you're letting her do to you. This isn't you."

I spun to the mirror. When stared back at myself, I was more than embarrassed, I was appalled. My brows were furrowed over my huge, glowing green eyes. They usually showed an inviting emerald, now glowing like Christmas bulbs. My jaw trembled and my lips quivered. I blinked a few times, moving past the anger onto something I didn't want to face. Shame.

I looked down at my hand. Pieces of black flesh were charred to my palms. My stomach churned and guilt washed over me. "Oh my god." I ran to the bathroom, flicked on the water, grabbed a rag from the shelf above the toilet, and scoured my hands. I scrubbed and scrubbed, trying to get the smell of burnt flesh off of my skin.

The water was so hot, it would have burnt anyone else. But it wasn't the temperature that hurt. It was the rag scrubbing the surface of my skin until it bled. But I couldn't stop because it felt right.

I deserved it. I melted the flesh off of her neck. I let my anger pull out the worst in me. Regardless of what she'd done, that didn't make me any better by burning her fucking neck off.

This was why I didn't want to see her. Not only because it hurt. But because I knew who I could be. I knew what I could do when I was angry enough.

Jeremy grasped my wrists, pulling them from the sink. "No," I pulled away and put hands back to the water. He grasped me by my shoulders, turning my body to face him.

"It's okay. She's alright." He lifted my chin to meet his gaze. "It's okay."

"No it's not," I said, tears welling in my eyes. "What's wrong with me?" Shaking, I hauled away. My breathing picked up speed. "I almost killed her. I would have killed her."

"But you didn't. And Leah's healing her right now. She probably won't even have a scar."

"I wanted to kill her." My chest heaved up and down. "I almost killed her." I held my racing heart behind my ribs. My teeth chattered, my palms began to sweat, and my vision grew blurry. I braced myself against the wall, knowing that feeling all too well.

The hyperventilating began. I fought the air around me to enter my lungs. My hands shook as I slid down the cool tile wall. I wrapped my arms around my knees, struggling hard, almost too hard, to return my breath to its normal rhythm. My teeth clattered and my hands wouldn't stop shaking.

"Hey, hey," Jeremy said softly, lowering himself next to me. "It's okay, baby. It's okay."

"I can't breathe," I said between dry heaves.

"Yes you can." His hands gently cupped my face and his eyes met mine. "You're having an anxiety attack. You've had them before." He wiped cold sweat from my forehead. "It'll pass. Just slow breaths. Don't think about anything else. Just breathe. Breathe in for five seconds, exhale for seven, in for five, out for seven."

I followed his directions for a few moments, breathing and holding his gaze. His hands held my neck gently, pushing sweaty hair from my face behind my ears. It took time, but I was starting to regain feeling in my numbed extremities. My breaths started to flow freer and more natural with each passing moment.

Truthfully, the bitch deserved everything she got. But attacking a possibly innocent person the way I just had—stacked on top of the hell this week had already been—was my breaking point. It was too much. Everything that had happened was too much, and I lost control. That's why I was sobbing. Because I lost control.

Who was I? A lunatic with no internal compass? I needed to get it together. I'd risked exposure this week. I almost just killed someone.

If I wasn't careful, it wouldn't only be someone like Ally who ended up on the other side of my flaming hands, and that was why I had to get it to-fucking-gether.

When my breathing returned to normal, he put his arms around me, and I wrapped mine around him. "I don't know what to do." Tears burned across my eyes. "I'm losing my mind. I don't even know who I am anymore. I'm not the one who gets angry like that. I'm not that girl. I've never fought someone. Especially not over a guy."

His lips touched my forehead. "She was egging you on. She wanted you to attack her. I just don't know why."

"What do you mean?" I pulled back.

He looked between my eyes. "That shit she said about me. I don't remember it. I didn't have a drink with her, I don't drink. I didn't love any of it. If anything, I feel violated. And you're right about Maroon 5, I always hum. And I know I didn't ask her to come upstairs with me. But then again, I don't remember anything after we started singing together." He paused, thinking hard. "I just don't know why she'd try to encourage you like that when five minutes before, she was crying and begging you not to hurt her."

The back of my hand rubbed at the water in my eyes. I thought for a moment. "She was afraid of me before we started asking her questions. She must have thought I knew something that I didn't. Or maybe she was hoping I'd be so disgusted I'd make you take her somewhere and stop interrogating her."

He gave a hard nod. He wiped sweat from my forehead. "And we never asked why she was passed out on the floor and didn't want to go home. Maybe she'd rather you kill her than have whoever's after her do it."

"We're going to have to put twenty-four-hour surveillance on her," I muttered. "And I'd really prefer if neither you nor I take any of those shifts."

"Yeah. Yeah, I think that's a good idea."

CHAPTER FORTY-FIVE

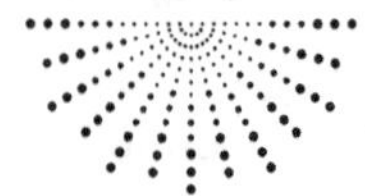

Warm chamomile slid over my tongue and down my throat. My hands were still shaking a bit, but the plushy comforter on Jeremy's bed sent a soothing sensation over my body. I drew in slow, relaxing breaths. I tightened my hands to fists, held for a few seconds, and slowly released them. It was anxiety control technique that my psychologist had suggested when I still went to her in high school. And it was working. The tightness in my chest had softened.

I just didn't get it. Who was this bitch anyway? What did she do to Jeremy? Why had she done it?

My eyes closed and I held the warm mug closer.

Just breathe, Laila. Breathe.

"You're savage as fuck, Lai." Hannah plopped onto Jeremy's bed beside me. "What you did to that bitch's neck. Wow, man, remind me to never piss you off."

I opened my eyes and met her gaze. A huff of a laugh left my nostrils. I placed the cup on the bedside table. "That wasn't pissed, that was infuriated."

"What'd she say? I mean, obviously I know she slept with Jeremy, but something must have pushed you over the edge."

"Honestly, you don't want to know. And I really don't want to think about it, let alone repeat it."

"Right. Sure. But why'd you and Jeremy put us on surveillance? She isn't dangerous, is she?"

"I don't know. I don't think so, anyway. I had a difficult time talking with her. You can try if you want. If she is dangerous, she isn't an immediate threat."

"I'll give it a try." She sat there, holding my gaze for a moment. It was an awkward look. The kind a child gives you after they've made a disaster and know they'll be in trouble.

"Is there something else you'd like to add?"

Her lips pressed together. "Kind of."

"Go on."

"Couple things actually."

"Shoot."

"Well, if you're not ready to answer this, that's alright. I completely get it."

I knew where this was headed. Little miss romance. She hadn't said much, but I knew what she was thinking. 'Please take him back, Laila, he loves you so so much.'

Not that I blamed her. I wanted that too. But there was a lot going on. A *lot*. My mind was racing, I was on the verge of a nervous break-down, and truthfully, I was ready to move past this too. But we needed answers first. I needed to know what happened.

"This about me and Jeremy?"

"I'm just wondering."

"More like hoping," I murmured.

"I just... I don't know, you guys are like yin and yang. Kit and kaboodle. Peanut butter and jelly. You're so happy when you're together and you're so depressed when you're apart."

"Hannah—"

Her hand raised in a 'stop' motion. "Now look, I know you're pissed and hurt and betrayed, but is your happiness worth your pride?"

"I see your point, Hannah. I do. But you have to see mine."

"I do, but—"

"No buts. Look at this subjectively. Don't think of it as me and Jeremy. Don't think about what we are, just think of it as any other couple. Or better yet, think about it as yourself. Would you just move right past this without knowing what happened?"

"I don't know. But I know you *aren't* just any other couple." I stayed quiet, listening to her. "I truly believe with every fiber of my being that he has never loved anyone as much as he loves you. More than he loves us, even. And I'm scared that if you leave him for good, he'll change." Her voice softened, big blue eyes growing dewy. "He'll revert back to who he was before he met you. Depressed and mopey, sleeping eighteen hours a day, or not sleeping at all, or even worse. He might relapse, and if he does, God, Laila, he's a whole different person. He just disappears and we don't see him for weeks. Last time, we only found him because he was underage, and the hospital called Aunt Annie and told her he'd ODed and he was unconscious. And the things he said when he was detoxing—you wouldn't even believe it was Jeremy."

"Hannah—" I frowned as she rambled, tears forming in her eyes.

"I can't lose him too, Laila. I can't. None of us can. I'm not saying that should be your reason for staying. If you didn't love him that'd be a different story, but I know you do. You both love each other more than life, and I—"

"I hear you, Hannah." I looked firmly between her eyes. "And I'm trying. I want things to go back to normal more than anything. Why do you think this slut is sitting in the room two doors down? I don't believe her, and I'm trying to believe him. But it's like the universe is telling me to run in the other direction. It feels like I'm fighting the cosmos, and just when I get my head above water, another wave comes through and holds me down. I feel like I'm drowning. I need things to settle down before I make any decisions. I'm planning a funeral, I'm trying to take over as the owner of a business, I'm trying to grasp every-thing my father hid from me before he died. I haven't even had time to accept that I have a brother, let alone get to know him."

"I get it." Then she looked down, twiddling her thumbs, as if there was something she wanted to say but didn't know how to ask.

I tilted my head to the side. "Is there something you'd like to add?"

"Yeah, but I don't know if now's the right time…"

"Oh, god. You're pregnant. I swear, Hannah. If you fuck up your plans for college—"

"What? No." Her brows creased over her bright blue eyes. "Why's that what everyone says when a girl has something to talk about? It's a very anti-feminist approach to—"

"What's this about then?" I asked.

She chewed her cheek. "So I'm not sure how you'll feel about this, and if you're uncomfortable with it, I'll leave it as is, and things will end where they are."

I was fairly certain I knew where this was headed. Kai had been here all week. Yet, I'd barely seen him. And when I did, Hannah was at his side. I hadn't given it much thought because of everything else that was going on. Also because of the fact that Hannah's three big brothers also lived in this house and wouldn't have let it go on if they'd seen a problem. Leah was in and out of our heads regularly, especially anyone new that was around. They could handle it.

I did have some reservations if I was right though. Hannah had never dated. And the first boy she did have an interest in is from an entirely different world? That could be a problem.

"Oh boy," I murmured.

She was quiet for a moment. "Kai and I kissed. And I know none of us know him very well, and he's your brother, and he's a good bit older than me, but I really like him. And in all fairness, you've kissed two of my brothers just in the past few days."

He wasn't that much older. In fact, it was the same age difference between Jeremy and me. The same ages when they met too. Seventeen and twenty.

"I thought I saw something going on there," I muttered.

"Really?" she asked. "Because I didn't see it coming. But like I said, if it makes you uncomfortable—"

I shrugged. "I mean, if you like him, I won't tell you not to be with him."

Her eyes shifted between mine. "But?"

"But he's practically an alien. He might decide to go home. And even if he doesn't, what can he do here? He has no diploma, no GED, primitive English. You're going to college next year, and I'll kill anyone that screws that up for you. And does he want something serious? Is he just looking for a fling while he's on Earth? I know he's my brother, but I don't know him. I don't trust him yet."

"I do," she muttered. "And I'm not saying we're soulmates like you and Jeremy. But we have this connection, Laila. He knew what I could do before I even told him. And he didn't act the way people here do. He said it was beautiful. Apparently one of the primary gods in that world had power over the abyss, and that ability is adorned. I don't have to pretend around him. He accepts me and—"

"Wait a second. How did he know about what you can do? I thought we kept that between you and I for a reason."

"He harnesses spirit. Way stronger than Leah, even. And in a way, so do I. A very different way, but he felt it."

Leah also harnessed spirit, but clearly not to the capacity that Kai did. Maybe that's why we were able to keep it from her. "Is that a thing?"

"In theory, I guess."

"Does he understand why no one can know?" I asked. "Because if he gives it up to anyone—"

"He doesn't understand why, but he's not going to tell anyone. He thinks I should tell them, but he knows I won't. And he won't."

I considered going into a lecture. Telling her to remember what she'd told me when I found out. That necromancy is a dangerous ability. That people in our world could—and would—hurt her to get to do what they wanted. Or that they'd kill her for the 'dark magic' she possessed. But she knew that. She was the one who told me it. Young as she may have been, she wasn't stupid.

Instead, I said, "Just be careful."

"I will." Hannah smiled. "So do I have your blessing?"

I huffed. "You can do whatever you want, Hannah. But I'm not giving you permission. You're old enough to make your own decisions."

She grinned. "Thanks, Lai."

CHAPTER FORTY-SIX

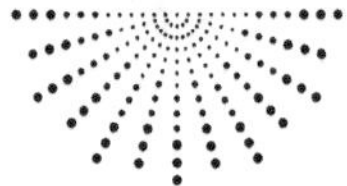

After a while of sitting in Jeremy's bed making funeral arrangements, my stomach rumbled with hunger. I stood and started from the bedroom. I made a left towards the maid stairs that led to the kitchen. As I walked past Adam's room where he was watching over Ally, giggling and whispers touched my ears. His door was closed, and it had been open when they headed in there.

Uh. Weird.

I turned the knob and opened the door. My mouth fell open.

Adam sat on his bed with Ally gently draped around him, both shirtless, bodies pressed firmly together.

"What the fuck are you doing, dude?" I grabbed his shirt from the floor and walked towards them.

Then I heard it.

Her voice. Soft, and smooth, a slow, gentle melody. And I just froze. Rationale left my mind. A rush of euphoria washed over me.

She stood from his lap, walked towards me—still singing—and my thoughts fumbled to a stop.

Her hand made its way to my hair, caressing it gently before moving to my neck.

Her lips pressed to mine, and I leaned into it. I literally could not stop. My underwear was instantly soaked, a different type of hunger rolled in the pit of my stomach.

I'd never been more attracted to someone in my entire life. It was like we were magnets, pulling into one another without control. It made no sense. She was the mistress who tore my relationship apart. Yet, there I was, standing in Adam's bedroom, making out with her.

After that, it's a blur. I remember kissing her, and then I remember hearing Hannah at the door.

"Uh, guys," she yelled. "I dunno how to tell you this, but I think Adam and Laila are about to have a threesome with that girl Jeremy slept with."

I heard Leah before she entered the room. "Oh." She awkwardly turned her head. "I know I should pull them away from each other, but this is pretty hot."

"What are you doing, Laila?" I heard Jeremy say. His tone was firm, but also confused.

But I didn't stop. It was as though I couldn't. When we kept kissing, he came into the room and physically pulled me off of her. Adam lay on the bed, rubbing his head, as if drunk and spinning.

I stood there for a second doing the same thing. I rubbed my eyes, trying to pull myself back into reality. I looked to Ally, who Hannah was now holding by her shoulders into Adam's desk chair.

"What just happened?" Jeremy looked between Adam and me.

"I...I don't know." I stared at Ally, trying to grasp it myself.

"She's a siren." Adam stumbled to his feet. "She has to be a siren."

Jeremy's eyes widened. Light gathered in his cheeks. He smiled wide. "Of course. Of course, that makes perfect sense. Why didn't I think of that?"

"We need to gag her," Leah said.

"No!" Ally screamed. "Please, don't. Just listen—"

Leah rolled her eyes. She reached into Adam's drawer and put a sock into the girls' mouth as Hannah held her down.

"Hannah, you're going to have to watch her," Leah said.

"What? Why me?" she asked.

"You're the only person in this house who isn't attracted to girls. She can't manipulate you," Adam said.

"What do you mean?" she asked.

My gaze stayed on Ally in the chair. A siren. I didn't even know they existed. I knew the Greek myths. I knew that they were beautiful women who sang a song and seduced men to their deaths. But I'd have never thought anything like this.

Jeremy didn't cheat. Whether he realized it or not, whether he'd admit it aloud or not, he was raped.

My stomach ached. I'd broken his heart because of something he had no choice in. He'd said it wasn't rape, but I should have put two and two together. I shouldn't have been so quick to hate him. I should have done better. He would've done better in my shoes.

"She can seduce anyone who's attracted to women. So obviously, I can't watch her. Clearly Adam and Jeremy can't, neither can Brody, and apparently, neither can Laila." Leah gestured between us.

"I didn't know you were bi," Jeremy muttered. "Learn something new every day."

"Really?" Adam chuckled. "I guess that makes sense. You didn't know Laila in her partying days."

I rolled my shoulders, bringing myself back to the moment. "I've never been the straightest of arrows, but..." My gaze narrowed at Ally. "That... That's horrible. How can you just..." I trailed off. "You're a glorified rapist."

"Pretty much," Leah muttered.

Suddenly, I didn't feel so bad about charring the bitch's throat. I wished I'd have burned her vocal cords out entirely. I wished she'd never be able to hurt anyone like she'd hurt Jeremy again.

"How could you do that?" I barked. "You didn't just sleep with someone else's boyfriend, you raped him."

"She probably doesn't see it as rape," Adam muttered. "In her mind, if her spell works, it just brings out a desire you already have. She's not creating the desire on her own."

"Desire isn't consent."

CHAPTER FORTY-SEVEN

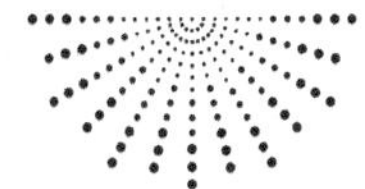

We all gathered around the kitchen island. Jeremy stared at the counter, eyes deep in thought. Long black waves hung in front of his brilliant blue eyes.

What was going through his mind? I thought about sliding in there. But he'd been violated plenty. I couldn't do the same. Dying to know what he was thinking or not, after what he'd just gone through, his thoughts were his own. Instead, I reached for his palm.

He looked up. His focused gaze softened. A smile raised at the edge of his mouth. He twined his fingers through mine and held tight.

I smiled back. But I felt like crying. How could I have treated him the way I had? Why did I have to make what happened to him any worse?

Jesus Christ, I'm a piece of shit.

Jeremy frowned. His hand dropped mine, he tossed an arm around my shoulder, and he yanked me into him. His lips touched my forehead.

No, you're not, his voice vibrated in my thoughts.

Oh, so he was in my head. Lovely.

I didn't believe that. I'd always feel guilty for the way I'd treated him that week. In his shoes, I wouldn't even consider wrapping my arms around him and hugging him tight. I wanted to pull away, because I didn't deserve that hug. But if I did, maybe that would just add to his pain.

"We know how she did it, but now we need to figure out why," Leah said at the other side of the island.

"What do you mean?" I asked.

"Sirens don't seduce for pleasure," Jeremy said. "They use it as a defense, the same way we use our powers to further our plans. If she wanted to be with me, she wouldn't have used her powers because it wouldn't be real."

"But what benefit would sleeping with Jeremy have?" Adam chimed in. "No offense, man."

Jeremy said, "None taken, wondering the same myself."

"Someone doesn't want us together." I gestured between Jeremy and I. Hannah squinted and I continued, "Like you said, Leah. And you too, Jeremy. It times out perfectly. She seduces him, Brody catches them, tells me, and I break things off. And if everything else that's happened this week hadn't happened, it would've worked. I wouldn't have dug any deeper."

"Alright, someone wanted to break you guys up so bad, they orchestrated all this. Fine." Adam's eyes shifted between us. "But what do we do now?"

Silence crept in. I didn't know either. However, I did know that someone was trying to hurt her.

"When we went to get Ally, she was unconscious on the floor of her apartment," I stated.

Jeremy paused, head shifting to the side. Then his eyes widened. "And she chugged a gallon of water when we got back here."

"So?" Adam said.

"So she made a deal for her legs." Leah smiled. "Of course."

"Not following," Adam said.

Ding-ding-ding, a lightbulb went off in my mind.

"Like The Little Mermaid," I murmured. "She's not a mixed breed. She's a fish."

"Only an Angel would have that kind of power," Leah murmured.

"Well, guys." Jeremy smiled. "Looks like we've found our method of torture."

"We won't be able to get anything out of her," Adam said. "None of us can talk to her. The second that gag is out, she's got all the power. And Hannah's too young to torture."

"It's not like it's physical," I said. "We just have to dehydrate her. It takes a human, what, three days to die without water? It might take her a day."

"Not even," Jeremy said.

"But do you think she'll even talk?" Leah asked. "You said she was passed out on the floor of her apartment. I'm assuming she had running water."

I thought for a moment. "She was terrified. What if they left her to die?"

"Who?" Jeremy asked.

"Whoever she's working for," I said. "Someone was there, someone prevented her from getting water in one way or another. Maybe they force fed her a diuretic or something, I don't know. But she didn't just end up dehydrated beside a working sink for no reason."

"They were covering their tracks. Kill her so she doesn't tell me what she did and do it in a way that won't look like murder so they can't be tried for killing an endangered species." Jeremy shrugged slightly. "They might have stayed there until she lost consciousness from dehydration."

"So she has nowhere to go," Leah said. "Home isn't safe, someone is after her. A couple days without water and she'll give us what we want if we can offer her something in exchange."

"We can interrogate her. But if she doesn't talk, whoever she was working with will come looking to finish her off." I nodded. "So one way or another, we have a lead."

CHAPTER FORTY-EIGHT

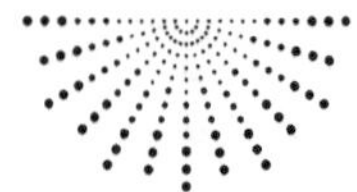

I knew what we'd agreed upon. We'd wait it out. Let her dehydrate, then question her once she was desperate. But my mind was racing, and I needed some answers. Or at least some clues.

The strong, clean scent of bleach touched my nose. Goosebumps rose over my arms at the drop in temperature. The hum of the furnace was the only sound moving through the space.

Despite its morbid nature, the basement was designed to be a perfect torture chamber. The floors had been paved with a thick, smooth epoxy to make blood clean up easier. The walls were stone but painted white, because the red stood out like a sore thumb on a white surface.

Chains attached to the concrete strong enough to hold the strongest man alive dangled from the walls. They joined to two hand cuffs as well as a set of shackles that connected to the feet.

An armoire filled with an assortment of torture weapons sat at the bottom of the steps. You name it, we had it. Knives, clamps, swords, bows and arrows, and some Renaissance weapons I don't know the names of.

My gaze traveled from her face down her legs. Her skin was pale and sweaty. Any beauty she'd had was dissipating before my eyes.

"You look thirsty." My feet met the ground from the staircase. "Poor thing. I actually feel bad for you. And I shouldn't, you're evil."

Her dreary, cross-eyed gaze met mine. It'd only been an hour without water and she already looked parched. Her head fell back onto the wall. She closed her eyes.

"Truth be told, I can't quite figure you out. You seem so sweet and likeable, but then again, I guess that's a part of your allure." I pulled a chair from the corner of the room and sat in front of her. "Ya know the worst part?" Her eyes opened, meeting mine. "All this time, Jeremy's been torturing himself for cheating on me. I've been torturing him. And that's just..." I let out a huff. "Wow, you're some serious levels of fucked up. You raped him, and he's the one being punished."

She murmured something from behind her gag. The curiosity was killing me.

"If I take that out, you still won't be able to go anywhere. I don't have the keys, so the most seducing me will get you is, well, ya know, fucking me."

Being the idiot that I was, I walked to her, pulled the gag from her mouth, and let the ball clank her teeth before it fell around her neck. "Don't you dare try that singing shit."

"I couldn't sing if I wanted to." Her voice was hoarse. "I can barely talk."

"Good." I said. "Good, you don't deserve to breathe."

Her gaze narrowed. "Then why are you letting me?"

"Because I need answers," I said. "And unfortunately for me, you have them. If you didn't, you'd already be dead."

She let out a chuckle. "You want me to be the villain, but I'm not. I'm just the middleman."

Looking back on it, she was right. She really wasn't the bad guy. In a way, she was a victim in all of it too. She still deserved punishment, but she was a mere pawn.

"Evil's evil." I leaned forward in the seat. "Just because you didn't devise the plan doesn't make you any less of a villain than the person who orchestrated the whole thing."

"Oh, Laila." She tilted her head, smile edging up her lips. "Have you never done a horrible thing to protect yourself?"

I'd done countless. I'd killed, I'd lied, nearly every bad thing in the book. But never rape.

I gritted my teeth. "Not at the expense of ruining someone else's life."

"No, just at the expense of *taking* someone's life." She let out a soft, quiet chuckle.

"Oh shut up." I laughed. She and I were on totally different levels of fucked up. Sure, I'd done bad thing but only for good reasons. "You don't know anything."

"I know you assisted in the murder of your best friend."

I stood up, walked to her, and gripped the bottom of her chin tightly under my fingers. "Then you should know that killing you would be easy. Fun, even."

"Maybe." She shrugged. "But you won't. You don't have the balls."

"Oh?" I gripped her face tighter. My fingers grew hot. The heat burned her chin and cheek. "I don't?"

Her teeth began to tremble, but she gritted them together. "Go ahead. Kill me."

I let the heat soar hotter until I smelt the flesh burn. Smoke slid between the tips of my fingers and her skin. But I dropped my hand, tightened it into a fist, and slammed it to her jaw. "Like I said, I need information."

She tightened her teeth to a hard line. "Well, I won't give it to you."

"You will. Or you'll wilt back into the cold-blooded bitch you really are." I shrugged. "That's your choice."

She huffed, head shaking. "You don't scare me."

I doubted that. She looked pretty damn scared back at the cabin. But alright, bitch.

"No, but someone does. Whoever you're helping left you to die. When they realize you're alive, they'll come looking. And that's all I need."

She laughed, biting her lip. "You're so blind. Your enemy could be in this room and you wouldn't see them."

Now, we're getting somewhere.

"What do you mean?"

She said nothing and turned her gaze to the wall.

"I might not have the most experience, but I have connections, Ally. If amenity is what you're looking for, I can work something out for you. I'm part Angel, I can help you."

She laughed. "Angel? You think that means something to me? Your kind is a disgrace to this earth. You don't deserve to share the air I breathe."

My eyes widened. Not that I disagreed entirely, but seriously? I couldn't help the laugh that escaped my lips. "Angels might be assholes, but, bitch, you're a serial rapist. And you aren't even supposed to breathe air. You're a fish."

"And you're a serial killer," she said. "And a racist one at that. You kill the Demons, and the Vampires, and the Wolves. Just for being who they are. Murder my family, the grazing cattle, the helpless creatures that roam this beautiful world. You commit murder every time that you eat. Meanwhile, the vile creatures you protect are destroying the only home they have and taking mine down with them."

Well, that was some hippy dippy shit if I ever heard any. Yeah. I killed things. But nothing that didn't deserve it. Nothing that hadn't made bad decisions that led to their own execution.

"What are you talking about?"

"I lived nearly two thousand years in the ocean. My beautiful waters, spanning more of the earth than any other substance. And these things, these *humans*, they do nothing but pillage and destroy. My babies, my children, dying because of your oil and your trash and your greed. In less than a hundred years, those people *destroyed* my home. I had nowhere left to hide. It was either die in the water from your poisons or help your precious Angels and move to the land and live with legs."

She was right. Humans were shitty. We let them destroy their home yet moaned and groaned about rogues killing them. But we couldn't force the human race to take care of their home without exposing ourselves. And if we did, if the Council and Elders came out from the shadows, the world would be in all out chaos. We'd be in war with them until we proved that we weren't hostile, but then it'd get to a point where they would lose their free will.

But in that little rant, she revealed something else.

"An Angel sent you." I smiled. "Which one?" She stopped, eyes wide and nervous. "Which one, Ally?" She shook her head. "Jesus Christ. They already left you to die. You'll die either way. Just tell me so that something good can come from your death."

"If only you knew. Your death would bring much more victory to this planet than mine ever could. You have no idea." Her gaze narrowed, teeth gritted together, vein pulsing in her forehead. She spat, saliva landing on my chest. "You can go to hell." I leaned forward and lifted the gag back to her mouth.

"And just for good measure." I raised my fist and slammed it to her cheek.

CHAPTER FORTY-NINE

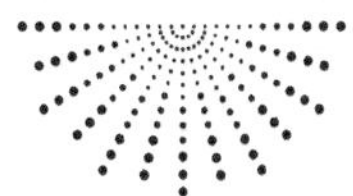

"What are you doing?" Leah asked as I trudged up the basement steps. "I thought we agreed she'd be used as bait."

"She will, but I had to ask some questions." I kicked my shoes off and shut the door.

"And?" She placed her hands at her hips.

I huffed. "And an Angel sent her."

"Well, we knew that. Did she say who?"

"Technically, we just suspected that," I said. "But no."

"Well, Mary sent Jeremy to Maine, and they were working on that case together. Maybe she'll know if Ally was working with anyone else." Leah leaned against the counter and crossed her arms against her chest.

My tongue ran along my teeth. A slow breath left my nostrils. I sat at the bar. "You heard Mary; she's not going to help us."

"She wouldn't help find your mom, but this is unrelated. We're trying to figure out who sent this siren, not who birthed you."

I paused, thinking for a moment. My fingertips ran through my hair, pushing it from one side of my head to the other. That line she'd said repeated through my mind. "*Your death would bring more victory to this world than mine ever could.*"

Someone had convinced my best friend to try to murder me. Someone wanted me dead. I didn't have the slightest clue why, but Ally did.

The chances of two Angels being out to destroy me and Jeremy's relationship as well as kill Moe seemed unlikely. It had to have been the same person. It was all connected. I didn't know how, I didn't know why, but now I knew for a fact. All of the bullshit from the last week all boiled down to the same person. Not some thousands of years old curse. Some bitch.

"What if my mother is whoever set this up?"

"But why wouldn't she want you to be with Jeremy? And why do so much to keep him from Ally?" Leah shook her head. "I don't get it."

That wouldn't make sense though. If she wanted me dead, she could have killed me easily the other day at the diner. None of it made sense.

Then again, no one had tried to kill *me* in the past week. Just people around me. Like Jeremy said. The common denominator in all of these things was that it hurt me. But it wasn't to kill me.

"I don't know." I ran my fingers through my hair. "I don't know, but I feel like we only have the tip of the iceberg here. There's more to this, there has to be."

"Yeah," she murmured, nibbling her lip. "Something definitely doesn't add up."

"It's like we're working on a puzzle with nothing but edge pieces." I rubbed my eyes and lowered my face to my hands.

Someone wanted Jeremy and I apart. Someone wanted each of us dead on separate occasions. My biological mother went so far as to kill Moe to disguise her identity. But again, why would that be the same person when she had ample opportunity to kill me?

Was it one person trying to ruin my life? Or two? Or more than that even?

Just then, a knock thudded at the door. "I'll get it," Leah murmured, heading towards the entry way.

I leaned my head to the counter, enjoying the cold granite beneath my cheek. That cool touch brought an ounce of relief to my racing mind. I tried to think of nothing. I tried to just breathe and let the rest fall away before I worked myself into a panic attack.

But my pause of relief lasted only a short moment, because then, Leah called, "It's for you, Lai."

I stood and headed to the front door. Ramirez stood there with a briefcase in hand. He seemed uneasy, probably because of something Leah had said.

"Hello, detective," I murmured. "What can I do for you?"

"I couldn't get the phone, but I took pictures of his schedule and texts. There's nothing notable in them." He gestured to the case.

"Great. How about we go to the diner? I'll whip up a pot of coffee and we can discuss."

"Sure."

I reached for my jacket. Leah caught my arm, telepathically saying, *What are you going to discuss?*

He has information about Moe's murder.

And he doesn't want anything for it?

No, he does. He needs help with a case.

Invite me.

But—

No, Laila, invite me. I have more experience with cops than you do. Let me help.

"Leah, would you like to join us?"

"Laila." Ramirez tilted his head downward slightly. "The matters we have to discuss are strictly confidential."

"Alright, Detective, let me tell you how this is going to go." Leah turned to meet his gaze. "If you and Laila are going to discuss a case, my assistance is more than helpful, it's necessary. I have much more experience than Laila and I'll be a much bigger contributor than her. No offense," she muttered to me.

"None taken," I murmured.

"Have you told her anything about our arrangements?" Ramirez asked.

"She's psychic, I don't have to," I replied.

"Lovely," he said. "So you're one of them."

Leah narrowed her gaze, firmly crossing her arms against her chest. "*Them*? What is that supposed to mean?"

"I didn't mean anything by it." His eyes widened. "Just that you're special. Which is good, I need help on this. Special help."

She rolled her eyes. "I'll get my coat."

CHAPTER FIFTY

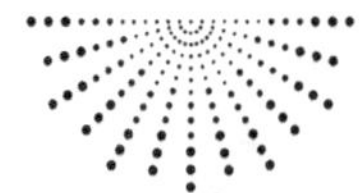

"Do you trust this guy?" Leah glanced at Ramirez in the side mirror.

Cutting the wheel to turn into Moe's parking lot, I said, "I dunno. I don't know him well. But he seems scared of us, I don't think he's a real threat."

"Have you scanned his mind?" she asked.

I put the car in park and fiddled with the door handle. "No, I haven't."

"And why the hell is that?" she said in a strong tone. "You wouldn't even need to help him if you read his mind. You could wipe whatever he's holding over your head—"

"I don't like going into people's heads, you know that. I don't want to see all of his fantasies and heart breaks."

"But you need to." Her darting eyes pierced mine. "You need to see if what he's told you is true. He could be the enemy."

"I don't think so," I muttered.

"Neither do I, but you can't just *think*. You have to check."

"Alright. You ask questions, I'll read his mind. I'll need to make contact though. I can only get fleeting thoughts without touching. For memories, I'll have to touch my skin to his."

"Sit next to him. You're wearing short sleeves under that, right?" I nodded again. "Take his coat when we go in. Your arm touching his should be enough."

"That should do."

Truth be told, the one power I had that I would gladly live without was telepathy. It was convenient at times, don't get me wrong. But it was also incredibly emotional.

When you hop into someone's head, you aren't seeing it from a third person perspective. You're reliving it through their eyes. You feel every breath, every emotion, even the temperature of the air in the moment that you're focusing on. It's more than just reading a mind, you *become* that person for the length of time that you exist inside of their thoughts.

Not to mention all the bizarre things that run through everyone's head on a day-to-day basis. After hearing a middle-aged man's thoughts about his pretty sixteen-year-old waitress, or a stranger's fantasies about homicide, you don't look at people the same. Even if they don't act on them, you quickly realize how disturbed people truly are. The pretense is easier than reality.

I fiddled with the lock on the door, pushing the old thing 'til it popped open. The cool air brushed my cheeks, and I tightened my jacket closer to my body. As Leah sat, I walked behind the counter, adjusted the temperature, and started a pot of coffee. I carried three cups to the booth and shivered.

Then I lifted my jacket from my arms. It was cold and I really wanted my damn jacket. But I needed it to look casual when I asked for his.

Ramirez stepped through the door, kicking snow off his boots at the entrance. "I'd offer coffee cake or scones, but they're probably stale by now," I said with a look over my shoulder.

"That's alright, I'm more of a doughnut kind of guy anyway," Ramirez said.

"Of course you are." Leah chuckled.

He narrowed his gaze. I cleared my throat. "Can I get your coat?"

He carelessly lifted it from his shoulders and handed it to me, completely oblivious to the fact I was about to intrude the most private place of his existence. I hung them on the wall hook next to the swinging steel door. I hurried together a pot of coffee, grabbed bowl of prepackaged creamers from beneath the bar, and a few mugs.

"So let's get down to business," Leah said. I made my way back to the table and set down the cups and creamer. "I know what Laila wants from you. But what is it that you want from her? Or us, rather?"

He nibbled his lip. "My wife and daughter went missing almost six years ago. I've searched high and low, but I've got nothing. Absolutely nothing. Considering what you all can do; I think you might stand a chance at finding them."

"How old was your daughter?"

"Four," he said. "Just turned four."

Leah pulled out her phone, jotting down notes. "And did you have any suspects at the time?"

"No. Absolutely nothing. No suspects, no evidence. The only DNA left at the house was theirs. Well, and mine, but I lived there so." He swallowed hard and shook his head. "But no. No suspects."

That sounded familiar. I couldn't place where from at first. But I knew it wasn't the first time I'd heard of someone with abilities disappearing without a trace.

"So what makes you think we can help you? If you don't have any evidence or suspects, our hands are a little tied too. And no offense, but it sounds pretty human. Nothing that you just told me screams Demons or Werewolves."

"His wife was Fae." I slid into the booth beside him.

She cocked her head to the side. "Really? She told you that?"

"Not exactly," Ramirez said. "I never heard that word until Laila said it the other day. Amy didn't know what she was. She had premonitions and a really strong sense of empathy. Lydia could make things grow."

Another peculiar detail I needed to meditate on further. Abilities are genetic. If the girl was in touch with the earth aspect of her abilities, why was her mom only in touch with the spirit? Had Amy just not realized how to use her earth abilities? Or did she simply rely on the spirit? I wasn't much different, in fairness. I relied far more heavily on fire than anything else.

"What kind of things?" Leah asked, typing again.

"Plants. Once when she was really little, around eighteen months, I think." He smiled at the memory. "The three of us were sitting on the porch in the dead of winter. And Lydia toddled over to the edge, reached her hand through the railing, and touched a dead rose bush. I jumped up to grab her but then I looked at the bush. And she brought at least half a dozen dead buds to a bloom. With a simple touch. It was the most amazing thing I'd ever seen."

"Definitely Fae then," she said.

"But it's not just that," I said. "Tell her what you told me."

"Right. Before she went missing, about a month or two, I think, Amy told me something bad would happen to her."

Leah looked up from her notes. "And you didn't take steps to prevent that from happening?"

He turned his gaze downward. "I didn't take her seriously; she was mumbling and irrational after a premonition. She always said things that didn't make sense. And she didn't say how or when. But she did… she insisted there was nothing I could do. She said her visions always happened. That it was destiny. And she didn't say what 'bad thing' would happen to her. It could've been cancer for all I knew." He cleared his throat. "But there was something else, too. She said she'd be gone for a long time, but the girl who" —he made air quotes— "'held fire in her hands' would bring us back together. She said I'd find the girl, then I'd find her. And I did." He glanced at me.

Leah huffed. Then she walked to the bar, grabbed the pot of coffee, and filled her cup. She walked back to the booth with the brew. "Well. That's bizarre."

"I know," he said. "I know, I didn't even believe her when she said it. Seemed pretty bizarre when the two of them disappeared, but I didn't know how to look for the 'girl who held fire in her hands.' I just...I don't know, I kept living. Then the other day, I saw that video and it clicked. You can help me find my family. I don't know how, and I don't know when, but I know you can."

I leaned in closer to him. Just a touch. Just enough for my shoulder to touch his bicep.

It was more than enough. I focused, searching for the memories of his wife and his daughter.

First, images of their wedding day flashed behind my eyes. "I, Amy, take you, Ray, to be my..." Their wedding vows. Her beautiful dress. Her long, flowing, copper hair. Her bright smile.

Then images of his daughter lying on her mother's chest for the first time. Tears of joy running down both of their faces. "So what's it going to be?" a voice asked.

"Lydia," Amy said quietly. "Her name is Lydia."

Then the sound of Lydia's bubbly laughter as he tossed her into the air. Two pale blue eyes and locks of curly black hair against his same shade of medium brown skin.

Like a tape on fast-forward to the bloodied house. Dripping from the knob of the door to the magnificent cherry hardwoods. Crimson smeared along the walls, as if intentionally spread across them for shock value. Broken glass all over the ground. A tree branch jutted through a shattered window. Like the toddler had prayed to Mother Earth for help but was no match for the intruders.

I felt his heart crumble when he ran to his daughter's room. The toddler bed still made but dusted in a layer of shattered glass and an aerosol of blood. Spewed against the walls, all over the floors.

He collapsed to the ground. His knees ached. The sound of his scream echoed like a gunshot in a tin can. His shaking palms raised to either side of his head and he thought, *Why didn't I believe her?*

"Right, Laila?" Leah pulled my attention from the dream like memory.

I struggled to slow the racing of my heart. "I'm sorry, what did you say?"

"Your powers. They only set in the year before last," she said.

"Almost three years ago actually," I corrected. It may as well have been last year for the poor handle I had on them, but it'd be three in January.

"Then wouldn't it have been more helpful for me to have met you people?" Ramirez asked.

Leah raised a brow at his word choice. "My *people* probably would've been more helpful, sure. But premonitions aren't science. I don't necessarily believe in the destiny story, but if that is accurate, if Laila is destined to return you to your family, it may not be as simple as it sounds. It could be metaphoric. She could guide you to them. She could be the one to lead you to their bodies. Hell, she could kill you and the three of you reunite in death."

His eyes widened.

"She's joking. Tell him you're joking, Leah."

"Sure." She gave a sadistic smile. "I'm quite the comedian."

He glanced at her, then at me. After an awkward moment, he cleared his throat. "What can you guys do though?" he asked. "I've cross checked all the data I have more times than I can count. It's all dead ends."

"Well, that's without magic," I muttered. "Not making any promises, but you'd be amazed at the things we can do."

"It isn't magic," Leah said. "Just biological advantages."

"Yeah, yeah. But it looks a hell of a lot like magic," I said under my breath.

"But don't you owe us something, Detective Ramirez?" Leah said. "If we're helping you, you've got to help us. We're on the same team, after all."

"I agreed to help Laila with the investigation of Moses Baker's death so long as she's helping with the investigation of my family."

Leah nodded in agreement. "Sure, of course. But here's the thing. If you're working with Laila, you're working with me. You're working with our family."

"There she goes," I muttered.

Leah's tirades always amused me. The eyes that could cut steel as she told someone how it was going to go regardless of how they felt. She may have only had two abilities, but her attitude was one in and of itself. That's still one of my favorite things about her.

"And we don't play well with cops. We do things that don't make sense to you. We operate on a separate set of guidelines. There will be times you see us covered in blood like you did the other day. We might even have a body in our house. But if we're working for you, you're going to have to work for us too. I'm not asking you to just keep your mouth shut about what you see around us, you'll have to participate with things we need."

"I don't follow," he said, crossing his arms.

"If we're helping you, we'll need more than your help on just one case."

"What kind of help?" he asked.

"Well. First of all, I'm going to give you a flash drive. And I'll need you to plug it into your computer at work."

Ramirez leaned forward. "What? Why?"

"Primarily, to cover your ass. I don't want to have to go through you every time I need to look something up in the police data base. Because believe me, this thing you have me working on is going to require a lot of research. Most of which Google won't be much help for."

"So you want to install a virus on my computer?" His head tilted to the side. "I could lose my job."

"I just told you we might have a dead body in our home, and you're worried about a cyber-attack?" She laughed. "It's not like I need access to missiles. I just need information. Don't think of it as a virus, think of it as a bridge between two computers. And I'm a programmer. I know how to cover my tracks. Even if someone did find it, there's no way to prove someone didn't break into your office and install it. And aside from that, if you're going to know all of our shit, we'll need some dirt on you. We can't work with a cop if you're the only one with a leg to stand on."

He sat quietly for a moment. Then he lifted his shoulders. "I guess I don't have a choice then."

"That a boy," Leah said.

"But if I'm going to be your puppet, then I'd like to know a couple things."

"Like?" I asked.

I expected him to ask about Adrian. Or more details of what I knew about Moe's death. Questions I wouldn't give him answers to. But a smile crept at my lips as he began.

He leaned forward, gaze shifting between us. "Like what you are? How you do what you do? Do you all have the same powers? Are they genetic? What are the limits? I know one of you can teleport, but how far? Anywhere in the world, just places you've been? And do you have to know where you're going? What about weight limits, how much can be carried when teleporting? Does it interfere with electronics? Do GPS satellites understand how you jump from place to place? And your fire. Does it burn you? If not, does regular fire? Or is it explicitly the fire you create that you're immune to? And you're psychic. How does that work? Can you read my mind right now? Can you turn it off? Do people think in words, or pictures, or both? Can you put thoughts into my head too? What about the water I saw that guy with? Does he extract it from the air around him or—"

"Jesus Christ," Leah said.

I laughed. He sounded just like I did when I got my abilities. Most of those thoughts, I did have answers to. But some I still puzzled on myself.

"You'll figure it out over time. But for now, we'll stick to the basics," Leah continued. "I'm one hundred percent Fae. To my knowledge, anyway, I was adopted so we don't know for sure. But Laila is one quarter Fae, one quarter Guardian, and one-half Angel. Yes, Angels are real. So are Elves and Fairies. No, they aren't like Tinkerbell, but yes, they do have wings. Some can fly, but not all. Demons are real, and no, you wouldn't stand a chance against one. And no, Santa and the Easter Bunny aren't, so don't get smart with me."

"I didn't say anything."

"You thought it, which is close enough." She sipped her coffee. "Look, if you aren't going to take what I say seriously, then you might as well walk away now because—"

"No, I am. I'm sorry. I'll be more thoughtful next time."

"Good. Thanks. Think we about covered it then," Leah said. "But about your wife and kid. Do you have any of their personal items? Hairbrush, a necklace they wore a lot or anything along those lines?"

"I have Amy's engagement ring; she only wore it on special occasions. And I think I have an old hairbrush of Lydia's. Would that work?" he asked.

"That'll do. Bring it by the house."

CHAPTER FIFTY-ONE

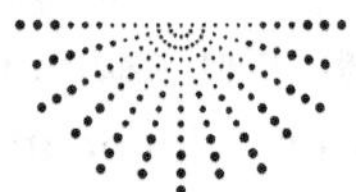

"So what do you think?" I asked Leah as we started onto the main road.

"That depends. Did everything he say check out in his head?" She clicked her seatbelt into place.

I gazed out over the roads. The snow had started to clear up a bit, it was mostly water now. "Yeah, it was all true. I didn't see any inconsistencies."

"Then I think it's a good idea. We need the law on our side. He'll be able to cover our ass if we ever get in a rut."

"And his family?" I asked.

She shrugged. "I don't know. It's weird that his wife knew about you well before you had your powers. But it's not unheard of. Fae don't normally have premonitions, but she may have been more than Fae if she didn't know what she was. When we get home, I'll start some research and give Helena a call. She can get me a spell to scry for them."

"Will it work?" I asked.

"It should. If they're alive, anyway. We'll see."

We were about halfway up the drive when Leah turned the radio down. She cleared her throat.

"So," Leah said. "What are your thoughts on all that shit with Jeremy?"

"Well, I mostly feel like a victim blaming piece of shit."

"Eh, you were manipulated."

"I guess. It just pisses me off that I fell for it, you know?" I shook my head. "Either way, I'm still confused. Why do so much work to keep Jeremy and I apart? And why not kill the siren sooner? Why kill Moe? And why take my book?" I paused. "It's just... Confusing."

"Moe knew who your mom was. And I think, whenever he saw you with Kai, he knew he'd have to tell you. Then she realized what he was going to do, so she intervened," Leah said. "But I'm at a loss over the trying to keep you and Jeremy apart issue."

"Yeah. Yeah, me too. What's the intent there?"

She shrugged. "Beats me. But we do know that par animos haven't existed for a really long time, at least not to the public eye. Maybe this is why, someone tries to wipe you out before you get your happily ever after. The stories do say that they're cursed."

"Huh," I muttered. "But this can't be a curse. Someone is doing this, Leah. There's a face behind all of this, and I don't think it's a wrathful god."

"Who knows," she said. "But next time something shady goes down between the two of you, at least we know with certainty that some-one's pulling cords behind the curtain now."

CHAPTER FIFTY-TWO

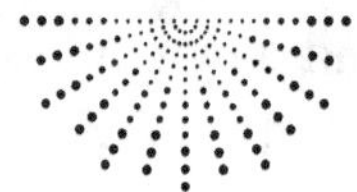

"Whose car is that?" Leah nodded toward the house.

I squinted, seeing the snow dusted, black Ford Focus. "I think that's my mom."

"What is she doing here?" Leah asked. "Shit. I wonder if she can hear the siren in the basement."

"She's got a gag in her mouth. I don't think anyone can hear her." I pulled in next to mom. "And she knows about all this anyway. She's not turning us in."

"That's true," Leah said.

As we walked in the front door, I called, "Mom, are you here?"

"In here," she hollered from the living room.

I walked that way, slushy tennis shoes squeaking beneath me. Mom sat comfortably on the couch, legs crossed, and purse on her lap. My head cocked to the side. "Hey, what're you doing here?"

"Well, I'm happy to see you too." She stood, took a few steps forward, grabbed my upper arms, and looked firmly between my eyes. The same way she had when I was fifteen to check if I'd been smoking grass under the bleachers. "You haven't been returning my calls. And I was worried, so I came to check up on you. Had a nice little chat with Jeremy while I waited too."

I glanced at him on the love seat. He pressed his lips together and widened his eyes a bit. "Kinda figured it'd be best if you explained the details."

"Right," I muttered. "But you didn't have to come all the way out here, I could have—"

"I did, because you haven't returned my calls since you told me there was someone in the diner like you were in some hostage movie," she said quickly. "I haven't slept in two days because I've been so worried about you. And whether you like it or not, you're going to talk to me. And you're going to tell me everything. And then we're going out to dinner. Or we can order in. I don't care. But you need to fill me in."

"I'm fine, Mom—" I said.

"Maybe you are, maybe you aren't. But one way or another, we are going to talk. Okay?" She insisted, eyes moving quickly between mine.

I looked to Jeremy. He nodded. Then to Leah. She nodded too. "Alright. Well. Where should I begin?"

"You could start with what you know about Moe. And then explain what's going on with the two of you." She gestured between Jeremy and me.

"Right."

<hr>

I went on to tell her everything I had gathered in the last few days. It started with Moe, detailing what I'd read in the journal, and then the events that led to the journal being stolen. Then I started on the subject of me and Jeremy. How someone had tried to kill him and what we learned about the siren. It was confusing, but she kept up.

Then, I told my mom the truth about Adrian. She said she'd suspected something other than what I'd told her before—that Adrian had never arrived at the party—but she didn't question it because she didn't want to raise any eyebrows or point any fingers.

We ordered pizza and sat around discussing where life had taken us over the past week. We talked about Moe's death, and then Moe's life. There were tears and there were laughs. Then, she told me things about my dad I'd never known.

Like how his "truck driving" job was only partly true. It was a cover for what he really did. Trafficking Fae from the other dimension to the Earth realm, taking over in his father's place.

Then about how he also worked with the Angels from time to time, assisting on jobs when his powers could be used. Since he controlled all five elements, he was a commodity. He could complete a job in the fifth of the time another Fae may be able to.

She went on to explain that Dad never wanted me to use my powers because he didn't want me to get hurt. I still resented that decision, but I was starting to understand. People die doing what we do. All the time.

Although I didn't agree, I tried to put myself in his shoes. He wanted me to have a normal life. I would never bind my child's powers, but I could understand his perspective.

***

Eventually, Kai made his way downstairs with Hannah. As Mom heard his voice, her wide eyes shifted over her shoulder and her jaw hit the floor.

"Hey, Kai," I called. "There's someone here I'd like you to meet."

"That so?" he asked, heading to the living room. "Who might that be?"

I stood, Mom following. "Kai, this is my mom. She met you once when we were babies but, well. You know."

He smiled. "Pleasure to meet you, ma'am."

Kai extended his hand, beginning to learn our human customs. Mom shook her head, lifted her arms around his shoulders, kissed each of his cheeks, and allowed him to kiss her forehead. As was the custom in the Fae realm, he'd said.

"I cannot put into words how great it is to see you standing here." She took a step back. "You look so much like him. The similarities are... Wow. Just like your father did fifteen years ago."

"My mum used to say that too." He smiled. "She said it looks like I got all of him and none of my mum."

"I don't know about that; you have her eyes. The shape at least, the color is all Luka," Mom said, looking over him carefully. "And the texture of her hair too. But the color, that's your dad." She quickly blinked tears away and took a step back. "Let me see the two of you together. Side by side, let me see you."

I laughed, stepping beside Kai. A tear dripped from the corner of her eye. She wiped it with the edge of her thumb. "I never thought I'd get the chance to see you together like this again. You're so beautiful. If your dad could see you now... He wouldn't believe it. *I* can hardly believe it. And I'm looking at you." She laughed. "I may hate that woman, but she did make some beautiful children."

CHAPTER FIFTY-THREE

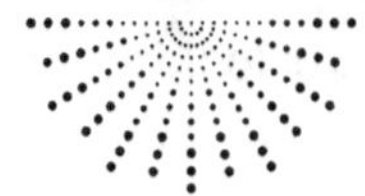

Around 9:30, Mom left, saying she had work in the morning. I kissed her goodbye and went on with my night. I took a long, hot shower, collapsed to Jeremy's bed, and took in a slow, deep sigh.

Jeremy's hand found mine, lifting my knuckles to his lips. "You alright?" he asked.

"I am, actually."

"Yeah?" He smiled.

I smiled back. "Yeah. Yeah, it was nice to clear that stuff up with my mom. Especially the stuff about you. I wasn't even going to tell her at first, but Jenna brought it up the other night and..." I looked over his dreary gaze. "We should probably talk about that."

His lips flapped together in a trill. "Yeah, we probably should."

I cleared my throat. "Well, first of all, I'm sorry. I'm so, *so* sorry. I should've listened to you; I should have had more faith in you."

"No, don't apologize." He reached for my hand. "In your position, I probably would have thought the same thing."

"I am going to apologize because I feel horrible. You... You were violated. And I just... I let you feel like shit. Hell, I blamed you. And that was fucked up. I never question a victim, but I wouldn't even try to believe you. And I'm sorry. I feel so bad that happened to you. It's not..." He struggled to meet my gaze, swallowing hard and shaking his head slightly. "How are you? Are you okay?"

"Yeah. I'm fine. It's just weird to think about, ya know?" He shrugged. "It's stupid."

"It's not stupid."

His fingers ran through his hair, still not meeting my gaze. "I don't know. It feels wrong. I didn't realize what had happened. I just... I thought I just fucked up. I mean, I knew it didn't add up, but *I* didn't even think I was raped. I didn't even blame Ally. But it's just... I don't know. I, uh... I don't know if I really want to talk about that right now."

"Sure. Sure, you don't have to."

After a quiet moment, he pressed his lips together and turned his gaze up to mine. "Okay, can I be completely honest?" I nodded and he continued, "I *was* attracted to her. There was a part of me that did want to sleep with her."

He said it as if I'd be mad or hurt. And sure, I felt a tinge of jealousy, but I thought the same thing when I saw her. It was just the human, monogamous brainwashing we all convince ourselves is normal when it ultimately boils down to a fairy tale mindset that doesn't exist. There's no harm in being attracted to someone who isn't your partner.

"I guess that's why I believed that I did... ya know, cheat. I... I didn't want to... It's just different for guys, you know? It's hard to admit something like that happened to you." He raised his hand to rub his eye. "God, I don't know if that even makes sense."

"No, it does," I murmured. "And it's okay. That you were attracted to her, I mean. I see good-looking people and I think about it sometimes too. But if I used my powers to get one of them in bed, it'd still be wrong. Even if they said yes. Using your abilities to violate someone isn't okay."

"Yeah. Yeah, you're right. I just feel bad. Not just about that, but her too. I guess I shouldn't, all things considered. But I... She's tied up down there dying, because of me and—"

"We aren't going to kill her, if that's what you're worried about."

"No, no. Not that. I mean, yeah. I don't want her to die. But I just… Wow, this is hard to say out loud."

"It's okay," I said, gently touching his shoulder. "Take your time."

"I'm not just some victim. And I feel bad that she's down there, literally dying, and here I am, acting like my problems are so bad. But I don't even remember it." A dry laugh left his lips. "I don't know, just feels gross. I don't even know if this makes any sense."

"It does," I murmured. "Following trauma, there's often an instinct to tell yourself that you weren't hurt. It's a defense mechanism. We try to stay strong and preserve our dignity by denying it."

"Alright, please don't psychoanalyze me. I'm not broken, okay? I don't even remember it. I'm not…Don't look at me like I'm a victim."

I paused, gaze shifting over him carefully. "Alright. Alright, I'm sorry. I just want you to know that this isn't your fault."

He chewed his lip. "Yeah. Yeah, I know. I just don't feel great about this whole situation. Locking her up down there and everything." He shrugged a bit. "We need to. I know that. But she's just a pawn in all of this too. She doesn't deserve to be tortured, not like this."

I did not feel the same. That bitch deserved to rot. Jeremy was doubtfully the only person she'd taken advantage of and if she wanted to, she could do it again.

She was where she deserved to be. But it was his call.

"We could try interrogating her in the morning," I murmured. "If she gives us what we're looking for, if you… if you want to, we could let her go. If you want, I mean. It's up to you."

He pressed his lips together and gave a nod. "Yeah, maybe. I'll think about it. But I'm pretty tired. Do you want to lie down?"

"Yeah. Yeah, let me just brush my teeth real quick."

CHAPTER FIFTY-FOUR

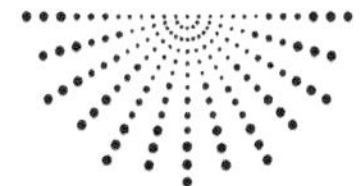

Jeremy was out the moment his head hit the pillow. But I tossed. Then I turned. I got up to pee and climbed back into bed. Then I tossed again.

I just couldn't get my brain to shut off. The past week had been a total shit storm. I was mentally and physically drained, but I just couldn't sleep.

When I closed my eyes, I saw Moe's body sprawled out on the floor behind the register. Warm blue eyes turned cold, frozen in terror. Blood against his cheeks, decorating the room like confetti.

Then they shot back open. I looked around the darkened room and panted out deep breaths. I took a hit off the burnt bowl on the side table and felt my muscles relax a bit. Eventually, my heavy eyes began to shut again.

But then I relived the memory from Brody's mind. That bitch's smug gaze. Her bare ass. Then Jeremy's confused and terrified expression, begging his brother not to relay the message to his girlfriend back home.

Then the look on his face when he pleaded with me to hear him out—and I threw him into a brick wall.

A long breath left my nostrils as I sat forward in the bed and looked him over. Had the roles been reversed, I'd have called him a misogynistic piece of shit for not hearing my side of the story. But I was a self-entitled little bitch. All I saw was the black and white. I didn't pay attention to the hurt in his eyes. I didn't care about his trembling hands.

I was sickened with myself.

After a few minutes, I decided I wouldn't be getting to sleep any time soon. I stepped into my slippers and started downstairs for a midnight snack. And drink.

I sat on the counter of the dark kitchen downing my third shot of Crown Royal. The back of my head rested against the cool cabinet. I rubbed my eyes and let a yawn escape my lips. Admittedly, I probably should have settled for the Oreos. But it'd been a hell of a week. And I'd rather see the room spin than my thoughts.

The pitter patter of footsteps made their way to the kitchen. A light flicked on. Brody stood there in his boxers, heading towards the fridge.

"Boo," I said. He jumped and I smiled. A laugh echoed from my mouth.

"Jesus Christ." He grasped his chest. Then he continued to the fridge. "Why are you up so late?"

"Couldn't sleep." I raised a cookie to my lips. "What about you?"

"Same." He reached for the bottle by my knee. I passed it to him, and he took a long chug. "How's Jeremy?"

I shrugged, running my fingers through my hair and grasping a chunk near the back. "He's okay, He says, anyway. But I don't know how he could be after something like that, ya know?"

"Yeah. Yeah, I can't imagine what's going on in his head. And you?"

"I'm drinking alone in the dark at four a.m. on a Thursday." I laughed, shaking my head. "Kinda speaks for itself, don't ya think?

"Five." He hoisted himself onto the island top across from me. "And I think it's Friday."

"Huh. Ya don't say," I muttered.

He laughed and took another gulp. "And you're not drinking alone."

"What a delight," I mumbled. "I just feel bad. Like I failed him, ya know? I mean, if I was raped, I wouldn't expect him to hold that against me, right? So what I did, acting the way I did—"

"Well, yeah, but you didn't know that's what happened. I was there and I didn't realize it was rape. Shit, neither did he."

"Still shitty." I outstretched my palm for the bottle. He handed it to me, and I took a swig. "I'm a shitty girlfriend."

"I'm a shitty brother," Brody said.

"I threw him into a brick wall," I muttered. "That was really mean."

"I told the love of his life that he cheated on her. Then I kissed her." He let out a quiet laugh. "We've never been close. But still. That was bad. Who does that?"

"You got me there, man."

"I... That was a real shitty thing to do," he muttered.

"It makes sense, though."

"Me calling out my brother for fucking another girl makes sense?"

"Well, you have feelings for me."

He licked his lips. "What's your point?"

"Think about it. For whatever reason, you're trying to break this couple up." Pieces of Oreo flew from my lips. "So you orchestrate one person in the couple, Jeremy, to do something unforgivable to the other person in the couple, me. But wait, how is Laila going to find out about this unforgivable thing Jeremy did?"

Brody's eyes moved between mine, waiting for me to go on. "Well, I'll have to find someone to relay it back to Laila. Obviously, Laila's friends and family won't simultaneously appear in the town where Jeremy's cheating a few states away. Of course, any of Jeremy's family will eventually tell Laila, but they'll give Jeremy a chance first. But Brody? Well, Brody is in love with Laila. If he sees an opportunity to swoop in and be the hero, he'll take it. No offense, of course."

"Yeah. Well yeah, I guess you're right. But who would benefit from you and Jeremy not being together?"

I shrugged. "No one that I know of. That's what I'm still trying to figure out."

He laughed and took a gulp from the bottle. After a quiet moment, he let out a slow sigh. "I'm really sorry, Lai."

"For what?" I asked.

"Instigating all that the night he got back. I know you're glad I did and everything, but if I would've held off." He turned his gaze downward. "If I would've let Jeremy figure things out first, maybe there would've been less heart ache. Not just for you, but for everyone."

He wasn't wrong. Had Jeremy told me what happened with that terrified, confused expression, I'd have had a totally different reaction. So yeah, it did suck. But honestly, I wasn't sure that Jeremy would've ever admitted to it. He'd probably have been so ashamed that he buried it.

"Maybe. But I dunno, I don't think Jeremy would've figured this out without me."

Brody raised a brow. "I know you helped, but Jeremy's been doing this for a long time. He isn't entirely incompetent."

"I'm not saying he's incapable. I just don't think he would have kept digging if he hadn't lost me. He wouldn't even admit that it was what it was until he saw me kissing the bitch. That, and I think that whoever's behind this must be kind of afraid of me. At least on some primal, existential level."

"Why's that?" he asked.

"When Ally realized who I was, I think she was afraid. Not even just scared, but, like, petrified."

"I don't know, if I was meeting the person whose girlfriend I just raped, I'd probably be pretty scared too."

"It was more than that," I muttered. "Like she was *told* not to meet me. I don't know. I just think there's more to the story, ya know?"

"Well, that much is obvious," Brody said.

I thought for a moment. "When Jeremy's car flipped, it must have been because he was going to see Ally, right? And then, by the time we got to her, she was dying. Whoever's behind this is trying very hard to cover their tracks. But on the other hand, at the diner, the person was caught on tape. Barely. Almost entirely indistinguishable, but it was literally as I was pulling into the diner, and Moe had already been dead for some time. They waited for me to pull up so that I couldn't be blamed. So that I had an alibi."

"Well, an Angel wouldn't want you arrested. That would just incriminate an agent of theirs."

"I'm just so confused. It's all so confusing."

He reached across the aisle to hand me the bottle. "Me too. If we knew who your mom was, we'd have so much more intel."

"If we knew who my mom was, I'd tie her to a chair and burn her alive."

Brody laughed uncomfortably. "Well look at that. You've grown into a little psycho, just like the rest of us."

I took a sip and shrugged. "She deserves it. She killed Moe. And threatened my mom."

"Can't disagree with you there."

My head plopped to the cabinet behind me. "Why does everything have to be so complicated?"

"Wish I knew," he muttered.

"I just don't get it. We're good people, aren't we? I mean, aside from the occasional homicide when necessary, we're good people."

"Aside from the murder and torture. Yeah, we're not too bad."

"It's like we're cursed or something. Like the universe doesn't want us to be happy." I raised the bottle to my lips. "Why doesn't the universe want us to be happy?"

His eyes locked with mine. He gently nibbled his bottom lip. "I really wish I knew. Maybe we pissed God off in a past life or something."

I held his gaze, heart breaking for him. To have to see me every day. To be one of my best friends and care for me the way that he did. "I'm sorry, Brody."

"What for?" His head cocked to the side.

"I don't know. For loving Jeremy? For the way you feel about me?" I said. "I can't imagine what that's like."

He shrugged. "You guys are supposed to end up together. It's destiny. I can't be mad at destiny."

"Sure, you can," I said. "I'm mad for you. As your friend, I want to go smack the bitch that hurt you, but it's really hard to smack yourself. You can though. You can smack me as hard as you want. I'll take it like a man."

He laughed, shaking his head. "No, I don't want that."

"Please? It'll make me feel better. Just hit me." I sat up and leaned forward. "Just do it. Right in my stupid face."

He laughed again, that time for longer, more genuine. Not so much because it was fitting to the conversation, but because for a moment, he really was happy. That made me happy. I laughed too, and for a second, that's all that mattered. Two friends, laughing together, tipsy on the kitchen counter in the middle of the night.

"I should probably go lie down," I muttered. "I'm starting to spin a bit."

He gave a nod. "Yeah, that's not a bad idea. Need help up the steps?"

"Nah, I got this. Thanks though."

He laughed. "If you say so."

I threw my feet over the edge of the counter and attempted to hop to the floor. But I underestimated the distance and stumbled. I toppled over. I slammed down. My head banged on the edge of the granite countertop.

"Holy shit." Brody jumped off the counter and lowered himself to the ground beside me. My head pounded and I laughed. "Jesus, Lai, are you okay?" I laughed louder, noting the bit of blood that was spilling from my forehead, puddling on the tile beneath my hands. "Jesus Christ, what are you laughing at?"

Still laughing, I said, "I said that I didn't need help, and then I cracked my head open." A cackle left my lips. "Apparently, I do not got this."

He laughed. "Should have let me teleport you."

"I'm a little nauseous, I might've hurled." I raised my hand to my throbbing temple. "Fuck, that really hurt."

"I bet it did." He headed to the cupboard, slid out a drawer next to the sink, and returned with a dish towel. "Are you alright?"

I laughed. "Yeah, I'll be okay."

"You need to be more careful, lady."

I gave a nod, repositioning myself to lean against the cupboard. "I should probably stop drinking so much too."

"Yeah, we both should." Brody kneeled beside me. "Want me to help you to the couch?"

"No. No, that's alright. Just give me a minute."

"Sure."

"Lai? What was that?" I heard Jeremy say from the steps. He rubbed his head, blinking hard as he scanned the room.

I raised my hand. "Guilty." I turned to Brody. "Could you maybe get me some ice?"

He stood and walked to the fridge. Jeremy made his way to me. His jaw fell open. He dropped to the ground. "Jesus, baby, how they hell'd you manage that?"

"I was sitting on the counter and I went to jump down and—Well. I fell."

He bit back a laugh and shook his head, hand lifting the towel from my forehead. "Are you okay?"

"Yeah, I'm fine. Just a dumbass."

"Damn, Lai. Really got yourself there."

"I'm an idiot, I know."

"Leah can heal it tomorrow," he muttered. "You really need to be more careful though."

"That's what I said," Brody chimed in, handing me an ice pack.

"Can you take me to bed?" I asked Jeremy. "I'll try not to barf."

He put his hand to my shoulder. "Night, Brody," I muttered.

"Night, guys," he said.

CHAPTER FIFTY-FIVE

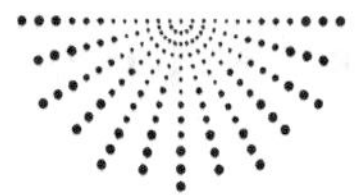

The two of us sat on Jeremy's bed. He taped a piece of gauze to my forehead. As he did, I studied his beautiful blue eyes. I thought about what had happened to him. I thought about everything I'd said. How awful I'd been. My chest grew tight. I fought tears that welled in my eyes.

"I'm sorry," I murmured.

"For what?" he asked quietly.

"Throwing you into the house," I said.

"What?" He chuckled.

"The other night. When you got back," I said. "You grabbed my shoulder and I flung you into the wall, and I'm sorry."

"Oh. That," he said. "It's okay."

"No, it's not okay. You were punishing yourself enough for something you never should have punished yourself for in the first place, and I'm so sorry because I should have trusted you and—and I should have given you more credit. You deserved that. More than you—"

He leaned forward, clutched the side of my neck, and pressed our lips together. He opened his against mine, five o'clock shadow scratching my chin. My hand moved to his neck.

After a long moment, our lips pulled apart. Jeremy carefully rested his forehead against mine. Our eyes met beneath his thick black eyelashes.

"You quit apologizing. And I'll quit apologizing," he whispered. "And we can move past this. You and me. We've made it through all of this shit, and we'll make it through more. We'll be okay. I promise. But we have to leave all of this behind us. We can't let it get to us. That's what they or it or he or she, or whoever it is that's manipulating us— that's what they want. They want us to hold onto this anger and pain and take it out on each other and I don't want to do that. I *won't* do that. I won't let anything or anyone get between us. I love you and I'm not going to lose you. Okay?"

My lips pulled up. "Okay."

He smiled back at me for a moment. Then he scooched up the bed until he lay beside me. I rolled onto my side and so did he. His arms tightened around my stomach. "Jeremy?"

"Laila."

"I love you," I whispered.

"I love you, too," he said.

He twined our fingers together and lifted my knuckles to his lips.

CHAPTER FIFTY-SIX

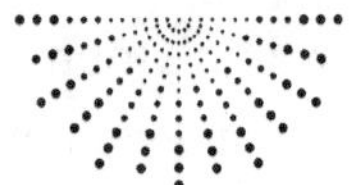

Loud, echoing screams ripped me from my sleep. I sat up quickly, too quickly, head spinning, blinking hard.

"What the hell was that?" I said.

"God only knows around here," Jeremy muttered. He scurried to his feet and I followed close behind. We didn't even get dressed, just rushed downstairs, taking two steps at a time.

As we made it into the kitchen, my eyes rested on the open basement door. Every light on the first floor was flicked on. We heard voices downstairs and followed them, fast, nearly tripping over each other.

The moment I realized where the sound was coming from, I had a good idea of what we were about to find. Hannah was great for resurrecting the dead, but not so great at being a watchdog.

There at the landing Hannah stood burying her head against Kai's chest. Sobs left her narrow frame. Kai struggled to soothe her. My eyes traveled to the siren.

Still strung on the wall with chains and cuffs, but now, blood spilled all over the smooth ground before her. Leah stood beside the body, rubbing her temples with the tips of her fingers.

Her pale throat hung open; flaps of skin covered in murky crimson.

It looked almost black the way the light hit it. Cuts ascended her wrists, sliding from side to side.

"Jesus Christ." My hand lifted to cover my mouth. I slowly approached the girl. Her head hung to the left; all color drained from her face. The ball gag still rested between her teeth. If she'd screamed, no one would have heard it.

"What the hell happened?" Leah yelled, looking at Hannah. "You were supposed to watch her, not get her killed."

"I only left for a minute; I swear. I went up to go pee and I came back down and...and she was like this," she cried.

Well, this was great. We'd successfully lost every lead we'd gathered this week. Maybe Mary was right. Sometimes, we just weren't so great at solving mysteries.

"Laila, get me a pair of gloves out of the drawer, would ya?"

I headed to the cupboard, reached in, and grabbed a couple pairs. As I handed them her way, she asked, "Think you can burn her body?"

I shrugged. "Maybe. We'll have to move her outside though."

Leah nodded, pulled on the gloves, and rolled up her pant legs so that they wouldn't come in contact with any blood. "Jeremy, have Brody go stand watch at the entrance. We don't need any surprise visits from Ramirez while Laila is cremating this bitch."

Jeremy stared at the corpse hanging from the wall. His jaw clamped shut, shaking hands balling to fists at his sides. Then he turned up the steps.

I felt for him in that moment. Despite what she'd done, the two of them were friends. He'd just been talking about how he felt bad for her and then we found her dead in his basement. I wasn't exactly happy about her death, but I certainly wasn't sad about it. I was sad for him though.

"Well, one thing's for sure," I muttered.

"What's that?" Kai asked with his arms around Hannah's weeping body.

"It had to have been an Angel. Nothing else would be able to get in the house through the barrier spells. Not in the time it takes for Hannah to use the bathroom."

"They had to watch and wait for Hannah to leave," Leah said. "And then get out quick. Damn it. We should have had two people on watch." She raised the girl's chin and examined the wound on her neck. "Whoever it was had to either be very strong or was using a very large blade."

"What do you mean?" I asked.

"Well, it wasn't a thin knife. Honestly, I don't think it was a knife at all. I'd say a sword, but the cut would've gone further into her neck. Something curved, maybe?" She looked at the wrists. "They were pissed too."

I examined them too. The cuts were horizontal. For a quick death, you go down the river, not across the bridge.

"Yeah. They wanted her to suffer. Otherwise, they would have slit vertically," I said.

"Can you get me the keys?"

I went back to the cupboard and grabbed them from the drawer with the gloves. I tossed them to Leah. She undid each lock, starting with the feet and then moving to her arms. Each arm fell. Then the body hit the floor. "I'll get Jeremy and he can transport her outside. Do you want help in here?"

"No, the less people the better. Just get me a tarp, a gallon of bleach and two rolls of paper towels. I'm going to change into clothes I can burn when I'm done."

"I'll cauterize the wounds here so nothing spills on the way outside."

"Good idea. Just be careful, don't get any blood on you. And if you do—"

"Wipe the body part with bleach and burn the towels with any soiled clothing. I know the routine," I said. Leah headed upstairs to change. I turned to Kai and Hannah at the bottom of the steps. "You're not going to want to see this. Head upstairs."

"I'm okay." she mumbled.

"It is going to smell really bad. Get her out of here, Kai."

He licked his lips and lifted his head. "C'mon, love. It's all right, let's go sit."

CHAPTER FIFTY-SEVEN

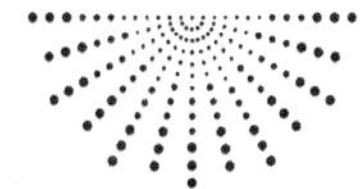

I went outside and laid a tarp to catch any blood from Ally's clothes and body. Jeremy followed, taking note of where the tarp was and returning inside to grab her. Then he went into the house and put on a pair of shorts and a t-shirt he didn't mind burning. He returned and laid the body onto the tarp. He lifted his shirt over his shoulders and tossed it onto the corpse.

Then he pulled his shorts off and dropped them into the pile. Shivering, he kissed my cheek and muttered, "I'm going to shower. I'll come out when I'm done."

He disappeared.

I brought a flame to my palm. Then I lowered my hand. I started at her core, moved upwards to her head, and then back down to her feet.

That wasn't the first time I'd burned a body, and it was far from the last. Although, it was the first time I felt guilty for doing so.

The first body I'd seen murdered was Adrian. Given my state at the time, I didn't take part in the cover up. I didn't burn the clothes. I didn't hide her car.

Typically, the bodies I burned were brought to that state in hand-to-hand combat. It wasn't hard to dispose of the body of someone who'd been trying to harm me or someone I loved.

You'd think that Ally's death would have been at least somewhat of a relief considering what she'd done to Jeremy and our relationship. But I felt bad for her. She made a deal with an unforgiving force of nature, and she was punished for her loyalty. Because to them, she was just a loose end. As Jeremy had said the night before, she was nothing more than a pawn.

Her body began to char, and over the coming minutes, each limb slowly turned to black coals. But I didn't stop there. I kept the heat steady, blasting for about forty-five minutes. Then I heard Leah yell behind me, "Incoming."

A plastic bag of blood covered clothes plopped onto my pile of ash. This was the part I hated about what we did. Having powers was fun. Burning bodies—and cute clothes—was not.

"Damn, how do you go for so long?" She gestured to my flame as I ignited the clothes.

"I don't know really. Fire comes naturally. Working with air is more exhausting."

"I wonder why that is." Leah took a few steps back and sat on the stairs. She lifted a cigarette from her pocket and lit it at her lips. She didn't smoke often, but when she did, it was usually after something shitty went down. "I wonder if Kai goes through that too."

"I doubt it. His powers flow so effortlessly. It's like he's not even trying."

"Yeah, but so do yours with this. Maybe over time, you'll be as skilled with air as you are with fire. I wish I could heal without practically dying."

"Maybe one day you will. You don't get exhausted with telepathy. And you can control people, that's amazing."

She laughed. "It's horrible. Do you know how awful it is to eternally be stuck in other people's minds? I'm a homebody for a reason, you know. It's not so bad here around everyone who has their mental blocks up. But going out into the world, hearing all those people's thoughts..." She huffed, took in a deep drag, and shook her head. "Sometimes I feel like I'm going crazy. But no. Just feeling other people's crazy."

I gave a laugh, still burning the body. My eyes shifted over Ally's palm. It morphed to ash and fell to the ground beside her.

After a moment, Leah said, "Do you think we're going to figure it out?"

"I hope," I muttered. "I don't know though. She can really cover her tracks. Which narrows it down to every Angel we've ever met."

"We've learned a lot though," she muttered. "I mean, you were face to face, we have to be on the brink of figuring it out. Or at least, figuring out *something*."

"Yeah, I guess," I muttered. I turned back to the burning body. A long pause crept in. After a moment, I cleared my throat. "Did your research get you anything useful? About Ramirez, I mean."

"Not really. His story checks out. Wife and kid went missing from their home. Lots of blood, but no DNA that didn't belong to the three of them. I haven't scryed yet. I'll do that once this mess is cleaned up."

"It's strange, isn't it? What she said about me?"

"Yeah. But I don't know, it could mean something entirely different than he expects. There's a good chance they're dead, dude. With the amount of blood they found... I don't know how they wouldn't be. I feel bad for the guy though. This is the only thing keeping him going. I'm afraid that if we do confirm their deaths, he might hang it up. He's definitely thought about it."

"Should we keep an eye on him?"

"If we put surveillance on every person who's thought about killing themselves, we'd never sleep."

CHAPTER FIFTY-EIGHT

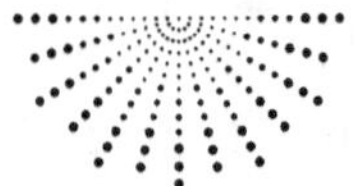

I plopped onto the couch after a shower. Jeremy sat beside me and gingerly wrapped an arm around my shoulders. He didn't say anything and neither did I. I rested my head against his chest.

We just sat there, not knowing what to say. Our only lead was gone. We were back to square one.

Eventually, Jeremy's crackly voice broke the silence. "She'd still be alive if I hadn't brought her here."

I turned my gaze up to him. "She was dying when we got to her, baby."

"I guess," he muttered. "Yeah, I guess. But she would've been in her home. She wouldn't have suffered, at least not as much as she did. We just prolonged the pain. She would have died peacefully, ya know? And someone slit her wrists and let her watch herself bleed out before they slit her throat."

That was definitely a shitty way to go. I wish I could say I felt bad for her. But after what the bitch had done... I just couldn't. Maybe she had some good in there. Jeremy saw it. But I hadn't. All I'd seen was a raging cunt. It hurt that he was hurting though.

I said nothing, just held his gaze. He rubbed his eyes.

"But on the other hand, we wouldn't be together right now if we

hadn't brought her here. And that should be the side I'm looking at."
He huffed. "But no, I just keep thinking about how she's dead. And
how that all comes down on me."

We were good at that. No matter what happened, we always
blamed ourselves. None of it was his or my fault. Ultimately, destiny
was to blame. But destiny didn't have a face, so we shifted the blame
onto the only person we could. The person whose gaze we met when
we looked in the mirror.

I pushed hair behind his ear. "This wasn't your fault, Jeremy."

"I didn't hold the knife." He shrugged. "But I put her on a silver
platter. And this whole thing was set up around me. What she did was
fucked up, I know that, but we were kind of friends. And I don't hate
her for it. I don't even blame her, she did what she had to do to survive.
I've done some fucked up shit to come out on the other side, too." He
was quiet for a moment. "Never raped someone to get there, but I've
killed to. I get it, ya know? I don't know. It's just fucked up. She didn't
deserve to die, and she wouldn't have if it weren't for me."

"*We* put her on a silver platter. It was all of us. Not just you," I whispered. "This isn't any more your fault than it is mine."

"I guess," he muttered. It grew quiet once more. He stared down at
our hands twined together in his lap.

He looked so lost. I wanted to help but I didn't know how. I was
just as off course as he was. The only compass we had was each other.

"I'm sorry," I murmured. "You're in the middle of a really shitty
situation."

A huff of a laugh left his lips. He met my gaze. "Just another day in
the life, right?" I managed a sad smile. He lifted our knuckles to his
mouth and kissed them gently. "We'll be alright."

"Guys." I heard Leah call from the kitchen. "Come here, everyone.
You're going to want to see this."

Jeremy and I exchanged a confused expression. We stood and made
our way to the kitchen. Leah leaned over the island with an array of
maps. Some of each continent and then one of the world on top.

"No luck using the ball?" I gestured over the counter.

"I tried but all I could see was darkness," Leah said.

"As in death?" Jeremy leaned against the sink.

"No, there would be something there if they were dead. Either a symbol, or a body, or the spot where they were buried. Something of some kind to symbolize death would have presented itself. But nothing did. Literally just a blank space. So I called Helena and asked about any other options I could use to locate someone remotely."

Jeremy rolled his eyes. "That Witch from Vermont?"

"Don't say it like that, you know as well as I do that her spells have helped us on countless—"

"Yeah, yeah. I know. She's good at what she does. What's your point?" Jeremy said.

"Well, she told me about this ritual. Basically, you combine some herbs and recite a spell, then you pour the mixture on to the map and start burning the edges. It burns the whole map and leaves you with a general vicinity."

"Okay, and?" I asked.

She turned back to the counter. "So I tried to light the map focusing on Ramirez's kid and wife, using their belongings as a guiding tool. And look what happens." She picked up the lighter, flicked it, and held it to the corner of the paper.

But the paper didn't burn. It didn't so much as singe. It acted the way that my skin did when I came into contact with a flame.

"That's weird." Jeremy stroked the paper.

"Did you try using the spell to locate someone whose location we do know?" I asked.

"Yeah. I figured what the hell, I'll try with Laila's mom. And sure enough, it worked. Did exactly what it's supposed to." She held up a quarter sized piece of singed map. The city of Pittsburgh, where my mom worked.

"So what does that mean?"

"I thought, okay, whoever's holding them must have a barrier spell of some sort blocking us out, right? Knowing we have barrier spells up here at home, I tried focusing on you, Jeremy, and it worked again." She held up another small piece of singed map with the word Somerset County. "Just like it's supposed to. But then a thought occurred to me."

She turned to Jeremy. "I figured I'd try. I didn't know what would happen, but it was worth checking out, right?"

"What was?" Jeremy turned his head to the side.

"I tried to use the ritual to find Chris."

Years ago, when Jeremy and I first started dating, I'd seen the photos of Chris hanging on the walls. He was almost the spitting image of Jeremy, just cleaner cut, so I knew he was his brother. Then I asked if he'd gone off to college or something. A dismal gaze moved over Jeremy's face and he shook his head.

Then he told me that Chris had died three and a half years prior. He mentioned that the anniversary was coming up soon. I told him I was sorry, then I suggested we go put some flowers on his grave. That I'd sit with him while he visited if he'd like. But he awkwardly cleared his throat and said they never recovered his body, so there was no grave to visit.

A lightbulb went off in my mind. That's what Ramirez's story reminded me of. A ton of blood, enough to confirm the person as dead, but nothing left behind. No DNA, no fingerprints, no foot tracks.

Jeremy's breath caught and his gaze narrowed. "Why?"

"Well, we've used how many other methods to try and find him and nothing has worked, and I figured it couldn't hurt." Her lips lifted in a smile. "And it didn't. It helped."

"What do you mean?" I asked.

"It did the same thing that it did for Ramirez's family. It won't burn. It's like impervious to the flame."

I pondered what was capable of doing something like that. Fae certainly couldn't, Angels couldn't either. Demons weren't exactly smart enough, nor did they care enough to go to such lengths to disguise a location.

But a Witch could. It'd have to be a damn powerful one, but there were intense barrier spells that hid magic. Meaning a Witch had to have been playing a part in disguising where he was.

"That doesn't mean anything," Jeremy said.

"Yes, it does," Leah said. "The MO matches perfectly, Jeremy. They were all taken at random, no evidence left behind, any humans involved left unharmed, just a shit ton of the victim's blood. Enough to legally confirm them as dead. And none of them were human. Not just that, but they went missing around the same time. Chris in May of 2012 and Amy and Lydia in February of 2012. That's only three months apart."

"Exactly. He lost too much blood for him to still be alive. It's not possible."

"But it is, Jeremy. It has to be. This wouldn't keep happening if they were dead. If they were dead, it would burn up completely. But look." She lifted the lighter to the map again. "It won't fucking burn. This has to be connected. It has to be."

"It can't be. It doesn't make any sense."

"Why not? The ritual came to the exact same outcome," Leah said. "How could that be a coincidence?"

As she spoke, I saw all the parallels she was drawing. There was too much in common for her not to make a connection. Disappearing without a trace within a few mere months of each other? That was just the cherry on top.

"They went missing from states away. They're two entirely different races, different genders," he said quickly. "The only similarity is the fact that none of their bodies were found. What would someone want with a Guardian and two Fae, anyway?"

"I don't know, but it can't be a coincidence. There were some differences but doesn't mean anything—"

"Yes, it does," Jeremy snapped. "He's dead. Leah. It's been almost seven years, there's no way he's still out there. There's just no way."

"What, you think it's all chance that the ritual resulted in the exact same outcome?"

"No, it must mean something, but that doesn't mean that it's a lead. And it damn sure doesn't mean that it's Chris."

"What the hell is your problem? For the first time in years, I might finally have something that could help us find out what happened to our brother—"

"My brother," he said. "Your cousin."

Jeremy was generally pretty kind and he rarely argued with Leah.

But he was always sensitive when it came to Chris. Still, his comment sent a chill down my spine. Technically, they may have been cousins. But not once had I ever heard him refer to her as such.

Her expression of anger and frustration softened quickly. She fiercely tried to pass it off as confidence, but I saw the hurt in her eyes. Then she sucked her teeth.

"Wow. Really? That's how it's gonna be? I am so incredibly sorry, I must have missed the part where my mom adopted all of you and we became siblings. But, oh that's right, I'm adopted too, so I guess we aren't family at all then, right?"

"That's not what I meant." His gaze softened.

"I just don't get it, dude." Her brows pulled further over her eyes. "We might actually be able to find him. We could bring him home. Don't you want that?"

"Of course I do but—"

"But what?!" she shouted.

"But he's dead, Leah!" he yelled. "He's been dead for almost a decade. You can't get your hopes up again. He's gone; he's been gone. You have to accept that."

She fell silent, teeth gritted to a hard line. "Not until I see a damn body."

"I don't want you to take on this false sense of hope and end up—" He stopped himself, biting his tongue.

"End up what?" She narrowed her gaze. "What? Like I was when he disappeared? Because if memory serves, I handled it a hell of a lot better than you did."

"Yeah, I know I fucked up when he went missing. But I didn't try to kill myself, you did."

"That wasn't just about Chris and you know it. I had a break down. My best friend disappeared, then my girlfriend died, and then Mom was right behind them. Who *wouldn't* lose their shit after that?"

"I don't want you to get like that again, Leah—" he began.

"Bullshit." She stepped closer to him. "Bull fucking shit."

"How is that bullshit?"

"You feel guilty. You're wondering what the fuck they've been doing to him all these years and you feel horrible because you spent all this time hating yourself and shooting dope into your veins instead of being out there fucking looking for him. You're too much of a pussy to admit that we shouldn't have given up on him." She extended her arm, angrily pushing his chest.

Jeremy looked above her at the cabinets behind her head, saying nothing.

"I'll find him myself then. But bet your ass, I'm *going* to find him. And when I do, I'll tell him all about how his little brother became a junkie and gave up on him." She angrily brushed past him, snatched her phone off the island, and stomped up the steps.

CHAPTER FIFTY-NINE

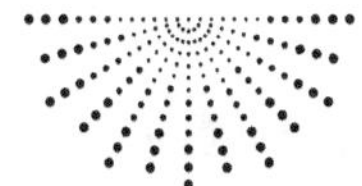

Standing in the bedroom doorway, I took Jeremy in for a moment. He sat with his guitar in his lap, humming along to the tune. I wasn't sure what the song was, but it sounded dreary. Just like he looked. Brows pulled together, stubble sprouted across his cheeks, messy hair in his face.

I understood why Leah was upset. I really did. She found something that had the possibility of bringing her brother home and Jeremy shut her down.

But he had so much going on right now. That fight didn't help. My heart hurt for him.

"Hey, you," I said.

"Hey." He glanced at me with a quick forced smile, then back to the neck.

"How are you?" I sat on the bed beside him.

He laughed. "I've seen better days."

I wrapped an arm around his waist and placed my head against his shoulder. "I'm sorry, baby."

"Don't be. You didn't do anything." He kissed my forehead and set the guitar on the floor.

"I'm just sorry for everything you have on your plate right now."

He shrugged and let out a quiet laugh. "It's not like our plates are ever empty."

"Ain't that the truth," I muttered. My lips flapped together in a trill. I pressed my lips to his cheek and pulled away. "I've got to head into town. Mom's meeting me so we can go over the details for the funeral. Do you want to come?"

"Do you want me to?" He turned his gaze to mine. "I don't know much about planning a funeral, but I'll be there for moral support if you need me."

"If *you* want to." I smiled. "Figured I'd offer in case you didn't want to be alone. But I'm alright, I don't need you there if you want to stay home."

"Are you sure?" he asked.

I smiled. "Yeah. Yeah, I'm sure. You just gonna relax here then?"

"If you don't mind. I'm just kinda stressed out. I don't really feel like going anywhere. I'm gonna try and write some music and chill out."

I stood. "Yeah, that's alright. Just call me if you're bored. Maybe we can go out for dinner tonight? I think I can get us a great table at this darling little diner. Might even be able to reserve the whole place, who knows."

He smiled. Then his hand caught mine. He pulled me closer, and his hands found my hips. "I think I'd prefer take out."

"Oh yeah?" I grinned.

He smiled back, head lifting in a nod. His hand wrapped around my waist. The other made its way to my neck, pushing hair behind my ear. Our lips touched for a moment. Then I smiled and pulled back. "Just call me if you need me."

"Likewise," he said. "But hey, you might want to ask Leah if she can heal your head before the funeral. Might look a little sketchy since you were a murder suspect and all."

"That is a good point."

When I left the house, I called the attorney to let him know I was heading that way to sign off on some documents. I stopped by Dunkin Donuts and grabbed a coffee on the way. Then I hurried inside, scribbled my signature, and shoved the carbons into my overflowing purse. Afterwards, I headed to the diner to meet up with Mom.

As I drove down the slushy, snow dusted roads, I turned the music up as loud as the speakers would allow.

I gazed out the windshield, watching the brown snow slush under the tires of the plow in front of me. He drove slowly, no more than twenty-eight in a thirty-five. I could have used the center lane to pass him, but I didn't. I didn't want to.

The loneliness was relaxing. It gave me a strange sense of peace. Because even if I couldn't control anything else in my life, I could control that car. If I wanted, I could hop on the highway and leave all my problems behind. I wouldn't. But I could. It gave me a false, but relieving, sense of freedom. A sense of freedom that let me begin to make sense of the rapid thoughts that spiraled my mind.

I'd started to feel oddly relieved at Ally's death. I guess it was kind of sadistic, especially considering Jeremy's view on the subject. I knew she wasn't actually a threat. Compared to the Angel orchestrating all of it, Ally was a simple, insignificant pest.

But most of me was genuinely happy that she was dead. She deserved punishment for what she'd done, regardless of how Jeremy felt about it. She couldn't hurt anyone else from the grave.

Then my thoughts travelled to the woman who'd birthed me.

I wondered how she could treat Kai and I as if we were simply orders given to her. I didn't understand how she could destroy our loved ones purely to protect her identity. How she took a bulldozer to our lives without a single shred of remorse.

My mind wandered to Jeremy and all the things Leah had said. She crossed a line calling him a junkie, but she made many valid points. The connections between Chris and Ramirez's family couldn't be overlooked. The disappearances could have been a mere coincidence, but the result of the ritual couldn't have been.

Then I wondered what had happened to Chris since 2012 when he was pronounced dead without a body. Then what happened to Ramirez's kid. She'd be at the tail end of her single digit years by then. I contemplated the effects of what had been done to her. What would she be like now? What kind of warrior could she become with the story she might have to tell if we did find her?

But then I pondered if the effects of wherever she'd been would leave her broken. And if Chris's situation would be any different.

Then I wondered if we'd ever find them at all.

Approaching the diner, I rolled my head against the headrest. I couldn't even get into the lot. The whole thing was two feet under snow. My old beaten-up Bug wouldn't make it a foot into that disaster. I made a mental note to call Ed Miller to get the diner's parking lot plowed.

I struggled my way through the snowy pit, gripped the handrail for dear life, and locked the door behind me. I made my way to the safe and leafed through the documents Moe's attorney had given me a few days prior. After a moment of flipping, I let out an exasperated sigh. I had no idea what I was even looking for. Then I pulled out my phone to call mom and ask which documents I'd need.

"I'm not sure, just get them all out," she said. "We'll figure it out. I'm hungry as hell though, do you have anything we could heat up there?"

"Yeah, that works. But maybe, I don't know what's still good here. The potatoes should be alright, I can make some fries. That reminds me, I need to call the whole sellers and put in an order. What day is the funeral again?"

"Well, as long as we can get the coroner to release the body, it'll be on Tuesday. But you'll have to call the police station with me since you're the executor. I don't know why Moe didn't just make me the executor. He could have still given the money to you. He should have known you wouldn't know how to do all this."

I rubbed my temples. "I don't know. He probably didn't think he'd die so soon."

"Well, I'm leaving work now. I should be there in an hour or so. We'll just order something when I get there. Maybe you should call your staff. We wanted to have the wake Tuesday after the funeral, didn't we?"

"Yeah. Yeah, I'm pretty sure that was the plan. I'll see if the employees can come in and do the food. I should hold a meeting anyway. I need to tell them about the new ownership. Oh, and be careful when you pull in. The lot's a winter wonderland."

"Alright, I'll park on the shoulder. I'll let you go make those calls then. Love you, baby."

"Love you too, drive safe."

First, I called Ed to set up a time for him to come plow the parking lot the next morning. I wrote him a check and set it in the mailbox outside.

Then I called each employee and told them to come in for a staff meeting that night. Everyone said they'd be able to make it except for one of the waitresses, Christie, because she couldn't find a sitter for her three kids at the last minute.

Since she wouldn't make it, I gave her a brief synopsis of what she'd miss. She said she could help with the wake Tuesday evening, and congratulated me on my new ownership. I told her she could still come pick up her pay if she needed to. She said she'd get it when she came for the wake.

Mom arrived just as I was wrapping up my phone calls. I put on a pot of coffee while she ordered Chinese.

We sat at the booth and worked out the kinks. I called Ramirez and told him I needed to know when Moe's body would be released for the funeral. He said he'd make sure we got the body midday on Monday so there would be enough time to prepare it to be laid to rest.

Once everything was worked out and we ate our lunch, Mom

headed home. I hugged her goodbye. Then I spent the duration of the day arranging the diner for our staff meeting. I made a big bowl of salad with the ingredients that weren't bad yet and prepared some chicken tenders to fry up. That was about all that I could scrounge.

Then I ran to the bank half a mile down the road. I made a sizeable withdrawal to prepare everyone's paychecks. When I got back to the diner, I counted out everyone's hours and calculated what their pays would have been had things not gone to shit. Then I tossed some cash into envelopes and locked them in the safe. After that, I went upstairs and started clearing out Moe's things.

I didn't know what I was supposed to do with them. There were some things I didn't want to get rid of. His book collection, for instance. But his furniture was so stained and outdated. His bed was sunken on either side, making it useless to keep. The frame was in good condition though. I thought maybe one of the employees could use it.

After a few moments of shuffling things around, something clicked. It wasn't Moe's apartment anymore. It was mine.

I had my own apartment.

It was the strangest realization of my life. I wasn't helping a friend move. I was rearranging and deciding where his things would go before he was even in the ground.

I couldn't help but think I was being greedy. It was too soon. I couldn't get rid of his things. Not yet.

Then I thought about it a moment longer and realized I wasn't being selfish. I was keeping busy.

I took a step back and lifted myself to the kitchen counter. Flashbacks to my high school psychology class and the therapy sessions Mom made me attend after Dad died blinked behind my eyes. I'd moved past denial. I was in and out of the anger, but there I was, bargaining his possessions to distract from the grief that crept up on me like a leopard attacking its prey.

My hands lifted to my head, cradling it for a moment.

"I'm sorry, Moe," I murmured. "If I would have known who you were, we...We could have talked about things sooner. You didn't have to tell me who she was. I wish you wouldn't have tried to. You'd still be here if you hadn't. I didn't need to know. Your life was so much more important than knowing who that horrible bitch is. We could have just talked about this life. What your gifts were. I could have gotten advice from you. You could've told me about my dad. About his powers."

I looked around the dusty old place. "I always thought of you as family, but it would have been nice to know that you *were* family." I shook my head, rocking it against the cupboard behind me. "I'm just gonna miss you, Moe."

CHAPTER SIXTY

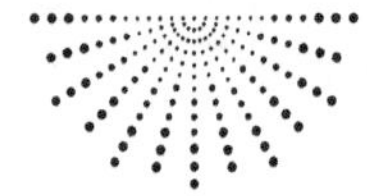

"I'm glad you could all make it in tonight on such short notice." I sat atop the bar while my servers and cooks found their seats. "I should have been more organized with all of these arrangements, but if I'm being completely honest here, guys, this has been a really tough week. But thank you all for bearing with me while I figured out Moe's funeral arrangements and what he wanted done here in the event of his death."

They sent nods with gentle gazes.

"Alright, where to begin. Well, first of all, I guess I should start with the new ownership of the diner. As we all know, Moe was an only child, his wife passed a long time ago, and he had no children. That being said, I suppose because of his close relationship with my dad, Moe left most of his possessions and assets to me. Otherwise meaning that nothing is really going to change here since I already run the place. There may be some renovations down the line, but nothing anyone has to worry about now. This week won't affect your paychecks, as you know, because you're getting your checks plus compensation for any tips you would have missed out on this past week."

"How can you afford that?" Max called from a table by the door.

"I've seen the books. You can't afford to pay us extra since we've had no revenue this week."

"I also can't afford to lose my staff, so I'll just bite the bullet. It is what it is. We won't go bankrupt."

"No, but if it means it's coming out of your pocket, that's not fair to you either." Max's eyes shifted between mine.

"I can cover it. Now that I own the place, everything comes out of my pocket."

He raised his hands in surrender. "Whatever you say."

"I have a question," Sophie said, awkwardly lifting her palm.

"Yeah, what's up, hon?"

She pushed hair behind her ear. "Is it true that Moe was murdered?"

I took in a deep breath. "Yes, unfortunately. He was."

"So is the diner safe?" she asked. "I mean, when I open by myself, it gets kinda creepy in here. Am I safe?"

"At this point, the cops think that whoever was responsible had a personal vendetta against Moe. They don't believe the diner to be unsafe. It wasn't a robbery or anything along those lines. Although if you're uncomfortable working alone, I can arrange the schedule to be at least double staffed when you're here, if that would make you feel more at home. Sound good?"

Everyone gave a nod or muttered a "Yeah." I looked over my notes and moved on to the next topic.

"Alright, guys. So the funeral is going to be Tuesday. There will be a viewing Monday night between five and eight, and then Tuesday morning between nine and noon for whoever wants to come. The final viewing is between one and three. Then the funeral will be at five. It will be short; it shouldn't go past six thirty. Afterwards, the wake will be here from seven until everyone is ready to go home. We'll cook some fried chicken, make some salad, and people will bring pasta salads and desserts. But I'll need a cook and two servers here to get stuff ready around six. Is anyone willing to do that for me?"

Max raised his hand, saying, "I'll cook."

"I didn't know Moe that well, so I'll stay here and prepare things for the wake," Sophie said.

"Okay, great. Christie said she would be here for the wake too, so we should be covered. If anyone does want to help with the wake, Max will open up so you can just come on in. If you're a waitress, you'll get paid ten-fifty an hour since you won't be making your tips, and if you're a cook, you'll get your usual pay. We'll resume normal business hours on Wednesday," I said. "But that pretty much covers everything I needed to tell you guys. Does anyone have any questions?"

"Yeah, actually." Cody, a server, raised his hand. "When are we going to start the concerts back up downstairs? A friend of mine was asking. She got cancelled for this upcoming weekend, but she wants a new slot whenever we open back up."

"Oh, shit," I muttered. "Actually, I completely forgot about the shows. Well, we have a full set lined up for next weekend. But I think we have a slot for the following weekend still open. That was Alex Woods, right? The folk girl?"

He nodded.

"I don't know if she'll want to open for Death Renegade, though," I muttered. "Let me look over the schedule and I'll let you know. We have an indie rock night in a couple weeks, I'll try and squeeze her in for a good time."

Cody laughed. "I'll relay the message."

"We got everything covered then?" Everyone kind of exchanged glances with one another, nodding. "Alright then. Get something to eat and then come to the office and I'll get you your checks. Again, thanks for coming by, guys. And thanks for bearing with me. This is going to be an adjustment for everyone."

CHAPTER SIXTY-ONE

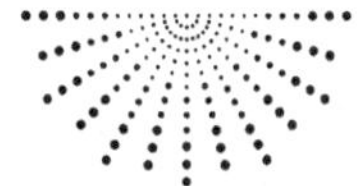

"Hey there," Max said in the doorway. He munched down on a chicken tender. "Congratulations on your new promotion, Boss Lady."

I laughed. "Thanks, I guess, if that's what you'd call it. Wish it were under better circumstances."

"I'll bet." He took a few steps into the office and sat on the other side of the aged desk. "How are you?"

"I'm okay, I guess." I shrugged, licking an envelope shut. "It comes and goes in waves, ya know? The weirdest part is all the responsibility. I mean, I had a lot to do before, but I always had Moe to call and ask questions. Now I'm on my own. It's surreal."

"Yeah. It's weird knowing he's gone. It's even weirder knowing someone killed him. Who would kill Moe? He was the chillest old dude I ever met."

"Yeah, I don't get it either. At first, the police questioned me since he left almost everything to me but there's footage of me pulling in as the killer is heading out the back door. So thank God for timing, I guess." I paused. "I don't know, man."

"How about things with Jeremy?" he asked. That's when I remembered I'd told him Jeremy cheated, forever changing the image Max kept in his mind of him. "You guys still broken up?"

I chuckled, putting my hand to my hair. "No, we're together."

"You took him back after he fucked someone else?" He made a face.

"It's complicated."

He made a *tsk, tsk, tsk* sound. "Of course it is."

"It's hard to explain. And either way, it's my life. I'm an adult, I can make my own decisions."

He squinted. "I'm not going to tell you how to live your life. But as your friend, I feel like it's necessary to remind you that having sex with someone else is usually unacceptable in a relationship."

I wanted so badly to tell him everything. After all, Max was my oldest friend since Adrian's death. But I knew I couldn't. Defending Jeremy's honor wasn't worth Max's life. Keeping my human and supernatural lives separate was more important. Jeremy would agree.

"It was a very complex situation."

"Oh, yeah?" He leaned back in his chair. "Go ahead and explain it then."

"You said I should hurt him, right?" I asked. He cocked his head to the side. "When I told you about it. You said I should get him back and then we could get better, right?"

"Yeah. I guess I did. What'd you do?"

"I fucked his brother." I lied.

"No way." He scooted forward to the edge of his seat. "You didn't."

"No, I didn't." I laughed. He huffed and sent a disappointed gaze my way. "Look, it's not like we erased it from the past. The slate isn't wiped clean. But I love him. And this has been a really hard week. And I mean, really hard. I needed him. I just…" I paused. "I decided that my pride wasn't as important as my happiness. Does that make any sense?"

"Yeah. Yeah, I guess it does. I'm not trying to be a dick, man. I just don't want you to get hurt."

"Well, you know what Bob Marley said. 'Everybody is going to hurt you, you just got to—'"

"'Find the ones worth suffering for.' Yeah, yeah, I know the quote. Well, regardless of how shitty your week has been, it's had some peaks too."

"Oh, yeah? Like what?" I asked.

"You just inherited a business." A boyish grin heightened up his round cheeks. "And god only knows how much money. Actually, how much money? You know what, don't tell me. I don't want to know. I'll get jealous. But we need to celebrate. Want to come over for a drink?"

"Maybe we should wait until after the funeral for celebrations," I said. "Moe's not even buried yet."

"Right, sorry. I keep forgetting you two were close." I made a face and he continued, "And I'm now realizing how insensitive that sounded. I'm sorry. You know I'm weird with this sort of thing. Death and I don't mix well."

"It's okay. I don't really know the right way to deal with all this death shit either."

He stood. "You sure you don't want to come get a drink?"

"Yeah, I'm okay. Thank you though. I've had way too much to drink this week. Hence this lovely little number up here." I pointed to the band aid on my forehead.

"I was wondering, but I didn't want to be rude. How did you—?"

"I fell off the kitchen counter."

He laughed. "You're such a dumb ass."

"Thanks, shit head. Get out of here." I smiled.

"I'll see you Tuesday. Do us all a favor and don't break any bones in that time."

"Hey, I'll do my best but I can't make any promises."

CHAPTER SIXTY-TWO

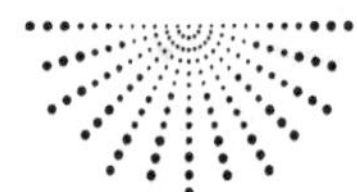

Once all the checks were passed out, I cleaned up, locked up, and headed home. I made my way through the front door, dropped my purse on the table and kicked off my boots. I heard arguing from the kitchen, so I headed that way.

There stood Leah, still focused on the maps she'd shown Jeremy and I earlier. Mary stood across the island, raising her voice. "You can't work with a human, Leah! Not one like this, not one that hasn't been briefed. It's unacceptable. What if he exposes you? What if he exposes the whole family?"

"You mean, if he *tries* to expose us?" She laughed. "No one will believe him. He was fired from his last position due to extreme paranoia. If he comes forward with anything against us, all I have to do is bring up those documents. Everyone will think he just flipped. Boom, psychotic break. No one wants to believe that monsters and ghosts are real, Mary. We have the power of disbelief on our side. And if it means I can bring Chris home, then it's worth it, isn't it?"

"It most certainly is not." Mary gave a firm shake of her head. "Discretion is absolutely everything."

"So what, Chris's life meant nothing? We just give up on him?"

"Of course it meant something, Leah. But the reality is, people in this world die. Sometimes, we have to put ourselves first," Mary said. "We have to choose our battles wisely—"

"I can't be as selfish as you are," Leah barked. "I have to keep looking for him. My best friend is out there somewhere, and I have to find him. I don't care if it gets me hurt or exposed in the process. I can't just say 'to hell with him' the way that you can. He was my brother. He was my best friend. I'm not giving up on him. Not until I've explored every possibility."

"Well, you should. All you're going to do is get yourself killed. And trust me, we'd all rather have one of you than neither of you."

"Fuck you."

Mary laughed, giving her head a shake as well. "You'll see. Mark my words."

She raised her middle finger, pushing it close to Mary's face.

Leah, although the fiercest of us all, had no offensive power. They were purely defensive; the ability to heal and telepathy.

So when Mary reached forward, grasped Leah's middle finger and twisted until there was a pop—followed by a crunch—I leaped across the room. I grabbed Mary by her shoulders and pushed her into the wall next to the wet bar.

I expected that to be enough. I'd pulled her away from Leah. You'd think she would realize that her efforts were petty. She should have stopped.

But she wasn't done. She reached for me, clasped my throat and slammed me backward into the kitchen island. I gripped the granite countertop, trying to grasp my breath as I struggled for air.

It totally blindsided me. I'd seen Mary in battle, she was ruthless. But that had never been used against one of us. I barely even realized what was happening.

"You need to mind your own business, little girl. Do you really think you stand a chance against me? You got lucky last time. You won't push me around, kid."

I gasped, trying to catch my breath. Leah struggled against Mary's inhuman strength. She tugged at her arm, screaming, but Mary and I were locked in a steady gaze.

I'm glad she did it. I'm glad she lost control for a moment. She was angry, and she lost it.

That's when she gave it all away.

"*You got lucky last time,*" the words rang in my mind. "*Thanks, kid.*"

Suddenly, I relived the moment I slammed the shapeshifted version of my mother to the ground.

"*You won't push me around, kid,*" her voice echoed.

"*Your enemy could be in this room and you wouldn't see it,*" Ally's voice vibrated in my memory.

Two different bodies. Two different forms. One person.

Then I remembered the morning we woke up to Mary in our room. She was standing over me, and Moe's journal was on my chest.

My book. She had my book.

It was Mary.

CHAPTER SIXTY-THREE

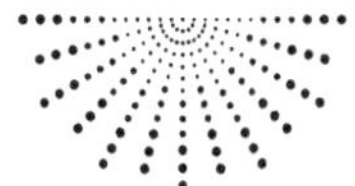

Adam stood in front of me yanking on Mary's arm. Her grip tightened around my throat. It couldn't have been long, because I hadn't passed out yet. It could have only been seconds.

But when those puzzle pieces all started to snap into place, a flood of adrenaline rushed over me. My body went numb. I couldn't even feel her hand around my throat. I shifted into a different being. My rage boiled out of my body like an overflowing pot of water on a stove.

All I could see was Moe's bloodied corpse strewn across the floor. The red specks all over the walls, the counter, the ceiling. All that blood.

Then I saw Jeremy. His perfect lips nearly white. Crimson pouring from his chest. Levitating him out of the car. His screams as Leah healed him.

Ally. And her moans as she bounced naked on Jeremy's lap.

The mass manipulation. The farthest from pure intent.

I reached out and grabbed her throat. My body temperature rose, blood boiling beneath my skin.

My neck burned her fingers. Mary cried out. She jolted back, looking down at her burned fingertips. I brought flames to my hands. My eyes brightened with heat in their sockets.

Heat soared from all over. I wasn't just angry; I had lost it. My body was a flame. I wasn't even visible at that point.

Then I reached out, trying to wrap my fire around Mary. Trying to hurt her. Trying to kill her.

She stopped me—or rather—slowed me. Telekinetically holding me away from her as she backed into the wall. But suddenly, I had an ounce of inhuman strength too. I stepped through her hold, grasped her throat, and squeezed.

I heard Leah screaming, begging me to stop. I heard Adam, insisting that she was too strong, that she wasn't worth it.

But they didn't see her how I did. They didn't know what I knew. They couldn't see her murdering Moe. They couldn't see her flipping Jeremy's car or killing Ally. They didn't see what she had done.

But that's all that I saw.

Kai rushed in from the stairs. He grasped me in a bear hug. Then he ripped me away from her—as he was the only one who wouldn't get burned by my flames.

"No!" I roared. "Let me go!"

"Go!" they all yelled to Mary. "Get out of here! Go!"

In that very moment, she realized that I knew. She held my gaze, like she was seeing me for the first time. Like she had no idea the kind of potential I held before that moment. Like for the first time, she was afraid of something that wasn't her god.

What I didn't realize then, and that I know now, is that that's not what was running through her mind at all. She always knew what I was capable of. But in that single instant, she realized nothing could prevent me from becoming who I was meant to be. And it wasn't fear for her own life that rushed over her.

It was fear for *me*.

Because she knew what came next.

"It's her!" I screamed. "She killed Moe! It was her!"

I heard a series of *what's*, and *huh?s*. Kai released me. I lunged toward her, but she disappeared.

Then I fell to the tile floor, still aflame, screaming, "It was Mary! God damn it!"

"What's going on?" Jeremy said from the steps.

The room fell silent. He made his way to me, reached out for my hand, burned himself, and pulled it back. "Baby." He tried to catch my gaze through the fire. Then he lowered himself beside me. "Baby, what's going on?"

"It's Mary." I tried to slow my flustered, angry breaths. "It was always Mary."

"What do you mean?"

The flames slowed at the sound of his voice. Limb by limb, they shrunk in size until they were back under my skin.

"It was all Mary. She killed Moe. She set you up with Ally. She stole my book. She flipped your car. It was Mary. It was all Mary." I made out between chattering teeth.

Jeremy pulled off his hoodie and wrapped it around my bare shoulders.

"Does that... Does that mean she's our mum?" Kai asked above me.

"I think it does." Leah reached into the freezer and tossed me an ice pack.

"What?" Adam asked. "Mary wouldn't do that. She wouldn't kill an innocent person. Let alone Jeremy."

"Put it together," Leah said. "Really think about it for a minute. Who was there the night Jeremy slept with Ally? Who made sure Brody walked in at the perfect time to catch the two of them? Who knew where Jeremy was headed when he was going to Maine? Who would've been able to watch the house to see when Hannah came upstairs when she was on guard? What other Angel would have known where Laila was at the perfect time to impersonate her mom and steal the book that Moe had written for her?"

"That morning," Jeremy murmured. "She-She was in our room. She was trying to get the book."

"And aside from that, in Mary's eyes, Moe wasn't innocent. He knew who she was. He knew she was Laila's mom. He knew about Kai. And even further aside from that, he was an illegal immigrant from the

Fae Realm. As far as she was concerned, he shouldn't have been here at all. But she never acted until he threatened her secrecy." Leah huffed, tongue running along her teeth. "Holy shit, I need a drink."

"This is wild." Adam leaned against the island blinking hard.

"She... She tried to kill me. She had Ally..." Jeremy whispered, dropping to the floor beside me. "How could she..."

"Jesus Christ." Adam squinted down at me.

"What?" I asked.

"This is probably a really bad time to say this." His eyes widened. "But holy shit, I can see it now. You look like her. Just hotter and with better eyes."

Jeremy lifted his hand and slammed the back of his fist against his brother's groin.

He moaned, lowering himself to the ground beside us. "Really bad timing, I guess."

CHAPTER SIXTY-FOUR

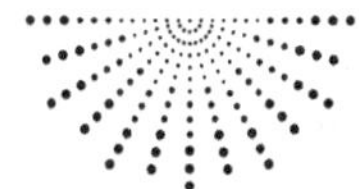

The evening was mostly silent. No one knew what to say. No one knew what to do. We all just sat there, pondering every conversation we'd ever had with the Angel we all knew as a part of our clan, a part of our family. Reliving each word, trying to understand how we missed it.

How could it be Mary? How could our ally be our enemy?

I couldn't face the fact that we shared genetic coding. I couldn't accept that she gave birth to me.

How could she be so evil? So self-centered, so horrible, that she would actually kill someone just for knowing me? Just for wanting to tell me the truth?

How could I have come from her?

Then I thought back to the first time we'd met. Or at least, the first time I remembered meeting her. Her wide eyes when she walked onto the back porch and caught me sitting on Jeremy's lap with his hand up my shirt.

She didn't yell at us for getting handsy. She didn't say a word, actually. She just stared at the two of us with her jaw open.

I hurried and stood, apologizing and introducing myself. Then she said, "I know who you are. Jeremy's mentioned you. You're the one who's friends with Adam."

Then Jeremy introduced her as an old family friend. She forced a smile. Then she told us to come in for dinner.

We all ate together. And after we were done, when I was getting ready to leave, she approached me in the kitchen. She asked me about my life. How it had been, what my parents were like, and if I was happy. I remember thinking that was an odd question, but I answered it regardless.

When I told her my father had recently died and I was struggling a little, her eyes grew so soft. Almost as though she was mourning him too. Then she asked about my mom. If I was happy I at least had her. I told her that Mom meant everything in the world to me, and I think tears welled in her eyes. Then she said that that was good. And that she was glad Jeremy found a girl like me.

When that memory flashed behind my eyelids, the past week began to make even less sense. She loved me. She did, I could see it in her eyes. And she loved Jeremy, and she said that she was glad we'd found one another.

So why would she want us apart?

I stood from the stool at the kitchen island and walked to the wet bar. I poured a glass of Jack Daniels and downed it. Without a sip or a gulp, I swallowed another down in one big slurp.

"Get me one of those." Leah gestured to my glass. I poured her one and poured another for myself. Gently, I placed it on the counter and slid it down to her.

"So what do we do now?" Adam asked from the breakfast nook.

"I don't know," Jeremy muttered.

"We can't kill her," Leah said.

My heart practically stopped. I turned to meet her gaze. "Why not?"

"Because she's an Angel," Brody said from his seat next to Adam. "She's protected. If we kill her, we'll be tried by the Council. And they won't care about anything she's done."

"But she killed Moe," I said. "He was innocent. He never did anything to anyone."

"He wasn't supposed to be on this realm in the first place," Leah muttered. "They won't care. And aside from that, he was in a blood bound treaty with her. If he told you who she was—"

"But he didn't. He didn't get a chance to."

"But she must have thought he was going to," Adam said. "And that's all they need to hear."

"That's bullshit." I gritted my teeth.

"It is." Adam teleported beside me and poured himself a drink.

"But she tried to kill me," Jeremy said suddenly. "That's punishable by death, clipped wings at the least."

Leah's eyes widened.

"You're right." She wagged her finger at him and took down her glass of whiskey. "You're absolutely right. I'll try and get in contact with some other Guardians. Hopefully, get in contact with another Angel. They should be able to set up a meeting with the Council. We might not get a conviction, but we'll at least get a trial."

"I should be able to get a hold of the Gagens. Manakel is one of the best Angels I've met. He'll be willing to help."

"Good. Get on it then."

He laughed. "Laila, it's three in the morning."

"So?"

"So, it's two there," Jeremy said. "We'll call in the morning. It's not like they'll be able to set up the trial tonight. It'll be months until anything formal takes place."

I guzzled my drink.

"In the meantime, everyone should head to bed," Leah said. "We'll deal with this in the morning."

Jeremy put his arms around my shoulders from behind. He rested his head on top of mine. "How about we go lie down?"

"What if she comes back?" I said.

"She won't," Brody muttered.

"How do you know?" I asked.

"Did you see her face?" Adam's forehead creased. "She was petrified. I'll be surprised if she ever shows her face around here again. And she's not gonna hurt you anyway, you're her kid."

"It'll be alright." Jeremy gently rubbed my shoulders. He kissed my hair and said, "Let's go get some sleep, baby."

CHAPTER SIXTY-FIVE

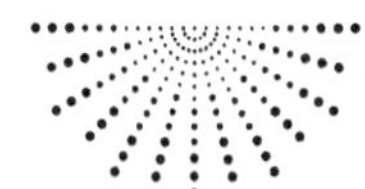

There it was. All laid out on the table. Everything clicked into place, but still, it didn't make much sense. Some things did, but others wcrc still floating around in the realm of possibility.

Why did she try to sabotage mine and Jeremy's relationship? Why did she flip his car? Why did she kill Ally? And what about Adrian? Surely, she fit into this equation somewhere.

I pondered the possibilities until the sun came up. I think I dozed off a few times, but as soon as I'd start to fall asleep, the thoughts started chasing one another like a game of tag.

I didn't understand what was going on. I *couldn't* understand. I didn't have enough information.

As the sun began to rise, I sat up. My stomach churned from the disgusting thoughts that looped around my mind. I wanted to forget it all. I wanted to wake up, because something this horrible had to be a nightmare. It had to be.

My belly tightened and my tongue thickened. I felt last night's chicken tenders making their way up my esophagus. I hurried to the bathroom. When I made it to the toilet, I bent over and emptied my stomach's contents into the porcelain bowl. Then I collapsed to the floor beside it. My face felt hot, and my skin was sticky and clammy.

I wasn't sure if it was anxiety or a hangover or if I was coming down with a nasty flu, but I felt like shit. I was nauseous and dizzy, very lightheaded. If I stood up, I was certain I'd fall over.

I knew I'd regret sleeping on the bathroom floor, but it was comfortable. The coolness caressed my cheek and arm, chilling my feverish skin. I'd just close my eyes for a minute. But as the moments ticked on, I dozed off, feeling more relaxed than I had in bed all night.

"Laila?" I heard Jeremy say in the distance. "Baby, what's wrong?" He collapsed to the floor beside me. He grabbed my face, fingers going to my neck. I opened my eyes. "Are you okay?"

I squinted, blinking a few times. My gaze shifted around. "Yeah. Yeah, I'm fine." I raised my hand to my neck, kneading out a thick, swollen knot near my left shoulder.

"Why were you on the floor?" He pushed hair from my face.

"I couldn't sleep last night and then I felt sick. I came in here to puke. Then I lay my head down for a minute and I guess I just passed out." A yawn passed through my lips.

"Do you think you're getting sick?" He felt my head with the back of his hand.

"Yeah, I must be. I didn't drink enough to be hungover."

"I'm sorry, babe. Do you need help getting to the bed?"

"No, thank you. I'm alright. Just a little queasy and stiff." I stretched and started to my feet. Jeremy gripped my hand, helping me to stand. "What time is it?"

He pulled his phone from his pocket, showing it to me, reading 1:36 P.M. "Well shit."

"Holy fuck," I muttered, another yawn escaping my lips. Then I walked to the dresser and fetched a pair of harem pants and a sweatshirt.

"Did you have plans today?" he asked.

"Just to get in contact with the Council." I threw my night shirt off and onto the bed, pulling the gray sweater over my head. I hurried my sweats off, yanked my pants over my feet. and stumbled to the bed. Jeremy gave a chuckle, leaning against the door frame to the bathroom. "Oh, real mature, mock my clumsiness."

He laughed. "I'm not mocking you; I'm just capturing you."

"What the hell is that supposed to mean?"

He smiled. "Nothing. Just making a mental note of how cute you are."

I rolled my eyes. "Quit being sappy. I'm too busy for your cuteness."

He laughed. "But you love how sappy I am."

I stuck my tongue out, stood, and grabbed a pair of socks. "I should probably shower, but..." I shrugged, brushing my hair back, biting the gum band around my wrist, and pulling it around my messy hair.

"You're fine." He leaned in and pressed his lips to mine. "I'd recommend brushing your teeth though. You smell like a bar's bathroom."

"Aww, aren't you just the sweetest," I said.

"You told me not to be sappy."

CHAPTER SIXTY-SIX

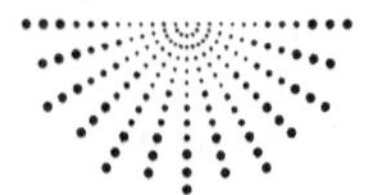

As I rounded my way down the steps, I heard Leah and Kai, then a third voice I didn't recognize.

"I don't care if she's your mother, Kai. What she's done is unforgiveable," Leah said.

"That may be, but she's the only tie to family I have aside from Laila, I won't take part in her murder. Are we any better than her if we do just as she has done?" Kai asked.

"Then don't take part. But I can't go on living in good conscience knowing what she's done. She was like family to us, and she tried to kill my brother."

"I don't think you have anything to worry about, Kai," the third voice said. "I doubt this will go past a slap on the wrist."

My stomach rumbled and my skin grew flushed. That's all that blackmailed rape would get her? How could that possibly be acceptable?

"A slap on the wrist, for attempted murder on one of the people she took an oath to protect with her life?" Leah asked. "Not to mention the collusion with a siren to sabotage the romance of two soulmates? You're kidding me, right?"

"I'm not saying I agree with it, Leah," he said. "But I don't make the rules. I just enforce them. And the term 'soulmate' is pretty subjective anyway."

I rolled my eyes. Like me and Jeremy just made up the bond that kept us linked to every ounce of pain the other felt. 'Cause that made perfect sense.

My stomach ached. I thought about running to the bathroom, but I wanted to hear what was going on.

"Then maybe the rules should change," she said quickly. "Typical, just blindly following the instructions of some holier than thou assholes, sitting high up on their thrones. Looking down at all of us—the ones doing grunt work for no reward—ever, only to be abused and beaten down by the very creatures sworn to protect us. What if she had succeeded, Raguel? What if she killed Jeremy? The only reason he survived was because Laila felt it."

"Had she succeeded, there would be an immediate execution. However, from what Mary has told me, her intention was not to kill him."

Then what the hell *was* her goal? Why would she flip his car if she wasn't trying to end his life and make it look like an accident?

"Right. Because you intentionally wreck someone's vehicle for shits and giggles." She let out a pissed off, annoyed laugh. I could practically hear her shaking her head. "You fucking Angels are a joke."

"That may be true, but I would highly recommend not speaking that way in a court room."

My stomach spun, growling maybe?

"A courtroom?" Leah asked. "We're getting a trial?"

"I may not make the final call, Leah, but I do believe in justice. And you all deserve such for the wrongs that have been done to you."

No. Not growling.

"Thank you—" Leah began. I darted through the kitchen to the garbage can. I wiped stray hairs from my face as I vomited into the trash bag.

"Jesus." Leah cleared her throat. "Raguel, this is our beloved, apparently hungover, Miss Laila Callidy."

I gagged, puking everything left in my stomach. Then I turned to the sink, grabbed a paper towel and wiped puke from my lips. I washed my hands and rinsed my mouth with water.

I turned around. "As if this past week could be any more hell, now I'm sick too," I muttered. "I'm sorry. I'm Laila. Raguel, Leah said?"

He gave a bare smile. "Yes, Raguel. Angel of—"

"Don't be modest, Archangel of justice, fairness and harmony." I smiled. "I studied the hierarchy very thoroughly when I found out what I was."

"Very good. Smart, like your father was."

"You knew my father?" I cocked my head to the side.

"I did. Vaguely, anyway. I conducted his trial as well."

"He had a trial? What for?"

"The trial that got him sentenced to life on Earth." He cocked his head to the side. "Oh. Yes. That's right. You didn't know what he was until after his passing. My apologies. He was smuggling Fae from their realm here to the Earth realm. Some Council members wanted him sentenced to death for treason, but I did what I could. In the end, they locked him here on Earth."

It was in that moment that I began to completely grasp the faults in the system we worked for. Ultimately, the way they operated went against everything I believed. I felt strongly about people's right to migrate if they were seeking a better life.

My opinion on the Angels, the Council, and the Elders, had already begun to shift after learning what Mary had done. I'd thought that they were good. That they wanted to help people. But it was all political. It wasn't about doing what was right, it was about following rules. Even if those rules were bullshit.

"Ye don't say," Kai said. "That explains a lot."

I let out a huff. "Yeah. Yeah, I guess it does."

He cleared his throat. "Well, I'd love to stay and chat, but I have many more places to be. I will set up a date and time for the trial and have the message delivered to you. It should be within two months. At least, I hope. Stay safe, ladies and gentlemen. I'll see you soon."

"Likewise," I said.

He gave a smile. Leah said, "Thanks again, Raguel."

He smiled back then turned to Kai. "I'm sorry you never got to know your father, son. He was a great man."

"That's what I've been told," he murmured. "Thanks."

CHAPTER SIXTY-SEVEN

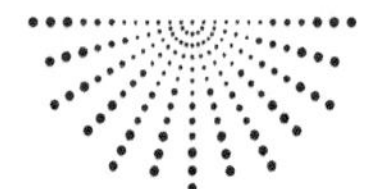

A FEW DAYS LATER - THE FUNERAL

I glanced over myself in the mirror. My knee length, black dress hung off my shoulders over black tights and a pair of black flats. I'd tucked my dark hair behind my head in a simple, elegant bun. I skipped the foundation, though my unusually pale and pasty skin probably could have used it. I wore a bit of waterproof mascara and a light red lipstick that framed my small, heart shaped lips. It was bright, but not hooker bright. Just something to dress up the lack of makeup. I didn't see the point in going all out, knowing I would cry it all off anyway.

Jeremy's arms made their way around my waist. They rested around my belly and he kissed my forehead. "You look beautiful."

I gave a soft smile. "Thanks. You look pretty good yourself."

He'd pulled his hair back into a ponytail at the nape of his neck. A long sleeve, black button up hung off his shoulders over a pair of black slacks.

"What can I say, I clean up nice." He smiled. "You almost ready to go?"

"Yeah. I just need to grab my coat and get Adam."

"Alright. Give me your keys. I'll go warm up the car."

I made my way to the hall and down the steps. Everything felt like it was moving in slow motion. I felt the ground beneath my feet, but not really. It was similar to spending an hour or two on a treadmill, then sitting down and still experiencing the sensation of walking. Almost like floating, but not in a good way.

I searched downstairs for Adam, from the kitchen to the living room, having no luck until I looked out the sunroom window. There he stood, wearing his nice black jacket, holding a joint and flicking its ashes over the balcony. I headed out behind him, pushing the difficult glass door with my hip.

"Hey," I said.

He turned with a smile. "Hey, lady." He extended the joint to me. "Want a hit?"

"No, I *need* a hit," I said.

He laughed as I took it. "It isn't disrespectful to smoke pot before a funeral, is it?"

"No one cares if you get drunk at a funeral. Everyone's eyes will be red anyway."

"This is true." He laughed and put his hand on my back. "So how are you doing?"

"I really..." I took a long drag off the joint. "I don't really know, man. I miss Moe. I miss my dad. I wish he could've been here to talk about all this. But other than that, I'm just numb. It's like he's just on vacation in Tampa or Bora Bora again. I mean, I would go months without hearing from him, so it isn't that I'm craving his companionship. I just keep thinking that he isn't really gone. And then I see the diner covered in his blood and I just..." I wiped tears from the corner of my eyes. "I just feel responsible."

"Mary's the one who put a knife in his gut. She's the one who should feel responsible. Not you."

"She doesn't give a shit. If she did, she wouldn't have done it in the first place. How do you... Jesus. How do you stab an old man that many times? A poor, defenseless old man. How do you bring yourself to put a knife through him?"

"I don't know, man. I don't understand how she could hurt him at all. Stabbing someone one time... At least someone you know... It does something to you. It's physically exhausting to stab anyone, even just once. But the wounds Moe had... Well, she must have been infuriated about something. There had to have been a fight."

"That's comforting." A cool chill ran down my spine.

"All I'm trying to say is that Moe hurt her somehow. No, he didn't kill her. But some way or another, Moe made his mark. It may not have been a fair fight. But he found a way to hit her where it hurt. I know it doesn't change anything or bring him back, but I hope you can find peace knowing Moe wasn't just someone's victim. He was tough, you know."

"Well. Like you said. It doesn't bring him back."

"Hey, guys." Jeremy rounded the side of the house and called to us on the porch. "Are you ready to go?"

"Yeah. Let's get it over with."

I couldn't walk up to the casket. I couldn't look at him like that. I knew that I should, but fuck. I didn't know how.

Every time I gazed over his profile and the side of his gray hair, I kept seeing it doused in red. I kept envisioning Mary slamming a knife through him. I'd seen her kill before and she was barbarous, frightening even.

Then I imagined her doing that to him. My eyes overflowed with tears. My hands shook and my stomach ached.

I loved him so much, like a second father. But I loved her too. I hated her then, but I loved her. And she'd ruined my life. She'd taken someone who meant the world to me away.

It felt like swallowing a pile of sewing needles yet burned within me like a forest fire. For the first time in my life, I felt true agony.

Dad's funeral was hard too. But it didn't touch the pain I felt at

Moe's. I was to blame for this death. He'd still be alive if not for me. Each time that thought crossed my mind, I erupted into violent sobs once more.

Jeremy held my hand. He rubbed my hair and held me close. I leaned against his shoulder and tears streamed down my cheeks.

Many people approached me, apologizing for my loss. People I'd known for years and others I'd never met. I recognized a few regular customers, too.

My mom sat to my right and my sister beside her. When the service started, I half paid attention, listening to some dumb shit about God, as 'the father of man' and Jesus. Moe wasn't even religious, let alone a Christian. But he wanted that pastor. I guess the sermon came as a package deal.

Then the man called onto the audience, saying that this was the time for anyone who wanted to share a memory of Moe to do so now. A few customers approached the pulpit, sharing moments they'd cherished over the years.

Someone talked about how when she was pregnant and didn't have enough money for her meal, Moe gave it to her for free.

A waitress I used to work with talked about how Moe gave her a loan for a down payment on her home after she left her abusive husband.

Max approached, telling the story of how he met Moe. That he was standing out back smoking a joint, and Moe approached him. He gave him a long dramatic lecture about how bad drugs were and that he shouldn't throw his life away on them. Then he took the joint from his hand and smoked it, all the while preaching to him about what he'd do to him if he ever caught him again. Everyone got a good laugh out of that one.

Mom spoke about when my dad died, when we were waiting for his insurance money to come in, and Moe paid for all the funeral arrangements and even covered the bills until we got back on our feet. Then when the insurance money did come, he refused to let her repay the debt. He had said it was his way of paying the obligation he owed my father for everything he'd done for him.

Then Jenna approached, telling about how Moe had given her her first job, at a wage she didn't deserve, so that she could graduate college without being completely drowned in debt.

That's when I knew I had to go up. Not because I wanted to, but because I felt obligated.

Jeremy gave my hand a squeeze. I stood. I counted every step as I made my way to the podium. Forty-eight. Then I cleared my throat, let out a deep breath, and began.

"Any person who was ever graced with the pleasure of meeting Moses Baker could tell you that he was easily the best person they'd met in their life. All of these beautiful stories we've heard these past few minutes just prove how amazing he really was.

"I wish I could say that this was Moe's time. I wish I could say he lived a long, happy life, and the circle of life has to end somewhere. Unfortunately, though, this wasn't Moe's time. He didn't want to go yet. He wasn't ready." My brows scrunched down, and my voice got heavier. "And that's why this is so hard. I want to stand here and tell a lovely, empowering story about him. But I'm having a hard time accepting that he's gone. I'm having a hard time accepting that anyone could hate my friend so much that they could hurt him the way they did. That they could stab him over and over and watch him take his last breath and let him bleed out on the floor of the diner he'd built from nothing."

I couldn't tell you when I started crying, only that by that point, I was wiping snot from my nose and trying to catch my breath. I paused for a moment, trying to regain my composure.

"I've spent the last week wondering if I had shown up to the diner a few minutes earlier, if he would still be here. Maybe none of this would have happened. Maybe it's my fault, because he was only down there so early because we were supposed to have breakfast together. We were supposed to catch up. He was supposed to tell me how his latest vacation went and brag about how beautiful all the things he had seen were. We were supposed to drink our coffee while I told him about my new ideas for the diner. He was supposed to sit there and eat with me and laugh about the good old days. Now there's nothing left of him, and I feel so bad that he's gone because he didn't deserve this. No one deserves this, but especially not Moe.

"He was just a sweet old man. An immigrant who fought so hard for everything he had. He created a life not only for himself, and not only without a single building block to get him started, but also, he helped build lives for so many people in this room today, and I'm sure others who aren't. He taught me to wash dishes, and then to swallow my pride and bite my tongue when dealing with a horrible customer, and then to run a business.

A sad smile came to my lips, tears still streaming from my eyes. "I remember when I was a kid, sitting at the creaky, red bar stools and spinning in circles while I sipped a milkshake out of a red and white paper straw with my dad. Thinking about how cool and exciting it was to have a restaurant like this, so old school and nostalgic, right down the street. I remember Moe standing behind the counter and kissing Agnes and smiling as he whispered something in her ear.

"There was this one time when I came in with my soccer team when I was seven after losing in the local championship tournament. My teammates were so mad at me because I was the goalie, and I wasn't able to deflect the other team's goal. And some girl, I can't remember her name now, but she told me that I was a loser, and no one liked me anymore because I was an idiot and ruined our chance at making it to states." I laughed. "And I ran to the back office and sat on the floor and started to cry when Moe came in. He picked me up and gave me a hug and told me that it was just a game. Then he said that it didn't matter what they thought, because I was the best player on the team, and it was their fault the other team got the ball in the first place. That if one player made a mistake, the whole team did. It was never just one person's fault. He said that if they were really my friends, they wouldn't have called me names. Then he told me I could let their words hurt me or I could be strong enough to let them go. Because I didn't need them anyway. If they didn't want me to be their friend, it was their loss.

"I guess that's when it occurred to me that Moe was a better person than almost anyone I knew. He didn't care about someone's failures or mistakes as long as they were going to try to do better the next time around. Moe taught me that if you aren't growing, you're dying. Even though he's gone, and I'll miss him terribly, I know that he'd want me, and everyone else in this room today, to keep growing."

I didn't look at the crowd, my eyes just held my own gaze in the reflection of my shoes as I made my way back to my seat. When I sat, Jeremy took my hand, kissed my forehead and whispered, "That was beautiful."

I said nothing, just lay my head against his shoulder.

———

We took our orange magnetic flag, attached it to the roof of the car, and climbed in. Jeremy drove because I just didn't feel up to it. I listened to the sound of the rain patting on the metal roof. It was a loud, obnoxious downfall that drowned out the sound of the music playing over the speaker, no matter how high the volume was.

I was in this strange place where I wanted to cry, but it felt like there was nothing left *to* cry. Like my eyes had gone completely dry. I leaned my head against the cool window, staring blankly at the wet, slushy snow on the mountain sides.

I felt a tap on my shoulder. Then I turned and Adam said, "Are you okay?"

"Yeah. I'm okay." Jeremy's hand made its way to my lap, squeezing my knee. I lay my hand on his, scooched closer to him and rested my head on his bicep. "I could just fall asleep."

"What's stopping you?" he said with a gentle smile.

He knew I hadn't been sleeping well, so I'm sure he was hoping I would. All weekend, I'd been puking my guts out. Last night should have been a good night of rest, but I tossed and turned in anticipation of the funeral.

"Hey, do you remember the day I met you?" I said quietly to Adam.

He laughed. "Yeah, it was at Moe's. You were just a server then."

"Yeah, and Adrian was always stealing scones from the serving dish on the counter."

"And I went to grab one and you slapped my hand and told me I had to pay for it. Then I dropped the lid and it shattered."

I smiled. "I made Adrian sweep it up while you went to the store to grab new ones."

"Adrian was so mad that night. She kept going on about how my dumb ass made her get her finger cut and ruined the rest of the scones. She was so pissed she had to wait until the next week to have another 'good' one."

I laughed. "And then she tried to make them herself and caught her parents five-thousand-dollar stove on fire."

"That girl shouldn't have been allowed in a kitchen." He made out between chuckles. We laughed so hard that my cheeks hurt when we were done.

As silence crept in, I murmured, "God, I miss her."

"Yeah. Yeah, me too," he murmured.

A few long moments later, we pulled into the cemetery to say our final goodbyes. Jeremy came to my door with the umbrella, held it up, and opened my door. I stood and clutched his arm. Adam tailed behind me.

We followed my Mom, who had ridden with Jenna and been in front of us on the car ride. I watched as the pallbearers lifted Moe's white casket from the hearse, gently carrying him through the slippery snow and rain.

That's when it occurred to me that this would be the last walk Moe ever took. That he'd never again see the light of day. The eyes I thought couldn't possibly contain another tear burst again. This time a loud, dry heave like cry left my lips. It felt so embarrassing in hindsight, although it was completely justified.

Jeremy held his hands tight at my waist. I don't know if I would've still been standing had it not been for his strong arms. My sister put her arms around me too, crying and wiping tears from my cheek.

"This sucks," Jenna whispered.

I cried a few moments longer, unable to keep walking towards the grave.

Just then, out of my peripheral vision, I saw her standing there. Dressed head to toe in a black pant suit, carrying a black umbrella above her head. But before I could react, Mom was already heading towards her.

"Don't hide in the shadows." Mom drew closer. "Twenty years wasn't enough for you?"

"No, Mom." My tears slowed. I pulled myself from Jeremy and Jenna's grip.

I darted after her, fearing for her life. I knew Mary wouldn't attack. At least not there. Not in front of all of those people. But given whose funeral I was at, it sent a chill down my spine.

"No, Laila, that's okay," Mary said. "Go on, Rachel. Say it. Whatever you need to get off your chest, just say it quickly. I need to talk to my daughter."

I'd never seen a look of such fury in my mother's eyes like I did in that moment. She raised her hand and slammed Mary's left cheek. The sound crackled. Mary's head reared to the side.

"Well, that stung," she muttered, wiping her face.

"Don't you ever call her yours." Mom wagged her finger. "The only thing you have done for my daughter is cause her pain. That's all you've ever done to anyone. You're a piece of low life scum. You weren't a mother; you were a dead beat. The only thing you ever did for her was give birth."

"'Only' generally speaks to one specific item or action. So I either *only* caused her pain or I *only* gave birth to her. If I only did both, well. You see where I'm going here." Mary gave an annoyed, half-smirk.

"You're a coward." Mom narrowed her eyes.

"Mom—"

"No, Laila. I didn't break my treaty. You already knew who she was. I just couldn't reveal it. But the cat's out of the bag now, isn't it, Mary?"

"Are you done?"

"No, I am most certainly not. You killed a man, a wonderful man. And for what? To protect your precious identity? The only reason she figured you out was *because* you killed him. If you would have just let things run their course, Moe would still be here, and Laila wouldn't have known who you are. Didn't think it through all that well, did you?"

"I'm not justifying anything to you, Rachel. I owe you nothing. I gave you my child. Nothing will ever put me in your debt. *Nothing.*" Her piercing gaze shifted between Mom's. "Laila, however, I do owe. So could you..." She made a shoo motion with her hand. Mom inched backwards, clearly against her will.

"How about you—" Mom began but I turned, cutting her off.

"It's okay, Mom. She won't hurt me. Go."

Mom gritted her teeth. "I'll tell Jeremy to stay close."

As she walked away, I turned to Mary. "What are you doing here? You kill a man and then show up to his funeral? That's low, even for you."

Mary's warm hazel gaze was unusually gentle. Almost apologetic. "I can't justify my actions to you. At least, not entirely. But I can tell you that everything I did, I did so with you in mind."

"Killing my cousin? Stealing his journal? Having my boyfriend, someone you've cared for his entire life, raped? Oh. And let's not forget the part where you tried to fucking murder him."

"I wasn't trying to kill him, Laila. I was just trying to slow him down. Send him a message to turn back. The road was icy, the bend was sharp. It was an accident. I love Jeremy like my own, I would never try to hurt him. I was just about to get him out of there and then you showed up."

Maybe she was telling the truth. But she'd lied to me for three years. I had no reason to believe her.

"The whole 'love him as if he was my own' bullshit doesn't mean a damn thing coming from you. Why are you here anyway? You want to talk to your kid, talk to Kai. He wants to have something to do with you. But I'd rather you choke on your lies and die."

"I'll speak with him soon, but I know you wouldn't disgrace Moe's funeral by trying to kill me here."

"Don't tempt me," I murmured.

She frowned. "I want you to know the truth, or at least, the parts of it that I can divulge."

I huffed. "Alright then. Tell me the truth, Mary."

Her eyes shifted over me quickly. "I don't want you to be with Jeremy. Not because you are a bad couple, but because I know things. Things that I wish I didn't. I did something I shouldn't have by stepping in, but I couldn't stand idly by while I watched you destroy your life. If you were in my shoes, you'd have done the same thing."

"I would never kill an innocent man."

Mary bit her smiling lip. "To protect your child, you'll do things you never thought imaginable. Far worse than I've done, Laila. You'd rather your child hate you than feel the pain I know you soon will."

"You want to talk about pain? Let's talk about how I found someone I considered to be a second father in a pool of his own blood, stabbed countless times. I still can't get the blood stains off the cabinets. I can't stop seeing it in my fucking head, Mary, and that's because of you. Every day, I think about what you had Ally do to Jeremy. And then I think about what you did to her, too. You turn your back on everyone."

She frowned. "That's not true."

"You bet your ass it's true."

Still shaking her head, she said, "You don't see the big picture."

"No? Then explain it to me. Paint this picture for me, nice and jumbo sized."

Her lips pressed to a line beneath her hazel eyes. "I can't."

"Oh, you can't." I scoffed. "Of course you can't. Because you don't have an explanation. You were selfish and you'd rather Moe die than me know who you are."

"You needed the money, Laila." She leaned closer and lowered her voice but kept it firm. "Yes, protecting my identity was a reason for killing him. But it wasn't my only reason. I wanted you to be able to leave this place and start over somewhere. Go to college, or buy a chain restaurant, or backpack around Europe."

My stomach swirled. She'd done this so I could get the inheritance. It really was all my fault.

I blinked hard. "My financial gain was worth his life?"

"No. That's not what I meant. I wanted you to be able to get away from Jeremy."

"What the hell does that even mean? You love Jeremy. He's a great guy. He's literally my soulmate, you're the one who told me that."

"He's wonderful. You're right."

"So what, then? In your bizarre, twisted mind, he isn't good enough for me?"

"No, that's not it at all." She pressed her lips together, as if trying to keep herself from saying something she couldn't. "You're a wonderful couple. But this wasn't about you. It wasn't about him. This was about the future. Although now I see I was too late anyway. It's already started."

I scrunched up my forehead, narrowing my gaze. "Too late for what?"

"You don't know yet?" I gave a slight shake of my head. "Don't you feel it? The force of life within you?"

"Are you on drugs or something?" I said.

Mary huffed. "Have you been sick recently? Mood swings? Smells you once loved making you nauseous?" She let out a bare laugh. "You're pregnant, Laila."

A laugh echoed from my lips. "No, I'm not."

"You are," she murmured. "But it doesn't have to be too late. You can get this taken care of. The procedures these days are—"

"Excuse me?" She stopped, waiting for me to continue. "First, you tell me I'm pregnant. Based off of no science whatsoever. Then, you tell me to get an abortion. When I'm not even pregnant." I shook my head. "How about you just leave me alone. I don't want to see your face again, Mary."

"Laila, please. I can't give you all the details, but you just have to trust me. Run away. *Now.*" Her eyes pierced mine. She grasped my shoulders. "Before it's too late. Pack the essentials. Load your car. Cash out everything you're getting from Moe's life insurance and just disappear. Everyone, *everyone* would be better for it. Please. This isn't a manipulation tactic. This is just me trying to spare you more heart ache than you can possibly imagine."

I shoved her palms from my biceps. "I can't trust you. Not after everything you've done. Just leave me alone, Mary. Leave us *all* alone."

I turned and started away. She called my name at least half a dozen times. But I didn't want to hear another word come out of her mouth.

As I stepped through the slushy snow, I tried to piece together everything she'd said. Making sense of it all wasn't possible with the bits of information she'd given me.

But one thing did make sense.

It had been a long while since my last period. I hadn't even thought about it until that moment. There was too much going on in my life to worry about my period. At least, that's how naïve I was at the time, to neglect something as important as my menstrual cycle.

I caught up with Jeremy and headed towards the burial for the final words. "What did she want?" Jeremy caught my hand and held the umbrella above our heads.

"I don't know. To apologize, I guess?"

"She admitted to his murder then?" he asked in a hushed tone.

"Among other things."

"You can give me the details later."

We approached the burial site and watched them attach the casket to a machine and slowly cranked it down into the dark hole.

I watched every inch slowly make its way into the ground. The pastor said a prayer, but I wasn't paying attention.

All I could think about was Mary. I was so angry at her. I was so offended at what she said about Jeremy. But most of all, I was terrified that she was right, and that I was pregnant. Not because that was the worst thing imaginable. But because I hadn't exactly been taking care of myself lately. And I had no idea what that would mean for a fetus.

After the ceremony, I asked Jeremy and Adam to teleport home before the wake, just so I could have a few minutes to myself. They understood and did as I asked. Jeremy kissed my cheek before he disappeared.

When I sat down in my Beetle, I noted something in the passenger seat. Moe's journal. With a green post-it on the top.

I'm sorry for what happens next.

I tried to save you from it.

My teeth gritted together, and my jaw tightened. I crumbled the post-it in a ball and tossed it to the ground. I placed the journal in my purse, started my car, and pulled out of the cemetery's lot.

Then I drove to Wal-Mart and bought two three-pack pregnancy tests. I scanned them at the self-checkout, swiped my card, and hurried to the bathroom. I snatched a cup from a cleaning cart outside the door, rinsed it out in the sink, and headed to the stall. I sat down, held the cup between my legs, and peed.

I put the stick in the cup and waited. When the time needed for the test had passed, I gazed down at it.

Pregnant.

I opened another package and followed the same procedure. Pregnant.

I repeated it again and again. Every test gave the same result. Pregnant.

"Shit." I raised my hand to my mouth, staring down at six positive pregnancy tests on the metal garbage can that connected between the stalls.

"Holy shit," I murmured. "Holy shit."

EPILOGUE

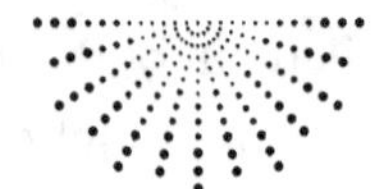

My gaze shifted around the room. I slid my fingertips over my belly. The large bay window overlooked the crowded parking lot. I couldn't walk around barefoot on the splintering hardwoods just yet, but the place had potential. Wouldn't be long and it'd be a nice home for the three of us.

It definitely wasn't Moe's apartment anymore. The cozy new sofa practically cradled me. Music played off the Google Home in the bedroom. It didn't smell like old people and mothballs anymore, either. Now, it smelled like sawdust, fresh paint, and new furniture.

Jeremy set a cardboard box of clothes on the couch beside me. "This place is really coming together."

"You don't think I've taken too much from it?" I stood and gestured around. "I think I've made it more modern than Moe would have liked."

"I don't think Moe would care that you redecorated. He hadn't lived here in years anyway. You think the condos he stayed at in Florida looked like this place did before we started?" he asked.

I shrugged. "I guess not."

"So what should I bring up next?" he asked.

"Maybe the twin bed for the guest room?"

The baby's room, I corrected in my mind.

I'd spent the last four weeks trying to find a good way to tell him. But it kept coming out wrong. He knew something was up because I hadn't smoked in weeks and I hadn't drunk since before the funeral. Although, thank god, the doctors said everything looked perfect.

"Sounds good to me." He kissed my cheek and disappeared. He reappeared a moment later in the guest room, hollering, "Do you want it on the frame or up against the wall?"

"On the frame is fine," I called. Then I headed to the baby's room. Jeremy set the bed down and plopped on top of it. I leaned against the doorway and smiled at him.

"Ya know, I really like the vibe in this room." He glanced between the walls.

"Oh, yeah?" I sat beside him. "Why's that?"

Smiling, he shrugged. "I don't know. I like the two windows on this wall, and where the door is located. It lets in a lot of light. Has good feng shui. What are we going to do with this room anyway?"

My hands trembled ever so slightly. I had to tell him. Time was running out. If he couldn't tell I was getting fat already, he would soon.

Something must have showed him that I was nervous because Jeremy chimed back in, "I mean, you. What are *you* going to do with this room? I'm sorry, I didn't mean to be presumptuous. I just figure that, well, you know. You consider my room your room. I mean, I know this is your place. I'm not trying to, like, you know, move in on you or something, if that's the message I was sending—"

"What?" I laughed. "What? No, that's not it. Of course this is your place. This is *our* place."

"What's wrong then?" he asked. I leaned my head back onto the bed and covered my face. "Laila, I know you well enough to know when something isn't right. Just tell me, baby. Whatever it is, I can handle it."

"I don't know about that," I muttered.

We'd never talked about kids. Not once. It just never came up. None of our friends or family had little ones so it never brought the conversation to light.

With the life we'd led until everything had gone down with Mary, it just didn't make sense to even think about children. Jeremy had been out of town so often, I worked a lot, neither of us had much money. It had just never been the right time.

But now, things were different. Jeremy and I both refused to work cases after what happened. We had our own place. There was money in the bank. The timing was right.

"You're killing me here." He pulled my hand from my face and smiled down at me. "What is it?" I sighed. Then I stood. "Where are you going?"

"I'll be right back." I walked to the kitchen and reached in my purse. I dug for a moment. Then I found the first sonogram print-out.

It was from the week before, only 10 weeks along. At that point, it barely looked like a tadpole. But I knew he'd understand when he saw the image.

I made my way back to the guest room, holding the picture behind my back. "Close your eyes and put your hand out in front of you."

Jeremy's eyes widened slightly. "Listen, you know I'm all about equality and women's rights but whenever the time comes, please let me do the proposing. It's just this thing I've always—"

"I'm not asking you to marry me, damn it. Just close your eyes."

He harumphed, closed them, and laid his palm out in front of him.

I carefully placed the picture in his hand. "Alright. Open them."

He did so. His gaze turned down to the photo. He stared at it for a long while, then he cupped his hand over his mouth.

"I know we're young. And it wasn't planned, but with the life insurance I got from Moe, and inheriting the business, we have more than enough to be comfortable. But I get it if you're not ready for this. I'm doing okay, I can do it on my own if I—"

"Laila, shut up." He stared down at the sonogram a moment longer. I swallowed hard and waited. Then he stood.

I studied his blank face. My heart thudded against my ribs. For a second, I thought, "Oh, fuck. Looks like I'm about to be a single mom."

But then he leaned down and twisted his arms around my waist. My racing heart slowed. I tightened my hands against his back.

After a moment, he pulled away. His gaze turned to my stomach with a boyish grin. "Is it weird to touch it this early?"

I laughed. "I don't think so."

He smiled. He gently placed his hand on my belly. "I'm gonna be a dad."

My smile heightened. "You are."

He blinked fast, still smiling. "And you're gonna be a mom."

I laughed.

"How far along are you?" he asked.

"Eleven weeks. I've been trying to find a way to tell you, but it was such a big thing and I didn't know how—"

"It's okay. It's okay." He reached up and cupped my cheek in his hand. "Just tell me before you go to your next appointment. I want to be there."

My lips lifted higher. I nodded. "Okay. Okay, I will."

His smile stayed wide. He looked down at my belly. "This is kinda scary."

"You're telling me," I muttered. "I gotta squeeze this thing out of my vagina."

Jeremy laughed. He cupped my cheek in his hand and looked gently between my eyes, still smiling. "But we'll have a baby when you do."

The way those words slid off his tongue made my stomach flip. His smile was so big, his eyes so full of joy. He wanted this. Maybe even more than I did.

Happy tears burned across my irises. "Yeah. We will."

He wrapped his arms tight around me and kissed my hair. Blissful butterflies flapped away in my tummy. Or maybe it was the baby.

Then Jeremy said, "I thought your boobs got bigger."

Laughing, I shoved him away. "You're an asshole."

He laughed and pulled me closer into him again.

In those few seconds, I thought everything was perfect. We'd take over Moe's. We'd live in our small but adorable apartment. We'd watch the baby grow, maybe even have a few more. We'd get married. Maybe buy a house with some land. We'd teach our children our ways, to use their powers to help and further human society. We'd live happily ever after.

I thought we would have a beautiful, sweet life.

But I had no idea what atrocities would come before I birthed that baby.

I had no idea how important the child within me would become, not only to me, but to the entire world.

I thought this was the end of a tragic story, but I would soon realize it was only the beginning.

This was a drop in the ocean of time. Losing my dad, and Adrian, and then Moe, were the hardest things I'd faced so far. But it was nothing compared to what the future had in store for me.

Soon enough, I'd understand exactly why Mary had done what she did. Not that I agreed with every detail. But we were on the same page about one thing.

I would do horrible, unspeakable things to protect my children.

The story continues in *The Horrors That Created Us*. Turn the page for a sneak peek, or click the link below to download now:
https://www.amazon.com/dp/B08T17G7S2

Sign up for Charlie's newsletter and receive a free copy of the Eluding Destiny prequel, *Blood Bar*:
https://liquidmind.media/eluding-destiny-prequel/

If you enjoyed this story, please consider leaving a rating or review on Amazon:
https://www.amazon.com/dp/B08J8FKLMZ

Join Charlie's private reader group on Facebook and discuss all things Eluding Destiny and Charlie Nottingham:
https://www.facebook.com/groups/661440911724435/

THE HORRORS THAT CREATED US — CHAPTER 1

JANUARY 8TH, 2019 - JEREMY- THE TRIAL

The rumors did the place justice. The Elders Hall was older than anyone who stood within it that day. The winged babies painted on the domed ceiling saw more people led to their deaths than I'd ever want to acknowledge. Everything was trimmed in gold paint and intricate woodwork above the white marble floors.

The eyes of the many statues situated around the pews seemed to stare at me anywhere I sat. I didn't see any books laying around, but somehow, that's what it smelled like. A library. It even had the same chill in the air. The whispers around the room were just as quiet.

From an outside perspective, it just looked pretentious. Rich and fancy, not scary. But something about that place chilled me to my core.

"I don't know what the point of this is," I muttered to Laila. "They don't give a shit. This is a child's problem."

"Moe's murder is a child's problem? What she had Ally do to you. That was a child's problem?"

"Not to me, not to you. But to them." I glanced up at the twelve old men and women situated around the semicircular table, murmuring amongst themselves. "Yeah, baby. We don't matter. The only reason we got this hearing at all is because we have connections to Angels that rank higher than her."

She ran her tongue along her teeth. "Well, let's just hope they're as wise as they claim to be. That bitch doesn't deserve to have wings after what she did."

I licked my lips and gave a nod. She wasn't wrong; Mary did some fucked up shit.

What happened last year tore me up more than I'd ever be able to admit aloud. But I knew that didn't matter to them. Mary would walk. And truthfully, I didn't want her to get kicked out of Heaven either.

I wanted to understand why she did it. I wanted to understand what I did that made her hate me. But I didn't want her to lose the one thing that she loved about herself.

"Ladies and gentlemen, please have a seat," the woman in a white robe at the center of the large wraparound desk said. "Would the accused please come to the stand?"

The whispers of the small audience—primarily made up of my family members—fell silent. We turned and watched as Mary stood from the front row. She walked in silent humbleness to the center of the semicircle before the Elders.

"State your name, age, race, occupation, and accused crime for the court, if you would," the woman at the center seat said.

"My name is Mary. I have no surname." She held her hands folded together in front of her hips as she spoke. "My exact date of birth is unknown, but I believe it's somewhere over two thousand years in the Earth realm. I'm an Angel for the Skoulda Guardian clan, or was, rather, before these events ensued. I stand accused of the murder of a Siren named Allisia from the Atlantic coast of the Americas."

"Pleasure to see you again, Mary." The woman smiled. Mary gave a civil nod as Laila scoffed beside me.

"They know each other? And she gets a say in all of this?" She spoke in a low whisper.

"She probably knows every one of them up there," Leah murmured beside Laila.

"That's bullshit," Laila said.

Not that I disagreed, but I expected nothing less. Mary was well known and well liked. My family? Well known, certainly. But never well liked. At least, not my generation of it.

"And how do you plead, Mary?" the woman asked.

"Guilty, your honor. I did it. I killed that girl."

The woman leaned back in her chair and sucked her teeth. "Care to explain why you felt it necessary to kill an endangered creature?"

"Ally wanted to inform one of my children that I was her mother. It was only a matter of time before she did or before one of the many psychics close to my daughter would have figured it out."

"Well, that's a crock of shit," Laila blurted.

"Excuse me?" the woman at the table said.

"Laila." I put my finger over my lips. But she was already standing.

"I said that's a crock of shit." Laila put her hands at her hips.

I rubbed my tense forehead. The love of my life. The defiant, obnoxious, out-spoken love of my life.

"And who are you?" the woman said.

"Laila." She gestured toward Mary. "Her daughter. Can I get called to the stand here? Because—"

"When you learn to talk like a lady, I may allow you to speak in this court."

Laila curled her lip in disgust. I wanted to laugh but I bit it back. 'Acting like a lady' was never Laila's strong suit. And I understood her frustrations, but in this court, our frustrations meant nothing. Gender meant a whole hell of a lot. Our opinions though? Practically useless.

"No, I'm curious," a man said a few seats down from the first woman. "What did Mary say that was 'a crock of shit?'"

"The Siren wasn't telling us anything and Mary knew that," Laila said. "We weren't questioning Ally because we wanted to know who my birth mother was. We were questioning her to figure out who gave her legs in exchange for raping my boyfriend. And to see if she knew who tried to kill him. Just so happened that Mary was responsible for both."

"Is your boyfriend in the court today?" the man asked.

She turned to me. I awkwardly ran my hand along my mouth as I stood. "That's me."

"Is that what happened?" he asked.

Mary looked at me over her shoulder. Her brows were pulled together, her throat bobbed with a swallow. She felt guilty. And for some reason, it hurt to see her that way. I should've been as angry as Laila was, but I wasn't. I was just... hurt.

But I cleared my throat. "Yeah. Yeah, that's what happened."

"*You* were raped." One of the women laughed. "How does that work exactly?"

I didn't care for the word either. Technically, that was what had happened. But I didn't want to talk about it. I didn't want to explain it, especially not to them. It made me feel gross and violated, and I hated even thinking about it. But what did it matter now? Ally was dead. She couldn't do it to anyone else. I had no recollection of the event. The only reason I was even there was because it *might've* helped Laila get justice for Moe's murder.

"Um, well, if you use your powers to get someone in bed, that's not exactly consent," Laila said.

"Did you say no?" the man asked.

"She did something to my head. I don't really remember it."

"So, you didn't say no then?" another voice from the table said.

"Well, I didn't say yes."

"And I take it she didn't drug you to..." She glanced toward my pelvis. "So, there must have been some attraction on your end."

"Is that so?" the first woman said. "Were you drugged?"

I turned my gaze to the marble floor. "No. I wasn't drugged."

I knew this was what they'd say. I knew that in their minds, I had no right to feel the way I did. To them, I was a man who'd gotten my dick wet. It didn't matter that I was forced. It didn't matter that I hadn't wanted it. It didn't matter that it was assaulted, because I was a man. What did they care? I didn't remember it anyway.

Although, having expected this, no matter how much the reminder ached in my chest and made my skin crawl, the fact remained. This was the reaction I'd anticipated. Which was why I'd hoped Mary trying to kill me would warrant some sort of punishment.

"Were you tied down? Was there a knife at your throat?" the woman asked.

"You're kidding, right?" Laila said. "A Siren's primary ability is to sing a song that makes people want to take their clothes off and—"

"Only if there is attraction," the man said. "So. Were you attracted to her?"

I licked my teeth and moved my shoulders in something of a shrug. "I didn't find her unattractive."

"That settles that part then," the woman said.

"What?" Laila said. "But she—"

"He has no recollection of the events, and it was at least somewhat mutual, or something wouldn't have worked." The man shrugged. "This is irrelevant."

The outcome I'd expected.

"Are you serious right now? You *condone* this?" Laila's voice was filled with disgust.

The woman turned to Mary. "Did you try to kill this boy?"

"No." Mary looked at me over her shoulder again with that same guilty expression. "No, I would never do that. I love Jeremy, I watched him grow from a child to the man standing here today. What Laila is referencing was a misunderstanding. I did accidentally hurt him, that is true. But I did not try to kill him. I was just trying to slow him down to give me more time to get to the Siren. I put morion inside of his car and caused an accident. The intent was only to halt his arrival at the Siren's home. The morion made it so that he couldn't teleport the vehicle when he started to crash. When I saw how bad the accident was, I started to help but then Laila arrived with Jeremy's brother. They took him back to his sister to be healed and all was well."

"You arrived." The woman made a face at Laila. "How did you know he was in an accident?"

"He's my par animo. I felt it."

The Elders looked between us. "Is that so?"

"It is."

"They're right, your honors," Mary agreed. "Chamuel confirmed it about three years ago."

The woman in the middle leaned back and crossed her arms against her chest. "I see."

"But ultimately, Mary," another Elder said, "you did these things to keep your identity confidential, as you swore an oath to do before this child was even conceived."

"I did," Mary murmured. "Above all else, I am loyal to Heaven and our father, the one true God. Although I do agree that many of my methods were less than humane, I was following orders."

"And who are we to argue with the lord himself?" The woman in the center smiled. She glanced at Laila and I with an expression I had a hard time placing. Contempt, perhaps.

"We are not," another Elder said.

"You've done as you were told, and you will not be punished for doing so," the woman in the center said.

A deep breath fell from my nose.

Was I surprised at the way this was heading? No, it was exactly what I'd anticipated. I also hadn't wanted to see Mary die for this, nor did I want her to get kicked out of Heaven, but I wanted her to face *some* form of punishment. At the very least, a slap on the wrist. But it looked like she was going to get off completely free.

"Are you serious?" Laila blurted with a darting gaze. "This woman stabbed an old man more than a dozen times for the purpose of—"

"Protecting her identity, no?" one of the men said. "Moses Baker, I presume, is who you're referencing."

Her teeth gritted to a line. "And that's just okay with you people? That she murdered someone in cold blood to protect a secret I figured out anyway?"

"Moses Baker had no place on this land," the woman said. "He had no rights the moment he crossed to this realm. I certainly won't condemn a loyal servant of God for an alien."

"Then you're a cunt," Laila snapped.

My heart palpitated and my eyes shot open.

I'd been a part of this world my entire life. And from the moment I could remember hearing my Dad talk about the Elders with a terrified gaze in his eyes, I feared ever standing within that room with those men and women. They worked directly with the Archangels and God himself. They had more power than anyone. Killing the love of my life would be like swatting a fly to them.

Mary turned to me with the same expression.

"Talk to me that way again and I'll have your tongue, little girl," the woman said with a piercing gaze.

"Oh, fu—"

I leaned over and put my hand over her mouth. She swatted it away. I widened my eyes further.

"Mind your woman there, boy," the first man to speak said.

"Before someone does it for you," another man blurted.

Laila scoffed. "I don't know what time period you're living in but—"

"Stop." I turned to her with eyes bigger than the ocean and shook my head.

I almost never told her what to do. But I wasn't about to end up in a blood bath with some of the oldest, most powerful leaders in the supernatural world. I'd rather her be mad at me than end up without a tongue. Or worse, not walk out of that hall at all.

"Are you done now?" the woman in the center asked. "Or do you need a little time out?"

Laila glared.

"Let's just go," I murmured with a hand on her back.

She clamped her teeth together. She took my hand. I looked to my siblings in the pew beside us. We all teleported back home in pairs.

***

"No, that was bullshit." Laila's nostrils flared. "They made it out like what Ally did to you was perfectly acceptable."

"I'm a man. Kinda figured they would," I muttered, raising a paint brush to the corner of the baseboard. "Don't know if you noticed but gender equality is pretty irrelevant to them."

"No shit." She lowered herself to the floor beside me and picked up another brush. "I just... I thought that something would happen to her. Some form of punishment. In the human world, she'd get at least twenty years."

"She'll get hers. What goes around comes around." I took the brush from her hand and met her gaze. "But you shouldn't be in here. All these fumes are bad for the baby."

"It's a little paint." She rolled her eyes and snatched it back. "The baby's fine."

"If you say so," I said.

Gliding the brush along the window frame, Laila said, "Just sucks that he's never going to get justice."

Ever since Moe died, all she'd talked about was Mary getting what she deserved for killing him. And I understood. Mary told her that she killed Moe so that Laila would inherit his business, and that burden weighed heavy on her shoulders. In her eyes, she was responsible for his death. I knew that she wasn't. I was sure that Moe, wherever he was, knew the same. But that was a heavy cross to carry.

"Is that what you want? Justice?" I sat the brush down and touched her cheek. "Or is this about the blame game you've been playing?"

Her voice was soft, a bit sad. "I just want to go back in time and keep it from happening."

"It'd be nice if it worked like that. But do you think Moe would want you to hold onto all this resentment? Because I knew Moe too, and he wasn't the vengeance type. He was the live and let live type."

"Well, I'm not."

I smiled and touched her hip. "Well. I think that if Moe were here, he'd tell you to be happy and not to worry about something you can't change."

"I think he'd tell me to find a man who knows how to paint." She squinted at the top of the windowsill. "We just stained these and here you go painting all over it."

I looked to the speck of green on the cherry wood. "Are you talking about that little, tiny drop smaller than a pinhead?"

"It's bigger than a pinhead." She pulled away and brought herself to the tips of her toes. I looked over the little bump starting to protrude from her flat stomach and smiled.

Even though we'd lost in court that day, I was so happy. *We* were so happy.

I had her, she had me, we had our diner, and nothing else mattered. Life was better than it'd ever been. I was ready to shut the door on what happened a few months before, the paranormal bullshit helping Angels track down rogue supernaturals, and move onto better days. Maybe that was why my reaction wasn't as volatile as Laila's. She wanted all of the wrongs made right regardless of how we both knew the hierarchies in our world operated.

I wasn't naive enough to expect anything more than what we'd gotten, but I was *done.*

I wouldn't waste another second fighting for them. If all of this had shown me anything, it was how little I mattered to the facilities I'd given years of my life to.

My trauma, Laila's trauma, meant nothing to them.

That was the catalyst I needed to leave that life behind.

The Chambers, the Council, the Angels... all of that shit was my past.

This was my future.

As awful as the path that led us there was, we finally had what we wanted. We were done taking orders. We were focusing on ourselves and what *we* wanted.

A family. A good one, not like the one I'd had. With a mom and a dad more in love than anyone else. Full of love, and passion, and peace. The two of us and our child, living happily ever after with a simple, human existence. Not that we'd forget what we were, but to leave the past in the past. To stop worrying about Demons and vamps that didn't matter to us anyway.

They were all that mattered. They were all I wanted. A happily ever after with my family.

"Now you're just nit picking." I smiled.

"No, you're just messy." She licked her thumb and began scrubbing.

I ran my tongue along my smiling lips and lifted the brush from the can. I reached around her and brushed a streak of green paint across her creamy cheek.

She gasped before she turned to me, mouth open as wide as her eyes.

"Oh, geez, I'm sorry." I grinned. "I'm just so messy, I don't know how that happened."

"Oh yeah?" Her mouth curved into an unwilling smile. I took a step back and held my grin as she leaned down to grab the other paint brush. "Come here."

"No." I laughed and took another step back.

She lunged forward on her tip toes, sliding the brush from my forehead to my chin. "Oh, geez, I'm sorry."

"That's it." I leaned down and stuck my hand into the bucket of paint.

"Don't you dare. If you fling that across this baby's room—"

"Fling it?" I asked. "Who said anything about flinging it?"

I teleported in front of her and pressed my lips to hers. I raised my hand to her cheek and slid my dripping hand to her neck.

"There ya go." I smiled, moving my hand to her hip. "No drips or anything."

She tried to force down her smiling lips before she reached up and wiped her cheek. She leaned forward and slid it along my chest.

"Do you want to take this outside?"

Laila grinned. I laugh, grabbed ahold of her hips, and tugged her into me. She laughed and rested her head against my chest. "I love you, ya know that?"

"I do know that." I kissed her hair and tightened my arms around her waist. "And I love you too."

Happy. We were *so* happy.

THE HORRORS THAT CREATED US
— CHAPTER 2

JANUARY 21, 2019 - LAILA

Kai Callidy, Celena Jones, Adalyn.

Three names printed in the back of Moe's Journal. My brother, and my two sisters.

On the other side of the glass pane stood one of them. Unfortunately, the one with a last name. The one I likely would've been able to track down on my own.

Her long blond hair dangled before her tired blue eyes. A red flush warmed her round cheeks. She held her strong shoulders high, proud, but I knew the weight she was carrying all too well.

We'd gotten a call this morning from one of Jeremy's friends. Wyatt Braxton. Although we'd left the Chambers behind, if a loved one was in need, we helped however we could.

That call had been about her. Celena Nicole Jones.

She was bitten by a Werewolf, and her cousin saw Celena's first shift. The girl didn't want knowledge of the supernatural world, so I'd just wiped her memories.

Looking at Celena on the other side of the glass pane though, I wished I could make her forget too.

That wasn't possible. Not really. Becoming a Werewolf was irreversible. She had no choice; she had to accept what she was.

But fuck, I wished I could take this pain away. Showing her that page in Moe's journal, explaining my theory that we were related, certainly hadn't made this any easier.

Jeremy's fingers found mine, dragging my attention to his gaze. "You got her blood?"

I thumbed the vial in my pocket, giving a nod. With her permission, I was taking it to the underground hospital to run some tests. Obviously to confirm if she was the girl Moe cited in that book, but also to see if she had any other dormant powers we didn't know about.

He frowned. "You okay?"

I was in better shape than she was, that was for certain. But my chest was tight, and my hands were shaky.

Maybe I was worried for her. Maybe I felt bad for making her bad day worse with my theories. Maybe I felt like shit because I knew how it felt to be roped into this world and feel like your entire life was a lie.

"Yeah, I'm alright."

He gave a smile. "Good, because we're gonna be late if we don't leave now."

***

The strong smell from the car air freshener wafted to my nose and made my stomach spin. Gazing out the passenger side window, I watched the snow-covered trees whoosh past in a blur of gray and white. The tips of my fingers coasted over the bump of my belly that had just started to appear a few weeks prior.

Jeremy pulled our hands to his lips and kissed my knuckles. I turned to meet his gaze and gave a smile. "What?"

"What's going on up there?" He pointed toward my head with a grin. "You've barely said a word since we left."

I thought it was obvious.

My mind was on the barely eighteen-year-old girl who'd just been turned into a Werewolf against her will. She was just immersed in a world she never knew existed, she was scared, and I wanted to help her.

Aside from that, the pack who'd turned her was a barbaric one. I'd had many interactions with Werewolves, and for the most part, I liked them. But these fuckers were beasts, and I was scared for her safety.

"I'm just worried about her."

"Celena?" he asked. I nodded, and he shrugged. "I wouldn't be. She's smart. So is Wyatt. They're tough kids, they can handle themselves."

That wasn't just it. Maybe they were big kids, maybe they could handle things on their own. But she was my sister. I felt connected to her. And even if she wasn't my sister—although I was fairly certain she was—I had a bad feeling about this. She needed me. And I needed to be there for her.

"Wyatt's just a wolf though. And Celena has no idea how to use her powers. They don't seem to be connected to anger and fear like they are for me. She doesn't know what her powers are yet, she can't protect herself," I said. "I don't know. I just feel like I have to do something. I have to help her."

"If they ask for it, we'll do what we can. But it isn't our battle."

"We're supposed to protect people, aren't we? Isn't that the point in having all of these powers?"

"I know how hard it is for you to see someone who needs help. I know you want to dive in and fix it. I get that you want to go in guns blazing and right wrongs and save people, but you're pregnant, Lai. Just relax for now. Enjoy the peace while we have it."

"I'm pregnant, Jeremy. I'm not defenseless. I'm more powerful now than I've ever been and—"

"Do you have any idea what that alpha did to Wyatt's girlfriend because he told her what he was?" Jeremy met my gaze with furrowed brows. He looked back to the road. "Damon's smart. He knows the rules. The Council and the North American Monarch know about what they did, and they let him get away with it because he said he was preventing exposure. They would do the same to you, if not worse. Any shitty creature in our world would do just about anything to see you dead. They keep their distance but only because we stick to ourselves. Killing a couple rogues is one thing. But you can't go up against a pack that's been around for hundreds of years and has hundreds of wolves to back them up," he said. "Not while you're carrying our baby, Laila. You just can't."

"Oh. So you're putting your foot down? Is that it?"

He rolled his eyes. "You make your own choices, you know that. But I think we both know you wouldn't forgive yourself if something happened to this baby because you rushed into something you weren't ready for."

"She's my sister, Jeremy. You would do just about anything to keep your sister safe, wouldn't you?"

"You literally just met her, Laila."

My already defensive gaze grew raged. He was right, I didn't know Celena yet. But that didn't matter.

I felt how scared she was. I could see how alone she felt.

"What's that supposed to mean? I should just let her die?"

"She's not going to die," he muttered with a shake of his head. "Trust me, they want her alive. She was turned by one of them, she's a part of their pack. And she was a hybrid before she was turned. She's a commodity, they aren't killing her."

"It's those two against everyone else and she has no idea how to control her powers," I said. "They can't do this on their own."

"I'm not saying we won't help them, Laila. But even with all of us combined, it's not enough to take them on. For us to win against them, she needs to figure out how to use her powers. Even then, I still don't know. With as big as their pack is, not to mention their mates... We'd lose. There's no way in hell we wouldn't. And who knows how many of us would go down in the process. Plus, are you ready to slaughter families? Because that's what we'd be doing. We'd be pillaging an entire community, not just a few wolves who don't want to stay in line."

I turned my gaze out the window. I saw the point he was making. In Jeremy's eyes, we'd left the Chambers, and none of this was our concern anymore. But if Celena was my sister, it *was* my business.

Although, I supposed he was right. I wasn't one for slaughtering villages.

"If she needs my help, I'm not going to turn my back on her," I said.

"I never said that we would. But we're not going on a suicide mission either. If they want to take the pack down, it'll be planned. We're not walking blindly into a battle we can't win. Especially a battle that isn't ours."

"I guess you're right." My fingers ran along my firm stomach. "I just want to make sure she's going to be okay. I was in her head; I saw how dark her life's been. She's so gloomy and jaded. She has a lot to heal from, you know?"

"If she's your family, she's my family." He turned and met my gaze as we came to a stop light. "I'll make sure nothing happens to her. But I don't want you to get involved with this pack shit. Not while you're pregnant. I'm not trying to be controlling. I just need you to be safe. I need our baby to be safe. I'd do anything to protect you guys, and if that means I'm being a dick, or controlling, I'm sorry. But at least the two of you'll be safe."

"That doesn't make you a dick." A slow exhale left my lips. I watched the snowflakes hit the windshield and melt to little water droplets for a long, quiet moment. "You're right. The baby comes first."

His tone softened, smile coming to his lips. "Let's not argue, okay? Today's supposed to be a good day."

"We might not find out the sex today, ya know." I smiled as I turned toward him. "And what does it matter anyway? They can be a boy, they can be a girl, I don't care. You can't put so much emphasis on gender. That just fills kids heads with sexist and outdated linear views of sexuality and gender identity."

"It's not that I really care. I just have a feeling he's a boy. And I want to win the pool." He gave an excited grin, hand moving to my belly.

I chuckled, looked down, and held either side of the baby bump. "They're already betting on you, kid."

Jeremy had been the perfect parent since I told him I was pregnant. I never saw him as excited as he was to be a father. He'd already read four books on pregnancy and one on birth. He spent hours on parenting blogs reading everything from whether or not I should eat my placenta to caring for my nipples while breast feeding.

He recently took over most of my duties that I couldn't do from my desk at Moe's. He obsessed over the nursery as we remodeled. He made sure to use stains and polishes on the hardwood floors that had the least numbers of carcinogens possible. He painted with the mildest paints, bolted furniture to the walls, and baby proofed every sharp edge and cabinet door that he could. He even put a lock on the toilet seat—which got to be a real pain in the ass with how often I was pissing those days.

I always wanted to be a mom, but I think Jeremy wanted to be a dad even more. Considering he lost his parents when he was young, I understood why he was so obsessed with doing it right. I'd never thought Jeremy would be the PTA sort of guy, but that parental instinct that'd kicked in only made me fall for him harder.

Enthralled by *The Horrors That Created Us*? Click the link below to download now:

https://www.amazon.com/dp/B08T17G7S2

ALSO BY CHARLIE NOTTINGHAM

The Eluding Destiny Series

Eluding Destiny

The Horrors That Created Us

Aftershocks

The Precipice

Land of Light

The Quiet Army

Sacred Sins

Flash Back

The Shift

Lost to Time

Gods Among Us

The Cover Up

Blank Slate

Eluding Destiny Prequels

The Last Beginning

Blood Bar

Raven's Cry Series

(MMFM Paranormal Romance)

Raven's Cry

Raven's Song

Celena's Story Duology

(Completed—paranormal romance, urban fantasy)

New Normal: Celena's Story Part 1

Reprisal: Celena's Story Part 2

Origins of the Gods

(Completed Trilogy—fantasy romance, more information on the origins of the Fae and Angels, how life began on earth, where Guardians came from, and—most importantly—a badass forbidden romance)

Origins

The Thrones of Ore and Ice

Creation

Stand Alone Novels

Curse of the Gods: The Bridge Between Origins of the Gods and the Eluding Destiny Series

Sign up for Charlie's newsletter and receive a free copy of the Eluding Destiny prequel, Blood Bar:

https://liquidmind.media/eluding-destiny-prequel/

A NOTE FROM THE AUTHOR

Thank you so much for reading. From the bottom of my heart, truly, thank you. These stories have existed in the caverns of my mind for more than a decade and I can't put into words how excited I am to share them with the world.

If you want to stay up to date on my new titles, click <u>Follow Author</u> on the Kindle Store when you exit. **You'll be instantly notified when a new book releases.**

Anyway, if you're interested in more info on upcoming books, please click the link to my website and sign up for my newsletter!

Also feel free to find me on Facebook, Instagram, and Tiktok. I love hearing from readers. Share any questions you have and comments you'd like me to hear. Seriously, I stay up way too late on a regular basis responding to emails from readers, and I love it(:

If you don't mind, it'd mean the absolute world to me if you'd leave a review. Reviews make a world of a difference to indies like me.

It'd also be deeply appreciated if you shared my work with your friends and family that like this sort of genre. Gaining a following as a new author isn't an easy feat and I need all the help that I can get!

I'll let you get on with your day now. Or let you go on to binge read the next book in the series!

Much love,
Charlie

Sign up for my newsletter here!
https://liquidmind.media/eluding-destiny-prequel/
Find me on Facebook here
https://www.facebook.com/charlienottingham1224
Oh, and find me on TikTok!
I love it there!
https://www.tiktok.com/@charlienottingham1224?lang=en

ABOUT THE AUTHOR

Charlie is a... Okay, talking about myself in third person is weird.

Nice to meet you! My name's Charlie Nottingham, and my whole world revolves around fantasy. When I'm not writing a new book, I'm either hanging out with my dogs, talking with my fans online, or reading some amazing urban fantasy, paranormal romance, or fantasy romance series (always a series, never a stand-alone, because I hate to fall for a character and never see them again). Or re-watching some Buffy or Supernatural. (They never get old!)

www.ingramcontent.com/pod-product-compliance
Lightning Source LLC
Chambersburg PA
CBHW072042190726

48294CB00005B/1373